R... ...ING

By Stephen Hunter

PALE HORSE COMING

HOT SPRINGS

TIME TO HUNT

BLACK LIGHT

DIRTY WHITE BOYS

POINT OF IMPACT

VIOLENT SCREEN: A CRITIC'S 13
    YEARS ON THE FRONT LINES OF
    MOVIE MAYHEM

TARGET

THE DAY BEFORE MIDNIGHT

THE SPANISH GAMBIT

THE SECOND SALADIN

THE MASTER SNIPER

TAPESTRY OF SPIES

STEPHEN HUNTER

PALE HORSE COMING

POCKET STAR BOOKS

New York   London   Toronto   Sydney   Singapore

A Pocket Star Book published by
POCKET BOOKS, a division of Simon & Schuster, Inc.
1230 Avenue of the Americas, New York, NY 10020

ISBN 978-0-671-03546-4

First Pocket Books printing December 2002

21

POCKET STAR BOOKS and colophon are
registered trademarks of Simon & Schuster, Inc.

For information regarding special discounts for bulk purchases,
please contact Simon & Schuster Special Sales at 1-800-456-6798
or business@simonandschuster.com

Front cover illustration by Rod Hernandez
Cover photo by Joe Sohm/Chromosohm/PictureQuest

Printed in the U.S.A.

At last, for Jean

The belief in a supernatural source of evil
is not necessary; men alone are quite capable
of every wickedness.

—JOSEPH CONRAD

The human target element always stimulates
interest.

—ED MCGIVERN

. . . and his name that sat on him was Death, and
Hell followed with him.

—REVELATION 6:8

ONE

Sam's Journey

1

In mid-1947, Jefferson Barnes, the prosecuting attorney of Polk County, Arkansas, finally died. Upon that tragedy—the old man fell out of one of those new golf cart things on vacation in Hot Springs, rolled down a gully screaming damnation and hellfire all the way, and broke his neck on a culvert—Sam Vincent, his loyal Number 2, moved up to the big job. Then in '48, Sam was anointed by the Democratic party (there was no other in western Arkansas), which ran him on the same ticket with Harry S. Truman and Fred C. Becker. As did those worthies, he won handily. For Sam, it was the goal toward which he had been aiming for many years. He had always wanted to be a servant of the law, and now, much better, he *was* the law.

Sam was six foot one, forty-four, with a bushy head of hair and a brusque demeanor that would not be called "lovable" for many years. He stared immoderately and did not suffer fools, idiots, Yankees, carpetbaggers, the small of spirit or the breakers of the law gladly. He wore baggy suits flecked with pipe ash, heavy glasses, and walked in a bounding swoop. He hunted in the fall, followed the St. Louis Browns during the summer, when he had time, which he hardly ever did, and tied flies, though he fished rarely enough. Otherwise, he just worked like hell. His was classic American career insanity, putting the professional so far above the personal there almost was no personal, in the process alienating wife and children with his indifference, burning out secretaries with his demands, annoying the sheriff's detectives with his directions. In what little time remained, he served on the draft board (he had won the Bronze Star during the Battle of the Bulge), traveled five states to interview promising high school seniors who had applied to his beloved Princeton, played a weekly round of golf with the county powers at the country club, and drank too much eight-year-old bourbon. He knew everybody; he was respected by everybody. He was a great man, a great American. He had the highest conviction rate of any county prosecutor in Arkansas, Oklahoma, Missouri, or Tennessee for that matter.

He was not reelected. In fact, he lost in a landslide to a no'count lawyer named Febus Bookins, a genial hack who smelled of gin all the time and meant only to rob the county blind during his term of office. He called himself a reformer, and his goal was to reform his bank account into something more respectable.

Sam had made one mistake, but it was a mistake which few in his home state, and in fact not many elsewhere, could ignore. In 1949, he prosecuted a man named Willis Beaudine for raping a young woman named Nadine Johnson. It was an unremarkable case, save for the fact that Willis was a white person and Nadine a Negro girl. It is true she was quite light, what some would call a "high yeller," and that she had comely ways, and was, perhaps, not normally so innocent as she looked when she appeared in court. But facts were facts, law was law. Certain evidence had been developed by Sam's former investigator, Earl Swagger, who was now a state police sergeant and was famous for the big medal he had won during the war. Earl, however, risked nothing by testifying against Willis, for Earl was known to be a prideful, bull-headed man who could not be controlled by anyone and was feared by some. Sam, on the other hand, risked everything, and lost everything, although Willis was convicted and spent six months at the Tucker Farm. As for Nadine, she moved from town because even in her own community she was considered what Negro women called a " 'ho," and moved to St. Louis, where her appetites soon got her murdered in a case of no interest to anyone.

Sam had taken his defeat bitterly. If his family thought he would see them more often, they were mistaken. Instead, he rented a small office on the town square of Blue Eye, the county seat, and commenced to spend most of his days and many of his nights there. He worked such small cases as came his way, but mainly he plotted out ways to return to office. He still hunted with Earl. His other friend was Connie Longacre, the smart Eastern woman whom the county's richest, most worthless son had brought back from his education at Annapolis in '30 and his failed naval career thereafter. Connie had soon learned how appetite-driven a man her Rance was, and while trying to raise her own hellion son, Stephen, fell to friendship with Sam, who alone in that part of Arkansas had been to a Broadway play, had met a gal under the clock at the Biltmore, and who didn't think Henry Wallace was a pawn of the Red Kremlin.

Sam was never stupid, not on a single day in his life. He understood that one thing he had to do was to regain

the trust of the white people. Therefore he utterly refused to take any cases involving Negroes, even if they
only revolved around one dark person suing another.
There was a Negro lawyer in town, a Mr. Theopolis
Simmons, who could handle such things; meanwhile,
Sam worked hard, politicked aggressively, kept tabs,
sucked up to the gentry who had deposed him so gently,
and tried to stay focused.

Then, one day in June of 1951, an unusual event occurred, though nothing in that day or the day or week
before had suggested it would. Sam, alone in his office,
worked through probate papers for a farmer named
Lewis who had died intestate and whose estate was now
being sued for back taxes by the state, which would
drive his widow and four children off the property to—
well, to nothing. Sam would not let this happen, if only
he could figure out a way to—

He heard the door open. In the county's employ he
had always had a secretary; now, on his own, he didn't.
He stood, pushed his way through the fog of dense pipe
smoke, and opened the door to peer into his anteroom.
An elegant gentleman had seated himself on the sofa
and was paging absently through an old copy of *Look*
magazine.

"Sir, do you have an appointment?" Sam asked.

The man looked up at him.

He was tanned softly, as if from an expensive vacation at the beach, balding, and looked well tended, of an
age that could have been anywhere between thirty and
fifty. He was certainly prosperous, in a smooth-fitting
blue pinstripe suit, a creamy white shirt and the black tie
of a serious man. A homburg, gray pearl, lay on the seat
beside him; his shined shoes were cap-toed black
bluchers, possibly bespoke, and little clocks or flowers

marked his socks. The shoes were shined, Sam noticed, all the way down to the sole, which was an indication that a professional had done them, in a rail station, a hotel lobby, a barbershop.

"Why, no, Mr. Vincent. I'd be happy to make one, or if you prefer, to wait here until you have the time to see me."

"Hmm," said Sam. He knew when money came to call.

"I am currently in the throes of a case," he said. "Mr., ah—"

"My name is Trugood, sir."

"Mr. Trugood. Have you a few minutes while I file and clear my desk?"

"Of course. I don't mean to interrupt."

Sam ducked back in. Quickly he gathered the Lewis papers up, sealed them in a file, and put it into a drawer. His desk was a mess; he did some elementary rearranging, which meant he'd have to derearrange after the man left, but Sam could use a fee, he didn't mind admitting, for any return from the poor Lewises, or the Jenningses, or the Joneses, the Smiths, the Beaupres, the Deacons, the Hustons, all that was in a future that seemed quite distant. More or less prepared, he removed a fresh yellow legal tablet from his cabinet and wrote the word TRUGOOD, and the date, atop it.

He opened the door.

"Sir, I can see you now."

"Thank you, Mr. Vincent."

Trugood stood elegantly, smiled at Sam as he walked through the door, pretended not to notice the debris, the mess, the strewn files, the moth-eaten deer's head, or even the fog of sweetbriar gas that hung, almost moist, in the air.

Sam passed him, gestured to a seat, and as he moved around the desk to sit, watched as the man placed a business card before him on the desk.

"Ah," said Sam. "A colleague."

"Indeed," said the man, whose card announced him to be Davis Trugood, Esq., of the firm of Mosely, Vacannes & Destin, 777 North Michigan Avenue, Chicago, Illinois, Hillcrest 3080.

"Mr. Trugood? I am at your service."

"Thank you, Mr. Vincent. May I say, I've heard a great deal about you, and I've worked some to find you."

"I've always been here, sir. I had no idea any reputation had spread beyond our little benighted state. Certainly not as far as a big sophisticated city like Chicago."

"Well, sir, possibly it hasn't reached that far. But it has reached all through the South, or, I should say, a *certain* South."

"What South would that be, sir?"

"That South occupied by our population of color, sir. Our Negroes. They say you are the rare white lawyer who is fair to the man of Negro blood."

"Well," said Sam, somewhat taken aback, "if by that they mean that as a prosecuting attorney I laid the same force of law against white as against black, then they are correct. I believe in the law. But do not understand me too quickly, sir. I am not what you might call a race champion. I am not a hero of the Negro, nor do I ever mean to be. I believe history has dealt our American Negroes a sorry hand, as do many people. But I also believe that sorry hand will have to be corrected slowly. I am not one for tearing things down in service to various dubious moral sentiments, which in fact would turn my own race against me, which would unleash the savagery of the many embittered whites of the South against the poor Negro, which would in fact result in destruction everywhere. So, Mr. Trugood, if you thought I was someone to lead a crusade, change or challenge a law, throw down a gauntlet, burn a barn, sing a hymn, or whatever, why, I am not that man, sir."

"Mr. Vincent, thank you for speaking straight out. I must say, most Southern lawyers prefer to speak a code which one has to have attended either Ole Miss or Alabama to penetrate. You, sir, at least speak directly."

"I take a pleasure in that. Possibly the product of an Eastern education."

"Excellent, sir. Now, I need a representative to travel to a certain town deeper in the South and make private inquiries. This man has to be extremely smart, not without charm, stubborn as the Lord, a man of complete probity. He must also be somewhat brave, or at least the sort not turned feeble by a show of hostility. He also has to be comfortable around people of different bloods, white and Negro. He has to be comfortable around law enforcement officers of a certain type, the type that would as soon knock a fellow's hat off as talk civilly to him. The fee for this service, perhaps lasting a week, would be quite high, given the complex diplomatic aspects of the situation. I would suppose you have no ethical objections to a high fee, Mr. Vincent."

"High fee. In my career those two words rarely appear in the same sentence. Yes, do go on, Mr. Trugood. You have my attention, without distraction."

"Thank you, sir. I am charged with executing a will for a certain rather well-off late Chicagoan. He had for many years in his employ a Negro named Lincoln Tilson."

Sam wrote: "Negro Lincoln Tilson" on his big yellow pad.

"Lincoln was a loyal custodian of my client's properties, a handyman, a bodyguard, a gardener, a chauffeur, a man whose brightness of temperament always cheered my client, who was negotiating a business career of both great success and some notoriety."

"I follow, sir," said Sam.

"Five years ago, Lincoln at last slowed down. My employer settled a sum on him, a considerable sum, and bid him farewell. He even drove him to the Illinois Central terminal to catch the City of New Orleans and reverse the steps by which he arrived up North so many years ago, for Lincoln's pleasure was to return to the simpler life from which he had sprung in the South. Lincoln returned to his birthplace, a town called Thebes, in Thebes County, Mississippi."

Sam wrote it down, while saying, "That is the deepest part of the deepest South, I would imagine."

"It is, sir."

Thebes, as a word, rang ever so slightly in Sam's imagination. He recalled that the original was a Greek town, city even, much fought over in antiquity. For some reason the number seven occurred in concert with it.

"I see puzzlement, sir," said Trugood. "You are well educated and no doubt think of *Seven Against Thebes,* by the Greek tragedian Aeschylus. I assure you, no army led by seven heroes is necessary in this case. Mississippi's Thebes is a far distance from Aeschylus's tragic town of war. It is a backwater Negro town far up the Yaxahatchee River, which itself is a branch of the Pascagoula River. It is the site of a famous, or possibly infamous, penal farm for colored called Thebes Farm."

"That's it," said Sam. "It is legendary among the Negro criminal class, with whom I had many dealings as a young prosecutor. 'You don't wants to go to Thebes, they say, don't nobody never nohow come back from Thebes.' Or words to that effect."

"It seems they have it mixed up with Hades in their simplicity. Yes, Thebes is not a pleasant place. Nobody wants to go to Thebes."

"Yet you want me to go to Thebes. That is why the fee would be so high?"

"There is difficulty of travel, for one thing. You must hire a boat in Pascagoula, and the trip upriver is unpleasant. The river, I understand, is dark and deep; the swamp that lines it inhospitable. There was only one road into Thebes, through that same forbidding swamp; it was washed out some years back, and Thebes County, not exactly a county of wealth, has yet to dispatch repair."

"I see."

"Accommodations would be primitive."

"I slept in many a barn in the late fracas in Europe, Mr. Trugood. I can sleep in a barn again; it won't hurt me."

"Excellent. Now here is the gist of the task. My client's estate—as I say, considerable—is hung up in probate because Mr. Lincoln Tilson seems no longer to exist. I have attempted to communicate with Thebes County authorities, to little avail. I can reach no one but simpletons on the telephone, when the telephone is working, which is only intermittently. No letter has yet been answered. The fate of Lincoln is unknown, and a large amount of money is therefore frozen, a great disappointment to my client's greedy, worthless heirs."

"I see. My task would be to locate either Lincoln or evidence of his fate. A document, that sort of thing?"

"Yes. From close-mouthed Southern types. I, of course, need someone who speaks the language, or rather, the accent. They would hear the Chicago in my voice, and their faces would ossify. Their eyes would deaden. Their hearing would disintegrate. They would evolve backward instantaneously to the neolithic."

"That may be so, but Southerners are also fair and honest folk, and if you don't trumpet your Northern superiority in their face and instead take the time to listen and master the slower cadences, they will usually reward you with friendship. Is there another issue here?"

"There is indeed." He waved at his handsome suit, his handsome shoes, his English tie. His cufflinks were gold with a discreet sapphire, probably worth more than Sam had made in the last six months. "I am a different sort of man, and in some parts of the South—Thebes, say—that difference would not go unnoticed."

"You have showy ways, but they are the ways of a man of the world."

"I fear that is exactly what would offend them. And, frankly, I'm not a brave man. I'm a man of desks. The actual confrontation, the quickness of argument, the thrust of will on will: not really my cup of tea, I'm afraid. A sound man understands his limits. I was the sort of boy who never got into fights and didn't like tests of strength."

"I see."

"That is why I am buying your courage as well as your mind."

"You overestimate me. I am quite a common man."

"A decorated hero in the late war."

"Nearly everybody in the war was a hero. I saw some true courage; mine was ordinary, if even that."

"I think I have made a very good choice."

"All right, sir."

"Thank you, Mr. Vincent. This is the fee I had in mind."

He wrote a figure on the back of his card, and pushed it over. It took Sam's breath away.

"You are sending me to be your champion in hell, it sounds like," said Sam. "But you are paying me well for the fight."

"You will earn every penny, I assure you."

2

IT took Sam but a few days to bank the retainer, re-arrange his schedule, book a ticket on the City of New Orleans, and spend an afternoon in the Fort Smith municipal library reading up on Thebes and its penal farm. What he learned appalled him.

On the night before he was to leave, he finally faced the unsettled quality of his feelings. At last, he climbed into his car and drove the twelve miles east along Arkansas Route 8 toward the small town of Board Camp; turning left off the highway, he traveled a half mile of bumpy road to a surprisingly large white house on a hill that commanded the property. The house was freshly painted as was the barn behind, and someone had worked the gardens well and dutifully; it was June, and the place was ablaze with the flora chosen to flourish in the hot West Arkansas sun. A few cows grazed in the far meadows, but much of the property was still in trees, where Sam and the owner shot deer in the fall, if they didn't wander farther afield.

Sam pulled up close to the house, aware that he was under observation. This was Earl's young son, Bob Lee, almost five. Bob Lee was a grave boy who had the gift of stillness when he so desired. He was a watcher, that boy. He already had made some hunting trips with them, and had a talent for blood sport, the ability to understand the messages of the land, to decipher the play of light and shadow in the woods, to smell the weather on the wind, though he was some years yet from shooting. Still, he was a steady presence on the hunt, not a wild kid. It was Sam's sworn duty as godfather to the boy to draw him into the professional world; Earl was adamant that his son would do better than he and not be a roaming Marine, a battlefield scurrier, a man killer, as Earl had been. Earl wanted something more settled for his only son, a career in the law or medicine. It was important to Earl, and when things were important to Earl, it was Earl's force of will that usually made them happen.

"Howdy there, Bob Lee," called Sam.

"Mr. Sam, Mr. Sam," the boy responded, from the porch where he had been sitting and looking out over the land in the twilight.

"Your daddy's still on duty, I see. Is he expected back?"

"Don't know, sir. Daddy comes and goes, you know."

"I do know. How you got such a worker as a daddy I'll never figure, when he has such a lazy son who just sits there like a frog on a log."

"I was memorizing."

"It doesn't surprise me at all. Memorizing the land? The birds. The sky, the clouds."

"Something like that, sir."

"Oh, you are a smart one. You have received all the brains in the family, I can see that. You'll end up a rich one. Is your mama here?"

"Yes, sir. I'll fetch her."

The boy scooted off as Sam waited. He could have walked in himself, for he was that familiar with the Swaggers. But something in his mood kept him still and worrisome.

Junie Swagger emerged. Lord, a beauty still! But Junie was, well, who knew? The childbirth had been a terrible ordeal, it was said, and Earl not around to help, at least not till the end, and so the poor girl fought her way through fifteen hours of labor on her own. She had not, it was also said, quite ever come back from that. She was somewhat dreamy, as if she didn't hear all that was said to her. Her great pleasure was those damned flowers, and she could spend hours in the hottest weather cultivating or weeding or fertilizing. It was also said that she would have no more children.

Now, a little wan, she stood before him.

"Why, hello, Mr. Sam. Come on in."

"Well, Junie, thank you much, but I don't want you making no fuss. I have to have a chat with Earl is all. You needn't even consider this a visit, and there's no need to unlimber any hospitality."

"Oh, you are so silly. You sit down, I'll git you a nice glass of lemonade. You'll stay for supper, I insist."

"No, ma'am. Can't. I'm in the middle of getting ready for a business trip to New Orleans. I'm driving over to Memphis tomorrow to catch the train."

"You know, Mr. Sam, Earl sometimes gets so caught up he doesn't get here 'til late."

"I do know. It seems a shame after all he's been through that he can't have a quieter life."

Junie said nothing for a second, but her face focused with a surprising intensity, as if some spark had been struck. Then she said, "I fear he has other things on his mind. I know this Korea business has him all het up. I'm scared he'll get it in his head he has to go fight another war. He's done enough. But I can read his melancholy. It's his nature to go where there's shooting, under the impression he can help, but maybe out of some darker purpose."

"Earl is a man bred for war, I agree, Junie. But I do think that he'll sit this one out on the porch. He's still in pain from wounds, and he knows what a wonderful home you've made for him and the boy."

"Oh, Mr. Sam, you can be such a charmer sometimes. I don't believe a word you say, never have, never will." She laughed and her face lit up.

"Now you sit here, Earl will be along shortly or not, as he sees fit. I will bring you that lemonade and that will be that."

So Sam sat and watched the twilight grow across the land. He could have sat all night, but on this night Earl had decided to come home as quickly as possible, and within a few minutes Sam saw the Arkansas Highway Patrol black-and-white scuttling down the road, pulling up a screen of dust behind it. Earl had meant to asphalt that road for four years now, or at least lay some gravel, but could never quite afford to have it done. Sam had volunteered to front him the money, but Earl of course was stubborn and wanted no debts haunting him, none left for his heirs to owe if his melancholy about the true nature of the world ever proved out and he turned up shot to death in some squalid field.

Earl got out of the car with a smile, for he had seen Sam from a long way off. He loved three things in the world: his family, the United States Marine Corps and Sam.

"Well, Mr. Sam, why didn't you tell me you were coming? Junie, get this man a drink of something stronger than lemonade and set an extra place."

Earl lumbered up to the porch from his car. He was a

big man, over six feet, and still so darkened from the Pacific sun after all these years some thought he was an Indian. He had a rumbly, slow voice famous in the county, and his close bristly hair—he'd removed the Stetson by now—was just beginning to gray. He was near forty years old, and his body was a latticework of scar tissue and jerry-built field-expedient repairs. He'd been stitched up so many times he was almost more surgical thread than human being, testimony to the fact that a war or two will write its record in a man's flesh. His hands were big, his muscles knotty from farmwork on weekends and plenty of it, but his face still had the same odd calmness to it that inspired men in combat or terrified men in crime. He looked as if he could handle things. He could.

"He says he won't stay," Junie cried from inside, "though Lord knows I tried. You tie him to a chair and we'll be all set."

"Bob Lee's going to be disappointed if old Sam don't read him a story tonight," Earl said.

"I will stay to read the story, yes, Earl." In his stentorian, courtroom voice, Sam could make a story come more alive than the radio. "And I wish this were a pure pleasure call. But I do have a matter to discuss."

"Lord. Am I in some kind of trouble?"

"No, sir. Maybe I am, however."

It was such a reversal. In some ways, unsaid, Sam had become Earl's version of a father, his own proving to be a disappointment and his need for someone to believe in so crucial to his way of thinking. So he had informally adopted Sam in this role, worked for him for two years as an investigator before Colonel Jenks had managed at last to get Earl on the patrol. The bonds between the two men had grown strong, and Sam alone had heard Earl, who normally never discussed himself, on such topics as the war in the Pacific or the war in Hot Springs.

The two sat; Junie brought her husband a glass of lemonade, and he in turn gave her the Sam Browne belt with the Colt .357, the handcuffs, the cartridge reloaders and such, which she took into the house to secure.

Earl loosened his tie, set his Stetson down on an unused chair. His cowboy boots were dusty, but under the dust shined all the way down to the soles.

"All right," he said. "I am all ears."

Sam told him quickly about his commission to go to Thebes, Mississippi, and the tanned, smooth-talking colleague who had put it together for him, and the large retainer.

"Sounds straightforward to me," said Earl.

"But you have heard of the prison at Thebes."

"Never from a white person. White folks prefer to believe such places don't exist. But from the Negroes, yes, occasionally."

"It has an evil reputation."

"It does. I once arrested a courier running too fast up 71 toward Kansas City. He had a trunkful of that juju grass them jazz boys sometimes smoke. He was terrified I's going to send him to Thebes. I thought he'd die of a heart attack he's so scared. Never saw nothing like it. It took an hour to get him settled down, and then of course another hour to make him understand this was Arkansas, not Mississippi, and I couldn't send him to Thebes, even if I wanted to. I sent him to Tucker, instead, where I'm sure he had no picnic. But at the trial, he seemed almost happy. Tucker was no Thebes, at least not in the Negro way of looking at things."

"They live in a different universe, somehow," Sam said. "It doesn't make sense to us. It is haunted by ghosts and more attuned to the natural and more connected to the earth. Their minds work differently. You can't understand, sometimes, why they do the things they do. They are us a million years ago."

"Maybe that's it," said Earl. "Though the ones I saw on Tarawa, they died and bled the same as white folks."

"Here's why I'm somewhat apprehensive," Sam confessed. "I went up to Fort Smith the other day, and found out what I could find out about this place. Something's going on down there that's gotten me spooked a bit."

"What could spook Sam Vincent?"

"Well, sir, five years ago, according to the Standard and Poor's rating guide to the United States, in Thebes, Mississippi, there was a sawmill, a dry cleaner, a grocery and general store, a picture show, two restaurants, two bar-and-grills, a doctor, a dentist, a mayor, a sheriff, a feed store and a veterinarian."

"Yes?"

"Now there's nothing. All those businesses and all those professional men, they've up and gone."

"All over the South, the Negroes are on the move. Mississippi is cotton, and cotton isn't king no more. They're riding the Illinois Central up North to big jobs and happier lives."

"I know, and thought the same at first. So I picked at random five towns scattered across Mississippi. And while some have had some social structure reduction and considerable population loss, they remain vibrant. So this does seem strange."

Earl said nothing.

Sam continued.

"Then there's this business of the road. There was a highway into Thebes for many years and it too supported businesses and life. Gas stations, diners, barbecue places, that sort of thing. But some time ago, the road washed out, effectively sealing the town and that part of the swamp and piney woods off from civilization, well, such civilization as they have in Mississippi. You'd think a civic structure would get busy opening that road up, for the road is the river of opportunity, especially in the poor, rural South. Yet now, all these years later, it remains washed out, and as far as I can learn, no one has made an attempt to open it. The only approach to what remains of Thebes is a long slow trip by boat up that dark river. That's not a regular business either. The prison launches make the journey for supplies on a weekly basis, and to pick up prisoners, but the place is sealed off. You don't get there easily, you don't get back easily, and everybody seems to want it that way. Now doesn't that seem strange?"

"Well, sir," said Earl, "maybe it's a case of no road, no town, and that's why it's all drying up down there."

"It would seem so. But the decline of Thebes had already begun three years earlier. It was as if the road was the final ribbon on the package, not what was inside the package."

"Hmmm," said Earl. "If you are that worried, possibly you shouldn't go."

"Well, sir, I can't not go. I have accepted a retainer and I have a professional obligation I cannot and would not evade."

"Would you like me to come along, in case there's nasty surprises down there?"

"No, no, Earl, of course not. I just want you to know what is going on. I have here an envelope containing my file on the case, all my findings, my plan of travel and so forth. I leave tomorrow on the ten forty-five out of Memphis, and should reach New Orleans by five. I'll spend the night there, and have hired a car the next morning to take me to Pascagoula. Presumably I'll find a boatman, and I'll reach town late the day after tomorrow. If I can find a telephone, I'll call you or my wife and leave messages on a daily basis. If I can't find a telephone, well then, I shall just complete my business and come on home."

"Well, let's pick a date, and if you ain't home by that time, *then* I'll make it my business to figure out what's happening."

"Thank you, Earl. Thank you so much. You saw where I was headed."

"Mr. Sam, you can count on me."

"Earl, if you say something, I know it's done."

"I'd bring a firearm. Not one of your hunting rifles, but a handgun. You still have an Army forty-five, I believe."

"No, Earl. I am a man of reason, not guns. I'm a lawyer. The gun cannot be my way. Logic, fairness, humanity, the rule of the law above all else, those are my guidelines."

"Mr. Sam, where you're going, maybe such things don't cut no ice. I'll tell you this, if I have to come, I'll be bringing a gun."

"You have to do it your way, and I have to do it mine. So be it. Now let's read a story to Bob Lee."

"I think he'd like that. He likes the scary ones the best."

"You still have that book of Grimm's?"

"His favorite."

"I know there's a dark tale or two in there."

"A dark tale it will be, then."

3

THOUGH Sam loved New Orleans, he was moderate and professional the night he stayed there, avoiding its temptations. He took a room in a tourist home, ate at a diner, went to sleep early after meticulously recording all his expenditures for his client. The next morning, he rendezvoused with his car and driver, and commenced the drive along the gulf coast down U.S. 90, passing quickly from Louisiana into Mississippi.

It was, at first at least, a pleasant drive, with a driver named Eddie, who knew how to keep his mouth shut, and his big, comfortable LaSalle.

"It's a 1940," Eddie said, "the last and the best." And that was the only thing Eddie said.

Sam had removed and folded his coat, rolled up his sleeves, put his straw Panama on the seat next to him, and let the cooling air stream in through the open windows of the big black car. Of course he did not loosen his tie; after all, one did not do such things. There were limits. But he got out his pipe and lit up a bowlful, and simply watched the sights. On his right, the gulf's blue tide lapped against the white sands, and small towns fled by, each quaint and cute enough for a tourist trade that was beginning to catch hold. The small cities along the way were white, sunny places, Gulfport and Biloxi, further given over to tourists. He could see young couples on the beach, some of them beautiful, some not so beautiful. Beach umbrellas furled against the gulf breezes and homes had rooms to let, many of them with FREE TELEVISION as the signs proudly proclaimed.

But beyond Biloxi, it changed. No one came here for the sun or the sand, and no beaches had been cleared. It was just mangoes and ferns and scrub pine and vegetation whose only distinguishing feature was its generic green viney quality, down to a strip of soil before the water which, Sam fancied (maybe it was his imagination) had changed in tone from carefree blue to a dirty brown. The sediment this far down floated unsettled in the water, giving it the look of an immense sewer. It smelled, also, some pungent chemical odor.

Pascagoula, it turned out, was a city of industry. Paper plants dominated, and shipbuilding came second, and it was a city that had once strained mightily to produce. Now, hard times had hit it. The paper industry was down, and shipbuilding had stopped with the end of the war. It was a sad place; the boom of the war years had dried to bust, but everyone had a taste for the big, easy money of before.

Again, maybe he was imagining too much, but he thought he saw despair and lassitude everywhere. The streets felt empty; signs were not freshly painted, and commerce was not active. It all baked under a hot sun, the stench from the paper mills enough to give a man a crushing headache.

"Sir, do you have a particular destination? Do you want to go to a hotel?"

Sam looked at his watch. It was only 11:00 A.M., and, yes, he did want to go to a hotel, have a nice lunch, lie down in a room with a strong fan or maybe some air-conditioning, take a nap. But it was not in him to do so. He was rigid about everything, but most of all about duty and obligation.

"No, Eddie, I've got to push on. Uh, do you know the town?"

"Not hardly, sir. I'm a N'Awleens boy. Don't like to come out to these here hot little no'count places."

"Well, then, I suppose we'd best start at the town hall or the police station. I'd like to confer with officials before I venture further."

"Yes, sir. B'lieve I c'n hep you there."

Eddie located the single municipal building quickly enough, a town hall on one street, a police station, complete to fleets of motorcycles and squad cars parked outside, on the other.

Sam chose the administrative before the enforcement. He suited up again, tightening all that could be tightened, straightening all that could be straightened, and implanting the Panama squarely up top as befit his position and dignity. Eddie left him in front of grand stairs that led to not much of a door; he climbed them and ducked between statues of Confederate heroes facing the gulf.

He entered to a foyer, consulted with a clerk at a desk, got directions, entered a set of hallways to look for the city prosecutor's office. It was not at all hard to find, and he went through the opaque-glassed doors to find a waiting room with leather chairs and magazines under the rubric WHITE ONLY. Through a doorway that bore the sign COLORED ONLY he could see another room, ruder and filled with more rickety furniture, all jammed up with pitiful Negroes. He turned to the white secretary behind a desk, whose hair was tidy but who ruled by right of a harsh face and too much makeup.

He presented his card.

"And, sir?"

"And I wonder, ma'am, if I could have a word with Mr. . . . ." he struggled to remember the name painted on the door, then did. "Carruthers."

"What is this in reference to?" she said, with a Southern smile that meant nothing whatsoever.

"Ma'am, I am a prosecutor myself, only recently retired on the basis of electoral whimsy. I wish to speak with my colleague."

"You from here in Mississip?"

"No, ma'am. Up a bit. Arkansas, Polk County, in the west. It's on the card."

"Well, I'll see."

It wasn't Carruthers who came to get him but a Mr. Redfield, an assistant city attorney, who made a show of ignoring the unfortunate Negroes in the back room and shook his hand heartily, escorting him back to a clean little office. As they walked, Sam searched his memory, and at last realized why Redfield admitted him: they'd met at some convention in Atlantic City in 1941, with a group of other prosecutors, all having a last fling before the war did with them what it did.

"Glad to see you made it back, Mr. Redfield," Sam said.

"Never got the chance to leave, alas," said the man, as they walked into the door of a clean little cubicle. "Four-F. Stayed here prosecuting draft dodgers while you boys had all the fun. Where'd you end up? Europe, wasn't it?"

"Finally. Ended up in the artillery."

"Win anything big?"

"No, just did the job. Glad to be back in one piece."

Redfield broke out the bourbon and poured himself and Sam a tot. Tasted fine, too. They settled into chairs, chatted somewhat aimlessly on the subject of the others in attendance of that long ago convention, who was dead, who divorced, who quit, who rich, who poor. Redfield then segued neatly into local politics and gossip, his chances for getting the big job in the next election or maybe it would be better to wait until '56, local conditions, which weren't good, except for, he laughed heartily, the coming of some Northern fool's waterproof coffin company to the South, which would put the ship carpenters to some good use until it failed, ha ha ha, or the gub'mint lost so many destroyers off Korea it needed to build some new ones. Sam didn't really care, but down South here, it was the way business was done, until finally, when a ten-second pause and a second drink announced it to be the time, he launched into particulars.

He explained, concluding with his unease about the upcoming trip.

"Well," said Redfield, "truth be told, I don't know much about Thebes. That's two counties up the river, and not much between but bayou and wild niggers and Choctaws living on 'gators and catfish, then finally your piney woods, thick as hell. Too thick for white people."

"Ah, I see."

"Don't know why any feller'd go up there he didn't have to."

"Well, Redfield, I really don't want to. But I've accepted the job. I was hoping you'd write me a letter of introduction or give me a name of a colleague to whose good offices I could appeal."

"Most counties, that'd work just fine, that'd be the

way to do it. But Thebes now, Thebes is different. It's the prison farm, and that's about all. You'd have to git into our state corrections bureaucracy, and I do know those boys run their territory very tight and private-like. Don't like strangers, especially strangers from up North—"

"Arkansas? Up North?"

"Now, mind you, I ain't saying I'd be in *agreement* with that sentiment, but that would be how their minds work. I'm only clarifying here. They're a clannish bunch. They've got a system full of colored men, some of whom may be het up on juju, some on booze, some on Northern communist agitation, all that plus your natural Negro tendency toward chaos, irrationality and ol' Willie thumping Willie on Saturday night just for something to do. So them boys got a whole lot on their minds, hear? I wouldn't just go poking about now."

"I see," said Sam.

"What I'd do, you'll pardon me for presuming, I'd just turn around, head back up North. Yes, sir. Then write that fellow in Chicago, tell him everything's fine, he don't got to worry, the death certificate be on its way. I mean, it's only probate now, isn't it? Then I'd forget all about it. Come time, he'll write some angry letters, but hell, he's a Yankee, that's all they know how to do is act all indignant."

"Well, see here, Redfield, I can't do that. I took the money, I must do the work."

"Oh, come on now, Vincent. Wouldn't be the first time someone took a retainer, wrote a letter, and forgot all about it. I just wouldn't be messing about in Thebes. They got their own ways of doing things up there, they don't want nobody getting in their bidness, no sir. I'd write you a letter, but to who?"

"Whom," corrected Sam.

"Who, whom, it don't matter. Thebes up there, up that dark river, ain't nobody up there to write to, ain't nobody up there to sit down nice and polite, sit under a fan, have a sip of rye whiskey, and palaver. They're sitting on a goddamned powder keg, what they're doing. A nigger powder keg. They got to keep it from blowing, and, way I see it, that's a hero's job."

"Redfield, I have been in a variety of prisons, white and Negro both. The men who run them are many things, but heroic is about the last word I'd employ. Necessary is about as far as I'd be pleased to go."

"Well, it's all clear and dandy to y'all up North, with all your answers. Down here, where it never snows and things change slow except when they change fast and ugly, it's a lot less stamped out. It can be downright messy. That's why there has to be a Thebes. The niggers have to know there's a Thebes, and by God if they get uppity, Thebes is where they'll be sent. So in its way, Thebes is more important than Jackson or Biloxi or Oxford or Pascagoula. Without Thebes, wouldn't be no Jackson or Biloxi or Oxford or Pascagoula. Without Thebes, Mississippi is the Congo and America is Africa. Thebes is what keeps the lid on. I'd hate to see you get your nose all a-twitch because you saw one guard knock a nigger down and you make a big thing over it. It just won't do. I say as one white man to another, you best stay far from Thebes. Nothing going on in Thebes you got to see or know about, you hear?"

"Well, Redfield, I am sorry you see it that way. I can tell you're a man set in your ways, but I am equally set in mine. I have a job to do, that's all. I am an attorney, I took on a client, and goddammit, that is what I will do, so help me God, Thebes or no Thebes."

He stood and walked out, without looking back.

* * *

THEY drove for a while, and Eddie read Sam's gloomy mood.

"Sir, any directions? I'll take you anywheres."

Sam said, "I suppose we're looking for a waterfront, or a marine district or some such. I have to hire a boat and just get this done on my own."

"Yes, sir. I'll try and find it for you, I surely will."

It turned out Pascagoula itself had only a marine industry focused on the deep waters of the gulf; what they needed was a smaller satellite city called Moss Point, up the river a few miles, where boats ventured out into the bayous that lay to the north.

Eventually, after more starting and stopping, they found a place, an old boatyard administered from a peely shed near the water. The boats were moored along docks, and they floated and bobbed on the vagaries of tide and current, bumping into one another, none of them particularly impressive craft. Sam had traveled to England on the *Queen Elizabeth* and across the Channel on an LST on D-Day. Even when the latter came under fire as it neared the spot to deposit him, his men and his six 105-mm howitzers on the dangerous shore, he'd felt more comfort than he did confronting this wooden fleet rotting in the sun.

The boats were all some form of fishing craft, their engines inboard, their cabins low to the prow, their comforts all but absent.

FISHING, the sign said.

And the place smelled of that commerce, with lines looped everywhere, and nets hung to dry, the sand shifty under the foot, crab husks and fish spines abandoned everywhere, the gulls flappity-flapping overhead for a bite of flesh or cake, but otherwise still as buzzards on the wharf.

Sam ducked inside to find an old boatyard salt, with bleached eyes and a face gone straight to the quality of the dried plum called a prune.

"Howdy," said Sam, to no answer, but only a sullen stare. "I'd like to hire a boat."

"You ain't dressed to fish."

"No, not for fishing."

"You just want to piddle around? See the sights?"

"No, sir. Trying to get upriver to a town called Thebes."

"Thebes. Don't nobody go there, except the prison supply boat once a week."

"Could I hitch or hire a ride aboard it?"

"Ain't likely. Them boys are coolish toward strangers. They run tight and private-like. What would be your business in Thebes?"

"It's a confidential matter."

"Ain't talking, huh?"

"Look, I don't have to answer anybody's questions, all right? Let's just find me a boat that'll go upriver. That's your job, isn't it? You run this place? I'm not one for Mississippi lollygagging in the hot sun when there's work to be done."

"Say, you're a cuss now, ain't you? A stranger, too, from the way you talk. Well, sir, I can git you a boat and a man to take you deep into the bayou after big catfish or brown bass or whatever; I knows men who'll take you far into the gulf where the big bluefish play, and maybe you'd hook one of them and be proud to put it on your wall. Maybe you just want to lie in the sun and feel it turn your pasty face a nice shade while sipping on an iced Dixie. But nobody here is going up the bayou to the Yaxahatchee and then to Thebes. Nothing up there but blue-gum niggers who'd as soon eat your liver with the spleen still attached as smile and call you sir. And if one of them blue gums takes a bite out of you, sure as winter, you goin' die before the sun sets."

"I can pay."

"Not the boatmen around here you can't, no sir, and that's a fact. Nobody goes up to Thebes."

"Goddammit, nobody in this fool town will do what they are told to do. What is your stubbornness? Is it congenital or learned? Why such simplicity everywhere in Mississippi?"

"Sir, I would not take our state's name in anger."

Sam—well, he near exploded, but the old coot just looked at him, set in ancient ways, and Sam saw that screaming at a toothless geezer had no point to it, not even the simple satisfaction of making a fool uncomfortable.

Instead, he turned, went back to the car.

"No luck, sir?"

"Not a bit of it. These Mississippians are a different breed."

"They are. Must be all the swamp water they drink, and that corn liquor. Makes them stubborn and dull."

"Just drive, Eddie. Drive along the bayou here. Maybe I'll notice something."

The shiny LaSalle prowled among riverside shacks and cruised past the hulks of rotted boats tied up and banging against weathered docks. Overhead, the gulls pirouetted and wheeled and the hot sun beat down fiercely. Sam soon forgot he was in America. It was some strange country, particularly when the color of the people turned black, and little ragamuffin kids in tattered underwear and worn shorts raced barefoot alongside the big, slow-moving car, begging for pennies. Sam knew if he gave one a penny, he'd have to give them all a penny, so he gave none of them pennies.

Then even the Negroes ran out, and they were alone;

the road's cracked pavement yielded to dirt, the river disappeared behind a bank of reeds, and the whole thing seemed pointless.

But it was Eddie who saw the road.

"Bet there's a house there," he said. "Bet there is."

"Go on down, then. Maybe there'll be a boatman."

At the end of the way, he did in fact see a shack, cobbled together out of abandoned or salvaged materials, with a tar paper roof, and tires everywhere lying about. The boxy skeleton of an early '30s Nash sedan rusted away on blocks. Clam or oyster shells in the hundreds of thousands lay about like gravel. The place was rude and slatternly, but behind it a boat lay at anchor a few feet out in the wide brown river.

"Hello!" Sam called.

In time, an old lady leaned out, ran an eye over the man in the tan suit sitting in the backseat of the black LaSalle, then heaved up a gelatinous gob from her lungs, expelled it through a toothless mouth and grotesquely flexible lips so it flew like one of Sam's well-aimed 105s and plunked up an impact crater among the clam shells and dirt.

"What you want?" she demanded. The accent was French, more or less, or rather the Cajun corruption of the French accent.

"To talk to a boatman."

"You come wrong place, Mister. Who told you come here?"

"Madam, nobody told me to come here, I assure you. I see a boat. Therefore there is a boatman. May I speak with him, if you please."

"You from revenooers?"

"Of course not."

"Po-lices? You the po-lices?"

"No, madam. Nor FBI nor the state in any of its manifestations."

"You wait there."

The door slammed.

"Well," Sam said to Eddie, "it's a start. Not much of one, but who can say?"

A few minutes passed. Some ruckus arose from the interior of the shack, and finally an old fellow popped out. He was nut-brown, wore dungarees and a torn, loose old undershirt and a pair of shoes that might have, years ago, been designed for tennis but were now a laceless ruin. His toes flopped out from the gap between last and sole in one of them. A few crude tattoos inked his biceps. His hair was a gray nest of tendrils, this way and that, and most, but not all, of his teeth remained. His face was a crush of fissures and arroyos from years in the sun, and from his own squinting.

"You want?" he said, scowling.

"The boatman. Are you the boatman?"

"Nah, not no boatman. You go on, git out of here now. No boatman here."

"You look like a boatman to me."

"Agh. What you want?"

"Lazear," cried the old lady from inside, "you talk to the guy now, you hear. He gots money."

The old man squinted at him up and down.

"I want to go upriver. Through the bayou, up the Pascagoula, to the Yaxahatchee. Into the piney woods. Up to the town they call Thebes."

"Ah! Sir, nobody go to Thebes. Nothing there but nigs and dogs. Oooo-ee, nigs don't git you, dogs do. Dogs chew you real good. Whichever git you first, the other clean up after."

"I understand there is a Negro town there and a

prison farm. I have business. I wish to hire a boat."

"You been everwhere. No one take you. So you finally come old Lazear?"

"Where I've been is of no account. I need passage up, I need you to wait an hour or a day, and I need passage back, that is all. I am prepared to pay the prevailing rate plus a little extra."

"Million dollars. You got million dollars for Lazear?"

"Of course not. What do you usually get by day? I'll double it."

"Sir," Eddie whispered, "I'd offer him a sum first and let him negotiate from that position."

But Lazear quickly said, "I gits a hundred dollars a day guiding in the swamp."

"I doubt he's seen a hundred dollars in his life," muttered Eddie.

"Two hundred then. Two hundred there and back."

"Four hundred. Two up, two back. Is tricky. Lost in the bayou, eaten by 'gators, you know. No fun, no sir. Four."

"A hundred is a month's wages. Take two hundred or I'll find another boat."

"Two then. Two. You pay now, you come back tomorrow night."

"I pay fifty now, I don't go anywhere, we leave now. We leave immediately."

"No, sir. Long trip. Day's trip, maybe day anna half. Lazear got to load up the boat."

"I am not leaving," said Sam, "now that I am here. And that is final, sir."

"Oh, crazy man from the North. Crazy Northern man. You from New York or Boston, sir?"

These people, thought Sam, they are so ignorant.

4

THE bayou soon swallowed them. If there was one river here, it was lost to Sam. There seemed to be dozens of them, tracks through marshy constructions of thorns or brambles, islets of gnarled green trees, thickets of vines, barricades of bristles. Though it was still light, the sense of day soon vanished.

Lazear's boat crawled through this wet maze, chugging along uncertainly, its engine fighting to breathe, terrifying Sam each time it seemed to miss a beat or pause to take a gulp.

"You know the way?" he heard himself say.

"Well as my own hand, Mister," responded the old man, who quickly sweated through his clothes as he navigated under a faded blue ball cap that may have borne an allegiance to a big league team, though the insignia had long since disappeared.

"I thought this was a river. It's a swamp."

"Oh, she straightens out up ahead, you'll see. Best relax, sir. Nothing good comes of hurry in the swamp. You hurry, you be a dead fellow, sure. But it be fine;

probably no snake be biting you, or no 'gator eat your hand off, but I cannot say for sure."

Then his crumpled old face lit with glee and Sam realized it was a joke, that humor was a part of the man's madness.

"Hope them Choctaws ain't in no drinking mood," said old Lazear over the sound of the motor. "If they be, sometimes it make them hungry and they eat a white fellow. Leave me be, I'm too tough, like an old chicken been eating bugs and grubs its whole life. But you, Mister, figure you'd taste right good to them red savages."

"There isn't enough salt in Mississippi to tenderize me," Sam said. "They could chew me, but they could never swallow me. They'd choke on me."

It wasn't only the weather. It was also the darkness, not of the day but of the overhanging, interlinked canopy. The leaves and vines knotted up, twisted among themselves, invented new forms. Strange vegetation grew on other strange vegetation, a riot of life forms, insensate, unknowable.

The seal of the canopy had the effect of a greenhouse on the two men trapped beneath it; the heat rose even beyond the heat of Mississippi, and in no time at all Sam had sweated through his shirt and coat. Off came the coat, up went the sleeves, rolled tightly. He left his hat on, however, for its brim trapped the sweat that grew in his hairline and kept it from cascading down into his eyes. And of course he left his tie tight to his neck. There were certain concessions to the jungle one simply could not make.

He settled into the rear of the boat, uncomfortable, nestled against a gunwale on a pile of ropes. Luxury was out of the question, and an inch or two of water perfumed with gasoline sloshed around the bottom of the boat as it chugged onward, radiating nauseating fumes and a slight sense of mirage. Or maybe it was his splitting headache.

"Cheer up," cried old Lazear. "We got another five hours or so before true dark, then we lay up in a bay I know. You can sleep on dry ground, Lazear he sleep on the boat."

"I'll stay with the boat, thanks," said Sam. He imagined himself alone in this place. Alone: dead. It followed.

The old man now and then took a tot on a bottle of something, and once or twice handed it to Sam, who politely turned it down, until at last curiosity got the better of him.

Argh! It was some hellish French stuff, absinthe or something, with the heat of fire and the tang of salt; it burned all the way down, and he suddenly shivered.

"Ha! She got bite, no?" exclaimed Lazear.

In time, the light dwindled further, until it seemed impossible to go onward. Lazear found a little cut in the land, a miniature cove, surrounded by high grass and a copse of gnarled trees of no identifiable features, and there put in.

"I rustle up some grub. You eat."

Sam was in fact ravenous. The scrofulous old man disappeared into the disreputable hatchway that led to the boat's forward interior and threw pots and pans around. He came up a few minutes later with white chunks of bread, a lump of butter at some indeterminate stage between liquid and solid, a warped segment of cheese, greasy, waxy rind still affixed, and a knife and fork.

"Fancy food for a fancy guy, no?"

"I've eaten worse," said Sam, who remembered K rations in the snow during the Bulge, when it was so cold he thought he'd die of it, and the Germans were said to be everywhere, and all he wanted to do was head back to Arkansas and practice law. Instead, he'd gathered his six

105s into a tight formation atop a low hill, dug them in, and waited for targets. A German panzer unit obliged, grinding through the gray snow and the gray fog a mile out, and Sam and his men stayed cool and blew it off the face of the earth in three minutes of concentrated fire. Only burning hulks were left.

He slept in his clothes, feeling the drift of the boat against the slop of the river and the dampness of his feet where the water had at last overwhelmed the leather of his brogues, penetrating them. But it was good, dreamless sleep, for the temperature at last dropped and the air seemed cooled of the corruption that so embalmed it during the day.

HE awoke to the ritual of the coffee. Lazear had woken early, gone ashore, made a small fire. Now, as Sam watched, he boiled a pot of water, then moved it off the flame. With an old soup spoon he scooped coffee from an A & P bag, and spread it on the water. Next he produced a Clabber Girl baking powder tin, popped the lid and scooped out roasted and ground chicory root and again spread the material on the surface of the water until it seemed right. Then he swirled the black mix and let the grounds settle and steep. The smell of coffee and wood smoke made Sam's stomach rumble.

The old man sloshed through the water and handed Sam up a tin cup of the stuff; it cut to the bone, hot, raw and powerful. The French and their coffee; they were good at it beyond arrogance.

As Sam tried to focus, he found the fog was not in his mind but in the swamp. Tendrils of cottony moisture lay low on the water, curled through the trees, licked at the leaves.

"How much longer?"

"We hit the big river soon enough. Then we bear right where she splits, and that part takes on the name Yaxahatchee. That one's wider open so it'll go smoother. Don't you be falling in. That water deep and the current can be strong. Suck a man down, spit him back with his soul missing, his nose blue, his fingers shriveled and his false teeth out and floated off somewheres."

"Sir, I have no false teeth."

"Whatever you got, if you go in, the river, she take it. She's a black bitch of a river, you see. You don't be messin' 'round with her, or she fuck you good."

"My trust in you is absolute," Sam said.

He settled back, got through a few shaky moments when the old man seemed to have trouble interesting the engine in life again, until at last it sputtered, coughed, shivered, then began to pull the boat back out from the shore.

They coursed through the blackness, passing in the morning fog a ghost town, its rickety houses mossgrown and semifallen.

"What happened there?"

"Oh, dey got through Indians and plague and flood okay, but then some dogs, wild dogs, tore up some kids there. Kilt three. Little girls, I think, caught 'em in the open, kilt 'em fast, bled 'em out. The people just gave it up after that. The swamp, she be a cruel bad place."

Sam looked away, trying to banish the horror of the idea of it from his mind. The girls, the dogs, the screams, the smell of blood. He shook his head.

"Yah! Ha! Ain't no picnic out here, no siree. You ain't where you from, not by no long shot."

At last the swamp seemed to diminish its grip on the earth. The gnarled trees, the jungly vines and dinosaur vegetation gave way to longleaf pines arrayed over ridges of land, saw grass and other green clutter, all lead-ing to bleak shores. The river widened, deepened, turned ever blacker, grew swifter.

Then it split. It broke into two forks, one headed east, the other west. Neither looked promising: highways of dark river, the texture no longer smooth as oil or glass but now ever so slightly giving evidence of disturbance, as if strong currents lurked beneath, hungry to pull a man to his death.

"You hang on now, Mister, she can be rough," the old man cried, as he steered the weathered craft to the right-ward of the two torrents, and took them dead up the center.

They progressed steadily against a current that sug-gested they try elsewhere. The piney woods sealed them off from any evidence of life except the pines themselves, low, heavy with gum and tar of some sort. They were turpentine trees, bled in the fall for the chemical that oozed out of them. The weather remained malignant, even as the sun burned the last of the fog away, and if pines had ever reminded Sam of Northern glades as in Wisconsin or Minnesota, these were not such pines. They seemed to form two walls and a long, winding cor-ridor, a madman's dream of nothingness, while above the sun scalded them and no wind dared stir.

Sam glanced at his watch, feeling the itch of sweat and bites all over his skin. He even thought about loos-ening his tie, but he'd fought the Battle of the Bulge in a tie, so that was really only the last thing one did before accepting death.

It was by now nearly 11:00 A.M.

"How much further?"

"Be patient, Mister. You cannot rush the river. The current's agin' us, she don't want us going there. Be glad you gots planks beneath to keep your bottom from what's under, yes sir."

And so it went, seemingly endless, until at last, unbidden, as if out of a dream, Thebes revealed itself on a far shore.

He wondered: Am I in Africa?

For what he beheld was something out of a dream of a lost place, a place so benighted and run-down it seemed to have no right to exist in the country he knew to be America. Not even the meanest Negro shanty-towns of Arkansas seemed so raw and sad. It was a collection of slatternly dogtrot cabins, tar-paper roofs scorching in the hot sun, low, rotting warehouses off to a side by docks, mud streets that were too congealed to sustain wheels of any sort, much less automobiles. The ruins of what must have been a sawmill stood isolated a bit farther down the river, most walls gone, nothing but decaying frame and unturning wheel left.

It seemed somehow to have devolved, to have gone backward in time.

"She ain't much. Why you want to come all this way for this place, I don't know. *Merde.* Do you know? *Merde,* shit you say in English. It's shit. A town of shit. Who could live in such a place?"

As the old man's boat maneuvered toward dockage, Sam thought the place was as abandoned as the last town, where the wild dogs had killed the little girls. But at the same time, he felt the presence of eyes.

A boat was so rare, he assumed, it would be remarkable to such a place. Every eye would be upon him, and indeed he felt every eye upon him, but again he saw no evidence of life.

Lazear got in close, set the course, and stilled the engine.

"You get up front," he commanded, and Sam did what he was told. There, on the bobbing prow, he found a coil of rope. When the boat glanced off the dock, he leaped, pulling on the rope, tightening boat to dock, then looping it to a post set aslant in the water. He glanced back, saw that the old man had gone aft to secure the stern by similar method.

He walked back.

"I don't know how long this will take. You stay here. You stay out of bars or whorehouses or whatever temptations they have here. I have business; if it seems to run long, I'll notify you somehow. You do not leave without me. Do you understand?"

"Oh, yah, I stay forever. I got nothing to do but stay till the lawyer man gits his money."

"Get me my briefcase."

Lazear found it, the one pristine object aboard, and handed it over. Sam straightened and tightened his tie, pulled his coat to cure it of wrinkles, made sure his hat was set straight, and went to work.

WAS it only a town of children? Little Negro scamps tracked him from behind the first line of buildings. He could not see them, but he heard them scurrying in the mud, and several times, drawn by flashes of movement, glanced over, but his look drove them back. And if he advanced on them, they scattered.

Otherwise the town was seemingly deserted. There was no commerce, nor any sidewalk. A few storefronts were abandoned. Mostly the places were cabins, many to his eye as abandoned as the storefronts. Yet still he had a queasy feeling, a sense again of being looked at, inspected. It brought a shiver of discomfort.

As he climbed the slope from the river, he at last came

upon an adult woman. Her eyes were big, her face a ruin. She was swaddled in a dress of many layers and colors, all pulled into one tapestry; her hair was bandannaed tightly to her skull, and she had no teeth at all. She was a Negro mama, a formidable figure in the Negro community, Sam knew. And she didn't seem insane, but regarded him with only sullen dull hatred.

"Madam, excuse me, I am looking for a county seat, a municipal building, the sheriff's department? You could possibly direct me?"

She responded in a gibberish alien to his ears. Was she still African? Had she not been Americanized?

"Madam, I do not understand. Could you speak more slowly?"

He picked out a word or two of English in her mewl, but she grew frustrated with the stupidity on his face, and shooed him away with a dismissive, abrupt gesture, then gathered herself with dignity, pulled her shawl tight about her, and strutted away.

But she stopped and turned, then pointed down an alley.

She said something that he deciphered to mean: down that way.

He walked down it, the mud sucking at his shoes. Here and there a door slammed shut, a window closed, people not seen clearly hastened away. He felt as if he were the plague, Mr. Death himself, with a scythe, behooded, a pale slice of darkness, and all human things fled his presence.

Then he came to it, or what had been it.

Fire had claimed it. A blackened stone wall still stood, but the timbers were all scorched and collapsed, and rogue bricks lay about in the weeds of what had once been a public square. No pane of glass remained in the ruin, once upon a time some kind of courthouse building after the proud fashion of the South, with offices and departments and lockups and a garage or stable out back. Scavengers had picked it clean, and moss or other forms of vegetation had begun to claim it for their own.

So this was why there was no "official" Thebes County, why no letters were answered. It had burned, and perhaps with that the will that claims civilization out of nothingness was somehow finally and permanently broken.

Now what? he wondered.

It's all gone? It burned, most everybody left town, and only a few hopeless cases remain. Those that do must eke out a living somehow from the prison farm yet another mile or so upriver.

He walked on, not out of purpose but more in the hopes of encountering an inspiration. Then, progressing a bit farther, he noticed a low, rude shack whose door was open, and from whose chimney pipe issued a trail of smoke, thin and white.

Batting at a fly that suddenly buzzed close to his face, he leaned in to discover something of a public house, though a rude caricature of it. It was empty but for an old man at the bar and an old man behind the bar. No array of liquor stood behind the bartender, only a motley collection of dusty glasses. Beer signs from the twenties dustily festooned the dim room, and dead neon curled on the wall, which could be decoded, with effort, into the names of the commercial brews of many decades past.

"Say there," said Sam, "I need some help. Can you direct me?"

"Ain't nowheres be directin', suh," said the bartender.

"Well, I'll be the judge of that. Can you guide me to what succeeded the town hall? Surely there's still some authority around. Possibly the registrar's office, the tax collector. Or a police or sheriff's station. This is the county seat, isn't it?"

"Used to be. Not much here no more. Can't help none. You g'wan, git back to that boat. Ain't nuffin here you want to know about."

"Surely there are sheriff's deputies."

"Dey fine you iffn dey want," said the other. "Best pray they don't want you."

"Well, isn't this the limit?" said Sam to nobody.

"It all burned down 'bout fo' years back, Mister. Everybody done left."

"I saw it. So now there's nothing?"

"Only the Farm."

"The Prison Farm, yes. I suppose I shall have to go there."

"Don't nobody go there but *gots* to go there, suh. In chains. Thems only ones. You don't want to go there. You best be on 'bout your business."

"Then let me ask you this," he said, and went on about Lincoln Tilson, the retired Negro whose fate he had come down to locate. But as he spoke, he began to sense that his two coconversationalists were growing extremely unhappy. They squirmed as if in minor but persistent pain, and their eyes popped about nervously, as if scanning for interlopers.

"Don't know nuffin' 'bout dat," said the one.

"Not a damn thing," chimed in the other.

"So the name means nothing to you?"

"No suh."

"All right. Wish I could thank you for your help, but you've not been any at all. Don't you respect white people down here?"

"Suh, jus' tryin' to git by."

"Yes, I see."

He turned and left, and began the long trek back to the boat. He knew now he had to go to the prison, where surely what records remained were kept, if they were kept at all. It seemed out of another century: the possibility that a man like Lincoln Tilson, a man of accomplishment and property, even by these standards some prosperity, could just disappear off the face of the earth, leaving no trace of paper, no police report, no death certificate, no witnesses, no anything. That was not how you did it.

Sam's mind was clearly arranged. He appreciated order above all things, for order was the beginning of all things. Without elemental order there was nothing; it wasn't a civilization unless undergirded by a system of laws and records, of taxes and tabulations. This down here: it was not *right*. He felt some fundamental law was being flouted before his very eyes.

He rounded the corner and began to head down the slope to the river. That's when he saw the dock, yet several hundred yards before him, and realized that Lazear was gone.

Goddamn the man!

But of course: this whole journey was a fiasco from the start, and how could he have trusted an old coot like Lazear? You'd as soon trust a snake in the grass.

He walked down, hoping that perhaps Lazear had taken the craft out into the deep water for some technical reason or other. But no: the boat, the old man, both were gone. Nothing stirred, nothing moved, behind him the ghost town in the mud, before him the empty river, and nothing around for hundreds of square miles but wilderness and swamp.

Sam was not the panicky sort. He simply grew grumpier and more obdurate in the face of adversity. He turned, convinced that he should find the first adult he saw and *demand* explanations. But to his surprise, almost as if awaiting him, the old mama lady stood nearby. How had she approached without his hearing? Was she magical?

Don't be a ridiculous fool, he thought. This isn't mumbo jumbo voodoo hoodoo, it was the blasted, backwater South, up some sewer of a river, where folks had degraded out of loss of contact with an outside world. He was in no danger. Negroes did not attack white people, so he would be all right.

"Madam, I have in my pocket a crisp ten-dollar bill. Would that be sufficient for a night's lodging and a simple meal? Unless there's a hotel, and I suspect there's not a hotel within a thousand square miles."

He held the bill out; she snatched it.

He followed her.

THE house was no different from any other, only a bit farther into the woods. It was another dogtrot cabin, low, dusty, decrepit and tar-paper roofed like the others. A few scrawny pigs grunted and shat in a pen in the front yard, and a mangy dog lay on the porch, or what passed for porch, but was just floorboards under some overhanging warped roof.

The dog growled.

She kicked it.

"Goddamn dog!"

Off it ran, squealing. It clearly wasn't her dog, only a dog she allowed to share space with her, and when feeling generous rewarded it for its companionship with a bone or something.

"Ou' back. You go where de chickens be."

"Why, thank you," he said, wasting a smile on her, a

pointless exercise because she had no empathy in her for him, and was only interested in minimally earning that ten spot.

He walked 'round back, and there was a low coop, wired off from the rest of the yard, and a few chickens bobbed back and forth as they walked onward.

"Home, sweet home," he said to nobody except his own ironic sense of humor, then ducked into the place. All the rooms were occupied, and the innkeeper, an orange rooster, raised a ruckus, but Sam, sensing himself to be the superior creature, stamped his foot hard, and gobble-gobbled as he did for his youngest children at Thanksgiving and the bull bird flustered noisily off in a cloud of indignant feathers and squawks.

Sam took the best bedroom, that being a corner where the straw looked cleanest and driest, and sat himself down.

Dark was falling.

He wanted, before the light was gone, to write out an account of his day for his employer. He filled his Schaeffer from a little Scripp bottle in his briefcase. Then he set to work on his trusty yellow legal pad, soon losing contact with the real world.

He didn't hear her when she entered.

"Here," she finally said. "Sompin' eat."

"What? Oh, yes, of course."

It was a foil pie plate, her finest china, filled with steaming white beans in some sort of gravy, and a chunk of pan bread. She had a cup of hot coffee with it and utensils that turned out to be clean and shiny.

"Thank you, madam," he said. "You keep a fine homestead."

"Ain't my home," she said. "Used to be. Ain't no more."

"It isn't your home?"

"It be the Store's."

"The Store?"

"The Farm Store. Onliest store dese parts. Da store own everything."

"Oh, you must be mistaken. If the Store is part of the state government, it can't loan funds against property, calculate interest, and foreclose, not without court hearings and court-appointed attorneys. There are laws to prevent such things."

"Da Store be the law here. Dat's all. You eat up them beans. Tomorrow you go about your bidness. I could git in trouble wif dem. Dey don't like no outsiders. You won't say I told you nuffin?"

"Of course not."

After that, she had nothing left to say, and he scraped the last of the beans off the plate. She took it, and left silently. He saw her heading back to her cabin, stooped and hunched, broken with woe.

Lord, I cannot wait to put this place behind me.

He made his plans. He'd clean up tomorrow as best he could given the circumstances, then go to the Store or the office of the Farm, where all power seemed concentrated. He would get to the bottom of this or know why.

Once he'd taken off his shoes and his hat and at last his tie, and folded his jacket into a little package that would do for a pillow, it didn't take long for him to fall asleep. For all its scratchiness, the straw was warm and dry. His roommates cooed quietly on their nests, and even the rooster seemed at last to accept him; it realized he was no threat when it came to fertilizing the hens.

He slept easily; he was, after all, near exhaustion. The dreams he had were dead literal, without that kind of logic-free surrealism that fills most sleepers' minds. In Sam's dreams, the world made the same sense it made in reality; the same laws, from gravity to probate, still obtained; reason trumped emotion and the steady, inexorable fairness of the system proved out in the end, as it always did. Sometimes he wished he had a livelier subconscious, but there was nothing that could be done with such a defect.

He was not dreaming when they woke him. He was in dark, black nothingness; the light in his eyes had the quality of pain and confusion. He sat up, bolt awake, aware of shapes, the smell of horses, the sense of movement all 'round him.

Three flashlights had him nailed.

"Say, what on earth is—" he began to bluster, but before he could get it out, somebody hit him with a wooden billy club across the shoulder. The pain was fearsome, and he bent double, his spirit initially shattered by it. His hand flew to the welt.

"Jesus!" he screamed.

"Git him, boys."

"Goddamn, don't let him squirm away."

"Luther, if he fights, whop him agin!"

"You want another goddamn taste, Mister? By God, I will skull you next goddamn time."

They were on him. He felt himself pinned, turned, then cuffed.

"That's it. Bring him out now."

He was dragged out. There were three deputies, husky boys, used to using muscle against flesh, who shoved him along, their lights beaming in his face, blinding him. The cuffs enraged him. He had *never* been handcuffed in his life.

"What in God's name do you think you're doing! I

am an attorney-at-law, for God's sake, you have no right at all to—"

Another blow lit up his other arm and he stumbled to the earth in the agony of it.

"That ought to shut him up," said the man on horseback, who was in command. "Load him in the meat wagon and let's go."

5

I T smelled of pines. The odor actually was not unpleasant; it was brisk, somehow clean, and pine needles, like tufts of feathers, light brown and fluffy, lay everywhere.

But it was still a prison.

Sam's arms were both swollen, and when he clumsily peeled away the clothes he wore, he saw two purplish-yellow bruises inscribed diagonally across each biceps, as if laid there by an expert. One was not harder than the other. In fact, they were mirror images. No bones were broken, no skin cut, just the rotted oblong tracing exactly the impact of the billy club upon his upper arms, each delivered with the same force, at the same angle, to the same debilitating effect. Sam's arms were numb, and his hands too unfeeling to grab a thing. He could make but the crudest of movements. When he had to pee in the bucket in the corner, undoing his trouser buttons was a nightmare, but he would not let these men do it for him, if they would, which was questionable.

He knew he had been beaten by an expert. Someone

who had beaten men before, had thought critically about it, had done much thorough research, and knew where to hit, how to hit, how hard to hit, and what marks the blows would leave, which, after a week or so, would be nothing at all. Without photographic evidence, it would only be his word against a deputy's in some benighted Mississippi courtroom, in front of some hick judge who thought Arkansas was next to New York, New York, the home of communism.

His head ached. His temper surged, fighting through the pain.

It was some kind of cell in the woods, and he had a sensation of the piney woods outside, for he could hear the whisper of needles rustling against each other in the dull breeze.

He said again to the bars and whoever lurked down the corridor, "I DEMAND to see the sheriff. You have no right or legal authority to hold me. You should be horsewhipped for your violations of the law."

But no one bothered to answer, except that once a loutish deputy had slipped a tray with more beans, some slices of dry, salty ham, and a piece of buttered bread on the plate, as well as a cup of coffee.

Was he in the prison?

Was this Thebes, where uppity niggers were sent to rot?

He didn't think so. There was instead a sense of desolation about this place, the stillness of the woods, the occasional chirping of birds. The window was too high to see out of, and he could see nothing down the hall. His arms hurt, his head hurt, his dignity hurt, but what hurt even more was his sense of the system corrupted. It cut to the core of the way his mind worked. People were not treated like this, especially people like him, which is to say white people of means and education. The system made no sense if it didn't protect him, and it needed to be adjusted.

"*Goddammit, you boys will pay!*" he screamed, to nobody in particular, and to no sign that anybody heard him.

At last—it had to be midafternoon, fourteen or fifteen full hours after his capture—two guards came for him.

"You put your hands behind yourself so's we can cuff you down now," said the one.

"And goddammit, be fast about it, Sheriff ain't got all day, goddammit."

"Who do you think—"

"I think you gimme lip, I'll lay another swat on you, Dad, and you won't like it a dadgum bit."

So this was the fellow who had hit him: maybe twenty-five, blunt of nose and hair close-cropped, eyes dull as are most bullies', a lot of beef behind him, his size the source of his confidence.

"G'wan, hurry, Mister, I ain't here to wait on your dadgum mood."

At last Sam obliged, turning so that they could cuff him, a security measure that was, in a civilized state like Arkansas, reserved for the most violent and unpredictable of men in the penal system, known murderers and thugs who could go off on a rampage at no provocation at all. It was for dealing with berserkers.

Once they had him secured, they unlocked the cell and took control of him, one on each arm, and walked him down the wood corridor, then into a small interrogation room.

They sat him down, and, as per too many crime movies and more police stations than Sam cared to count, a bright light came into his eyes.

The door opened.

A large man entered, behind the light so that Sam could not see details, but he made out a dark uniform, black or brown, head to toe, with a beige tie tight against his bulgy neck, and a blazing silver star badge on his left breast. He wore a Sam Browne belt, shined up, and carried a heavy revolver in a flapped holster, his trousers pressed and lean, down to cowboy boots also shiny and pointed.

"Samuel M. Vincent," he said, reading from what Sam saw was his own wallet. "Attorney-at-law, Blue Eye, Polk County, Arkansas. And what is your business in Thebes, Mr. Vincent?"

"Sheriff, I am a former prosecuting attorney, well versed in the law and the rightful usage of force against suspects. In my state, what your men have done is clearly criminal. I would indict them on counts of assault and battery under flag of authority, sir, and I would send them away for five years, and we would see how they swagger after that. Now I—"

"Mr. Vincent, what is your business, sir? You are not in your state, you are in mine, and I run mine a peculiar way, according to such conditions as I must deal with. I am Sheriff Leon Gattis, and this is my county. I run it, I protect it, I make it work. Down here, sir, it is polite of an attorney to inform the po-lice he be makin' inquiries. For some reason, sir, you have seen fit not to do so, and so you have suffered some minor inconveniences of no particular import to no Mississippi judge."

"I did not do so, Sheriff Gattis, because there were *no deputies* around. I spent most of yesterday *looking for them*. They prefer to *work after midnight!* I insist—"

"You hold on there, sir. You are getting on my wrong side right quick. Any nigger could have told you where we are, and if they didn't it's 'cause they thought you's up to no good. God bless 'em, they have the instinct for such judgments. So, Mr. Vincent, you're going to have to cooperate, and the sooner you do, the better. What are you doing in Thebes County? What is your business, sir?"

"Good Lord. You set up a system than *cannot* be obeyed, then punish when one does *not* obey. It is—"

Whap!

The sheriff had not hit him, but he'd smacked his hand hard on the wooden table between them, the room echoing with reverberation from the force of the blow.

"I ain't here to talk no philosophy with you. Goddamn you, sir, answer my questions or your time here will be hard. That is the way we do things here."

Sam shook his head.

Finally he explained: he was after a disposition or certificate in re the death of a Negro named Lincoln Tilson named in a will being probated in Cook County—that is, Chicago—Illinois.

"Thought you had a Chicago look to you."

"Sir, if it's your business, and it's not, I have never been in the state of Illinois and know nothing at all of it."

"What I hear, up there, the Negro is king. Ride 'round in fancy Cadillac cars, have white girls left and right, eat in the restaurants, a kind of jigaboo heaven, if you know what I mean."

"Sir, I feel certain you exaggerate. I have been to New York, and that town, progressive though it may be, is nothing as you describe."

"Maybe I do exaggerate. But, by God, that ain't goin' happen in Thebes. Down here, we got a natural order as God commands, and that's how it's goin' to be."

"Sir, I feel that change will come, because change is inevit—"

"So you are one of them?"

"Uh—"

"One of them."

"I'm not clear—"

"One of them. You talk like one of us, but you be one of them. Northern agitators. Communists, Jews, God knows who, what or why, but up to nothing good. Is that you, Mr. Vincent? Are you a communist or a Jew?"

"I am a Democrat and a Scotch Presbyterian. You have no right to—"

But the sheriff was off.

"Oh, we done heard. We done been warned. We onto y'all. Y'all come down here and stir our niggers all up. You think you doin' them a favor. Yes sir, you *helping* them. But what you be doin' is filling their fool heads full of things that can't never be, and so you be making them more unhappy rather than less unhappy, while you be gittin' it ready to tear down what we done built down here, on nothing but sweat and blood and guts and our own dying. Oh, I know your sort, Mister. You are the pure-D devil hisself, only you think you doin' good."

"I am a firm believer in the rules, and I—"

"The rules! Mister, I got a county full of piney-woods niggers who all they want to do is fuck or fight, don't matter much to them."

"Sir, I didn't say—"

"Now I'll tell you what. I will make inquiries. I will git you your certificate, and my deputies will get you out of our county. Don't you never come back, you hear? That's the goddamnedest best you're gonna git down here, and I am cutting you an exclusive deal because you are white, even if I believe you be deluded close to mental instability. Thebes ain't for outsiders. You want Mississippi hospitality, you go to Biloxi, you square on that, partner?"

"I see the point," said Sam.

"Yes, sir, I bet you do. Boys, move Mr. Vincent to holding, where he'll be more comfortable. He's 'bout to leave us."

SAM was no longer locked up, nor did he remain handcuffed. He was free to move about the general area, but had, under orders and strict observation, to stay close to the station, as it was called, and not to go near to or rile any Negro people.

They let him take a nice shower indoors, where they themselves kept clean, and he got himself back into some kind of civilized order. He was fed, and the food was better than anything he had eaten since leaving Pascagoula, beans and ham, fried potatoes, heavy chicory coffee, fresh bread. These boys here, they lived pretty good, in what was a kind of barracks in the woods, a good mile out of town, which, he now saw, was protected against attack by a stout barbed-wire fence. There was a stable here, for the deputy force seemed more like some kind of light cavalry than any law enforcement unit. The men lounged about like soldiers, keeping their uniforms sharp, riding off on patrol now and then in twos. There was a duty room with assignments and rotation, a roster board; in all, it seemed far more military than police.

Finally, a rider came, and after conferring with some of the deputies, he came and got Sam, who was put back into the wagon, though this time not bound or beaten. He sat up front with the driver, who drove the team through the piney woods—Lord, they were dense, seeming to stretch out forever into the looming darkness— and then through the town, dead now as it was then.

They approached the river, the big wagon and the thundering horses driving back what Negroes remained

in the street. As they passed the public house, Sam felt
the eyes of the two old men he'd spoken to watching him
glumly.

Down at the dock, a happy sight greeted Sam. It was
Lazear, back from wherever, standing by his boat, whose
old motor churned a steady tune. The sheriff stood there
also.

Sam climbed down from the wagon, on unsure legs,
then caught himself.

"All right, Mr. Arkansas Traveler, here is your official
document. You'll see that it's right and proper."

It appeared to be. Under the seal of the state of Mississippi and the state motto it was an official CERTIFICATE OF
DEATH for one LINCOLN TILSON, Negro, age unknown but
elderly, of Thebes, Thebes County, Mississippi, October
10th, 1950, by drowning, namely in the river Yaxahatchee. It was signed by a coroner in an illegible scrawl.

"There, sir. The end of that poor man. The river can
be treacherous. It takes you down and it does things to
you, and out you come three days later. Poor Negro
Tilson was such a victim. It's a miracle that after that
time in the water, he was still identifiable."

"Sheriff, who identified him?"

"Now, Mr. Arkansas Traveler, we don't keep records
on every dead Negro in the county. I don't recollect, nor
do I recollect the exact circumstances. Nor, sir, do I
fancy a chat with you on the subject, while you interro-
gate me and try to prove your Northern cleverness over
my simplicity."

"I see."

"You have been given fair warning. Now you get out
of our town, and don't you come back nohow. There is
nothing here for you and you have done your task."

Sam looked at the document; there was nothing to it

to convince him that it couldn't have been fabricated in the last hour or so.

But here it was: the out. The end. The finish. He had earned his retainer, and would file a complete report to his client, and what would happen next would be up to the client.

"Well, Sheriff, this is not the way I do things, but I see things down here are slow to change, and it is not my charge to do that. I fear when change comes, it will be a terror for you."

"It ain't never coming, not this far south. We have the guns and the will to make that prediction stick, I guarantee you. Now, sir, every second you stand there is a second you try my hospitality to an even more severe degree."

Sam stepped down into Lazear's boat and didn't look back as it pulled from the shore and headed out to the center of the dark river.

6

SAM sat in the prow of the boat, too angry to talk to Lazear, uninterested in the feeble excuses the man had thrown his way on the whys and wherefores of his seeming abandonment.

He felt two powerful, conflicting emotions. The first was relief. Thebes was enchanted, somehow, by evil. Who knew what secrets lurked there, what horrors had been perpetuated under its name, who was buried where and how they had perished? It was frightening, and escaping its pressures brought a sense of complete liberation.

So a part of Sam was happy. He was done, and now it was a mere progression of travel and he could return to his life, chastened, as it were, by exposure to the lurid and the raw, aware that the world in general was uninterested in his experiences and it would best be forgotten or filed away for distant future usage.

But there was also a powerful, seething anger. His mind was orderly yet not overly rigid. He understood that order was a value and from order all good, great things stemmed. Yet order was only a value when it guaranteed and sustained those good, great things. When it actively opposed them, where it destroyed them, where its rigidness was so powerful and its administration so violent that it was only concerned with its own ideas, something evil happened, and it filled Sam with rage.

He felt the thwack when the deputy's two expert blows had smashed his arms, and the fear when under the influence of pain all will to resist had fled him. He remembered the helplessness of being bound and forced into the wagon, the wait for the sheriff as that man took his own sweet time, the fear on the faces of the Negroes whom he ruled so absolutely, the brazenness of the phony document that had guaranteed the end of his days in Thebes.

And Sam finally wondered this one last thing: Did he have the strength, the guts, the steel, to stand up to it, to oppose the ways of Thebes?

He knew the answer.

The answer was, No.

It wasn't in him. It wasn't in anybody. You just got out and didn't look back and you went back to a better life, and soon enough the memories eroded and you won your election and you fathered your children and you won the approval of powerful men and you had a career, a set of memories, a fine tombstone, the respect of those who stayed behind when you had passed. That was enough.

He sat back, having at last faced and come to terms with his own weakness. On either side of the river, the piney woods fled by, diminished by the steady chugging of Lazear's old motor, the day a bit cooler than before. Before him the river wove and bobbed, dark, calm and smooth. It was growing toward late afternoon; he assumed that in a few hours or so, when they had penetrated the great bayou, they would lay up as before, then continue in the morning.

He began to calculate. They'd be in Pascagoula then by late afternoon; he'd call his wife and alert her that everything was fine. He could spend a night in a fine hotel—if there was such in Pascagoula . . . wait, then, no, a better idea. He could hire a car and zip down the coast a bit, possibly to lush Biloxi, and take a room there, where surely there'd be fine hotels. Maybe he'd take a day or so; the stipend he'd earned would certainly cover it, and possibly he could even expense it, as the recovery time from his ordeal was a fair charge, was it not? He saw himself having an elegant meal under a slowly rotating fan, amid ferns and palms; outside there'd be a sparkling beach. The meal would commence with oysters fresh from Mother Gulf, move on to fresh sea bass or trout grilled or poached in butter, all served by an elegant black gentleman in a white cotton jacket. The room would be full of beautiful people, happy people, the best kind of people that our great country could produce.

What a riposte. What a recovery. Then, the next morning, on to New Orleans, refreshed and restored; from there by rail up to Memphis, the drive over to Blue Eye and home, home, home, home.

Home, he thought.

Home, home, home. Then he saw the body.

He happened to be looking down, in the black water, and the shock was such that perhaps it was an apparition, something that his momentarily deranged mind had conjured. But he knew in the next second that no, this was reality, no haunt, no ghost, nothing from the subconscious. It was a Negro boy, a few inches under the surface, bled white by immersion, his features puffy, his body in the cruciform as if inflated, his fingers abulge, his eyes wide and empty, his mouth open black and empty, his clothes in tatters, gliding by. Then he was gone.

Sam blinked, stunned.

He saw something just ahead, floating, its low silhouette just breaking the surface, and as Lazear's old craft fled by, he made this victim out to be a girl child, also Negro, but facedown to spare him those open eyes staring into nothingness.

He looked: on the surface of the water appeared to be the remnants of a massacre by drowning; bodies floated everywhere, as if a vessel had capsized and all perished. There had to be at least ten, drifting, riding the currents, bobbing this way and that.

"*Stop the boat! Goddamn you, stop the boat!*" he screamed, over the beating of the engine.

Lazear looked up, surprised, yanked from whatever crude reverie had occupied him.

"*Stop the boat, you idiot!*" Sam cried, and rushed back. Lazear didn't stop it, but reined in the throttle so that the boat merely idled, drifting.

"What you say?"

"There're people in the water! Look, look around, people. A Negro family, all gone, all lost, stop the boat."

Lazear just shook his head.

"Sir, I done tol' you. In de river, de currents is ugly and mean. Suck people down all de time. Send 'em back bloated and dead. Nothing we can do but press on. Can't do them no good. Make a report when you gets back to civilization if it makes you feel good. I can't be wastin' no time on this."

And with that he bent forward and readjusted the throttle to a steady roar and the boat lurched back into—

But Sam took him in two strong hands, shook him once malevolently, then almost quite literally threw him into the rear of the boat.

The old man raised a hand in fear as Sam advanced upon him.

"Don't hit me, sir! I didn't do nothing to them people, I swear. They's fleeing the Store, they got in trouble, and the river done et 'em up, is all."

Sam declared, in the full stentorian powers of his voice, "You slimy little maggot, you turn this boat around and we will recover those that we can. Then we will head back to Thebes and we will get that good-for-nothing sheriff off his fat ass and all his deputies and we will come back here with full lights running. There may be a child out here, clinging to a branch or ashore in the weeds. We will save that child, or by God, we will die trying, and that is the way it'll be."

Now he bent, and with one hand pulled Lazear up, and propelled him toward the boat's cockpit, and the old man hit it, and sank to the deck.

"Get your ass up, and get going, sir, or I will make you wish you had never ever been born."

"Yes sir, yes sir," said Lazear, pale with terror.

As it turned out, Sam quickly realized there was no point in recovering any bodies. It would take too much time, and it was a job for professionals with the right equipment. He realized those bodies therefore might never be recovered.

Thus, as newly proclaimed captain of Lazear's vessel by right of mutiny, he determined that the correct course of action was to return to the Thebes dock as swiftly as possible. He gave these directions to Lazear.

"And if de motor burn out, what then?"

"Then I will whip your scrawny ass until it bleeds. You just get us there faster than you got us here, you wretched old fool."

"Yes, sir."

"What did you mean when you said 'fleeing the Store.' What was the meaning of that comment?"

"Sir, I don't recollect saying nothing 'bout dat."

"Listen here, you brainless idiot, you said it flat out in plain English just minutes ago. Now explain it, or once again I will shake you 'til your teeth, all three of them, rattle like dice in a cup."

Glumly Lazear looked ahead. A bitterness settled over him. He acted as though God had selected him alone to bear this monstrous cross. He sighed.

Sam kicked his scrawny ass.

"Does that help? Clear the memory, does it?"

"You din't hear nothing from me. Dey kills me dey know I talkin' their business. Okay? Kill me dead. Kill you dead as well."

"Talk, damn your soul."

"The Store own everything the nigs got. Nigs take credit from the Store, fall behind, they don't get this interest thing, the Store forecloses, and then they owned by the Store. Heard the nigs talking 'bout it once."

"Yes. And so?"

"And so, dey gots to work it off. Dey works for de

man. Never can leave, never can go nowhere, tell no-body, no nothing. Stay and work for food is all.

"Every once a while, nigs git fed up and sneak off at night. Some make it, some don't. Dat family, dey no got no luck. The river et 'em. Maybe dey's better off, though."

"Good Lord," said Sam, disgusted.

7

How did they know?

But they did. Somehow, in Thebes, they always knew.

The old boat maneuvered its way in and Lazear lined it up just fine and laid it up next to the dock. There, Sheriff Leon Gattis and no less than four deputies, all uniformed and heavily armed, awaited. Their horses, lathered and nervous, milled behind them. Together, men and horses, they looked like some apocalyptic drawing out of Doré, along the four-horsemen-of-death motif.

But Sam did not care.

"Sheriff," he cried, as he climbed up, "you'd best get your boys onto the river. A Negro boat has overturned some miles down, and there yet may be survivors. You'll need powerful flashlights, for I fear the light will be gone by the time—"

"Didn't you and me reach a agreement, sir? You's to leave town, and not never come back on no account. And on that bargain, you would not be prosecuted for resisting arrest or generally stirring up the population."

"Sir, I am not here to quibble. People's lives may be at

stake. For God's sake, time's wasting. Get those boys of yours on to the goddamn water and get them going. This is a river town, surely you have boats. This is not some paltry charge, this is a public safety emergency."

"Goddammit, Mister, you must be thick of the skull or water-brained or some such. Didn't know they growed such knotheads in Arkansas. Heard it was an all right place, though I can see now it produces too many of the daft persuasion."

"Sheriff, I insist that—"

"Mister, I am not sending boys out on that dark river to look for fleeing Negroes. The currents are tricky, the fog comes in and twists things around, and before you know it, you have white men in trouble as much as black ones."

"My God, we are talking about human beings!"

"If they go out there after dark, they know damned well the chance they take."

"Sheriff," a merry deputy called, "bet it's Jimmy and Glory and them all."

"That Jimmy, never was no good," said another. "That one always be in trouble. Lord, he done got Glory and the chilluns drowned, too."

"We'll ride over and check in the morning."

"Sheriff," Sam implored, "am I to understand you'll do nothing? Nothing at all. Possibly a child—"

"Ain't no children out there, sir. The children are all dead. These people flee their responsibilities and they make plumb fool decisions and take terrible chances, and they pay the price, most of them do. Jimmy owed money, he should have stayed like a man and worked off his debt, 'stead of running off to welch on it."

"Sir, I have to tell you: If I don't see evidence of public safety activity on your part, I will myself make a report to the governor of Mississippi and—"

"Haw!" laughed one of the deputies, "ain't that a good one. He's gonna go to Jackson and tell old Bilbo 'bout a drownded nigger!"

The others hooted.

"Sir," the sheriff said, "tell who you wish whatever you want. In Jackson they consider that we do our job well down here. We handle the uppity niggers, or rather the prison does. We make the state run, and we do our part to keep order, and I'm a proud man because of it. Now I warned you to leave this town."

"Mr. Leon," Lazear suddenly proclaimed, "don't make us leave now. I don't know de river in de dark; we end up dead as them nigs."

About three different conversations seemed to explode simultaneously: the deputies continued to enjoy the humorous idea of Sam's audience at the state capital; Lazear enjoined the sheriff to let them stay the night so that he did not have to face the river in the dark; and Sam continued to demand action on the missing family.

The sheriff finally reached to his holster, pulled out a big revolver, and fired a single shot to quiet them all. Its boom clapped and whanged, rolled and reverberated. Total silence followed as all looked at the large man with the revolver in hand.

"Y'all, you git back on patrol," he told his deputies. "Old man, you stay here, moored to that dock. At first light, you be gone, or by God, I'll make you wish you had. And you, Mr. Lawyer, you git back on that boat, and don't you come off to step on the dirt of my county ever agin. If you do, I will personally have a knot beaten into your head that will last forever, and you can tell all your fancy Arkansas people, I got this knot in Thebes, Mississip, on account of some drownded niggers. And I don't care to speak again on this subject, no more, never."

"Sheriff, you are making a big mistake."

"Jed, you stay down here, make sure these two don't roam. And make sure they put off with the light. They give you any trouble, you can whip up on them any old way you want. Now I'm going home to get my supper."

Jed detached himself from his chums and swaggered down. He was a big ol' boy, with three guns, and cords and leathers and belts everywhere. He looked just dumb enough to take all this seriously, and wouldn't be convincible elsewise. He'd as soon hit you with the club he carried as listen.

He spat a wad into the water, where it popped wetly as it hit.

"Don't you worry, Sheriff," he said. "I'll take care of these boys, you can bet on it."

SAM awakened in the dark.

He had reached his conclusion at last.

He'd been building toward it for a long piece, fighting its implications, aware that he was troubling with the very stuff of his life, his destiny, his fate.

But now he knew he could not spend his time in Blue Eye, Arkansas, pretending to represent law and order, while three hundred miles away this chancre perpetuated itself, unseen, unmolested, uncontested.

He knew: Thebes must fall.

Somehow, some way, it must fall. In his mind, he sketched out a plan. It was orderly and well founded, almost certain to succeed. He would have to form a committee of well regarded, unassailably moral Southern prosecutors—he knew many of them—and very carefully review and accumulate the evidence. An unassailable report had to be created. Then, carefully, copies of this document must be given to selected press, which would reveal the findings on the day that his committee presented the report to the governor of the state of Mississippi, the speaker of the house in the Mississippi state assembly, Mississippi's two senators and five congressmen, hell, maybe even, for the publicity value alone, Harry S. Damn Truman himself, or, since all this was some years off, whomsoever bigwigged war general was in the White House.

It had to be done square and legal, one step at a time, with an eye toward reality, so that the final product had a rightness to it that transcended the seething angers of the South. He wanted the white Southern mill worker and small-patch farmer, the sharecropper, the feed-store clerks, the small-town politicos, the damn women (if they could control their goddamn crying!), the MacWhatevers and the Joneses and the Whites and the O'Whomevers; a new Confederacy, if you would, of the same ol' boys who marched up Peahawk Ridge or across the wide-open ground at Gettysburg behind the fool Pickett or thrashed and perished in the cornfields of bloody Antietam. They could do it, for they had it within them, if they were ably led; they and they alone could bring Thebes down and make the world a better place.

But he knew this too: he had to start with a document.

It was all so much palaver without a piece of evidence, a piece of paper, that made it clear as a bell's last dying dingdong: this is evil. This is wrong. This must be stopped.

He had to have something. He knew it, and that there was no way around it.

He thought: I have to get into that store.

And then he thought: that is insane. It is in a prison, it is carefully guarded, it will not give up its secrets easy, it is a mile away down a dark and windy forest road that I have never traveled and, top it all, I am no man for breaking and entering. I would get caught, and if caught I would be in deep trouble.

He thought again: I need someone to help me. I need someone to take the risk, to get me a document.

Then he remembered the old lady whose chicken coop he'd rented. She spoke a gibberish at first, but as he listened more carefully and got used to the rhythms and strangenesses in her words, he had begun to understand her. It was she who told him about the Store. She must understand the legal underpinnings of Thebes County, the original crime that indebted its citizens to work for little or nothing for the benefit of bossmen who kept his expenses in that way to a minimum while raking off the top, whose iron system of rule by violence lined his own pockets.

She must have a piece of paper. He remembered now, the weathered old face, the fierce eyes, the watchfulness; why, that old mama was the only one in the town whose spirit remained secretly intact, and Sam knew this to be in accordance with Negro ways, where authority frequently devolved on the sagacity of an old woman, who was smart and just and well-tempered by experience.

Sam squinted in the dark, and saw that it was near 4:00 A.M. If he could get by that behemoth on the dock, he could get to her house by 4:30 and back again by 5:00, and then he'd have it, something upon which to build. It was how a lawyer worked: go for the paper. Get the paper. Get the evidence. If there was any evidence.

He rose from his length of blanket on the prow of the boat, and carefully put on his shoes. Though it was warmish, he took his coat, which had been his pillow, and threw it on, to blot out the whiteness of his shirt.

Rising craftily, he crept down the length of the boat, and stopped for just a second to listen to the easy sawing of old Lazear's aged lungs as he snoozed away in the cockpit, in some impossible position that no civilized being could find rest in. But Lazear snored as if lung-shot and producing death rattles, each a mighty shudder through bubbles of phlegm, but otherwise unwakeable.

Sam made the climb to the dock and discovered that the guardian deputy, of course, had grown bored with the passing of the nighttime hours and had departed for whatever recreation he wanted, probably a willing colored gal in a crib somewhere, for all the deputies had the look of men who're whup-ass on colored in the daylight and cuddle with it in the night.

Sam climbed the slope from the riverside area to what amounted to the town's main drag, not really much of either main or drag, just shuttered storefronts behind which, on either side, lay the dogtrot cabins that made up the domiciles of the place before yielding to the all-encompassing piney woods. He tried to remember. This way or that? It's not that Thebes was a complex metropolitan zone, with byways and alleys that could lure a man to ruin, or at least get him lost. Still, in the dark, it seemed all different, and the vistas down the few streets were closed off to his eyes. But then he saw the public house where the two bitter old men had been and remembered . . . no, he didn't get to the woman's house until *after* he'd been there. Why hadn't he paid attention? It hadn't seemed important then, but it surely did now.

At last he thought he had it, as he projected a three-dimensional map of Thebes in his mind. He passed the public house, turned down an alley, walked amid silent cabins. Dogs scuffled and scurried, and occasionally barked, and he heard the slithery, feathery rattlings of chickens twitching in their coops. A pig or two was up, for whatever reason, maybe to shit in the mud or whatever. But of people the place was forlorn and empty.

It was a balmy Southern night. Above, towers of stars spangled in the pure black sky and a zephyr whispered through the pines, bringing relief from the day's brutal heat. The smell of the pines was everywhere, bracing and pure, almost medicinal. With the squalor and the despair blocked out by the darkness, Sam could almost convince himself he was in some healthy place, some nonblasphemed ground.

And then, yes, there it was. That was hers. It was different from the rest, being set farther back, almost in the woods themselves. But he recognized it by its shape and location, and as his eyes adjusted, and he moved just a bit, he made out that coop out back where he'd had the corner suite with the chickens and the disgruntled rooster.

Sam approached stealthfully. He didn't want it noted that the white lawyer from the North had visited old granny in the night. It would do old granny no good at all in Thebes County, Mississippi.

Of course the door was not locked. He slipped in and stood motionless for a bit, waiting for his eyes to adjust yet again, this time to the closer dark of the interior space.

When at last he could pick out impediments and chart a passage in the dark—say, the doorway into the bedroom to be aimed for, the stove in the middle of the room to be avoided, the rickety furniture not to be knocked asunder—he moved quietly, and slipped into her bedchamber. He was a prince come a-calling.

No, he was a soldier of the Lord, come to bring righteous vengeance and God's wrath to Sodom.

No, he was a scared white man in way too deep and playing with forces he could not even begin to understand.

He approached the bed, wondering how to waken her without making her scream and alerting the locals and the gendarmerie.

"Madam," he whispered, in a low voice.

There was no response.

"Grandma? Grandma, wake up, please, it's me, Mr. Sam, come for a talk."

That was louder still, but there was no response.

He bent to the bed where she lay swaddled and touched her arm, gently as he could, and rocked ever so slowly, crooning, "Mama, Mama, please awaken, Mama."

But Mama remained mute.

He became aware of an odor, and then, through the bedclothes, his fingers sensed damp.

He recoiled, but had to go forward.

He turned to the candle next to the bed and found a few stick matches next to it. He struck one on the bedpost, cupping the sudden flare, and brought it to the wick, where it clung, then held fast. Again, he kept his hand cupped around it, to cut down on the light, and brought it to her, and pulled back the bedclothes.

She had been smashed all to hell and gone. Her skull had the shocking aspect of deflation, for its integrity was breached mightily. Whatever oozed from it oozed black onto the bedclothes. Her eyes were distorted by the trauma done to her skull, and one had a bad eight-ball hemorrhage to it. It was too cool for the flies, but by midmorning they'd be here in waves.

He had been to murder scenes too many times before, so he did not panic, but a breath of air passed with a hiss from his lips.

Jesus Christ, he thought. Who could—

The flashlights from the window came on, several of them. Then, from the other side too. Men moved swiftly toward him, and he heard the creaking of leather boots and belts.

"Mister, you in plumb bad deep dark trouble now," said Sheriff Leon Gattis. "Boys, git this Yankee cuffed. We done caught us a murderer."

Earl's Journey

8

EARL called the town up through blur by focusing his binoculars, and watched as it swarmed into clarity. What he saw was of no surprise in the piney woods, a slatternly place in the mud, with its ruined waterfront, its closed sawmill ruin off to one side, and the residential zone, its warren of jumbled cabins, and the listless people who populated it.

He saw also the men on horses, six, seven, then eight of them on the big steeds, in the dark uniforms, lords and masters, rulers of all. He watched them thunder through the town when it so moved them, and could read terror in those they stopped to talk to. There were no easy encounters in Thebes; all confrontations were charged and difficult.

Earl therefore set out to do what he knew he absolutely must. He set out to draw a map.

He was across the river, possibly one hundred yards from the town, and he lay there, hour by hour, his binoculars focused, his handwriting steady and clear, the lines growing in his notebook. He noted also the times of the mounted patrols, the officers involved, the routes they took. He noticed the officers themselves, the fat ones, the quick ones, the mean ones. He wrote it all down.

He watched early in the morning as the Negro ladies all left. These, Earl guessed, were the prison cooks and seamstresses and whatnot, who picked up after the white men who ran the prison and, Earl also knew, provided comforts as they were needed. He knew at night men on horses would stop at certain houses in the town, enter, then leave an hour or so later. He didn't care to speculate on the drama of favor and fury that took place inside the cabins; down here, it was an ancient pattern, and maybe that's why so many of the children who roamed the wild streets during the day had a yellowish cast to them.

Earl's approach had been different than Sam's. Earl was no lawyer like Sam; he presumed, as Sam had not, the existence of no set rules of order and regulation, no rational system that would entertain inquiry with fairness and due deliberation and cough up, ultimately, a response, rational and complete. Earl was a policeman, but not really; he was still a Marine in his mind, and any territory was enemy territory until he knew otherwise. He acted deliberately and decisively.

For example, on the day that he and Sam agreed upon as the last day by which Sam could be expected back, Earl called Sam's wife and made his inquiry.

"No, Earl, I haven't heard a thing. I've begun to worry. Should I contact the authorities?"

Earl thought not, for who knew by what compass the authorities in swamp-water Mississippi steered?

"Did he tell you so?"

"He said no such thing about it."

"Then, Mary, I'd wait. You know how Sam hates a fuss."

"Earl, it's been long enough. What he had to do oughtn't to have taken this long."

"Well, Ma'am, these little towns, you just can't tell how they operate. As I understand, it's swamp country and communication might be tricky."

He then called Sam's other closest friend, Connie Longacre. Earl knew the two had a private relationship, though its nature was neither clear to him nor curious to him.

"Miss Connie?"

"Earl, have you heard from Sam? I've begun to worry."

"No, Ma'am. I thought possibly you had. You know how that man enjoys a good talk."

"Not a word, Earl, strange on its face for Sam. Earl, what should—"

"I will do something."

"Earl, I—"

"Miss Connie, I will."

Then Earl made another phone call. It was to Colonel Jenks, the commandant of the Arkansas Highway Patrol and his mentor beyond Sam.

"Earl, yes?"

"Colonel, sir, I've some leave time due. It's been on five years straight. Got a private situation I need to deal with. Would certainly appreciate it if you could help."

The colonel loved Earl, as did most who knew him, the others being those who only feared him. He knew that if Earl had a situation, Earl would need the time to deal with it. Earl didn't request things lightly; he was the kind of fool for duty that commanding officers have relied upon for thousands of war-filled years.

"Earl, I'll notify personnel. We'll see to it the county is covered."

"Yes, sir. Much obliged."

"Earl, you've earned it, you know you have."

It was true. Earl's record was embarrassingly without blemish. His problem: he worked too hard, he cared too much, he was too fair and too meticulous in his planning and deportment. It was as if the goddamned medal he had won demanded of him that he be perfect the day long, and by God, perfect the day long he would be, and he would die before letting it down, though of course he never, ever, to any man or woman, talked of it.

As for Earl, the next part was the difficulty, with Junie. Yet it turned out easier than he expected. He told her he'd be going off for a bit, and he watched as her face fell.

"You're going to that war," she said. "You are a fool for war. You cannot stay out of it."

"No, ma'am," he said, "I am not. They do not care for me; I'm too used-up for them these days." Then he told her he was only going to Mississippi, and only for a few days, and only to look after Sam, who might be in some trouble.

"Sam? In trouble? Why Earl, Sam could talk the devil himself out of hell."

"I know. But maybe Sam run up against something meaner than the devil. Don't you worry none."

He knew he had won; her deeper terror was the anguish he felt about being over here while the Marines were over there, in Korea. She knew he had been writing letters to congressmen and the commandant, and she worried that sooner or later one would be fool enough to let him back in, despite the wounds he'd picked up in the big war. So in a way she was relieved that it was only Mississippi.

That done, a few travel arrangements needed to be

made, and finally he had one last call, though he made it from a pay phone. He called a colleague named Wilbur Forebush, by rank a lieutenant in the Arkansas State Police and by authority director of undercover work, which was becoming necessary, as the crime tendencies grew more sophisticated. He and Wilbur had shared a pleasant few Saturdays in a duck blind over flooded rice fields these past several years.

He explained what he wanted but not why.

But Wilbur trusted him.

"All right, but Earl, if you git in a jam now, you call me. I will come quick for you."

"I appreciate it. I just don't want no tracks back to my family, when I don't know what's cooking."

"So I understand. I'll have it couriered down to you. Tomorrow morning okay?"

"That's fine."

What arrived was a pouch containing a driver's license, seemingly authentic, in the name of, as it turned out, one Jack Bogash, of Little Rock. Other authenticating documents included a social security card, a heavy equipment operator's license, and others. There was no Bogash, of course. The documents were high-grade fakes, meant for undercover officers in tough circumstances, and would pass scrutiny in every crime lab except the FBI's.

Earl then took the bus to Pascagoula, his belongings, including a .45 from the old days, in a pack under a sleeping roll, and a Winchester '95 carbine in a scabbard. He dressed in hunter's rough clothes and high boots, and wore a fedora. No one thought the rifle odd at all, for rifles rode in pickups and saddle scabbards everywhere in the South. On the ride down he studied what maps were available, the best a big color thing that was included in the WPA's 1938 *Guide to the Magnolia*

State. He scanned it carefully, looking to learn the land and the foliage, committing it carefully to memory.

He did not stop in Pascagoula, but went farther up the river still by bus until he was the only white person left aboard, to an old, nearly dead lumber town called Benndale close to Greene County. There he picked up some supplies at the general store, then went looking for a hunting guide. Of course it wasn't hunting season. Hell, he knew that, he was scouting for some rich fellows and wanted to find a place where he could take a deer lease, bring these boys in the fall, git them all fat bucks, pass some green around, and, dammit, everybody'd be better off. He was directed, eventually, to a hardscrabble ol' boy named McTye, who volunteered to canoe him up the Pascagoula, then up the Leaf. Earl said that sounded fine.

The trip through the bayou was without incident, but then Earl changed plans on the old fella. Instead of heading up the Leaf, he decided to have the boy put him off there, at the juncture of the three rivers, Leaf, Yaxahatchee and Pascagoula. He'd work up the Leaf on foot, looking for a sign, scaling out the terrain. The oldster would come pick him up a week hence.

"Mister, this here's dangerous territory," said the scrunched-up old man, McTye. "There's bogs and hollows, and hellholes, where the land has fallen and the trees are so thick you maybe get in, but you ain't getting out. Tricky currents in the water. No one's quite clear on who's hereabouts. Might still be some Indians, might be blue-gum niggers whose bite'll kill you. We got us a dog problem, too. Feral dogs, big as wolves, they travel in packs and can chew a man to bonemeal right fast. They got a prison farm thirty to forty miles away, and they didn't plan to build it there 'cause the territory was easy traveling."

"Well, sir, I am in no hurry to git close to a prison one way or the other. But I am an experienced woods fellow and believe I can hold my own. I ain't doing my job if I'm just looking at the ground from a canoe. Want to find and map the hellholes, see where I'd put up stands, where the deer paths are, where I might expect some heavy bucks, if this state done growed 'em.

"She does, I'll tell you, eight-points and more, big 'uns. So I can see I'll not be telling you what's for. I can see you're a hardhead. Okay, son, the funeral they be holding be for you, not me. You want to leave me word for your next of kin?"

"Yes sir, Mr. McTye," said Earl, and wrote out an address for Jack Bogash in Little Rock. "I will leave this here with you. You come back in a week. If I am here, so much the better. If I am not, then possibly I've left in another direction. Don't you worry none either way, until maybe some weeks hence, if my widow calls the state po-lice. Then you tell 'em where I started in, and if they can find the body, so much the better."

"Sir, I hope you know your stuff."

"Mister, I do too. But this is what a feller has to do these days to earn a living, and if this pays out, I'll be a happy dog."

The old man spat into the river, left Earl off on the shore of the Leaf, turned around, and in smooth strokes propelled his way back until a bend at last obscured him.

Alone now in the dark cathedral of the swamp, Earl wasted no time. He unlimbered the rifle, fed four .30-'06 150-grain cartridges into the magazine which, by the peculiarity of the gun, was not a tube under the barrel but a complicated internal spring-loaded well that took some care in the proper fitting of the shells, and jacked the lever to feed a cartridge to the chamber. That done, he lowered the hammer.

Next, compass: he shot an azimuth due east, meaning to carry him across the promontory between the upper-Y configuration of Leaf and Yaxahatchee and in seven or eight hours good traveling, locate up on the Yax yet still twenty or so miles downriver from Thebes.

This he did, the pack on his back, a canteen on his belt, the .45 still secured. Though not in combat shape, Earl lived a vigorous life and his body was entirely comfortable in the state of extra effort. He didn't feel now as if he were in Japanese territory, so he moved quickly, without a mind toward invisibility, on as straight a line as he could manage. The woods, once the waters had receded, were firm and piney, and it didn't take long for the heat to soak his shirt and the brim of his fedora. He kept his pace up steady for a good five hours, avoiding hellholes, always returning to his original due east heading. He finally took a quick break for tuna from a can (buried afterward) and a few swigs of water. Then onward. He reached the Yax by dusk, just where it began to widen and straighten for its last twenty-mile plunge through the piney wilderness to Thebes. He spent two hours with his good knife hewing pine boughs, then stripping them, working until well after dark, assembling a raft.

He slept without a fire, sitting up in his bag, the rifle across his knees, his eyes watching, never asleep enough to be unconscious but nevertheless nourishing his energy.

Breakfast, before dawn, was another can of tuna fish, followed by a can of cold tomato soup, the cans again buried. By the duck hunter's hour, he was on his fragile craft, poling his way along the shore, never venturing to the center, ready to dip into shore at the first sign of disturbance.

He reached what he felt must be Thebes well before dark, having pulled off the river only once, when the powerful churning of engines far off indicated a heavy craft; it was the weekly Mississippi Bureau of Prisons boat, a steam-driven thirty-five-footer, with its supplies and its cargo of human woe, a few more unfortunates destined for the penal farm. He studied the craft through his binoculars, noting nothing peculiar about it except a large white box with an odd insignia of red triangles arranged around a red dot, where a red cross would be if the box contained medical supplies. He'd never seen such a thing; he recorded it in his notebook, and having done so, promptly consigned it to his subconscious, forgetting it totally at his functional brain level.

Earl laid up across from the town, watching and waiting.

It became clear soon enough that there had to be some sort of station on that side of the river, near enough to the town for the officers to run their patrols, and they were aggressive enough and changed horses enough to suggest that they were close by.

And Earl could guess where it would be. To the northwest, equidistant between the town and the still unseen Thebes Penal Farm for Colored.

Earl knew it was there; he could tell by the barking of the dogs.

9

THE dogs.

At least they weren't free-roaming. Instead, they were kenneled at the back of the wire compound, and the deputies were so complacent that they didn't patrol the perimeter with them or any such thing, or keep a night watch, or any true security measures. That's how atop the world they felt. The deputies were like kings of everything, these boys, atop their horses, with their chained dogs, easy, confident masters of the universe of piney woods and bayou and cowed Negroes.

Earl studied the kennels: there he saw blue-tick hounds, low, slobbery, sinewy barking and sniffing machines. There were twenty or so of them, and they gamboled and played in their pen, but if they were put on his trail, he knew they'd be remorseless. It was the dog way.

Earl feared dogs. On Tarawa, the Twenty-eighth Marine War-Dog teams had sent their animals into blown-out bunkers in search of live Japs. The dogs' noses were so much finer than humans', they could pick out the smell of the living from the dead, and when they found a wounded man, they'd tear him up bad, usually to death. They'd drag them out of the bunkers or pill-boxes, swarming and yapping and biting, and you could see the Jap, bled out, sometimes concussed, the poor man fighting against them on some kind of general principle of survival but without much energy. As much as Earl hated the Japanese, he hadn't enjoyed seeing that; the packs of dogs ripping at the wounded man, usually by this time awash in blood that made the dogs even more insane. Meanwhile, their handlers, by nature brutal, urged the animals on, laughing at the spectacle. The dogs snapped and chewed, or they hung on and shook and twisted and pulled. No man, not even a Jap soldier, should die like that, torn to pieces by dogs as sport. Earl bet that after the war, those dogs had been destroyed. You couldn't have a dog like that in a civilian world, a dog encouraged to the furthest extremes of its savagery. Yes, they were our dogs, but still: he shuddered. Some things were too much.

These dogs looked the same. They were beautiful and sleek, but they'd been corrupted by men and nourished toward specialized forms of violence. In a way, they represented all the evil that men could wreak on the world, impressed upon the innocence of a dumb, brute animal. He saw that in the kennel where it was the rule of the pack, a rough-and-tumble world of tooth and fang. A big blue seemed to run the place, and he kept the young dogs away with the strength of glare and intensity. Just like in the human world. That's why Earl never wanted any part of a pack. Meanwhile, an old man who worked the dogs looked more dog than human; he was more an ambassador to the dog world from the human race than a full human himself. The other deputies kept apart from him. He'd be the master of hounds; he'd be the one tracking Earl if it came to that.

Earl found the compound at dawn by simply following the horse tracks. It was a rude building, made of
logs, more cavalry outpost than anything. For these
boys practiced their trade from horseback, and held
their whole operation together from a horse, with a dog
or two on chains.

So: a kennel, a stable, and a main house, all log, all secure behind a high barbed-wire fence in the piney
woods. And of course, no Negroes allowed near. Maybe
the dogs had been trained to smell Negroes. The main
house had the lock-up attached; that's where Sam had to
be, or else he was up the road in the penal farm itself,
and if he was there, there'd be no getting him out without a division of Marines. Earl watched from deep in the
trees, saw well-fed, confident men locked in routine. Patrols, lots of organized activity. Boss man was a big fellow he heard someone call Sheriff Leon, to whom all
others deferred. He was sure Sam was here, because
Sheriff Leon checked in to the lock-up, and it seemed to
be the point of a lot of energy.

Earl knew he had to get in. He studied on the place,
trying to figure out a way.

It had to do with the wind, he knew. The wind might
carry his scent. If the dogs picked it up, they'd throw up
a fit; that might agitate the deputies, and once agitated,
they might begin to nose around. They'd let the dogs out
to hunt him, and the dogs would find him, and that
would be that. He'd be taken and he'd be in with Sam.
What good would that do?

Earl patiently charted the breezes on the first night.
He learned it was most still between 5:00 A.M. and 6:00,
just before the dawn. He knew he had to come in on the
other side of the compound from the dogs, and that he

had to move slowly. If he sweated, the dogs would smell it; their noses were so much better, and they were creatures of pattern, used to things being just so and prone to acting up when they weren't.

At the same time as he exhibited a hunter's patience, Earl was himself becoming increasingly disturbed. It's one thing when deputies live with families, and go on duty and off, and when off go back to a civilian world, be with their kids and wives, go to church or the movies. But these boys weren't like that. Instead, they were kept living out here in the woods, isolated, in uniforms that sparked fear and mystery, behind wire and protected by dogs. They were more like a conquering army in an occupied territory than police officers.

And they were young, too. Somehow, they were paid enough to put up with the dormitory-style living far off in the woods, and the constant discipline of the military. So there was some money behind this, certainly more than could be justified by the paltry ruin that was Thebes County, a town locked in mud living off a penal installation upriver still a mile or so.

Earl didn't like it. The dogs, the horses, the guns, the fear of the townspeople, Sam locked up way out here. He didn't like it one bit.

EARL scrubbed himself in a cold-water stream until he shivered, then put on the last of his clean underwear. He would sweat some, though it was cold, but still he'd leave less man smell that way.

He slithered to the wire at 4:30, and watched. In the lock-up, a candle burned, meaning someone had night duty, but Earl bet he was asleep. The big log house was before him, between him and the dogs. Earl had patted dark mud against his face, as he'd done in the Marines with burnt cork, and stripped to his dungarees and a dark shirt. Getting through the fence was tough, and the barbs cut him in a dozen places, shallowly, but enough to sting like hell and leave a tiny blood track. Easier to simply cut the wire; but if he cut it they'd notice it the next day.

Earl lay inside the wire, waiting. He was unarmed, except for a K-bar knife, black-bladed and leather-gripped, which he might use in a pinch on a dog. But no dogs howled or barked, no one called. He lay still for the longest time. Then he stood, and walked.

He walked nonchalantly. He didn't sneak or dash or evade. If anyone should see him from the house, he looked like he belonged. He walked across the yard to the house, waiting every second for a challenge, but it never came. These boys felt secure in their place.

He skittered around the house to the lock-up, and peeked in; he could see a deputy asleep at the desk, the fire in the stove having burned low, and beyond three cells in the back, two open, one locked. That's where Sam would be. But Earl didn't enter. Instead, he crawled around, past the door to the back, then found purchase at a window and gutter and swung his way up, as silently as he could. Again, no challenge came. He eased to his haunches, then to his feet, and staying at the edges eased around until he thought he was over the locked cell.

Going prone again, he pulled the knife, and quickly set at cutting through the roof. He figured—rightly—that the roof would be the weakest part, unreachable as it was to the prisoners. It was old, rotted wood, the shingles soft, the tar holding them down softer, and digging assiduously, he quickly opened a seam in the roof, chopped through the wood, and at last got a bit of an opening. He could see down at Sam, sleeping restlessly on his cot.

Earl just loosed a gob of spit. It wasn't a nice thing to do, but it hit the man in the face, to the effect of minor irritation. Another followed, and the man awakened.

"Shhhhhh!" Earl commanded. "Mr. Sam, you keep it down."

Sam blinked, unbelieving. He looked around, dumbfounded.

"Earl, is that—"

"Shhhh!"

Sam was silent, and at last looked up. He saw the gap in the rotted wood and an eye behind it that could only be Earl's.

Quickly he rose, to close the distance between them. He stood on the cot, craning upward, until his mouth was but a foot or so from Earl.

"Good God, how did you find me?"

"It don't matter. What is happening?"

"Oh, Lord. These boys have me buffaloed on some fool charge of murder that wouldn't stand up for one second in a real court of law or even a grand jury room. What they're planning, I do not know, Earl, I want you to contact our congressman and then work through the—"

"Shhhh!" commanded Earl again.

"No, I have thought this out, and I know exactly how to proceed. Listen to me carefully."

"Mr. Sam, you listen to me carefully. I have eyeballed this setup, and you are in shit up to your nose."

"Earl, you must contact Congressman Etheridge, Governor Decker, Governor Bilbo of Mississippi, and then—"

"I will do no such thing. That would get you killed right fast. What I have to do is get you out."

"Earl, no! If I escape, I break the law. Then I am no better than—"

"And if you don't escape you are dead. Then you are no better than the worms that are eating at you and having a fine picnic at it, I might add. Mr. Sam, look hard at the cards you have been dealt: these boys will kill you. They have to. They're working up a plan even now: accident, drowning in the river, fall, quicksand, I don't know. It'll be crude but legal and you will be long gone to the next world. I guarantee you that."

"Earl, there are laws and—"

"Not out here there ain't. Now you listen. I can get you out. But you have to be ready, you understand? I have to set dog traps and figure us a course and cache goods along the way. I need something from you, your undershirt with a lot of stink on it."

"That I have."

"Good. You drop it out the window. Two nights from now, at two A.M. I will come git you. You will be awakened by distractions, which I ain't yet figured. Fires, explosions, something like that. Then I will kill that big blue boss hound and the hound master and I will come git you."

"Earl, you cannot kill anything. Not a dog, not a man."

"Either would kill you in a second."

"Earl, I have done nothing. If you kill, we've moved beyond a limit. There's no getting back. I could not forgive myself for pushing you to that situation. You of all men should not be made an outlaw. I would rather be sunk in the river than be the ruination of you."

"You are a stubborn old piece of buffalo meat."

"Earl, swear to me. No killing. No matter what these boys have done. They cannot be killed, for that makes us them sure enough."

Earl shook his head. Sam was set in his ways.

"Throw that shirt out, Mr. Sam. I will see you two nights off, at two. And then you and I will go on a little walk in the piney woods and go home and fall off the wagon with a big laugh."

EARL got back into the deep trees just before dawn broke and stole a few hours of sleep. Some internal alarm awoke him, and maybe the sleep was pointless, for he never quite relaxed enough to let it take a good grip of him.

But he awoke, washed again in the cold water, fighting a shiver that came through the dense heat of the place, and then set to thinking. He thought about direction, and looked through his effects until he found that goddamned 1938 WPA *Guide to the Magnolia State,* God bless them commies or whoever done the work, they done a good job. Besides the big map, he found on page eighty-three a nice map marked "Transportation." Squinting hard, he found what he needed, a rail line running north–south more or less, as it wended from Pascagoula to Hattiesburg, a spur of the Alabama and Great Southern. That's where they'd head, and hope to snag a train as it came by.

Earl knew it would be a close-run thing. The dogs would be on them almost immediately, and he had to throw the dogs off the track as many times as he could. The straighter the dogs tracked them, the worse off they'd be. They might never make the railway, or they might get there but no trains would come. Fortunately the land was too foresty for horsemen; the deputies would have to pursue on foot, and as horsemen they'd be slow and reluctant on their own two legs. They'd tire long before the dogs, but the dogs would drive them on, and that nameless hound master and of course that Sheriff Leon, who'd have all his pride on the line. He wondered if they'd have time to involve the prison security people. In a way, he hoped so, for that would take more time in the organizing, and time was precious for him.

He maneuvered his way through the trees until he picked his positions: where he'd enter the compound, how he'd move, how he'd get Sam out, which way they'd move, what their landmarks would be as they moved into the woods. He used his compass to orient himself, and when he reached a stream, he cached his pack, his rifle and his pistol, to be picked up on the outward trek. That rifle might be the smartest thing he'd brought, for with it he could kill the dogs that the boys sent after him.

Night came, and he penetrated the prison compound again. He went first to the stable and worked his way among the shifting, seething, beautiful animals. In a tack room, he found what he needed most of all: rope. Good, strong four-ply rope, which anyone who administered horses would pack.

Next he worked around back to the shed that housed the generator. The boys shut it down at night. He slipped in and found several twenty-five-gallon cans for the gasoline. He looked about until he found the gallon cans by which the tank would be filled and took three of them, loading them to the brim and screwing the caps down tight. Three gallons of gasoline. Fella could do a lot with that.

That done, he again slipped out before the dawn, to get some sleep. He had another hard day tomorrow. And after that, the days got harder still.

THE sheriff came by at 3:00 P.M.

"Well, sir," he said, "at last I've got some news for you."

"Well, that's wonderful," Sam replied. "And I have some news for you. Not only will I file formal complaints, Sheriff, with the state police and the Federal Bureau of Investigation, I will sue you and your men in a civil court of law. It'll be a great pleasure not merely to send you behind bars for a very long time, but to leave you destitute and without hope for gainful employment for the rest of your life. Possibly you can replace some of the Negro washerwomen at the prison farm when you get out."

"Sir, you have got a vicious tongue. I do believe I ain't never met a man with a golden voice and a poison tongue combined like you. You surely wouldn't fit in down here in Mississippi."

"When I am done with you, Sheriff, you will rue the day not that *I* set foot in this state, but that *you* did, goddammit all to hell."

"We shall see about that one. As for tomorry, you'll be moved downriver and sent to a small town called Lucedale. That's where we'll present our findings to the judge of the Third Circuit, and he will determine whether or not we have the evidence to try you on a charge of murder."

"You know I could not have committed that crime. There is no physical evidence, there was no blood anywhere on my person, I left no fingerprints. A coroner would have concluded that the woman's death was well in advance of my arrival."

"Well, maybe so, maybe not. Fact is, Vincent, you *was* found in a dead woman's house by my deputies and no one else was. Maybe you couldn't stand visiting a Niggertown without cashing in on some cheap cooze and thought that old gal be accommodatin'. But she wouldn't lie with you, and so you done poleaxed her head in. Seen it before. Now, if you's a local, we might just say, Old Vincent, he got to thinking with his little head 'stead of his big one, and let it go at that. Them kind of things will happen. But you's a big *outside agitator* so the rules are much different this time."

"This is *ridiculous*. Any prosecutor would scoff at that. Did you interview other witnesses, did you develop a timeline, did you quarantine the crime scene, did you investigate her standing in the community, her kinship relations, those who might hate and fear her? No, you just arrested—"

But Sam quit. He suddenly knew what this was all about.

It was as Earl had said. Tomorrow, on the boat, he'd be drowned. The river would eat him, as it had eaten the Negro family. This story, it was all to get him quieted.

"You'll have your day in court," said Sheriff Leon, with a smile. "You'll git your chance to call an attorney. We'll git all this straightened out, once and for all. It's all gonna be all right, and justice will be paid out, as it always is in Thebes County."

10

No moon, not much breeze. The dogs were quiet, and in Thebes, Mississippi, it seemed to be just another night in a long summer of nights, each the same.

But Earl crouched inside the wire at the sheriff's compound, checking his watch. He was not dressed seasonably, but rather for war: heavy dark hunting pants, boots, a dark navy sweater, a watch cap, his face muted by mud. The K-bar knife was sheathed at his hip. His Hamilton was upside down on his wrist so that the radium dial would not show.

By his reckoning, in exactly one minute a Molotov cocktail of gasoline and powdered soap would detonate when its cigarette fuse burned into the soaked rag in its nozzle in an outbuilding in Thebes less than a half mile away. That fire would spread through the abandoned building and lead to powder fuses, which in turn would track to firecrackers Earl had constructed from the powder of .45 shells. For a few brief seconds it would sound like a gunfight had broken out in all its fury in Thebes. The building would burn; a few more shots would ring out through the night as the flames ate the wood.

He expected the boys would be up in seconds. Whatever else they were, they were well-drilled troops, and that sheriff expected them to react fast. They'd be saddled up and out to fight the invaders in a matter of minutes. That's when Earl would kick his way into the lock-up and conk whomsoever there he found, and liberate Sam. They'd be off. But the time of freedom to move was short and chancy, and he knew he had to get as good a lead on the dogs as possible.

He checked his watch again, thinking briefly how many other times over the years he had checked his watch in dark places, waiting for a certain time to arrive, a certain signal to be given, and somebody's idea of what was necessary to begin. But this time, at least, it was his own idea of necessary, and he would save the man whom he loved most in this world or life itself would not be worth continuing. That is how his mind worked, and that is the only way it worked. It felt no deviation, no consideration of other possibilities, no reluctance, no doubt, no temptation to a softer course, and if there was fear it was buried under a willed aggression that was his one gift in the world.

He had committed to Sam. In a youth he cared not to remember, it was Sam who offered the only tenderness in an unpleasant world, far more than Earl's own father, a sheriff who enforced the will of God and the righteous Baptist Bible with a razor strop many times a week to Earl, his brother and his mother. But Sam was a good man who'd even once upbraided the father for his readiness to punish.

The years passed, Earl's in the Marine Corps, and then he came back from the war and got himself in another one, in Hot Springs, and again almost got himself killed. Sam came to him a second time and said, "Now, Earl, I do have a job open. I need an investigator in Polk. Don't pay much, but you'll be in the public safety sector and I will be making calls on your behalf. I want you working for me, young man. I don't want nothing bad happening to you."

So they worked together for a number of years, and Earl finally began to understand that in some way—no book would ever say this, but he felt it and knew it to be so, whatever the books might say—Sam was the father he'd always wanted. He couldn't put this in words, of course, for words were tricky things and never meant exactly what they said, or worse, never said exactly what they said, or worse, never said exactly what was meant. But Sam was steady and fair and honest and as hard a worker as Earl had ever seen, and it was Sam who got Earl a bank loan so that he could fix up his father's old place, and it was Sam who treated Earl's boy more like a grandson than an employee's son, and it was Sam who loved that boy, Bob Lee, and made the boy feel connected to family.

So now: we do it, goddammit, without looking back, we do this thing.

He looked again at his watch. Yes, any minute now and—

From far off the blast erupted. It wasn't a blast so much as evidence of a huge force being released. A glow rose up through the trees, and seconds later the crackers popped—Earl had set up twenty-five of them from thirty cartridges, the bullets painfully pried out of shells, then resealed with mud. They went off, powder and primer detonating simultaneously, and it sounded like the Dalton gang had decided to rob two banks in a town that had none.

Earl watched as the big log house stirred, and lamps were lit all around it. Someone fired up the generator, and then a man, then another, then three or four clambered out to see the ruckus. Someone started clanging on a big gong, and for a little bit it looked almost humorous—the term Chinese fire drill came to Earl's mind—as the boys, then the sheriff, tried to figure out what was going on.

A night patroller came thundering up the road and roared into the compound, gathered his sweated horse to a halt, and started screaming.

"Sutter's Store is burning and men is shooting the place up. Don't know what it is, maybe the niggers are getting a revolt going."

"Y'all git a-goin'," screamed the sheriff. "You got to stop these goddamn things early else they git wild and big on you. G'wan, git out there, you bastards!"

The horsemen saddled and mounted, and played with guns for a bit—revolvers loaded, shells inserted into shotgun tubes, levers thrown, hammers drawn back—and then, without much chatter, the unit roared out the gate, pulling up a screen of dust from the road.

Earl had placed himself at an angle to the house such that the fewest of the windows opened onto him. At the same time, he knew he couldn't slouch or scurry. Now he arose and walked purposefully forward, presuming that in the general melee no one would be focused enough to notice, or that no one would notice that as he walked, he had Sam's old undershirt knotted around the ankle of one leg. He made it.

He slid around the back of the house as another group of outriders, this time led by the sheriff himself, hurried off. Possibly the place was deserted by now; possibly it wasn't.

Quickly, he found the shed that contained the generator, which was plugging away and coughing up smoke as its gasoline engine drove its gears. He crouched to it and unscrewed the cap to the tank. He untied the bunched undershirt from his leg, rolled it thin and fed one end of the tube of cloth down into the gas. He wedged the shirt into the nozzle of the tank, knowing full well that the gasoline would diffuse upward until it had saturated the shirt. Except that he took out a Lucky Strike cut in half already, lit it, took a deep puff, and wedged it into the bunched cotton. It would burn down as the fuel spread up; in two minutes (he'd timed it with the other half of the cigarette), when they met, the tank would be lit off and the boys would then have two fires to think about, one that was burning up their own goods.

He left the shed, slipped along the house and into the lock-up. He tried to ease his way in, but an old guard was standing up, looking in the direction of the fire, fingering a large double-barreled sawed-off. The man smoked a cigar, shifted weight from one foot to the other uneasily, wiped his dry lips, scanned the horizon, and generated unease in all the ways a man can generate unease.

Earl removed his K-bar, feeling its familiar heft and weight, the worn smoothness of the leather grip. He knew exactly the length of the blade and what it was capable of.

Swiftly he walked to the old man, gripping the knife handle.

Earl struck, and he went down.

Earl hit him with the metal cap at the end of the grip, right where the jaw meets the skull, an inch below and an inch on the diagonal from the ear. It was the hay-maker. It conked the old boy so solid his lights went out before he hit the ground, and the shotgun clattered away into the dust. He'd be gone cold for a good five minutes.

Earl stepped in, grabbed the keys off the desk, and went back and unlocked Sam, who had dressed silently, even to the point of tightening his tie. His eyes bulged with anticipation or fear, and he was already breathing hard and shallow.

"Let's go," Earl hissed, and the two of them scurried out the door.

But before Sam could lurch himself off into the night, Earl had him under control.

"We goin' run out the front, trying to step in the tracks cut up by the horses. Step in horseshit if you see any. You got me?"

"How can I see? I can't see the—"

Whoomph!

It wasn't a blast so much as an unleashing; a blade of light ruptured up the shank of the dark sky, spreading illumination as it rose. When it rose high enough, it fragmented, sending flowers of devouring flame off in a thousand directions. Enough landed upon the house to catch its roof ablaze, and in this comforting glow, Earl and Sam found the cut and shit-caked tracks of the angry horses, and dashed out the front gate.

"Off here," he yelled.

They left the road and headed to the trees. It was a maze of interlocking pines, a complete bafflement in the dark. But Earl found an incline just where he knew it to be, and climbed a small hill, and at the top, oriented toward the east, found a brief interruption of meadow, and then another wall of trees. Where he thought it should be, he stopped, then snapped on, ever so briefly, his flashlight, until the beam disclosed a loop of rope around the trunk of a pine. He went to it, and with his K-bar cut it free and stuffed it into his belt.

"This way, you stay with me, goddammit. We got some hard travel ahead. We got twenty miles to go in about ten hours. You up to it? 'Cause if you ain't, I can't carry you, Mr. Sam."

"I will run till I die, Earl. You are a great man. You are a great American."

"That I doubt. But I do mean to get you clear of here, goddammit, so let's go."

And off they went into the woods, stopping every one hundred yards or so for Earl to find and cut a rope necklace from a pine trunk.

THEY got the fire out by dawn, but already the dogs had found the scent.

"He won't git far," Pepper told Sheriff Leon. "My pups got him lined up right fine. They'll be nipping at him by noon, Sheriff, and by four you can put him back in the cuffs and I can kick his ass for the knot he done give me." Pepper was the conked one. The left side of his head was swollen like a softball. He had a headache, and he'd swallowed a plug of Brown's Mule when he'd been hit. That was the worst, for he'd puked brown slop for an hour and it had emptied him of hunger for the 'baccy;

so he had two grudges going, one for the knot on the skull, the other for the wasted plug.

"Yessir, the pups be on his Arkansas be-hind."

But the sheriff was not so convinced.

He knew there had to be a second man and that the second man had to be mighty smart. Already the sheriff found himself behind the eight ball. The fire in town proved to be nothing but an old building burning and some kind of firecracker put together from some .45 shells. It was clever. This feller'd thought hard to come up with that one.

Meanwhile, as all the sheriff's deputies are hiding behind trees and looking for targets at what's nothing but burning lumber, whoever he is is back in the compound, jury-rigging a bomb out of the generator and freeing up that goddamned Arkansas lawyer.

He should have killed the dogs, though, the sheriff thought. He should have slipped in there and cut twenty dog throats. Why didn't he kill the dogs?

"Okay," he said. "Y'all got your sleeping packs? This may be a long 'un."

His deputies by now had switched to hiking boots, for there were no horse trails in the deep woods, and they all carried packs. It was the drill. They'd hunted men before. They also all had rifles.

"Sheriff, you want I should go on up to the Farm and tell Warden and Bigboy we gots a runner. They's got them good hounds, too."

"Hell, they hounds ain't no better 'n my hounds," Pepper put in. "My pups outtrack them mangy Farm mutts any day of the week, including Sunday and Armistice Day. Yes sir, my hounds the best hounds."

Pepper's hound pride meant little to the sheriff, and he considered telling Warden and Bigboy and getting the guards in on the hunt. Some of them were essentially professional manhunters, as they'd run many a nigger to ground their own self over the years. But again: that meant notification and coordination, it meant trying to rendezvous in deep, twisting piney roads and nobody had radios or anything, and it could just mess it up bad. Sometimes too many on a manhunt got in their own way and ended up chasing each the other.

"Naw, it's only one man, maybe two. Running through woods they don't know, toward what they ain't sure. We knows our land, and them dogs old Pepper has are good enough. You boys, let's git her going. And, let me say this again, man fleeing justice who done lit up a municipal building is a desperate man. No limit likely on what he's willing to do to taste some free cooze and a jar of lightning down the road. So if you git him in your sights, you jack. Okay? Understood? You shoot him dead. This boy's had the smell of mischief on him from the git-go, and his wagon should be fixed. Let's move it out."

With Pepper's six best hounds straining against their chains, driven almost insane by the thickness of the Sam-smell clinging to the earth, they set out, the dogs snuffling furiously at what they believed to be Sam's path out of the compound, around the back of the house and crosswise to the wire, where he'd obviously slid underneath.

The sheriff commanded the wire cut, for now that he'd started he didn't feel like backtracking to the gate, then circling around again to this spot. One by one his men slipped through, and then he followed.

"Cut the dogs free, Sheriff?"

"Cut 'em, Pepper. Let 'em hunt."

So Pepper clicked to his animals in some strange dog tongue he knew, and the old blue, the master of the pack, fought through his instincts and settled. Soon the others followed.

Pepper passed among them, freeing each, and though each had instincts that commanded onward, they had had their obedience beaten into them by Pepper's brutality, and so they knew they risked a thumping if they disobeyed, no matter how their loins ached to.

Finally Pepper said, "*Go!*" and the six took off like nags from a gate, yelping their excitement as they gobbled up the Samness of the track, and plunged, muscles working, jowls slobbering, toward the woods.

"Oh, they got it rich," Pepper said. "Watch them pups hunt. They are hunters and they got locked in on that ol' boy. Going to bring in the meat."

The dogs plunged ahead, almost in formation, so strong was the Sam-smell, and for just a second the sheriff allowed himself a whisper of pleasure.

They had it so strong. They were so sure. It was going to be easy.

But then the pack seemed to explode. Each dog picked a different direction. One raced into brambles, another circled back around, two more began barking at a tree, and the last two simply stood stock-still and began to whimper. They'd stopped before they'd even got going.

"What's happening? They lose it?"

"Goddamn," said old Pepper. "Goddamn him, that goddamned tricky bastard."

"What happened?"

"He done laid a false scent. He brings the dogs here where he's smeared up ever-thing with Arkansas scent. He must have had some clothes or something, and he riled up a big scent trap here, and my pups is all messed up in their heads. It ain't that there's no scent, it's that there's too goddamned many scents."

The sheriff felt the frustration rising in him like a column of steam, pressure increasing, heat rising, pain swelling.

"Goddamn him! Goddamn him all to hell."

"That goddamn lawyer is smart," said Opie Brown, one of the younger fellows.

"Lawyer nothing. Some other bird's in on this one, don't you see. He been watching us and thinking this thing through a while. Who else set that fire last night, God himself?"

"No, sir."

"Pepper, what we do?"

"Well, sir, got to start over. Got to run a perimeter until my pups can find the true scent, then we be off."

The sheriff knew this would take hours: he and his party and the dogs inscribing a large, slow circle around the compound until one of the dogs came up with a Sam-smell unaffiliated with this riot of Sam-smell here.

Then the hunt would begin in earnest.

"We'll get him, Sheriff," Opie cried. "Goddamn, I know we will!"

THEY ran out of loops of rope too early.

"Goddammit," said Earl.

"What?"

"We're ahead of schedule."

It was still dark in the woods. Around them loomed the shapes of trees rearing up, which men with undisciplined imaginations might have seen as monsters assaulting them, or foreshadowings of impending doom. But Sam didn't have enough imagination to let run wild, and Earl was too locked into the absolutely necessary. Though a flicker of dawn showed behind them, the sun was still more than half an hour away.

"That's good, isn't it?" said Sam, breathing hard.

"Nah, it's bad. Means we just sit here till it's light enough to take a compass reading, goddammit."

"You can't—"

"No, sir. Can't see far enough to set a compass reading, shoot an azimuth. Got to sit here till I can make out a landmark half a mile ahead."

"We're hours ahead of them, and they can't bring any horses in here."

"You'd be surprised how hard men can move when they're motivated. And that sheriff's got plenty of motivation. He's been humiliated in his own little world, and he don't want that getting out, 'cause everything he has is based on the idea that he is the toughest, smartest, meanest sumbitch in the territory. Seen it in my father, same goddamn mule-pride craziness. He will come after us both barrels, and now we're stuck just sitting here for a half an hour. How you holding up?"

"Ah. Okay. I've got a blister on my foot."

"Got bandages and some aspirin at my goods cache, but that's still a few miles ahead. That'll be some help."

"Good. I didn't wear the right shoes for a hike."

They both looked at Sam's leather brogues from Brooks Brothers in St. Louis, a smooth, beautiful shoe in rich mahogany, a successful man's shoe, and so out of place in the woods it was almost laughable.

"You just keep on pumping," Earl said. "You do that, I'll have you home to your kids in two days."

"The hell with my kids. I just want to see Connie Longacre."

"She is some gal—"

"Earl, an experience like this, gets a man to thinking, and I—"

"Save it, Mr. Sam. Not for now. Save your breath. You'll need every little bitty piece of it before this here thing is run out."

In twenty minutes Earl found just enough light to shoot his azimuth to a terrain feature, and they were off again, and an hour after that found Earl's goods cached out of sight behind a log, in some high, dry grass.

Earl unscrewed his canteen and Sam took a good long draft. Earl got clean, dry socks out of his pack, and a bandage, and Sam took off his shoes, threw away the socks, bandaged his foot and pulled on the dry socks, which, being thicker, fit not quite so well in the tight, sodden shoes.

"That's okay," said Earl, "they'll loosen, you'll be fine."

Then he reached further into his pack and pulled out a .45 automatic, which had been worked on a few years back: it had a larger than usual rear sight welded to the receiver and some kind of shelf on the safety.

"Here. This is for you."

"Earl, I can't accept that. I cannot kill to get away. That invalidates anything I have ever stood for, which is the law."

"Mr. Sam," said Earl, as he reached further into the dry grass to pull out his Winchester '95 carbine, "do you see much in the way of *law* out here? We are on our own, and no law's going to help us."

"Earl, I know you to be a moral man, a decent man, a good man. They say you are the best policeman in the state, and I know in the war you done fine work for our side. But I must say it amazes me how quickly and well you convert to the other side. It's as if your great gifts for action, well-conceived thought, for capability beyond all men, could go either way. I hope your boy grows up to be the straight and narrow you, and if you have another son, I hope he doesn't grow up to walk the crooked, violent road."

"Are you ready?" Earl said, returning the untaken pistol to his pack.

"Earl, you cannot kill with that rifle. Kill a man and you have crossed over."

"I will not kill except to save you, Mr. Sam. Except a dog. I may have to kill a goddamned dog or two. That I will not enjoy, but if it has to happen, it will."

And that was when they heard, far off and scratchy, the sound of the hounds.

"My, my," said Earl. "I do believe they are still in the hunt."

THE dogs had something.

"The pups got 'em. Yes sir, got one of 'em treed."

The pitch of their barking changed. It was not the unfocused yipping of the tracking animals who made noise to keep themselves amused and because it was their way. It was focused, ferocious, and intense.

As they came into a clearing, they all saw them gathered.

"Yes sir, by God, got a one of 'em treed, you can see, ha, goin' to git that sumbitch, yes, sir, oh, them wunnerful doggies!" cried Pepper, his throat phlegmy with glee.

The hounds circled a large pine, three on point, the other two trying to leap up the trunk, snarling fiercely. Only the big blue was apart, as if not sanctioning this development.

"Okay, fellows," yelled the sheriff, "now you git around 'em and be care—"

One shot sent a Winchester bullet blowing through the clusters of pine needles, and then they all opened up, shot after shot after shot laying into the tree, puffing it with green haze as the bullets ripped through. Dust and pulverized bark rose from the tree, a limb hit precisely tumbled off under its own weight.

"*Cease fire, goddammit!*" yelled Sheriff Leon, and one by one the men stopped firing.

"Take cover, and keep the tree covered, goddammit. Just wait and see what you bagged."

The men scurried to cover, and the dogs, who had scattered at the first reports, reassembled under the tree and recommenced trying to leap and nip at it.

The sheriff waited another three minutes, then slowly drew his Smith .38/44 Heavy-Duty.

"Y'all cover me."

"Yes, sir."

"Opie, you don't be shootin' me, you hear?"

"Yes, sir," replied Opie.

The sheriff slid on the angle toward the tree, and as a veteran of several gun battles—he'd worked on the New Orleans police force before being cashiered for corruption back in 1932, at which time he'd started his new career as a prison guard at Thebes, which led ultimately to this position—he knew what he was doing. Keeping the gun out before him aggressively, his finger caressing the trigger, he at last ducked under the skirt of boughs and pointed upward to see what he could see.

"Well," he finally said, when he emerged, "why'n't you boys come see what you have killed."

The deputies raced to the tree.

About ten feet up, hanging on a sheared-off limb and surrounded by the pock and puncture marks of too many rifle bullets, they could see two black socks hanging limply.

"You killed that lawyer's socks," said the sheriff. "Pity he ain't in them."

* * *

"THEY are truly a disciplined bunch," said Sam, when a mile or so behind them the firing eventually stopped. "You were right. They attacked my socks. They were fancy socks, too. I don't suppose I'll ever get them back."

"You never know," said Earl. "These backwoods fellows, they don't like to waste a thing. Probably someone named Billy or Ray Ed or something is trying 'em on right now. You could come down in ten years or so when everybody's forgot all about this, and probably find them on his feet on Sunday at the meeting."

The pines showed no particular tendency toward abatement, though now and then they'd come to a logged out area, which upset Earl; he would not let them pass through the open land, because a rifleman who got there before they cleared its bare spaces might get a good, clean shot off, and one was all it took.

"On the other hand," Sam had argued, "we can make better time, because the ground is less cluttered with these goddamned vines and weeds and things. We can advance our lead and—"

"But they can make better time too. They're following our smell. We go 'round, they go 'round. That's it. Either that, or you figure out a way to stop smelling. When you get that one done, you let me know."

"Should have known I couldn't outthink Earl Swagger on some tactics issue," said Sam.

"I got a bagful of tricks," said Earl. "Only goddamned thing I know at all in this world."

But he hadn't sprung his best trick yet. He'd been looking for just such an opportunity, which demanded the congruence of stout trees, not pines, but the occasional oaks that sprung up helter-skelter in the woods. He needed a dead one, with a nice spike of splintered trunk atop it.

And at last, on the far side of a gentle hill, he found it.

"Okay," he said. "You take a rest."

"Earl," said Sam, his face ashine with sweat, "you know those boys can't be that far behind."

"I got a little something here. This one's real pretty."

Earl knelt and reached into his pack. He came out with a big coil of rope. He diddled with it, until at last he'd fashioned a cowboy's lariat with its expandable loop just perfect for bringing down running steers from close-by horseback.

"We used to see them Western-type movies in the Pacific when we wasn't killin' Japs. You know, with that feller John Wayne, you seen any of them?"

"Yes, Earl, of course I've seen Westerns. But what on earth—"

"Oh, you just watch me now."

Earl swung the looped rope overhead, building up a nice rhythm and swoop, then let the thing fly and it soared the thirty feet or so to the spike and missed.

"Goddamn," he barked.

"I'll go—"

"No. You stay where you are."

Instead of retrieval, Earl snapped the rope back slowly so that it wouldn't catch on anything. Then he began again, flinging the rope across and—

This time he got it right, and the loop settled over the spiked trunk and slipped down.

"There we go."

With that he went to another oak, this one alive, pulled himself up a bit, got to the second branch, pulled the rope tight but not too tight, so that it had some spring to it, and secured it by a peculiar knot to the trunk.

He scurried down.

"Now you come on."

"What are you up to, Earl, this is the craziest—"

"You just come with me."

They forged ahead another hundred yards.

"That's fine. That's right good. Now come on."

They backtracked to the tree.

"Now sir, you git up that tree and you hand-over-hand across to the other tree."

"Earl, I don't see—"

"It's the scent. It's low to the ground. Them dogs can only smell what's on the goddamned ground. That's why they got to keep their noses in the mud. So we going across, we ain't touching no ground, and when we get across, we head off from over there. They go right on by and a hundred yards up so where we stopped, they run out of trail. It'll take 'em an hour of scouting to find us again."

Sam looked at Earl.

"Sir," he finally said, "if you weren't on the side of the law, you would make a very cunning criminal. You have it in your bones, no doubt about it."

"GODDAMMIT!" screamed the sheriff.

"Damn," said Pepper. "Ain't seen a thing like it never. Trail just stops. Did they fly out by spaceship?"

"Maybe it was one of them heliochopters," a deputy said. "Seen it in the newsreel. Them things can land straight down."

"Don't be no fool, Skeeter," said the sheriff. "Ain't no helicopters in Thebes County. They backtracked and someplace back they managed to jump trail. Don't know how they done it, but this fellow running this thing, he's as smart as they come."

"Sheriff, ain't nobody got this far before."

The sheriff knew that to be the case. It clouded his brow with darkness. Usually the runners headed the other direction, because for them the river meant freedom; there was something in the Negro head, something ancient and unperturbable, that connected crossing a river with freedom. The sheriff didn't understand it, but he knew that the colored went east, to the bayou, and because they thought the dogs couldn't track through water, but the dogs were really good and didn't lose a scent easy, and the runners left enough about on weeds and vines and wet logs and leaves for the dogs to stay with, and the swamp slowed them down and sometimes killed them, sparing the sheriff and his boys the trouble. Nothing personal: it was just that a running nigger was a guilty nigger, whatever the infraction might be, and a bullet was as easy a solution to the case as time in the Farm, and it meant a good deal less paperwork for everybody.

But this goddamn white boy had been smart. He'd gone out through the piney woods, which meant he had a compass and was good in the wild, and he'd thought hard about beating the dogs. He'd worked it out real solid.

No, nobody had gotten that far before.

"So, we got to circle until we pick up that scent again, is that right?" he demanded.

"Yes, sir," said Pepper.

"Tell you what," said the sheriff, thinking into the problem. "You put them dogs back on chains. I want two teams of three dogs each. You run one team, Opie'll run the other. Instead of one big circle, we'll each take a half. Whichever team picks up the scent first, whether it's one or t'other, you fire a shot. Then you mark it. You see. You mark it with a handkerchief or something, Opie, you can figure out to do it, right?"

"Yessir, b'lieve I can," said Opie.

"Yes. And the first team goes on after them boys, and the second team cuts cross the circle, finds the mark, and it commences after the first team. That seems like it could save us a mess of time, don't it?"

"Yes, it do," said Pepper. "Sheriff, you one right smart man."

"Okay, let's get her done. I figured out where they're headed, by the way."

"Where, Sheriff?"

"Track. The Alabama and Great Southern track cuts across the woods another six, seven miles out. So they goin' to catch a train ride, they think. You boys best catch 'em, you hear? We don't want nobody gitting out to tell fantastical stories about Thebes County now, do we?"

"How much further, Earl?" said Sam. The ordeal was wearing on the older man. He'd twisted his ankle back there a ways, and now hobbled painfully onward. The going wasn't easy, for vines and sawtooth clotted the passageways between the trees and palmettos with sharp leaves that cut at them like cutlasses. Worse, every now and then they'd come upon a trail, and the easy passage, beckoning them onward, tempted their spirits away from Earl's compass plot sorely and broke their hearts when they had to find the discipline to say no to its comely ways.

"We're getting close," said Earl, lying. He knew they weren't "close," only "closer." But no longer did they hear the barking of the dogs, and now it was just the two of them alone in the dark woods.

"I am running low on steam."

"I am, too, Mr. Sam. Neither of us banked on this. But by now them boys is goddamned good and mad, so we'd best keep going. If they catch up to us, there be all kinds of hell to pay."

"I'm only thinking we've done beat them. That trick

of yours buffaloed them good. We could take a rest, maybe."

"Mr. Sam, that earned us an hour. But the deputies is younger and stronger and well motivated. They will not be stopping, no sir. They will keep on coming, I guarantee it. Best thing is, don't think about other stuff. Keep your mind hard."

"I suppose you are right on that one. I—oh, shit."

"Goddammit," said Earl.

Far back, they heard a shot.

IT was the bitch Lucy who picked it up, and the sheriff's team, with Opie on the dogs, who got it.

Lucy began to shiver and whine; she leaped up, her wet tongue licking at Opie.

"Goddamn mutt," he said, pushing her back.

"No, she's got it," said the sheriff. "She wants her reward. Opie, give her a kiss."

"Ain't kissing no dog."

"Yes you is, Opie. Seen goddamn old Pepper do it. Get to it."

As Opie bent and faked love to the squirming, prideful hound, the sheriff turned and drew his Heavy-Duty and fired a shot.

"Okay, boys," he said. "Let me tell you how we goin' do this thang. That track can't be more that three miles ahead. So now it's a goddamned race, and I am too much a old man. I will slow you down. Opie, you and Skeeter take off them packs. We will leave the packs here. I just want you with your rifles running after them dogs. The dogs will show the way. They hunt good. They'll hunt 'em down, you hear? I will wait here for them other fellas. When they arrive, we'll run them dogs too, and they will follow along right quick, I do believe. But you our best chance. You get to them boys and you shoot 'em dead. I don't want no confusion here now, you understand. Your job is to bring 'em back dead and not alive, so that no one ask no questions, not now, not never. Got it, fellas?"

Both men were hunters; both men appreciated the opportunity that had been presented them; both men looked upon it as the greatest of fun.

"Now you go, dammit. I will wait for t'others."

Opie set the hounds free, and they bounded off. Packless, but carrying their Winchesters with the glee of men about to have some fun, the young deputies took up the chase.

"Dogs," said Sam. "Oh, Christ, dogs."

"Ain't as many of them," said Earl. "He done split up his team, and only a few marked us."

"Can we make it?"

"We got to pick up the pace. We can't tarry. Sorry, Mr. Sam, but it's going to be a running thing now."

"Then," said Sam, "I will give it my best effort."

They accelerated their movements, bucking ahead with more abandon now. Sam did something unprecedented as testament to the seriousness of his situation: he actually loosened his tie.

"Hope no supreme court justices see you with that tie all reckless like that," said Earl. "You could git in trouble with your career if that happens."

"Don't you tell a soul now, Earl. This one's between you and me, and as soon as we catch that train, the tie comes up again. You never can tell who you may run into hoboing on a freight."

Earl appreciated that Sam could still joke a bit. When a man's sense of humor went, it meant he was near going under. In the war, he'd always looked for a chance to make his boys smile at some fool thing or other. It made 'em that much looser and gave 'em, however tiny, just that much more chance.

The land began an incline, howsoever gentle, and the height worked against them as well. Soon both were bent double, puffing hard, feeling the sweat leak off them, lost in the intensity of the ordeal.

Earl had plotted onto a lone pine a half mile ahead. They increased their pace, achieving almost a jog, just the steady, easy lope of men at urgent extension, pushing themselves ever onward, trying to ignore the multitude of discomforts that built toward pain as they rushed along, their minds tunneling through everything toward the possibility of escape.

Earl had pieces of metal scattered through his body, most of it Japanese shrapnel. Now and then a piece worked loose and nudged a nerve or something and sent a searing pain up to his brain. He'd been shot in the war a whole bunch of times, treated roughly by combat as combat will do to a man. He thought he was beyond the rough stuff, and he wasn't.

Still, he clung desperately to the rifle. It was an old gun bought secondhand from a retiring trooper, what you call a trunk gun. It rode in the cruiser, wrapped in a blanket, picking up nicks and scratches over the years. But if a trooper ever needed something heavy to plow through the bones of a wounded animal or a barricaded robber, the heavy old Government .30 Model of '06 bullet would do the trick, and Earl knew he had but a hammer snick to accomplish before he fired the first of five packed in there.

He hoped he didn't have to shoot. But he knew if he did, he would. It was his way.

*   *   *

THEY reached the crest of the hill.

"Lookie, goddamn," cried Opie. "Seen 'em. They just ahead."

His eyes were good. They'd picked up on a flash of movement a quarter mile down the slope from them, nothing demonstrably human but nevertheless clearly the flash of something moving urgently.

"Them dogs be on 'em soon," Skeeter declared. "Tear 'em up real damn good. Then we pop 'em. Like bear huntin'. Hunt bears with dogs. Dogs drive 'em back, tire 'em out, bleed 'em, y'all git close and you can pot yourself a bearskin rug for the winter."

"You ain't never hunted no bears, Opie."

"Well, that's right, goddammit. My people wasn't bear-hunting people. But that's how it be done, by Christ, that I know. You ain't never hunted no bears neither."

"There, goddammit," Skeeter yelled. "Seen 'em too. Let's git them old boys. Whooooie, goin' to be fun a-coming!"

"Fun a-coming!" yelled Opie.

The two lanky youths gathered themselves heroically, and once again started loping through the pines toward the last view they'd had of the fleeing men.

The track was easy. The running dogs chewed up the soft pine needles where they galloped, and three of them left a big enough sign for an idiot. On the balls of their feet, Opie and Skeeter danced forward. The prospect of action, of success, of getting home after all this shit lightened their steps and their spirits. Their natural hunter's exuberance amplified the chemicals in their blood, and they soared ahead.

SAM stumbled and fell, caught himself, and kneeled, chest heaving, face wet with sweat.

"Earl, I'm about finished. I think I'm going to have a goddamn heart attack! You go on. You git. You leave me here. You done your best. I just wasn't up to this goddamn thing."

"Mr. Sam—"

"No, Earl. I formally relieve you of any obligation to me. It's the right thing. You go on back to Arkansas and raise that boy and—"

"Mr. Sam, give me your coat."

"I—"

"Your coat. Goddamn, we haven't much time at all. And that hat too, give me that goddamn thing."

"Earl, I—"

"Goddammit, Sam, do what I say!"

Sam was stunned that Earl, who understood the elaborate system of deference that underlay Southern society as well as any man, would actually raise his voice at him. It seemed so out of character. One yelled at Negroes or, occasionally, workingmen, women and male children, particularly of the teenaged years, but one never—

Earl lost all patience with the shocked man and picked him up by the lapels, spinning him, stripping him of his coat. Then he plucked the straw hat.

"Now your shirt."

"My shirt?"

"Your goddamned shirt!"

Quickly, Sam shucked the damp garment. Earl quickly shed his hunting coat and extended it to the bare-chested man.

"Here's what we do. I will lead them away. It's your scent them dogs has homed on. I will peel off to the right. You keep going straight to the track. Them boys will be on me. I will try to shuck them a few miles from here, and I will get to the train."

"Earl, you don't even *know* there's a train, you have no idea when on earth the train—"

"It's due in Hattiesville by six-thirty, which means it ought to be through this part of Greene around four, which gives you fifteen minutes. You think I'd do this goddamn stunt without a train schedule in my pocket? The whole goddamn thing is set up around that freight. Usually six cars, it slows down as it hits grade, and you ought to git aboard easy enough. I once rode from Little Rock all the way to Dago on the bum. Now, goddammit, you have rested enough. Get going."

"Earl, I—"

"Just go, Mr. Sam. I will see you in Arkansas."

"Yes, I—"

"And one last thing. If I don't make it, you will want to start your program. The governor, the congressman, the police chief, the newspaper joe, all that stuff. Well, I am giving you an order: don't you do it. If they nab me, one thing'll keep me alive, and that's them wondering who the hell I am. If big shots start asking questions, they will shoot me in the head and bury me out here in the piney woods. Do you hear? Do you understand?"

"Earl, give me a time frame? How long do I wait?"

But a train whistle sounded far-off, and Earl, rubbing Sam's sweaty clothes on bushes and against trees, began his maneuver to the right.

Sam picked himself up, pulling Earl's coat tight about himself, and was off.

IT was better now. Earl, alone, spread the Sam scent broadly as he worked his way back. He preferred to be alone. Alone, he could concentrate fully on what he had to do; he didn't have to pay attention to Sam. Regretfully he tossed his pack and pistol into a hollow log; he couldn't afford the weight.

The dogs were loud now. He knew they'd take the bait. That was the way their minds worked. But he had a moment where he wondered if he hadn't been wiser to have just set up and shot the dogs as they came upon them. But who knew when they'd be here and maybe he'd not have time after shooting them to get to the train himself. No, of the choices, all of them bad, this was the best.

He worked his way along but just below the crest of what appeared to be a low hill. On the other side of the crest, the land would drop away to the tracks, possibly half a mile ahead. That would be fine. Sam should have plenty of time. He checked his watch and knew that he had enough time now to get himself to the train. He would just dump Sam's clothes and dip over the crest.

He wadded them into a union of pine trunk and bough and laughed at the ruckus the dogs would set up when they reached this spot. Then he ducked over the ridge, ready for his own descent. It occurred to him suddenly: They were going to make it. It was—

At the crest, he made a terrifying discovery.

The trees had been timbered all the way down the slope. There was no cover at all. And he could see Sam, alone, amid a forest of stumps, picking his painful way down to the tracks, now plainly visible.

He knew what that meant.

A rifleman on the crest would have a clear shot at Sam all the way down. If he was any good at all, he'd have Sam dead three hundred yards before he got to the track.

Earl squatted to gather his breath for a second. It wasn't even a dilemma. Even though he was close enough to the limit of the timbering, and had at this moment technically escaped, and had only a last downhill plunge before intercepting the train, it never occurred to him to go.

Instead, he dropped back on the other side of the crest, and headed toward his pursuers.

Now he was hunting them.

SAM felt naked. He knew this wasn't good, but the nearest timber was a half mile in either direction, and if he raced for it he'd miss the train. He hoped and prayed the boys behind wouldn't get a good shot at him, and he stumbled ahead, feeling so helpless. He had no shirt, but only Earl's hunting coat, a waxy canvas thing, and his shoes were sodden, and his ankle still throbbed from the twist, and the breath came in hard, dry spurts, as if he hadn't enough room in his throat to get the proper right amount of air into his lungs.

He could see the track before him, glinting in the sun like a piece of ribbon on the floor, but at the same time bobbing in his perspective because of the spastic quality of his breathing and his downward lurching. The sun was hot. He seemed to be floating through thickets of moths or butterflies. Now and then a pine stump jabbed or poked at his already torn and battered legs, but the slope helped him immensely, as did his momentum, as did the prospect of gravity.

Suddenly he heard a shot.

THE first dog bounded into view. It was a hound, sleek and young, a beautiful animal, gobbling up Sam's scent as it plunged ahead.

It saw Earl, and it didn't pause a second, and went from tracking dog to attacking dog, flying at Earl with a fury no man could muster, its fangs bared, a guttural growl of pure insanity screaming from its throat. The eyes were red and narrowed as it leaped, and Earl took it from the hip, one shot, the bullet piercing its throat, blowing its brains out at an upward angle as it passed through the not-so-thick skull, and the dog, so beautiful, was also so dead. It collapsed in a heap.

A bullet kicked up a gout of dirt near him, a geyser of high-powered energy. One of the deputies had fired.

Earl threw his lever, jacked a shell out, and took up a kneeling position halfway behind a tree. The stupid boy ran ahead to see if he had bagged something and Earl put the sight blade in the center of his chest, and almost squeezed the trigger, but instead let it drop and fired a round at the running boy's feet, throwing up his own geyser. The boy dropped, both himself and his rifle, and if the other were aiming, he took a dive when he saw the closeness of the round.

But Earl saw none of this.

Instead another dog leaped and before he could get a new round levered into his rifle it was upon him so even in the motion of cocking, he wheeled and clubbed it with the butt of the rifle, feeling it shudder with the blow and sigh. But the dog after that was on him, and he felt its tearing snout burrowing through his shirt as it tried to rip his throat with its canines. There's something terrifying about the totality of the way an animal fights; it has no doubts or qualms and its fear releases a pure blast of chemicals into its blood, so that its muscles triple in their strength and its savagery quadruples. But the animal could not get purchase on the soft flesh of Earl's throat because he protected it with his chin, then ripped out his K-bar and got the blade into her.

She squealed in the sharp pain, and knew herself to be mortally hurt, but in a second she was back at him.

By this time he had gotten the rifle up and fired. He belly shot her, and down she went, and he could not stand the idea of so brave an animal suffering, and so he levered the rifle again and shot her in the side of the head.

The beaten dog came at him and got its jaws locked on his left wrist so he could not shoot. The pain flared through his arm. He transferred the rifle to his right hand, flipped it, then used it to brain the dog. The dog relaxed. He swung it overhead and brought the full weight of the accelerating rifle down upon its skull, and something broke. The dog lay still.

He sat back, leaking blood from a dozen ugly wounds. He could feel it in his eyes, running down the side of his face, darkening his shirt, running down his arms to his hands, making them so slippery they could hardly hold the rifle. He tried not to look at the ruined bodies of the animals. It seemed to cast a bad spell on this business. Killing something so beautiful that was only doing what it had been trained to do, well, it was nothing to be proud of.

As he sat back momentarily, he made another terrifying discovery. The force of thumping the last dog was so intense that the lever had popped, opening the action, and the remaining two .30-06 cartridges had spilled out to somewhere on the floor of the forest. He was unarmed.

"Opie! Goddamn, there he be."

"Wal, git him. Then we git t'other. And the sheriff be here with more dogs. Git that one down there. It's that goddamned law fellow, I know for sure."

Indeed they could recognize Sam as he worked his way toward the tracks, not going as fast as he should, a civilized man in rough territory without a clue. He was nakedly open to them in the distance, a tiny figure against the rawness of the timbered plot.

Both deputies dropped to prone and eased the hammers back on the Winchesters.

"You got to shoot high. You shoot over him, drop that bullet into him."

"You watch where I hit, and yell corrections."

"You ain't so dumb for a dumb hick."

"Only thang dumber than a dumb hick is a smart city boy."

Opie was the designated shooter. He was young, his eyes sharp, he had shot a lot and hunted his whole life. He could see his target hobbling along at what appeared to be a range of about six hundred yards, a far carry for a .30-30, but not impossible. Hell, he didn't even really have to hit him. He just had to scare him into dropping—and missing that coming train. If he done that, he done right good. The sheriff and the dogs and the other fellers could round him up.

He found the old man perched at the tip of his sight, and squeezed the worn, smooth trigger of Mr. Oliver Winchester's best gun.

The target was lost in the jump of the rifle.

He levered the gun quickly, tossing the empty, bringing a new one into the chamber.

"You's off seventy-five yards at least," yelled Skeeter. "You got to shoot high."

"I know that, dadgummit. Just gittin' a feel for it."

He held again on the man, then raised the rifle a good five man-lengths over his head and squeezed.

"Goddamn, that's close. Still a mite short."

"That's five men high. I am five men high. I'm going to six."

He levered, found the position, and fired.

The shot plunked up a spray of dirt not ten feet from the fleeing target.

"That thar be it."

"Six men high gits it done."

He fired again, and Skeeter saw the dust puff surprisingly near Sam, who dropped immediately, scurried a few feet in the low crawl, and took refuge in a gully.

"Whoooeee," said Opie. "Now you shoot, Skeet. Six men high, that's it."

S A M lay in the gulch, heaving for oxygen. It was quiet, and then, with a lazy puff, the earth just behind him erupted in a scuffle of dirt and broken stone. Something stung him in the neck, some fragment.

Oh Lord, he thought.

Then, a full second later, the pop of the report lazily reached his ears, as the sound took its sweet time following on the bullet.

Oh Lord, Lord, he thought.

He could hear the train. It was getting closer and he was but a hundred yards from the track. But he knew he had to stay until the very last second, calculate it just perfect, and get up and run helter-skelter like some sort of Crazylegs Hirsch to catch the train, climb aboard, and drop out of sight from the bullets. He knew he had a chance, at least a small one, but he didn't like that run, over the rough ground, trying to read the speed of the train and match his own speed, worried about stumps and potholes and stones, with those boys up there whacking away at him, just desperate to get close to him and pancake him with their sticks again.

Whop!

This one lit up about an inch from his face and filled his eyes with dust.

It enraged him.

Caught. Trapped. Stuck.

It occurred to him: I will die here and nobody will ever pay, and Earl will die, and for what, justice denied the heirs of a rich Chicago man who happened to leave money to a Negro who had worked for him.

It seemed so unfair, but then he counseled himself that life wasn't fair and that things happened as they happened, and you never knew what you were getting into.

He got ready to make his run.

EARL came upon them from the side, and they were so intent on shooting they did not hear him, as they had forgotten their own dogs in the excitement. He had lost blood and was no longer quick, but he was determined.

As he rushed at the deputy, the boy heard him and spun, but too late, and Earl knocked into him as he rose, pulling the rifle from his hands.

As he got it, he rose and hurled it at the other boy, who was now bringing his rifle to bear. But the thrown weapon crashed into the boy, knocking him backward.

Earl rushed to him as he rose. The boy absurdly raised his fists in classic fighting style, as if a boxing match were about to commence. There wasn't a lick of fear on his face, just pure meanness. He looked about nineteen.

Earl hammered him hard in the jaw and he went down, but then the other boy was on him, trying to drive him to earth with one arm and both legs, while pummeling him in the kidneys with the other. Earl twisted and shucked and got the boy off him, slipped and rose as the boy fired a good punch with his left fist that tattooed Earl in the jaw.

"Haw!" shouted the boy with glee, then spit a brown goober of 'baccy off into the woods and closed in, fists rotating crazily as he tried to line up a good shot, squinting as he hunted the angle.

Earl took two ineffectual blows on the shoulder, ducked a roundhouse, then dropped the boy with a right to the point of the jaw that would have him sipping meals through a straw for a month.

Both boys were down.

Earl gathered up the two rifles, quickly cranked the levers to empty each one, and threw each empty gun as far as he could.

He stood and waved. It was too far to yell, but Sam saw him, rose and returned the wave. Earl made a get-going gesture, as if flinging an imaginary football that far distance, meaning to communicate the idea that the train was almost there, the train, the train, and Sam turned.

The huge thing pulled into view as it emerged from the trees, pumping smoke, pulling four boxcars and two flatcars loaded with farm machinery.

Earl turned to the boys. One was awake, nursing a busted jaw.

"Sorry about the dogs, but they didn't give me no choice. Now you stay put or I will beat on you some more."

The boy had no interest in further fighting, and so Earl turned just in time to see Sam clamber aboard the train.

He knew he'd never make it, but he had to try.

He began to dash down the slope, and the train slowed, because it had to climb a bit here, and he thought he just might be all right, and then he heard the barking.

11

SAM rode for an hour, unmoving. He lay among chained pieces of equipment, the vibration of the track rattling upward, making his head buzz. No one came for him, no one inspected the train, there was no train detective; it was just him, alone, on the bed of the flatcar, between a thresher and what might have been a combine, each a brand spanking new example of McCormick's finest machines and speaking of hopes for the bright future.

Sam felt nothing. There was no joy available for him. He had not seen Earl. He did not know what had happened to Earl. Had Earl made the train? He doubted it. The last time he had seen Earl, Earl had been up the slope, waving him onward, and he'd turned and pulled himself toward the track.

The train thundered along. It was immense. You never appreciated from afar how big they were. Worse, it was terrifying, a contraption that vibrated the very planet as it crossed its surface, vast and deadly, and as Sam pulled near to it, he became aware of the hugeness of its wheels as they glistened and sliced along the track.

Helpfully, a little ladder hung off the rear of the flatcar, and he hoisted himself up it, banging a knee on something hard, experiencing a moment of horror when it felt that he was slipping off. But then he had it, he was up, and he clambered desperately for cover and fell between the chained machines and lay there, terrified.

When it occurred to him to look for Earl, he picked himself up and peered through the spokes of the machine. But it was too late. The train had passed beyond the timbered-out zone and was now in close, dense trees. He could see nothing but piney woods a few feet back from the tracks, and whatever secrets they concealed they would not surrender.

His mind was in a fog. He had not expected an ordeal so piercing this late in life, after having survived the craziness of the war and having at last found his place in the world. It was as if he couldn't wrap his mind about what had just happened to him, unhelped by the terrifying reality that nothing yet was settled. Earl was still out there, somewhere, somehow. That ate a large hole in Sam's digestive tract and would not stop hurting, like an ulcer gnawing away on him.

He tried to reason it out. Earl probably got away. Earl, in the woods on his own, was a match for any ten men. Earl survived, for nothing could kill an Earl Swagger, state police sergeant, Marine war hero and all around the most capable of all men on the planet.

But that presumed . . . the rational universe. A place that made sense, where order prevailed, where justice was paid out. Wherever they had been, it was not a rational universe but some haunted zone of Manichaean savagery, as if out of some ancient tale, where survival was not for the just but for the lucky, and one's antagonists were unbound by civil logic or the stays of the human heart.

I put Earl in that, he thought, and his heart broke again, as the tide of guilt, like a kind of phlegm in the soul, molasses-thick and greasy, pure sludge, oozed over him. He thought of what he had done to Earl, where he had put Earl, and for what?

His self-loathing exploded, and he worked himself over pretty hard, wondering if the right thing to do hadn't been to jump off the train and head on back to help Earl. But even as he conceived that idea, he knew it was impossible. He could not have done so. He could not leap off a moving train (leaping on had been hard enough) and gone back to face Sheriff Leon Gattis and his deputies and their educated billy clubs and their dogs. He already had seen the battered skull of that poor black mama. Who could have killed her but them? He had seen the fear among the Negroes at their powerful and confident ways, their occupier's arrogance, their complete self-assurance in their mandate to rule by force. He could not face that again, not without a shirt, with a twisted ankle, exhausted beyond any exhaustion that had afflicted him in the war, when he was so much younger and stronger and had believed so much more firmly.

So it was not until 8:30, when the train pulled into a freight yard at Hattiesburg, that the last reality suddenly occurred to him: he was a wanted man. The police would be hunting him. Bulletins had gone out, possibly by radio or radio telephone or telegraph. There would be a manhunt. And there he was with no money, no local connections, nothing to sustain him.

It was at this point that his hand closed on something hard and round and crisp in the left pocket of Earl's canvas hunting coat, and he pulled whatever it was out to discover a roll of bills. He quickly slipped the rubber band off and discovered over four hundred dollars,

mainly tens and twenties. With that he could buy lodging, a shirt, some new shoes, but he knew he had to be
careful, and that the cops would have all forms of transportation covered. He formulated a plan: Connie Longacre could drive down here and pick him up. He could
hide in the trunk of her car and hopefully get through
the roadblocks that way. Connie would do it. Connie always liked a big adventure, as if being married to the
worthless but wealthy Rance Longacre wasn't adventure enough, or was perhaps too much adventure.

It wasn't much of a plan. Earl would no doubt come
up with a much better plan, as Earl was a natural man of
action, whereas he, Sam, had a tight legal mind focused
on the stratagems of the law, but at the same time somewhat indifferent to the physics of the natural world.

But he knew one thing: he had to get away from this
rail yard. That would be the first thing to be reported,
the first thing the police would think of. In fact, he realized with a start, they were probably combing the place
now.

He looked around. It was dark. He saw nothing. He
gathered the coat up around him and slipped off the flatcar, dropping a few feet and again feeling a twitch of
amazement at the hugeness of the thing. Of course he
was unobserved by anybody, except for the three police
officers who happened to be strolling along the way at
precisely that moment.

"Well," said the first one, "ain't you a bit old to be
bumming the rails, Dad?"

"Ah! Well—"

Sam's mind, normally so filled with words, so glib,
swift, logical, eloquent, powerful, emptied. It purged.
He felt his mouth gibbering soundlessly, his lungs inflat-
ing with air, his lips drying in the breeze.

He was caught.

"I, uh, er—"

"Cat got your tongue, buster?"

"It's, ah, er, you see—"

"Bet he don't got no ID neither," said the last officer. "Bet he don't know nothing about nothing. They never do."

But the cops didn't seem menacing. None of them put their hands on their revolver butts, which is, Sam knew from experience, the first thing an officer does if he's not feeling right about a situation. Nobody unlimbered a billy or a kosh or a sap, no knuckles went white, nobody started breathing hard or squinting or hunching and coiling at the prospect of violence; there were no signs of aggression whatsoever.

"Well, let's go, bud, or I guess we'll run you down to the drunk tank to sleep it off all night long."

"Sir," Sam finally found the voice to say, "I am not inebriated."

"Well, he's got a voice and he knows some big words, by God!"

Sam was amazed at how quickly he had recovered, and at how quickly he was analyzing this: do they know? Have I been reported an escaped prisoner? If so, wouldn't they be quick to the gun and the club, in full cop manhunt posture and tension, which he'd seen in his time, too. No, these boys were pretty relaxed and seemed to think he was a funny old goat.

"Bet there's a helluva story on how he lost his shirt," said one. "Something involving a farmer's daughter, a farmer, a shotgun, and some city feller knows too many big words for his own good."

Sam realized: they don't know. They can't. They wouldn't be acting like this.

So he reached back ever so slowly and removed his wallet.

One cop took it; he put his flashlight on it.

"He's an Arkansas lawyer. Mr. Sam Vincent, Esquire, of Blue Eye, Arkansas. Hell, don't that beat all."

"Mr. Vincent, sir, you are a long way from your stomping grounds. Ain't Blue Eye way to the west in Arkansas, if I recollect correctly?"

"You do, sir."

"Well, sir, I'm afraid we got to ask you how come you're riding the rails into our little city? Without a shirt and looking like the devil hisself just got done throwing a party for you."

Sam never knew where the inspiration came from, or why, or how, but there it was, and in a second or so he even had himself convinced.

"Officer, I was on a business trip to New Orleans. You know that town. I'm afraid I gave in to certain low temptations, after denying for years I felt them at all. In a certain house I met a certain young woman. She was a Negress. A yellow Negress."

"A high yeller. Them's the worst. They can make a man act like a dog faster'n hell."

"Yes, sir. I would confess also that alcohol played a part. In any event, the next day I believed myself to be in love and went back to the house to rescue her from it, and take her home with me. I admit I hadn't yet figured out how I'd explain her presence to my wife of seventeen years and my five children. In any event, it was made clear to me that I wasn't wanted, but I learned she was from Pascagoula, her name was Vonetta Louise, and thence she had returned. I imagined it was because she was so profoundly moved by my love for her and hers for me that she had struck out a new path in life."

"Haw! Heard that one before! Knowed plenty of white boys thought they could rescue a nigger gal from being a nigger."

"It don't never work. God won't let it work."

"Anyhow, before I knew it, I had hired a car and traveled to Pascagoula, and began to make inquiries. I found her. I also found her boyfriend and his gang of brutish young Negro fellows, her daddy, her granddaddy, and most fearsome of all, her grandmama. They were not moved by my declaration of love, nor the whiskey on my breath. I seem to recall a scuffle, some rough thrashing and rolling, and the next thing, I was fleeing. I found myself without a shirt in a rail yard being hunted by large men of a dark persuasion interested in administering what I believe they referred to as a 'big ol' ass whuppin.' That didn't sound like much fun to me, and suddenly my love for sweet Vonetta Louise acquired a somewhat tarnished patina. I managed to sneak aboard a flatcar and lay still for the longest time. Then white men came and the Negroes left, but there was too much agitation for me to escape and I had no desire to explain my presence to them, either. Soon enough the train pulled out, and here I am."

"Shee-it, don't he tell a purty story!" one of the boys guffawed. All three had enjoyed it immensely. It connected with experiences they had either had or heard of, and it amused them no end to see a fancy talker, a man of education like Sam, brought low by the twin furies of drinking whiskey and high-yeller tail, which had been the ingredients in many a poor man's destruction in the houses of New Orleans.

"The niggers will teach you a lesson if they catch you alone and there ain't no other whites 'round. Way it is don't mean jack to them in that sityation. Way up where you live, y'all don't see that part of 'em. You just see 'yassuh' and 'nossuh,' but let me tell you, sir, they's got it in for us, always will."

"I fear I have learned that lesson the hard way. You know, I am not without means. I have some money. I require only a night's lodging—preferably not in the drunk tank, as I can afford a hotel room—a shirt and some clean underwear, and I'll be on my way by bus tomorrow."

THEY took Sam to their prowl car, and then to Hattiesburg's best hotel, where a brief intervention got Sam a fine room, though of course he had to pay cash up front.

"Want you to see Mississippi hospitality at its finest, sir. Don't want you to think all's we do down here is fight the niggers for control. It's a wonderful place to live and raise up your kids. You'd best call your wife with some story or other, 'cause I'll bet that old gal is all upset."

This was the youngest, nicest and smoothest of them.

"I certainly will, Officer."

"Dave, Mr. Sam. I'm Dave."

Dave appeared to have conceived of some major affection for Sam, along lines that Sam would never understand. Perhaps it was that, being discovered at a total disadvantage, Sam never got into his more usual powerful personality, where he was the best of all men, the smartest, the most capable, the boss prosecutor. Or perhaps it was as a residue of his experiences that he no longer quite believed so fiercely in those attributes as his birthrights, having seen how quickly and totally the world will dispense with them, and allow mean young deputies the privilege of beating a tattoo against your skull with a nightstick. In any event, whatever it was, the young officer responded to it.

Sam called home; he spoke to his oldest son, who

seemed not to have noticed that he had been gone three weeks instead of one and then his wife, who had made the observation, but just barely. He then called Connie Longacre, got drunken Rance instead, but left a number, and she called back and they had a wondrous conversation, as they always did. Sam loved her; he knew he'd never quite have the nerve to blow up his life and then hers in order to make a change, and this thing between them, this fondness, was all that he would ever have.

The hotel sent a room service meal to his room; he slept, dreaming of Earl, convincing himself that Earl would make out just fine, Earl was all right, not to worry about Earl.

At eight someone knocked on the door, and he had a brief seizure of horror imagining that the news he was in some sense a wanted man had caught up to him, but opened it to find merely a portly gentleman from the Longbow Men's Apparel Shop with a selection of coats, shirts, and ties, from which Sam selected a new outfit and paid for it in cash.

After a nice breakfast in the hotel dining room, Dave the cop came on by and drove him to the bus station. Dave had done some checking and discovered that the 10:00 A.M. bus to Meridian would get Sam to the airport in time for a 3:00 P.M. flight by DC-3 to Memphis, where his car was parked. After the cross-state drive, he'd be home in time for a late supper.

Dave drove him through Hattiesburg, talking amiably of his life, his children, his hopes for the future—he hoped to go to night law school and asked Sam some keen professional questions, and Sam gave him forthright but encouraging answers.

Finally, in a lull, Sam tried a bit of a probe.

"Say, Dave, you ever hear of a place called Thebes

Prison for Colored. Seemed like them black people down in Pascagoula was talking about it. Got my curiosity up."

"Well, sir, best bet is, don't get curious about Thebes. They got a big set of work farms over at Parchman in the Delta, but they send the truly lost niggers down there to Thebes. You don't want to know what goes on down there. It ain't a purty place, no sir."

"Ah, I see. You'd think if conditions were so rough, they'd worry about escapes."

"Sir, ain't nobody never escaped from Thebes. Never. It's so hellish a place, it breaks a man's spirit to be there, and he don't got the spunk for no escape. Plus, it's in the worst jungle on earth, and I hear they got the best hounds in the state, and a crew of guards that can run dogs and track like dogs themselves, all big boys who git extry pay to work that camp. The state likes it that way: a place for sartain bad niggers, you know, so that the niggers always have a fear of it, when they hear the word, and that fear keeps 'em fine. It's better that way. Better for us, but better for them, too, in some ways. They don't git their hopes up so high, and therefore live in constant disappointment and bitterness. They always know there's a Thebes somewhere."

Sam nodded sagely, and said, "Yes, very interesting sentiments," by way of seeming to agree but not really having committed to a position.

The rest of the trip went pretty smoothly, and indeed he slept that night in his own room next to the indifferent form of his own wife, just down the hall from the indifference of his children. He'd thought he'd never make it back to such comforts, and yet he had.

And tomorrow he'd see Connie for lunch and have a fine old time.

But that was not the main condition of his mind. The

main, the inescapable condition of his mind had to do with Earl. Over and over again, he confronted Earl's dictate: do not tell anybody, raise a ruckus, start a thing to come get me. That will get me killed soonest.

He parsed those words, as imperfectly as he remembered them, for a provisional escape clause, an intellectually justifiable principle of dispensation or modification, and concluded in the end that the contract was fairly drawn and that he must obey it. He did feel he had to make a report to his client, which he would do in the morning, and send off by special delivery, and he resolved to discover options within the framework of Earl's command that would enable him to engage the issue. That was all he could do.

Earl, he thought, and it would not leave his mind: What of Earl?

12

THE dogs took Earl down hard. It was their nature, but it also may have had to do with the blood that they smelled on him, his own and their cousins' and brothers'. They hit him simultaneously, strong young hounds in full power, growling savagely as they flew upon him like blurs, and in the next tenth of a second he gave up on any idea of catching the freight and concentrated only upon covering his vitals.

He went into a fetal ball, his knees locked to his forehead, his arms swaddling his head and throat, his face buried. This drove the dogs more insane. They knew how to kill him and their frustration was immense. But there was no way they could get their muzzles and teeth into a vulnerable, soft area, so they attacked his arms and legs, knowing that if they hurt him bad enough by reflex he'd unsnap from his protected position and they could get him where he would bleed out. So for a few moments, that's all it was, the dogs biting to get him to spasm while he fought the pain and the anger of them to stay locked up in himself.

But then the dogs were pulled off by men, and a general kicking commenced. At first it was just two men, and then three more, and they kicked and stomped at him, and cursed and spat and threatened. This went on for a few minutes until, finally, a last fellow arrived and imposed some order.

"Goddammit, boys, let him be, let us see what we got," and the blows stopped whacking into him.

"Mister, you best get up or I will finish you as you lay there."

Earl rolled over and uncoiled, looked up to see six men, that is, four deputies, the hound master and the sheriff, all of them sweated up and crazy-eyed from their ordeal.

"Don't hit me no more, please," he said. "I didn't do nothing."

Whack!

It was a kick in the ribs, delivered with visible pleasure by the dog man.

"Kilt three fine dogs, you did, goddamn your black soul. I'll see you a-swing before this damn day is done."

Two bent to him swiftly and rolled him over. He felt his arms being pinned behind his back and the cuffs coming on.

"Git me them leg irons, too. This fella's a kicker, you can double bet on that!"

The leg irons were yanked tight around Earl's ankles.

"There, he ain't goin' nowheres now, no sir."

The young deputies sat back from their work, then rolled Earl over.

"Who are you, Mister?" the sheriff asked.

"I, uh—"

Earl could not recall the name on his phony driver's license.

"Hah? Who are you, goddammit, when I speak to you, you damn well better answer me right smart, you whelp."

"His name's Jack Bogash," yelled a deputy, who'd evidently found Earl's wallet off to the side, "and he's another goddamned Arkansas fella."

"Ain't that something? You Arkansas fellas seem to stick together, don't you? Ain't you just the fanciest things, y'all? You come down to rescue that old—"

"Sir, sir!" screamed Earl, "I don't know what y'all are talking about. Please don't hit me no more. I'm bleeding plenty bad. I need a doctor. Please, sir, oh God, I will bleed to death I don't get a doctor."

"You will be okay. You may lose some blood, but if you can't lose no blood, you oughtn't to be playing rough. And that is not nothing to do with your problem. You have a much worse problem, and that problem is me."

This was the sheriff, screaming in his face.

"Sir, my name is Jack Bogash. I am an unemployed truck driver trying to get a hunting camp going. I came down here 'cause I heard there was unleased land about, with lots of whitetail. I meant to lease the rights, build a cottage, and see to bringing some Hot Springs or Little

Rock high rollers down here for the season. That's all there is to it."

"Son, we done chased you twenty miles. You burned down a coupla buildings, coshed a guard, kilt three dogs, beat the Jesus out of two strong young men and run us a merry old time."

"Wasn't me, sir. I swear to you. Was them other fellas."

"Other fellas?"

"Yes, sir. I's set up camp about two mile off. Looking for deer sign. Hoping to learn the land, figure on where to build my stands. These two fellas come running out of the piney woods with some story about blackies chasing them for some hellfire reason. They offered me cash money to help 'em git to the tracks. I admit now it don't make much sense, but they offered me money. The old boy talked a blue streak, he did, and before I knowed it, he'd talked me into helping. Don't recollect now why I done it, but he was a persuasive son-of-a-bitch, I will say. He done twisted up his ankle, so I helped him move along, sort of a human crutch. Don't know what happened to that other fella. When I got the old man to the track, I was headed out when them dogs done hit me. That's every true word."

"He's lying," said Opie. "I seen him shoot the dog. I seen him take a shot at me. He jumped Opie and me, and he out-boxed us both and put us both out without busting sweat, like some sort of champion. He's a lying bastard, and he's dangerous as hell. He's playing scared now, but he's just figuring on how to kill us all, you can bet. He's a goddamn gangster."

"I think he's a red. I think he's a red sent down here to rile up the niggers."

"I think he's one of them FBI boys, sniffing around. Looking for trouble."

"Sheriff, best thing is, you just string him up."

"Please, please, fellas. I didn't do nothing. Young man, I *swear* to you wasn't me hurt your dogs and took a shot at you. That was that other feller, the one still loose. I don't hardly know how to shoot a gun at all. I done some boxing once, that's the only thing, and if I hit you it was because you had a gun and was fixing to shoot at me, that's all. What choice did I have?"

"You say you are leasing hunting properties. That would make you a hunter, and unless I miss my bet, them are hunting boots you're wearing. But you don't know how to shoot a gun? Yet someone shot three dogs moving fast. That would be this other missing fella, who left no tracks or scent for the dogs to track. Then at your age, you outbox two strong strapping young fellows, but you are just an Arkansas truck driver without a job. Mister, your story got more holes than a piece of angel food cake."

"He's a goddamned plenty dangerous man."

"I've had enough. Sir, you are too much for us to handle. Boys, take him to the tree, that's all. I will be done with these Arkansas people for good and all."

IT took an hour, but they knew exactly where they were headed; Earl realized they had been there before. It was a hanging tree. He guessed if they caught a runaway out here, that's where he went. Or if someone talked against them in the town, that's where he went. These boys didn't like the shooting close up, they couldn't stand the look of a man's skull all bashed in by a .45 and blown out on the other side. The hanging tree killed easy and bloodless.

"Sheriff, I'm telling you—"

"You shut up now, Mister. I don't want your words

confusing these boys. You keep your mouth shut or I'll have Pepper do some work with his knife on your tongue, and that'll shut you up right and proper. You'll have to meet your maker without no tongue."

"I'll do that right now, Sheriff, you want. That's what we do to a dog killer down here in Mississippi. You kill a dog, you got to pay. Dogs is valuable, and them three was like my brothers."

The convoy marched on through the pines, and Earl tried to lag, but rifle muzzles prodding him urgently kept a spring in his step, and the blood oozing from the many dog bites wouldn't let him relax. Eventually, the group found a path, which speeded matters up considerably, and then they encountered a hill. Up there, at last, was one of the rogue oaks that this piney woods somehow allowed to grow, a stout tree with a limb heavy enough to support a man's full weight, a task for which no pine could be counted on.

It was barren and windswept, as such places inevitably are, and no pine would grow close to the old oak, which was barkless and crooked like a broken bone, climbing twisted into the blue sky.

"Okay, boys. You know what to do."

"You should make him dig his grave," said Opie, "so's we don't have to."

"Yes, let's put a goddamn three-foot shovel in the hands of a man that capable, and see which of us he kills with it and if he can git all of us before we get him. I swear, boy, you don't think a lick before you speak your mind."

"Sheriff, this ain't right," Earl said. "I ain't done nothing. I just helped two boys say they was running from a mob of colored."

"That's another thing. You ever hear of white boys running from niggers? If you actually heard that story, which I doubt, and you were so stupid to believe it, then you are getting your neck stretched for being a dumb bunny, too blame ugly stupid to live. But more likely you think we're the dumb bunnies who'd believe such a crock of sawdust. Now, I think you're some kind of hero type, down here to rescue that old goat. Hired by his family, maybe, for cash money. I hope you spent it already. You paid the goddamned price for it, and see what being a hero does for a fella in Mississippi?"

The rope went over the limb, and was then looped by one of the young fellas he had outfought around his neck, and pulled tight. Of course there was no horse for them to drive out from under him, and nothing for him to fall from; he'd die, not by the merciful snap of a neck giving way to gravity, but slowly, pulled aloft by strong stupid boys, to asphyxiate slowly, twitching, twisting, shitting, pissing, gagging.

Yet Earl was not particularly frightened now, at the last. He and death were old friends, and as a professional man killer for the Marine Corps he had sent that old gentleman many a customer in his time. He had known it would come for him, sooner or later, and now he faced it, as before, the way a predator does—without much fear, with much coolness, with the bull-goose drive to do this last thing well and give these boys, squalid as they may seem, something to remember him by: the one who was a man and died a man.

The rope pulled taut, lifting him onto his toes.

"Usually they be beggin' about now," someone said.

"Cold day in hell afore I beg to white trash like you Mississippi peckers."

"Ain't he a hard one?"

"Give him credit, he ain't got no cards to play but he is playing them out just as they lay on the table."

"You got anything to say?" said the sheriff.

He swallowed and could find nothing at all of interest.

"You got any regrets, sir? This'd be the time to make 'em, and face the Lord at peace."

That inspired him. "Yes," he said, feeling the tautness loosen just a shred, so that his voice could find words. "Here's my regret. I regret that I tried to get this one done without killing no human man. I told somebody that's how I'd do it. And that was a mistake. If I'd done what I knew was the right thing, and shot you boys dead, beginning with them two lunkhead baby shits, and then you, dog man, and you two yassuhing deputies, and finally you, Sheriff—"

"Big words for a man standing under the tree whar he'd a-going to swing," said Pepper, spitting a gob out on the dirt.

"And finally," said Earl, "I regret for them living dogs, 'cause I know when you boys finish with me, you're going to liquor up, and sooner or later you going to git on them poor animals like they's women and—"

The rope came up, closing up his larynx, and he was off the ground, the world gone to black nothingness, his vision gone, his hearing gone, his feet kicking the breeze. He fought for air but there was none, and the full muscles of his arms and legs kicked and jacked, but only to the effect of opening yet more wounds in his flesh where the unyielding steel bit it. He thought at least he had a son, and by all indications a good one, and he loved his wife and wished he'd been better to her, and he thanked God he'd done his duty in the Marine Corps all them years, and as far as he knew he'd only killed men who were armed and wanting his death, and he'd never raped no one or fought a man who couldn't defend himself, and he thought of blue Pacific seas and the smudges that became islands when the smoke cleared, and how it felt afterward when you had made it and you had just a little bit of time to feel the joy of surviving a bad one once again, and he realized that was as happy as he had been, and it was a kind of happiness few men had felt.

He fell to earth.

He sucked the air.

He heard shouts.

He opened his eyes, saw new men had arrived, six or seven of them, and saw a fellow in command screaming at the sheriff. This one was huge: he had shock-white hair and a pinkish skin, and he wore sunglasses and the uniform of a some kind of sergeant.

"Warden wants this boy, Leon, goddammit, and you back off, because you know what the warden wants, I make sure he gets."

"Yessir, Bigboy, I do know that," the sheriff was yammering as he backpedaled. "But you watch him, 'cause he's a tricky bastard, yes, he is."

"Oh, I don't think he'll be any trouble," said Bigboy, and he turned and smiled at Earl, who had collapsed to the earth, retching and breathing raggedly. "You won't be any trouble now, will you, sir?" he asked, and then hit him hard and flush in the side of the jaw, putting him dead-out cold.

THREE

All
the Houses
of Thebes

13

EARL'S brain saw water: he was underwater. Above him, the green surface undulated; he gasped for air and there was none and then he remembered where he was. Tarawa, off Green Beach 1, and the Higgins Boat had tied up on a reef a quarter mile offshore and he was walking the platoon in while the Jap tracers, blue-white, flicked across the surface, and their howitzers and mortars tossed big boomers down and their Nambus cut puffs into the water. The world was liquid and fire, chaos and fear, nothing but, and he tried to hold it together, keep the boys moving, get in toward cover, because there was nothing here for anyone. A moment came when he slipped and went under, with all that equipment, the pack, the Thompson, and the weight just pulled him down in green silence, and he almost quit. He was underwater. Above him, the green surface undulated; he gasped for air but there was none. But he didn't quit. That wasn't in him for some reason, and so when he really awoke, he realized he wasn't in the warm salty Pacific off Green Beach 1, but in some other hellhole. Then he remembered.

The pain was general all over his body, from the rips in his flesh where the dogs had chewed him to the aches in his ribs where the deputies had kicked him. His own blood tasted salty in his mouth and his muscles were throbbing in discomfort; worse still, where his wrists and ankles had cut against the cuffs, he'd opened wounds too, and those flickered hot as fire. But it was his head that hurt the most. As he swam to consciousness, he was aware that something was wrong; it was as if the left side of his head had doubled in size. He opened his eyes and in the left one, the vision was blurred toward blindness. He moved to touch his wound there, but was bound by the chains. Instead, he lowered his head and touched it against his shoulder; it erupted in pain, and he realized the oddness he felt was a swelling. The left side of his head was swollen like some kind of fruit, and his eye was crushed shut. He remembered a fight on the deck of the old U.S.S. *Philippine Sea* in Shanghai Harbor in 1938, against a Seaman Second named Kowalachik, where each man had battered the hell out of the other for fifteen rounds. He remembered it, but he didn't recollect if he'd won it or not, and then realized you don't win a fight that hard, you merely survive.

Details began to accumulate, and through the buzz and the glare and the pain, he pieced together where he was. That rough jostling: that meant he was in a wagon, being jounced along a country road. The green overhead: the road ran through forest, no, really more like jungle, for it had a Guadalcanal aspect to it of overhanging canopy, and there was tropic vegetation, moisture and heat in the atmosphere. The jinglings and janglings: those were the chains that bound him, hand and foot. He couldn't move a step, one way or the other.

They were in jungle. No pine trees anywhere; that

meant they were close to that dark river. He rolled over, nobody paying him any mind at all, and saw two guards ahead of him, up top the wagon, driving the team of six horses as they juggled along.

On either side, the jungle climbed and vaulted; it was like some cathedral of green, dense and hot and steamy.

He rolled over just a bit, and using his elbow lifted himself until he could see over the rough wood of the wagon. On either side rode three guards on horseback, each with a drill instructor's flat-brimmed hat low over the eyes, each with a big revolver on his belt, each with a Winchester '07 .351 self-loader in his scabbard. The guards rode well, men at ease on horseback.

He turned and craned to see what was ahead.

Whack!

Someone smacked him hard in the arm and he leaped back in pain, knowing that two weeks' worth of bruise had just been laid on him. He looked at a guard who'd leaned down to supply a little discretionary discipline with a billy club. Earl sat back, well away from the wagon's timbers. As if he'd had a chance to escape anyhow, with all these chains entwining him, and also, he saw now, running through iron rings pounded into the wood, so that he was moored to the wagon no matter what came.

"You see it soon enough, boy," said the guard. "And come time, you'll wish you ain't never seen it and that them fellows had hung you straight up."

And see it now he did: red brick walls, crumbly and ancient, in disrepair, wearing a brass plate kept shiny amid the ruin, where the letters gleamed:

THEBES STATE PENAL FARM
(COLORED)

"Welcome home, nigger," said the guard.

The wagon passed through the brick gates, and Earl saw something else. It had been added recently, crudely welded together, an ironwork arc curving overhead, in the clumsy penmanship of the unlettered, presumably under the direction of a firmer hand exactly certain of the message.

"WORK WILL SET YOU FREE," it said, and it had a weird familiarity to Earl, but he could not place it in time or locale.

Then the ironwork arch was gone and they had progressed into the belly of the beast itself, into Thebes State Penal Farm (Colored).

He saw a ghastly old plantation house, its columns still soaring and fluted, speaking of a grand old age, but speaking as well of rot and decay, for what had once been jet white was now mottled with brown stain, the taint of algae and corruption, or possibly only moss. It had the look of a ruin, though a curtain flapping in an upstairs window next to the portico suggested some form of provisional habitation, perhaps a more engaged owner would have seen it repainted and restored to a glistening white. Who would leave it so decadent? And why?

Next to it was a newer structure that had the look of wartime improvisation, a barracks-style military building of one story, low and busy. It looked like some kind of store, for it, not the old house, was the center of activity, and a line of free Negroes waited patiently for admittance. Earl wondered what could be in there so important to these people, lined up in complete obedience, as if the key to their provenance lay therein. And perhaps it did, for a Negro woman stepped out, and someone admitted her replacement; she had sacks suggesting goods or merchandise, and Earl recollected that he had seen no store alive in Thebes from the far trees, his observation point. This must be the only store around.

Other decayed brick outbuildings stood, some in ruins, some in better repair, all somehow moist in the closeness of the jungle and the overhang of the thick canopy. Beyond that the compound proper, that is, where the convicts must live. He saw a gate and a barbed-wire fence more efficient by far than the crumbled old brick plantation wall. In the distance he could make out barracks, again military-style, presumably the homes of the convicts when they returned from their day's toil in the farm's fields. But he saw something else, which struck him as queer: that is, four towers, each a story tall, each with a shed atop and gaps in the shed walls, where men looked out with binoculars. Hard to tell from here, but he was sure from one of the gaps he saw something he knew well: the water-cooling jacket of a Browning .30 caliber machine gun. Four towers? Four Brownings? That would bring considerable firepower to bear on whoever challenged authority here at Thebes Penal Farm, and it did surprise him, for such guns might have been common in big Northern pens like Alcatraz or Sing-Sing, but down here in the backwater South? They didn't even have any of those at the big penitentiary in Arkansas.

The wagon headed to one of the outbuildings and pulled up short.

Goddamn, he thought, we are here, wherever in God's name *here* is.

The guards dismounted and unlimbered the wagon. His chains were freed from the rings that pinned them, and, roughly, he was dragged off toward the door of a two-story brick building, dating from at least a century before, shabby but clean, as if well-maintained by men who feared lickings if they didn't clean it well. He was pulled indoors.

"Okay, chief," someone said, "you cooperate or them bruises you got will seem like Sunday school so far. You catch my drift?"

Earl said nothing as he was pulled into a room, and a man with a knife appeared, and without any ceremony at all, began to slice away at his clothes.

"Jesus," said Earl, as his nakedness was finally revealed.

"Shut your mouth, boy," said one of the huskies, and there were no less than five of them for this task.

"See, he got a tattoo," another added.

Someone bent close at the blue ink faded into Earl's biceps.

"He's a Marine. 'Semper Fi,' all that good shit. You a war hero, boy?"

Earl didn't answer; you can't talk to some people.

Then the hose hit him, hard, a jet of screaming water that knocked him backward. Hygiene wasn't its real purpose, though possibly it did some work to that effect. It beat him badly, pinning him against the floor, and purifying him in a rough way. Finally, it stopped, and he began to shiver in the sudden cold, feeling wilted. No clothes were offered. Naked, he was dragged to his next destination.

"My name," the man said, "is of no importance. I want you to know, however, that I have one. I have a real name, but you'll never know it."

Earl now sat on a wood chair. They wanted him naked, in chains, feeling powerless before this guard sergeant, who was, not to put too fine a word on it, something to see.

"In case you're wondering where you are," said the sergeant, "let me tell you. You are in what is called the Whipping House. This is where I do the business of this institution. It's ugly work, but it's necessary. I am very good at it. The convicts know one thing. Well, two things. One is to stay out of the Whipping House. The other is to avoid the anger of Bigboy."

It was the man who had rescued him from the hangman's noose, then knocked him cold with a blow that blew up the left side of his face. Earl looked at him, though he suspected it would be better to keep one's eyes averted in the presence of this fellow.

The sergeant went 240 to 260 pounds, but it was not fat; it was muscle. He had to have spent hours hauling dead weights up and down to get bulges like that. He had his sunglasses off, and Earl could look into his little red eyes, bloodshot and weak, clearly his one vulnerability. His skin was pale and would burn in tropical sun as if set aflame, so he wore the hat with the big brim, gloves, and kept his olive green shirt buttoned up to the top. His hair wasn't blond in the yellow sense, but a new snow's fresh white.

"Bigboy. You will become quite familiar with that name," he said to Earl, "so I would mark it well. Bigboy. It's a nickname. The men I command call me that. Some of the trustees call me that, our doctor, the colored help who run the jobs in this place, the cooks, what have you. The convicts call me that, but not to my face, for they know the penalty for disrespect. Now, do you know where I got that name?"

Earl didn't think the question required an answer, but in the next second, *whap,* a cosh from another guard in the shadows, slapped hard against his wrist, curling his wrist in pain, almost, but not quite, breaking bone.

"No," Earl finally said.

"No *what*?"

Whap! Another blow.

"No *sir!*" Earl responded instantly, shivering with the intensity of the hurt.

"Much better. Anyhow, you might think I got that name because I am big. But that's not true. For many years I had another name. In those days I wasn't big. I was weak. I was food. I was free lunch. I was everybody's favorite target. Are you listening?"

Insane, Earl thought. The man is clearly out of his head.

"I was a fat weak boy, with red eyes and white hair, a disorder specifically called oculocutaneous albinism. I had a cute little upturned nose. I grunted when I ate, and sometimes I farted. My hygiene was questionable. So I was called *Pig*boy. It fits, doesn't it? Pigboy. My papa called me that, so did my mama and my three brothers. Until I was fifteen years old. So do you think I was happy?"

"No, sir."

"No, sir. Pigboy was not happy. 'Pigboy, git your goddamn ass in here, you goddamned worthless piece of pig shit!' So Pigboy one day in his fifteenth year got himself an ax and he cut Mama and Papa and three brothers up into tiny pieces. The happiest day in Pigboy's life. This was in another state, far far away, under a different name, but nevertheless, it happened, I can assure you. I escaped. I fled. I remade myself many times and had many adventures and learned to trust myself, and at a certain point, I decided I would never again be weak or frightened. I got myself a job on a railroad, laying track. Five years I laid track, getting bigger and stronger. I discovered the gym. I lifted a million pounds of iron and discovered I had a certain kind of muscle tissue that responded spectacularly to lifting. I worked. I learned. I started fighting. It turned out I was good at it, because I have all that hatred stored up in me, and I like to hurt people and see them bleed. I like to make them cry and teach them they have no chance in the world. So where would such a fellow go? Why, there's only one place: I joined the Mississippi Bureau of Corrections, where my talents were not only appreciated, but encouraged. Now I am a sergeant and I run this whole goddamned mighty engine of retribution and justice. And my friends call me Bigboy, and every time I hear that, I think of how Pigboy became Bigboy, what it took, how it hurt, what strength and determination it demanded. I tell you that, convict, so you will understand that you are not dealing with a normal man. You are dealing with a creation of pure will who will do what is necessary to get the job done. You have no rights. You have no recourse. You have no hopes. There is nothing for you anywhere in the universe except that you accept the power of my will, the totality of my domination, the hopelessness of all resistance. I am superior to you physically, morally, mentally and spiritually. If you resist me, I will destroy you and never think of it again. Do you understand?"

"Sir, I am no convict. I am—"

Whap!

The beatings started. They didn't even ask him any questions, not at first. They just beat him.

EARL lost contact with the very concept of time. It was neither day nor night, it just was.

"Name?"

"I told your, sir."

"Tell me again."

"Jack. Jack Bogash. Of Little Rock. Unemployed truck driver. Looking for hunting leases, that's all.

Seemed like a start on something new. Some fellows come out of the woods, screaming of being hunted by wild darkies, or maybe Indians, I don't know. Needed my help. I done helped the old one, for money, and the other fellow, he circled around and—"

Whap!

Bigboy himself never struck Earl. Somehow it was beneath him. Another guard or two, shadowy figures that Earl never saw, administered the blows. They used short cudgels and were expert, with flexible wrists and fast hands, and could hit him a blow that hurt exquisitely and forever, yet broke no bones. They were quite practiced in this. They were professional.

"There was no other man," Bigboy said, "and it angers me that you think I am stupid. Convict, I am not stupid. No tracks of him, no scent of him that the dogs picked up, nothing. You penetrated the Thebes lock-up, you set up diversionary devices which you had to have improvised, you conked a guard in just such a way that he was knocked cold but not killed, you rescued a man, you led him out over miles and miles of rough territory, you set up several clever traps to confuse the dogs, you circled back and killed three dogs in about two seconds with incredible shooting and knife skills, you closed on two powerful young deputies and outfought them in a matter of seconds. If the second pack of dogs hadn't arrived, you'd have made it scot-free. This is very impressive work. It's the work of a trained man, a professional. Who are you?"

"My name is Jack—"

Whap!

"Are you an FBI agent? Are you a communist spy? Are you still a Marine? Are you some sort of super Marine? Are you investigating us? What are you up to? Why are you here? Where did you learn your craft?"

"Sir. My name is Jack—"

Whap!

They threw him in a cell, and just when he drifted off, they pulled him out for more.

Hoses.

Head in a bucket, gagging for air underwater.

Exhaustion, bright lights, hideous noise.

The smacking of the expertly administered cudgels, which produced such excruciating pain.

Sometimes it was Bigboy, sometimes it was others. They passed him, shift to shift to shift.

He got through it all on the strength of the one idea that permitted him survival. It was that he could make it only if he kept his identity quiet. They could not kill him until they broke him, and as long as he defied them he hurt them. His stubbornness was a weapon of ferocious power.

"We checked. Ain't no Jack Bogash. That address. A phony. Who are you, boy? What you doing here?"

"My name is Jack Bo—"

Whap!

This is how he figured: they had to know who was investigating them. It would be crucial to their survival. They were smart, they were cunning, they had connections, but they knew they had enemies and they had to root them out and destroy them. A man like Sam was no enemy, not really; he was a normal fellow, indignant but not heroic. Besides, he knew nothing of the prison, only of a corrupt rural Mississippi county, which, really, was no more corrupt than any other rural Mississippi county. Earl, though, tantalized them. They somehow instinctively believed that he represented a powerful threat, and it both terrified and infuriated them.

"*Jack!*"

"Huh? What?"

"Jack, I called you by name twice, you didn't even look around. You forgot your name was Jack. If I called your real name, you'd have looked around fast."

"Sir, my head is all achy and fuzzed up. Don't know nothing no more, not even my own name."

"Which is?"

"Jack, sir. Jack Bo—"

Whap!

"Jack, you are a stubborn piece of shit, I'll say that for sure. Damn, you are a piece of stubborn shit."

"I ain't stubborn at all, sir. I am just telling you the truth."

Earl clung to it passionately, even as he forgot the rest of his life, for to think of that would be to weaken. He could not weaken. If he weakened, he was dead. If he let an image of his wife or son into his mind, he was poisoned.

"Jack, who you work for?"

If they knew he worked for nobody, if they knew he was just a man sworn to help a friend, then they'd put a bullet in his brain and bury him deep and forget where. Because a nobody was no threat to them. But if he was somebody—an agent of some sort, an investigator— then he represented an enemy institution and that institution had to be identified.

"Who you work for, Jack?"

"Sir, I don't work for no one. I am a poor man trying—"

Whap!

AND sometimes it wasn't even him they beat. One night—or maybe it was day, he could never tell—he was stirred from the blurry sanctuary of light, sporadic sleep by screams from somewhere else in the Whipping

House. He wasn't sure how this building was set up, but he believed he was on the first floor in a little warren off a corridor, but up above was bigger, more expansive. It was from that direction the sounds fell through the floorboards. He heard the screams of a black man.

"Suh! Suh! I swear, suh, wasn't me took them things. Suh, I knows the rules. Suh, please, I—"

He heard the sounds of physical struggle, and somehow moans, low sounds that seemed involuntary, as if they seeped out of a living man from some other orifice than his throat, as if some secret fear ducts had been opened.

"You know the rules, Willie."

It was Bigboy, his almost accentless voice, his surprising command of the language, his lack of excitement or fear, his insistence on defining his pleasure as some kind of duty for the betterment of humanity.

"Oh, God, no, suh, please, I—"

When they hit Earl they used hand cudgels, short billy clubs, and got their power from a lot of practice and a flexible wrist. The theory behind it was to not build up too much speed, to inflict a short, sharp, incredibly painful blow to the outer muscles and the nerves, but to break no bones and rarely cut the skin.

The whip was different. The whip, wielded by an expert as it now seemed Bigboy truly was, gained incredible velocity as the snapping of a powerful wrist amplified itself as it traveled down the nine-foot leather braid to the tip, which ultimately reached supersonic speed, and when it struck it tore, brutally, gaps in the flesh, penetrated, and by the roughness of the leather pulled through the already explosive pain of the wound increased that pain even more.

Earl could tell by the sound that something obscene was happening, for the whip thrummed almost musically as it accelerated, and when it struck the snap was like a gunshot, yet there was a curiously muted quality to it, for the flesh of Willie was absorbing the complete energy of the blow.

Willie screamed and screamed and screamed. No transliteration can quite capture the agony of those utterances, for they were beyond the power of an alphabet or a writing system to record. It was just an agony, untethered by restraint and encouraged by fear, that burst alive and pulsating from his lungs.

A good whip man can keep you at maximum pain for the longest time. With control and an awareness of the human nervous system he can hit you where a previous blow's nerves aren't already sending out signals; he can make each blow, that is, a new blow.

Willie struggled to provide drama for the lesson, as Bigboy, proving a very good whip man, crooned to him, but he was not with it, and couldn't keep up his part. Earl heard what he knew was a death rattle, for he had heard it in the islands so many times, a kind of low gurgle as some valve or other lets go while life passes from the body.

"Sarge, he's out," Earl heard one of the assistants say.

"He's not out," said Bigboy, who knew of such things, "he's dead. He's gone."

"He didn't last long, did he?"

"It's hard to tell," said Bigboy. "Sometimes the scrawniest ones, they last for hours and hours. And the big fellas, they just go fast, because something in their brain tells 'em it's too much and it clicks off."

"You know more about niggers than any man alive, sir," said the assistant.

"No, it's the warden who knows niggers. I learned all this from him," said Bigboy.

LATER that day—or maybe later that month or year—he was alone with Bigboy. The guard lit a Camel from a fresh pack, passed it over. Earl took it, though he couldn't look Bigboy in the eyes, for Bigboy had begun to preside over his mind, to loom, to move through his dreams. He felt fear, because he had no power.

"Go on, boy. Smoke that cigarette."

Earl smoked hard. The first glimmer of pleasure in what seemed like years, though really it had only been days.

"Look here," said Bigboy, "you've done well, even I have to admit it."

"Sir, I haven't done nothing. Just tellin' the truth, that's all."

"So here's what we'll do. You tell us who you are. Okay? We'll have to check it. For a few days, we'll let you alone, move you to a nicer place. Food. No discipline. Plenty of smokes. You like the girls? We'll git you a nice dark field gal for a night of fun. We have a part of the setup here we call 'ho-town. You know what that means, don't you? Let me tell you, Jack, she'll make you forget all your bruises. If we can make some sort of deal with your agency, a kind of you-scratch-my-back-we-scratch-yours arrangement, then we'll let you go. You can look back on all this as a character-building exercise. Hell, we didn't break any bones. You lost some sleep, that was all."

"My name is Jack Bogash. I am—"

And so it continued.

14

THEY took him to the hose room and hosed him down, blowing the filth and excrescence off of him. His chains, finally, were unlocked. He was given a prison uniform, newly laundered, a rough, striped garment, and a pair of old boots to wear. When he was done, he was chained again, but more lightly: not festooned with chains so much, but merely handcuffed and ankle-cuffed, the two bonds joined by a single strand of chain.

He was led out of the Whipping House, his home for however many days it had been. He blinked. The sun was hot. It was daylight, when there is no night or day in the Whipping House. Bigboy ran the convoy, with two guards on either side and another behind him with a riot gun, in case Earl had breakaway designs.

They walked from the Whipping House past what Earl had identified as the Store, and Earl felt as if he were some kind of freak show all his own, the man with two heads or six arms or three noses, visiting town. All the Negro women in line to get into the Store stared at him, for they had never seen a white man in chains before and were committing the image to memory, to tell their grandchildren about, that day at Thebes where a white man was treated like a Negro.

They came to the once grand house whose Doric columns seemed romantic proclamations of a time past. That house rose above them all, something out of one of those movies full of belles in fancy dresses and young Confederate cavalry officers heading off to fight the blue bellies and defend a way of life. But there were no liveried Negroes in service at the doors to hold them open, and up close the old house showed how rotted it was, how forlorn, how its paint peeled; some of its windows were boarded over, its shrubbery and bushes were not tended at all, were overgrown and weedy. If a hundred years ago this house had commanded a plantation, today that memory was a ghost.

Up the three steps they went, and into a foyer, where the furniture lay under sheets. In rooms and corridors beyond, Earl glimpsed other rooms and corridors, also shrouded and dusty. But Bigboy led them to the right, through a single door, into the one room that was functional. It was the warden's office, where the man himself sat behind a desk.

He looked up, so mild, at Earl. He was baby-fat plump, bald with a spray of white hair on his temples, maybe sixty or so, eyes distorted behind glasses. He wore a battered linen suit, a white shirt gone to gray, and a black string tie, like a hero of the Confederacy in his declining days.

"Here he is, Warden," said Bigboy.

Earl stood before the man, who looked him up and down.

"My, my, my," he said, "you are a strong one, aren't you?"

Earl had no words for this man. He said nothing.

He was prodded.

"Convict, when Warden says something you reply right quick."

"I ain't no convict," said Earl. "This here's all a big misunderstanding."

Something jacked him hard in the ribs.

"And you call him sir, convict."

"Sir."

"My, my, my," said the warden. "Well now, convict, you seem to have raised a right smart ruckus in our little pea patch. Yes, sir, you do have a talent for chaos."

"Sir, my name is Jack Bogash of Little Rock, Arkansas. I come down to your state in quest of deer-hunting leases in unhunted areas, with the idea of starting up a hunting business. I don't know what these fellas have told you, but some men come out of the woods in a powerful sweat and offered me money to help them, and the one was very convincing and I did need money, so I got involved. I had no idea no law-breaking was involved. This is all just one big misunderstanding."

"I see, I see," said the warden. "And what happened in our county, a detained man being broke out, a chase through the woods, some tricks played on some dogs, all that I have had reported to me, all that didn't happen then, that's what you're sayin', is it?"

"Sir, there was—"

"Another man. Yes. Well, convict, I just don't know what to do here. You say one thing, the reports say another. Now what am I supposed to do?"

"Sir, I don't know nothing about no report. I only know what happened."

"Now, convict," said the warden, "if that is so, can you 'splain to me one damn thing?"

"If I can, sir. My brain ain't working too well with all the pounding it's been getting."

"It seems to me that if you were who you say you are and were not who *we* say you are, you would be screamin' bloody murder for a lawyer. That is what all innocent men accused unjustly demand, for they understand that the lawyer is their emissary before justice. They demand phone calls, they demand to call their wives and see their children, they demand to return to the world they claim they have been unjustly removed from. The world means something to them, it means a lot. They cannot in any way quickly make an adjustment to their new surroundings. That has been my experience."

"Sir, I just tried to cooperate with the deputies and then the guards, sir. That's all I—"

"Now, a natural criminal mind, or some kind of trained man, on the other hand, he doesn't waste time in mourning. No sir. He understands right fast he's in a new world with new rules, a new system, with new lords and masters, new traditions, new possibilities. And he sets about as fast as a skinned cat to master what he's got before him. He's used to quick thinking, quick adaptation. Hell, that even may be why he got in the business he got in, 'cause he's so dadgummed quick at it. Your undercover man—and here I could mean on whichever side of the law, for it is my theory that detectives and criminals bear a marked similarity in personality—is above all a realist. They tell me you are a realist, convict. That you play weak and scared and stupid, but underneath it all, you're calculating your next move, trying to figure out what's going on, aiming at your best chance of survival. You ain't done one thing, not one thing, the man you say you are would have done."

"Sir, I don't know what you're talking about. I am Jack—"

"Now, see, there you go. Bigboy, did you see that?

He's playing stupid again. But if you watched his eyes as I spoke, as I did, as I know you did, what did you see?"

"Warden, what you see all the time," said Bigboy. "His pupils narrowed and darkened, his head got real still, and he put it down a bit, as if it could help him hear better. His eyes didn't move, he was concentrating so hard. And when we brought him over here and in here, you should have seen him looking and memorizing."

"How many Negro women were out front at the Store waiting admittance, Bigboy?"

"Warden, I don't know."

"I'll bet he does. Convict, how many?"

"Don't know, sir."

"Five or six?"

Actually it was seven.

"Don't know, sir."

"I watched his eyes again, Bigboy. He didn't involuntarily respond to either five or six, because he knows it was seven."

"Sir, y'all are way beyond me."

"Well, you have presented me with a problem here, boy. Now I want you to work it through that achy brain of yours what I should do. Okay? You with me?"

"Yes, sir."

"Okay. What I see before me can't be Jack Bogash of Little Rock. There's no Jack Bogash in Little Rock. Documents phony, but very fine phonys. Skills highly developed. Marine background. Tough, smart, violent. No, you'd be Mr. X. Mr. X is an agent. Maybe he was hired by someone in Arkansas, or maybe in Washington. He's a white man, he's very smart, he's been around. He's what you might call a professional operator. Yes, sir. Now, we can't do anything with him until we figure out who he is, why he's here, what his goal is. Unless we know that, we don't know a thing, but if we know that, then suddenly there are possibilities. Without that, we're just stuck with another convict. And being a convict here, sir, is no picnic, for we believe that convicts should suffer for their crimes against society."

"My name is Jack Bogash—"

"*Damn!* I thought I explained it to you. There is no Jack Bogash. Jack Bogash doesn't help a thing. Jack Bogash isn't here. Jack Bogash doesn't exist. Jack Bogash is a fantasy, or a professional identity, well camouflaged, well thought out. I don't want to hear that again from you, convict. You understand. You are pulling a stunt, and you know how we deal with stunts."

"Sir, I am Jack Bo—"

"Okay, Secret Agent X. You have made your choice. Sergeant Bigboy, take Secret Agent X to the coffin."

15

SAM sent his letter of report to his client, Davis Trugood, in Chicago and waited anxiously for a reply. He thought a telegram might be the fastest way, or a long distance call, which would come on the third day, but on that day there was no response. Then came the fourth, with nothing either.

In the meantime, he fretted wretchedly, and was unpleasant to everybody. But he was hardest on himself, and for the intense relief he felt at being out of Thebes County, even if Earl was still there. He wished he didn't feel such pure joy in simple survival, in small things like his wife's grits on the table in the morning and his children's sullenness.

He had punishing horrors to be got through still, the worst of which was a terrible session with Junie and little Bobbie Lee, in which he assured them that Earl was fine, he was on confidential business regarding a legal matter for Sam and in no danger. He would report in soon, if he didn't reach Junie first.

Junie had become somewhat passive by this time in her life. She knew Earl's ways and his nature, and if she didn't accept it or understand it, she had made peace with the fact that her life would in some way be shaped by his needs.

"It's some war thing, isn't it, Mr. Sam? Earl is a man who somehow needs a war. He saw too much war and now he has no other way to feel fully alive. His wife and child just don't supply what he needs. He tried to get to Korea, you know."

"Yes, Junie, I know."

"But they refused. They did not want a man with his record getting shot up on some terrible ridge in a little country nobody ever heard of."

"I suppose no, they did not."

"So Earl has gone looking for another ridge upon which to die, and this time, I'm sure, for even less. For nothing at all, in fact. Mr. Sam, no man that I have ever heard tell of is like that. Why is Earl like that?"

"Junie, I assure you, he is not in desperate, warlike circumstances."

"Oh, Mr. Sam, you are such a bad liar for a man so good with words. Or maybe it's that you yourself see the truth of what I am saying regarding Earl, and so you can't lie with the usual polish. But we both know Earl is in some terrible mess and may well die. I hope if he dies we know about it, and so can go on with our lives. I cannot have him simply disappear. That would be too cruel. Death would be hard enough, and for this boy to have no father, that would be so tragic. But for him just to be gone; no, I could not get through that."

"He will return. I promise."

"You cannot promise, Mr. Sam. You know Earl as well as I do, and you know no promise can cover his behavior. He makes his own choices on his own needs, for reasons about which I know nothing. No one does, no one ever will. That is the way he is."

On that displeasing note, the conversation concluded, and Sam went out to his car. The boy, Bob Lee, was sitting on the running board.

"Whar my daddy?" the child asked sternly.

"Son, he is off someplace doing something important. He will return as soon as possible, but your father is a particular man of duty, and will do what must be done or bust. That is why he is such a good policeman."

"What's 'duty'?"

"I can't explain it. It's doing the right thing, no matter what it costs. If it's easy, it's not your duty, it's your job. Most people do their jobs, but only a few, like your daddy, do their duties."

"I want my daddy."

"Son, if it is possible, he will return, I swear to you."

The boy fixed Sam with unblinking eyes and stared almost through him. For a second, Sam thought he was confronted by the father himself, and then he concluded that little Bob Lee probably had it in him to be just such a man as Earl, as would any of Earl's sons, if he had more.

When Sam got back to his office on the town square, he discovered yet another surprise: what he recognized, outside, as the limousine owned by or rented by Mr. Trugood. That gentleman himself awaited indoors, in Sam's office.

"Mr. Trugood, sir."

"Mr. Vincent, I came as soon as possible. This is very disturbing news."

"Sir, I am as upset about it as you are."

"You have to admit, please: I did not authorize the involvement of another man. This was your doing? I am not here to evade consequences, but I do have to have that acknowledged at the start."

"Mr. Trugood, are you seeking to avoid a lawsuit?"

"No, I am not. I am more concerned with my own conscience. I would not have put another man in such jeopardy on so trivial a matter. That's my concern, and only that."

"Then you may rest. Earl did what he did for me, not for you. He doesn't know of you. But he is a man of great loyalty who may feel toward me what could be similar to a son's feelings, even though we are close in age. It was his decision to risk all on my behalf."

"I do not mean to separate myself from him, but only to support him on my own moral compass. Is that fair? I seek to be fair. I know a good deal about unfairness."

"Yes, sir. That would be fair. Fair as fair could be."

"Good. I thought so. Then I am here to support him in any way possible. What can we do about it?"

"As yet, I don't know. I don't know if he was taken by the prison or the county authorities or by anyone at all. I have had no communication from him. But they are capable of anything. That is an evil place down there. I never knew such a place could exist in this country in this century after we fought a war to liberate men from these kinds of things all over the world."

"Should you call the police? Surely a Mississippi state police agency would intercede in local matters."

"Sir, in that part of the South, I'm not so sure. It's different. It's cut off, isolated, they have their own rough way of doing things, and I suspect certain folks in Jackson like it that way. But Earl did grab me hard, as I said, and made me promise not to instigate an investigation or raise a complaint. He thought that could put him in more, rather than less, danger."

"Do you share that assessment?"

"I don't know. Earl is a good judge of matters of force and violence, as I have indicated. He knows better than most how such men operate, and he can operate with the best of them. This is what he wanted. He was afraid that if outside pressures were brought to bear, they would result in his death rather than his release, assuming he's even been taken."

"I find it hard to stand by and do nothing."

"I do, too."

"We should set a time. Say, one month from now. If we haven't heard from him by then, then I would urge you to begin to apply every pressure you know how. Is that fair?"

"Yes, it is."

"I would advise this, too: If we are to in any way move to change events in Thebes County, then we will have to know all about Thebes County. Would it not make sense to begin some kind of research project, so that we could know all about how Thebes County became Thebes County, who is responsible, what local conditions ensue? Would that not be a wise course?"

"I've already begun, sir. Earl is my friend, and I am torn as to what to do, and I feel guilty as sin for being here, among my children and friends, comfortable and at ease, while he is in extremes. I say that even though I know him to be a man of superior capability, and that if he can in some way escape and survive, he will do it."

"Here is a check, Mr. Vincent, drawn on my bank in Chicago."

"Sir, I have not asked for money. Earl is my friend."

"Then he is my friend, too, and what he has done on your behalf he has done on my behalf, and on my client's behalf and on Lincoln Tilson's behalf. All of us in a row are beholden to him, and I cannot live with myself if I sit back and do nothing. So I want this check going into a sort of working fund. Any expense that is necessary for the rescue or release of Earl should come from this; I leave it to you to put some portion of it with his wife and child, for theirs can't be an easy lot while they wait. But use the money wisely, Mr. Vincent, and keep me informed. You have the number."

"Yes, sir."

"Mr. Vincent, I will say I am very pleased about your escape and impressed with the dedication you Arkansans have to one another. We could use some of that kind of loyalty up in Chicago. I know some families where loyalty like that isn't much applied."

"Thank you, sir. I will begin to find a way to crack this nut right away. I only hope we have not in our way declared a war, without even realizing it. Wars can be hard to control and too many of the innocent can die."

"Though if you must wage them, I take it Earl Swagger is just the man for such an enterprise."

"Yes. That is his genius. And also his tragedy."

16

IN the coffin it is not the heat, even though that is considerable. It is not your own filth, which soaks you, and the odor of your corruption, which assails you. It is not the darkness, though that is a special hell of its own. It's not the solitude, at least not for Earl, a man accustomed to solitude and able to endure it more lightly than most. It's not the rats, or whatever they may be, that skitter over your feet or may be felt examining your particulars, or the occasional insect bite. All of that is miserable in its own pure right, but it may be borne by a strong man who believes in what he is doing.

What it is, really, is the space. Or the lack of it. The sense of being crushed, of being utterly helpless. That is why they call it the coffin, and that is why it is so terrible.

The box is six feet long and about twelve inches deep. It is framed in concrete out on the harsh and pitiless yard behind the Whipping House, near some trees, but sited to catch the sun's full blast. Its floor is concrete and it has no comforts at all, just the rawness of the concrete beneath and the overwhelming encasement of the steel,

which draws and magnifies the heat and whose closeness permits no air circulation, so breathing itself becomes labored and sometimes a cause for panic.

Supine and stiff, with no room to flex any joint, Earl
found only a universe of corrugated steel. Above, it was
but two inches from his face. He could not move. The
sense of claustrophobia grew in geometrical degrees,
and came in a very short time to weigh immensely upon
him. In any case, he was not a man for stillness, and this
stillness, enforced by a wall an inch beyond his nose, an
inch beyond each hand, an inch from the top of his head
and the bottom of his feet, this sense of being pinioned,
of being trapped, locked, broken: this was difficult.

Earl tried not to scream. But panic was his constant
enemy. If he didn't work at relaxation, the panic, liber-
ated by the pain and the misery and the darkness and the
closeness, flew out of control. He yearned so desperately
to sit up. Sitting up seemed a paradise worth dying to at-
tain. Rolling over was too greedy a goal and stretching
seemed positively indecent.

Here the time passed slowly. It drained by, as he could
feel the tickle of the sweat as it departed his hairline,
drawing a tickly track of irritation down his face. That
was the only measure of time, except that by the excess,
brutal heat, he could tell it was day and by the endless
shivering of the dark, he could tell it was night.

No one came for him. No one fed him or watered
him. He pissed and shat where he lay and starved or
gulped dryly in thirst over time. He was alone in the
world, literally buried alive. In there, thoughts of death
came naturally to him, and he began to pray for the arrival of that old friend.

Then he rallied, at least a little. He tried to find a
place where he could go to relax, where memories could

overcome the present. He examined his life for oases of respite, where the sensations of well-being were so overwhelming they could even overcome this grotesqueness.

It didn't work, not even a little.

Each wonderful memory in a life soon produced a moment of pain, which jerked him down to the steel an inch away.

He thought of surviving the islands, and that only got him melancholy for those who hadn't.

He thought of the day his son was born, but he was so exhausted he somehow missed truly feeling that, and there was a look so soon in Junie's eyes that expressed some kind of disappointment.

He thought of a boxing match he'd won in a different world, before there had been a Second World War, and everything was different, and the joy had been so thorough: it was the first time he'd really ever won a goddamn thing, and he had been so proud. But then he knew his daddy would say "You was just lucky, boy," even if his daddy was a world away across the huge Pacific, but still that harsh truth sucked the joy from that pleasure and opened his eyes, and there was his steel wall in the blackness, an inch off, and the suffocating smell of his own filth, and the touch of some other form of life finding him fascinating, and horror that this would be his forever and ever, that all the things he had tried to do would come only to this, the coffin.

You can get through this, he told himself, to quell the panic that again flashed through his brain and made him ache for release, for freedom, for some other chance, even if he doubted he could get through this.

He was a physical man, used to the freedom of movement and the expression of his strength. Physical enemies he could vanquish, and he was used to them and to that process. He knew better than most how to fight, how to win a fight, where to look for weakness, how to exploit it, when to show mercy and when to close for the kill.

But here there was no enemy except his own immobility and the immensity of the steel and concrete crushing him. He tried to focus on Bigboy or the sheriff or the warden, or on old Pepper, the dog man, who'd kicked him so savagely when he was down.

He could not hold these images in his mind. They slipped away, as if he hadn't the energy to hate them now, he was too weak.

He was scared. So many thought he was so brave, but he knew bravery to be a kind of fraud. He was alone and terrified that now, at the end, he would disgrace himself. Even with the noose around his neck he had not been particularly scared, for he'd been anesthetized from fear by rage. He had just wanted to kill those crackers who were lynching him.

But now, again, his strength was meaningless and without an enemy to focus on, his rage deserted him and he felt defeated. It hardly seemed worth it.

He hated that, and possibly it was the warden's shrewdness that saw how this would plague him. In fact, he saw that that was the point of the coffin: it was for strong, active men, that is, violent Negro felons, who were so full of hatred they felt no fear. It was superbly designed to crush them so totally—both in the exact meaning of that phrase but also in the larger, more philosophical kind of way—that their minds gave up, and they were broken. It was an expression of the ultimate power of what the Negroes call "the Man," meaning the white boss, who was so all-powerful he could not allow a single threat, even in the form of a petty theft, to his rule. But even knowing that did not stop it from working so well.

He yearned to straighten up. He tried not to think of it, or of water, or of the pleasures of a good stretch, or of the simple dog's freedom to roll over and scratch your own butt, and these things, now denied, seemed more valuable than gold or diamonds or, possibly, even love.

Pain was everywhere, in places he hadn't known he had. His lower back itself ached tragically, for the tightness of the coffin held it at a wrong angle, against the concrete, and muscles unused to that tension soon rebelled. His elbows were rubbed raw, and so were his heels. His ass itched because of the foulness there, and that seemingly minor irritation tunneled deep into his brain and was possibly the worst thing, for it made him ashamed of being alive, and made him hate himself for his filth.

He tried not to give in to self-pity, but there was nobody to hide it from. He tried not to give in to rage at, of all people, Sam, for his stupidity, good-hearted though it might have been, in swearing him to a vow of not killing, and thereby dooming him, at the expense of Sam's own sense of morality. Sam got to feel moral; Earl got to die alone, paralyzed, in the suffocating heat, with ants and spiders eating him, and his wild and crazed yearning for the simple freedom of moving his head or turning his neck.

It grew and grew and grew, this big thing, this weight. He felt an urge to scream.

Tell them, he thought.

Tell them you're nobody; you're an Arkansas cop who came looking after his buddy, a man he owed much to, your boy's godfather. You meant no harm. They could just let you go and it would all be over.

Yes, and then they'll kill you and bury you and that's all there is. You'll never be heard from again. You'll be nothingness, and that's what got Earl through it: he refused to be nothing. On that issue alone he could fight them.

I will not be nothing.

I will fight you, even from the coffin.

He closed his eyes, but he could not sleep. He itched, he ached, he shat, he stank, he was lunch for something and dinner for something else and he could not move his face or his head or his shoulder and he didn't know how he'd get through it.

17

SAM recalled what he had learned of Thebes before his trip, remembering the decline in the town and the unrepaired road that cut the place off from casual visitors and dried up economic prospects. At the Fort Smith Public Library, he looked up the WPA *Guide to the Magnolia State,* and there refreshed himself on the subject of Thebes State Penal Farm (Colored) and Thebes County. It was listed on Tour 15, which drew travelers, however few of them there may have been, down into the southeastern corner from Waynesboro to Moss Point. It was the shortest tour in the whole damn book over a "remote backwoods section about which little has been written [where] economic and social development have been slower, perhaps, than in any part of the State." He looked up the Mississippi state guidebook and went to "penal system" in the index. There was a whole batch of numbers behind the subheading "Parchman Farms," the big complex in the Delta, but for Thebes there was only one page number, on which it was stated merely that the prison was founded in 1927 on the old Bonverite Plantation as a satellite of the Parchman Farms, as a place to segregate particularly violent Negro convicts. No visiting hours or amenities were cited.

That at least gave Sam two clues to work with, the old Bonverite Plantation and the year 1927. For this work, he decided he had to go to Jackson, Mississippi's capital, loath though he was to reinsert himself into that state's unwelcoming climate. But after once again checking the circulars in the Blue Eye police department (where he was still highly regarded and where everyone assumed he'd be prosecuting attorney again after the next election), he learned that no "wanted" bulletins had been sent out with his name on them, and so he went ahead, with his wife's sullenness, his children's indifference and Connie Longacre's blessings.

The trip there, by train and bus, was uneventful, though made livelier by far by what had been missing from the first part of his last trip, which is Mississippi hospitality. Everywhere he went it seemed he met people willing to help him with his business, to make calls and arrangements for him, to do what had to be done. His first appointment was with a Mrs. James Beaufueillet ("That would be 'bo-fwew-yay,' son") Ridgeway III, who turned out to be the state's youngest living Confederate widow, in that her late husband, whom she had married when he was sixty and she twenty, had run at the Yankee position with Pickett and his fellows, and carried a ball in his lungs ever since that day, Lord only knows how he survived it in the first place. Mrs. Ridgeway III, formidable in her own way as the German panzers Sam had blown to hell and gone that snowy day in

Belgium, was custodian of the memories, as a fellow prosecutor in Jackson told him. That is, she knew the social history of the old Mississippi, and it would be she who would verse him on the Bonverite Plantation.

Now in her seventies, she still had a belle's beauty amplified by theatrical makeup applied with a professional's precision, an elegant and completely perfect coiffure, and a manicure of uncommon beauty. She was a production still. She had those high, fine, sparrow bones of good breeding; she still wore dark, as if in mourning, though of course James Beaufueillet had died back in 1923 and she had married twice again afterward, each time acquiring a yet more sizable estate. She had therefore buried three husbands, given birth to eleven children, buried a few of them, been through the wars of '98, '17–'18, '41–'45 and now this Korea thing. She served him lemonade; they sat on the screened porch of her house in North Jackson, in the center of the antebellum district, where old porticoed mansions spoke of days past but not dead, while outside, amid the cars, surreys and two-wheeled dump carts driven by white-haired Negroes were seen on the streets.

There was only one problem: she could not be hurried.

She would take her own sweet goddamned slow-as-molasses time.

"Now they were a family," she began, her eyes locked firmly on that past, as if it were still within touch of her beautiful old hands, so slim, so elegant. "Timber family. The first Bonverite man was George, and he arrived in the eighteen forties, from Louisiana, I'd guess, the French in him, and he was an empire builder. Yes, sir, Mr. Vincent, where others saw gold beneath the trees where it never was, it was George Bonverite who saw the gold *in* the trees, where in fact it hid. But to timber you must have a mill, so George decreed a mill out of nothingness onto the Yaxahatchee, built with Negro slave labor and strictly applied discipline, and after building began to cut and ship the wood. Where the capital came from originally I don't care to know, and perhaps you would be wise to avoid investigating. If he was from Louisiana, gambling had to be involved, and duelin' and women, for the Bonverites, as it turned out, always had a taste for the women, their own and anybody else's with a comely set of ankles, dimpled knees and buttocks like buttered apples."

Sam took a deep breath.

She laughed.

"What a pleasure it is in this day and age," she said, "to discover a man I can still shock. These young men, they've been through the war and everything, so they've not had the time for a moral education. You have, sir, and I do approve, though as an old gal who's outlived them all, I may now and then give you two fingers of truth."

"Ma'am, I shall try and get through it without calling for my vapors."

Hurry on with it, old Circe!

"Oh, sir, you are a fine rascal, I can tell. Anyway, back to George Bonverite . . ."

And so the story crawled through the generations begat by begat, scandal and duel by scandal and duel as George and his heirs timbered in ever wider circles to feed the growing appetite of the state and the shipbuilders of Pascagoula, and for which they built themselves a grand house, called Thebes, after the storied Greek town of yore, presumably because old George the patriarch had a classical education somewhere in his abandoned background.

The Bonverites flourished, their great house Thebes flourished, and the town that grew to service it and the timbering flourished. Pascagoula ships sailed the world on Thebes lumber. But hard times, perhaps in payment for all the virgins deflowered and all the angered husbands slain by single .41-caliber pistol balls in duels, came in the twenties, when the region was all but lumbered out and the boom of the Great War had subsided. Though America was on the go then, the collapse of timber hit Thebes County hard.

"So old Joe," recalled Mrs. Ridgeway, "who was the patriarch then, old Joe had to contemplate giving up. The town was on the collapse, nothing was growing, there was no work. He would lose it all. It must have destroyed him, for down here we hold our land dear, as I'm sure y'all do up North in Arkansas."

"We do, ma'am."

Get on with it, you old singer of songs!

"Down here, a man'll do just about anything to hang on to his land. Without his land, he's nothing, he's got nothing, his family is nothing. So he had to come up with something. I don't know if it was his idea or if it was the boy's."

"The boy's?"

"The last Bonverite. Cleon, I b'lieve. Cleon Bonverite. Wonder what ever became of him? Anyway, either he or his daddy cooked up a way to save the house and the town. They had heard that over at Parchman, the nigras was escaping now and then, not a lot of it, but enough to get folks riled. Nobody got killed or anything, but you can't have that now, can you, that is, felonious Negroes on the loose? It just won't do, will it, Mr. Vincent?"

She batted her belle's eyelashes at him.

"No, ma'am. I can see how it would get people upset."

"So Joe reasoned, along with his boy, that Thebes had

one thing left to sell, one last product. Its isolation. It was Joe who went to the state legislature, spread some money around, called in chits, did what had to be done, and offered up the idea of a prison for the very bad Negroes, which the Bonverites of course would operate themselves at a generous stipend. So the state 'bought' the land, though not really. The land never changed hands; it just meant a generous stipend was paid out each month to the Bonverites, and that for the minimum investment of a few barracks being built, old Joe no longer had to pay his field hands, he now got them for free from the state. The taxes went away as if they were a bad dream. Joe and the Bonverites were now sellin' retribution against the angriest of the darks, and it was a product many people in this state were ever so eager for. It was a grand system, for it gave the white people a new and more terrible club to wield over the poor nigras, and the Bonverites had their place and their property assured, and new sources of revenue, and for a time the town once again flourished."

"This was 1927?"

"If you say so, Mr. Vincent."

"And then?"

"My, my, my, you are so inquisitive, aren't you," the old beauty responded. "Do pour me some more of that lemonade, won't you, Mr. Vincent."

"I will, madam."

She was flirting, *damned by vanity still!*

He did, filling his own glass too, more to assuage her than to drink, for the stuff was foully sweet, almost a paste of sugar that had yet to dissolve and flakes of lemon rind and melted little round blobs of ice cubes.

The old lady took a greedy drink, needing another blast of sugar to stir her dry old bones and, fortified, went onward.

"Joe died. Don't know why, or how, or by what hand. It was said he died in violence so terrible it could not be reported and that the nigras did it, though no man was accused, and in that part of the state an accusation was a guilty finding, and a trip to the nearest tree was a way to get your dried dead fingers sold as souvenirs. Yes, sir, even in the thirties such terrible things occurred."

"Yes, ma'am. And the boy Cleon? Are you imputing he killed his own father?"

"I would never say such a vulgar thing."

"But he vanished."

"He vanished. He inherited nothing, though by whose decision I know not. There were rumors."

"Rumors?"

"Of another."

"Another? Another what, ma'am?"

"Why, sir, such things can't be talked about. Not among decent white people. But since you are such a charming man, I will perhaps intimate that which should never be intimated. That is, there does seem to be something in the white man's brain, some ancient thing, perhaps curiosity, perhaps fear, perhaps bravado, who knows, that makes him wish to lie with the gals of color. Are you familiar with this phenomenon, sir?"

"Yes, ma'am," said Sam, "not that I've ever—"

"Of course not, Mr. Vincent, as any old fool could see so plainly. But not all are as strong and sensible as you, much less a lust-engulfed creature like a bull-stud Bonverite man. So that, perhaps, is the origin of the other, if there was another. For whatever reason—it was all hushed up, you can understand, with only the faintest reek of scandal—the boy Cleon disappeared. Or went away. The plantation with its great house Thebes, it was lost to the Bonverites. The state took it over, expanded it, put people in charge who care nothing about anything except whipping the nigra and cashing their checks. Why, I believe the new warden was named Jones, can you believe such a thing? And the people that run it to this day are uninteresting. They have no family, to speak of."

"And the Bonverites are all gone?"

"It would seem so."

"I see."

"Do you, Mr. Vincent? Why, it's our Southern tale, exactly the one that Mr. Faulkner up in Oxford has had such sport with, of generations of strong men with but the weakness of wanting to lie with the fetching high yeller, and of that weakness's inevitable result, which comes in the form of nigras with strange ideas of importance, and intelligence much inflated, and devious minds, natural antagonists to what must be and must be defended. Yet now it is hard to defend, for when bloodlines are confused, moral certainty disappears, which equals moral downfall, sir. The Bonverites were a great family; they ruled an empire from a great house and dined on china imported from London. They helled and rode hard and made things happen with their deep schemes and their courage, and they lost it all in scandal, a man dead, his son fled in shame, the haunting suggestions of a shadow brother also vanished. Chaos, loss, pain. New inheritors named prosaically enough Jones come and know or care nothing about what came before. But that is the tragic story of what happened in Thebes, and that is why to this day no decent folk will visit it, for it is blasphemed ground. Would you care for more lemonade, sir?"

"Ma'am, no, I wouldn't."

"I have so enjoyed this. I do not get audiences as once

I did when I was young and fair. It was so nice to have a gentleman caller."

"I had a very stimulating experience," *you old monster.*

SAM returned with a treasure. It was a name, the name Jones. How many Joneses could there be in Mississippi? And it turned out there were hundreds. He set about his task with a great deal of discipline, even though he was sure people would think him cracked if they knew what a thing he was up to.

He called the directory assistance or the switchboard of every single town listed in the gazetteer, and asked for the number of every person named Jones. It turned out there were over 450 of such people, and he called each and every one of them, acquiring a phone bill that set a record.

At each answer, he began the same way.

"Hello, I am Sam Vincent, Esquire, a lawyer from Arkansas. In regards to a law case, I am seeking a man named Jones who may have been for a time the warden of a penal farm in Thebes County, Mississippi. Is there any chance, sir [or ma'am, depending], I have the right Mr. Jones or at least a relative of that Mr. Jones?"

The answers he got ranged from the idiotic to the unprintable, but most were polite enough, though disappointing.

"No suh," the Negro Joneses would say, "don't know nothing about that Jones. Our people never had nothing to do with no jail."

"Thank you, sir [or ma'am]," Sam would reply, "I am very sorry to have bothered you," and another name was scratched off the list.

The white Joneses were more helpful; their sin was perhaps that they were *too* helpful. It turned out that most were obsessed with their own families, and kept him on the phone for what felt like hours as they took him through their family trees, and they were so flattered to have a listener interested in their lives, they spilled beans quite readily that hadn't ought to have been spilled to anyone, much less an unknown caller.

"Well, sir, we never had a Jones who worked in a prison, but I'm sorry to say, we had a Jones who served time in a prison. He was a lawyer like yourself, sir, my aunt's husband, and as luck would have it, his name was Jones too, like our family's name, Willard Jones, and it turned out he was overbilling an estate to which he had been appointed executor, and he had to resign the bar after he got out of the prison. He's now in Memphis, I think, and I believe he has passed the Tennessee bar, though of course there are no standards whatever in a primitive state like Tennessee," and so forth and so on.

Sam wearied quickly of his ordeal by Jones, but there was no quit in him at all, so he kept at it, though he could feel his energy and interest lagging, and his voice growing dull and charmless. Of course he was at his worst when he finally connected.

"Well, what would this be in regard to?" the Jones on the other end asked, the first time he'd encountered an upward tweak of voice, signifying a nibble.

Sam looked quickly at his list to figure out where the hell in the maze of Joneses he was, and discovered that this Jones was the third Jones of McComb, Mississippi.

"Sir," said Sam, "I am in the business of trying to authenticate the death of a Negro man at that prison much later, and I am trying to locate someone who could provide information about conditions there."

"Under my father, conditions was as good as they could be. He was a fair man with a hard job to do, and he done it like he done everything, which is true-blue steppin' to duty and our Christian god."

The edge of hostility gave Sam something to work with.

"That is what I had heard. I had heard that this Warden Jones was a fair and a good man. If I can establish that, if I can enshrine his memory and make the court see what a good man he was, then possibly I can demonstrate that what happened after he left—let's see that was—"

"It was forty-three. The gubmint took it over in forty-three."

"I see. So he was there—"

"Thirty-six to forty-three. He wanted so bad to run his own prison, and he'd been at Parchman quite a while, and when he got Thebes after, you know, old man Bonverite got roasted up like a weenie, and it wasn't much, but he worked it hard. He worked it so hard it damn nigh kilt him."

"He sounds like a great man."

"Nobody escaped under Wilson W. Jones and nobody died, neither. I'm not saying it was a nice place, now; it couldn't be."

"Of course not," Sam said. "After all, its mission was the incorrigibles."

"And I'm not saying no Negro wasn't now and then mussed up a bit by the guard staff, but they had a hard job, and a great responsibility. They didn't beat nobody so bad they died, and my pa was proud as hell of that. When they beat 'em, they beat 'em fair and square, lookin' 'em in the eye, I seen it my own self many a time. And b'lieve it or not, the Negro, he likes it that way, too. He likes knowing the rules and what's 'spected of him. You can't give no Negro too much freedom, 'cause it makes his head spin and there's all sorts of hell to pay."

"And the government came in, forty-three you say, what was his—"

"He was upset when the gubmint came in—"

"It was the state government?"

"No, no, the U.S. gubmint. The Army. They took it over in forty-three. What they needed with it, I do not know. I do know that my daddy never got another prison, and he was a bitter man. He took the worst job in the system and made a go of it, and had a perfect record, and he went on to be assistant warden at several places, but never got to be top man again. He died of a broken heart, I would say."

"Oh, I am sorry to hear that," Sam said, anxious now to get off the phone and pursue this new direction.

"I am sorry, too."

"So he is not alive and I could not get a deposition from him?"

"No sir, not unless you got a telephone number from heaven."

"Well, then, I am so sorry to have wasted your time. But may I thank you for your father's service. He sounds as if he were a good man."

"Thank you, sir. That's more'n he ever got from the state of Mississippi."

The government took it over in forty-three. What on earth could that mean?

Sam puzzled this one over for a bit, and recalled that nothing he had read anywhere spoke of such a thing. Perhaps it wasn't worth reporting, simply some temporary wartime measure like a supply depot or a reporting station of an ancillary training facility for some arcane specialty, like ball-turret gunning, that needed some isolation to practice in. Or jungle survival; that made sense. Maybe they brought in young naval aviators and gave them a crash course in jungle survival, for certainly parts of that bayou were as wild as anything in the Pacific.

He tried to think of who he could call, and then came up with the name Mel Brasher, who was a staffer in Congressman Harry Etheridge's office but had been a county chairman down here in Polk for a number of years before Harry had tapped his talents for the big D.C. job. Once Mel's wife, Sherry, had been picked up for drunk driving after an election night, and Sam had seen to it that the case never came to trial and that nothing had happened to Sherry's license.

So Mel owed Sam; now Sam meant to collect.

He got Mel, not right away, but soon enough, and after a de rigueur session of political gossip and a run-through of each fellow's family and prospects, Sam got to the point.

"Mel, I'm stuck on a case here and I wonder if—"

"You just tell me, Sam. You know you can count on me."

"Thanks. You want the long story or the short story?"

"Sam, it's D.C., so I have to have the short. I've got fifty phone calls after this one to return, and I've got to make sure Boss Harry gets to the Silver Spring VFW post tonight."

"Mel, I'm looking to find out what U.S. government installation was established at a Mississippi state prison in nineteen forty-three. For some reason, the Army came in and took the place over. Why'd they do that, when did they give it back and under what circumstances."

"A state prison?"

"Actually, a penal farm. For colored. In the bayous of

Thebes County, way up the Yaxahatchee River. No country for white men."

"I'll say," said Mel. "I'll have a kid in our office get back to you, Sam. You need this by—?"

Yesterday! Sam's brain screamed.

"Well, sooner'd be better than later."

"I'll get this kid right on it."

The kid, a pip-squeak voice that wore a name that didn't register, wasn't a fast worker, but he was at least thorough, and it was two days before he called back, two days, needless to say, of anguish for Sam.

After introductory preliminaries, the boy—Harold, that was the name!—got to the point.

"Yes, sir, I checked with the Department of the Army, and you're right, an army unit did move in down there."

Sam was all ears.

"It was actually Army Medical Corps. So I went over to Walter Reed and used the congressman's name and met a guy in records, and it turned out it was something called the 2809th Tropical Disease Research Unit. They were looking at the jungle diseases and cures for them, so they had to go somewhere where there was jungle, I guess."

"I see," said Sam, writing it down. "Yes, that's very good. Is there more?"

"Well, I couldn't see the file. I just got this fellow to look at it."

"Ah," said Sam.

"Yeah. But I did learn something. This unit, the 2809th, it was commanded by a Major David Stone. That would be Major Stone, M.D."

Sam wrote it down.

"But if you think you need a line on Stone, Mr. Vincent, you can forget all about it. I ran that through the

Department of the Army, and I found out that this Stone died in nineteen forty-five. So it's a dead end."

"Died of what?"

"Sir, I don't know. It didn't say and nobody knew. You'd have to get the records themselves."

18

A CRACK appeared in the darkness, and then spread to a blast of light, as someone pried the coffin lid open. Earl was too gone to notice or care.

"Whoa. Do he stank or what? No human man stank like that, no sir."

"Give it to him."

The next thing Earl knew, cold water hit him under great pressure, pushing him sideways as it smashed him. He withered under its force, which was in its own way a beating, for the power of the pressure tilted him sideways and mashed him against the rough concrete box. He felt the water going up and down him, then settling in his ass where he was filthiest, where it beat a steady hurting into him there, tearing at him where he was sorest and most delicate.

And the water was so cold it sent tremors raging through his body. He could make no sense of it for a second, of what was happening. It was like going for a sleepwalk and waking up from a dream when you stepped off that top step and started your long and horrifying tumble down the steps.

The water stopped. Rough hands got a grip on him and pulled him out, where they dumped him in the dust. He uncranked limbs that had been immobile for who knew how long, and felt those pains added, as muscles bent in shape were stretched for the first time. Yet he was so confused he could take no pleasure in it.

"Ain't he a sorry sight though?"

"He is. Ain't no white man let hisself git like that. He can't be white."

"He ain't white. He's another nigger, that's all."

"Hit 'em agin with that water, boys. Git his ass good, git that shit out of there so them flies don't go crazy. Bigboy wants him clean and right proper for the doctor. This boy goin' git his shots."

The water blasted Earl along the ground, but soon the men pinned him flat on his belly and the hose man really squirted him out. Then they pulled him to his feet, and he could not stand, and went to one knee, at which time he was yanked up again.

"Boy, no one here goin' carry you, that's for sure. You can move as we direct, or I can shoot you behind the ear right here and we'll let the hogs eat you."

Earl couldn't focus or speak. His lips were cracked, his muscles a-tremble. That he was naked before these uniformed men didn't even occur to him, and he felt no shame, for he was not human enough for shame. He just felt some strange sensation that had to be something like the recognition that he was alive. But it was not pleasing nor elating; it simply was. They shoved him along, and his feet dragged in the dust as they led him into the Whipping House.

There, in Bigboy's office, he was wrapped in a blanket. He waited.

Then Bigboy arrived, with some others, bent to him,

and lifted his chin in his big hands. Lights flashed in Earl's eyes; he blinked and jerked, but Bigboy had him in control and yanked his head back.

Something cold and round pressed against his chest, and Earl fought through jangled memories for a name, and came up with the concept of stethoscope, which was attached to the concept of doctor, which led onward to medical examination.

"Well, his heartbeat's remarkably strong. His pupils are all dilated, and they'll stay that way for a day or so. He needs nourishment, bed rest, gradual exercise, penicillin for all of those bites, in case he's infected. But he'll be all right in a bit. Nothing a few shots won't cure easily."

"Well," said Bigboy, "we don't got a bit. We only have right now."

But the doctor, if that's what he was, stared at Earl in some kind of rapt curiosity. Earl tried not to stare back, for such a breach of rules would get him a rap in the back of the head and his eyes weren't working very well. Some flashing seemed to cut through the room each time he blinked. But he eventually made out a man of surprising civility, neat, modest, hair perfect, eyes lit with probing curiosity, as he looked Earl up and down.

"He's strong," the doctor said. "You're strong, aren't you, friend?"

Earl was glum.

"He has fight in him still. You don't see many Negro boys that strong. They tend to give it up and hand it over. This one has some spirit."

"Can we do this, sir, and move on?"

"Of course. Secure him."

Strong hands moored Earl to the table he sat on, and there was in them a threat of violence.

The doctor opened his case. Earl caught just a

glimpse into it and made out tubes, many tubes. But then a tube came out, a paper sheathing was pulled away, and Earl saw a large hypodermic needle.

"Like shots, friend?"

Earl said nothing as the doctor drew some fluid into his syringe from a tiny bottle, then came around to him. He felt his arms slapped, felt the sting of powerful disinfectant, and then the steely prick of the needle. It felt about an inch wide as it slid in, and a numbness spread as its fluids were injected into his system.

Then came another needle in the other arm. Then he was bent forward, and took two shots in the ass.

"You'll be sore for a while. Now you've got penicillin, a common booster, a blood coagulant, and some vitamins that should get you around."

"Are you done, sir?" said Bigboy.

"I am. He'll survive."

He looked at Earl.

"Friend, I don't know what you got yourself into, but I wouldn't want to be in your shoes."

He rose, closed his case, and left.

Earl was alone with Bigboy. His mind was full of strange sounds, and he was having some trouble making much sense of all this. He felt pain from the needles and could already see the bruising beginning.

But he felt Bigboy looking hard at him, as if trying to figure him out. Finally Bigboy said, "You know how long you were in there?"

Earl shook his head.

"Seven days," said Bigboy. "Seven goddamn days. No one has lasted there more than four. You know, it backfired. You're playing to be somebody named Jack Bogash, unemployed truck driver, but I'll tell you what, nobody believes just any Arkansas Joe Truckdriver could get through what you got through. Only man who could get through that is some kind of hero, some police officer or Marine raider or agent or some other. You think you're helping yourself, you're only guaranteeing more rough treatment. So I'm now going to ask you again: Who are you? You tell me."

"Bogash," was all Earl could think to say after he finally found his tongue.

"Yeah, and my name's Jesus Christ."

He sat back, got out a cigar and lit it up, sucked in a big cloud of tobacco, let it sift from his mouth through a tiny channel in his lips.

"I told the warden this," he said. "See, I know how these boys think. This one thinks he's a hero. You beat him or drown him or make him think you're going to kill him, that just makes him stronger. You know what the heart of a hero is?"

"No sir," said Earl.

"You're lying again. Even as stretched thin as you are now, you're lying, playing dumb-and-stupid cracker who doesn't know a thing. You think no matter what, we won't kill you, not 'til we've figured out who you are, so that's what's keeping you alive. Yeah, I see that, nobody else does."

It didn't seem to require an answer.

"So, I'll tell you what the heart of a hero is, even though you know it. I just want you to know how far ahead of you I am. The heart of a hero isn't love or sacrifice or courage or anything fancy like that. That's for the funny papers. No, I've seen through that in my adventures. Here's what it is: it's arrogance. Vanity. Love of self. You think you're so special. Yes you do. And when we treat you special, when we do all this to you, it may hurt like hell but pain doesn't mean a lot to a tough cracker like you, been blown up in the war, and shot a few times to boot. You can get through the pain. No sir. Now I'll tell you what you *can't* get through. Are you listening?"

Earl didn't say a thing. He was concentrating on not passing out.

"Yes sir. What you can't get through is this: to be nobody. Take away what's special, make you nobody. Make you just another convict and you have the rest of your life down here among the lowest and crudest and most violent of the Negroes. This is just it, this place. No hope of escape or recognition, nothing at all *special* that's going to happen to you. You'll be anonymous, a face in the crowd, a nobody for ever and ever. Now how do you like that?"

Earl said nothing.

"You think about this. We're going to give you a nice day or so in a private lock-up with some food and a toilet; you get a shower twice a day. You can play the radio. We get you some newspapers. I won't even pretend to hide from you what I'm doing, because you'll see through it. All that's to make you think of the good stuff of life. Then it's over, convict. Then you go to the Ape House."

> It makes a long, o time man, o feel bad
> It makes a long, o time man, o feel bad
> It makes a long, o time man, o feel bad
> O my Lord, Lordy, when he can't get
>   a letter-a from home.
> O Captain George, he was a hard
>   a driving man
> O Captain George, he was a hard,
>   a driving man,
> O my Lord, Lordy, out on the Gulf
>   and Shelf Island Road

It wasn't music, not really. It was a chant, deep and from the heart, pounding with rhythm as hoes flashed and bit into the earth in unison.

Earl could see them far away. They were in the broad fields, chopping weeds from gullies, and they seemed to be engulfed in mist, as if legendary; but it was dust that rose and the men just fought through it, their hoes rising and falling to the sound of their song, as guards rode around them on horseback with guns.

"You don't look over there, convict," said Earl's escort. "You ain't going over there. Over there, them's got it *easy.* Where you're going, it be hard."

Earl walked along the dusty road, his wrists ensnared in chains, and his ankles too, so that the only steps he could take were mincing and pitiful. His arms still ached from the shots. Two men flanked his shuffle, and one was up front and one behind. The sun beat down, a Mississippi sun that seemed to have been put into the sky for one purpose alone and that was to fry the hell out of all men unfortunate to experience its blast full out.

He felt somewhat better now, at least in a physical sense. He'd had food and shots and was clean. His clothes were clean, if simple, cotton, striped as were all the convicts', and boots that fit.

But in other ways, he didn't feel better at all. Bigboy was right. Bigboy was smart. Bigboy had him figured out pretty good.

The two days of relative respite did more to hurt Earl than all the abuse that had been heaped upon him by Bigboy and the prison itself. He listened to the radio, he ate grits with butter in the morning, a ham sandwich in the afternoon and fried chicken in the evening, buttery biscuits and gravy. He saw now that his life didn't have to be circumscribed and brutal. They had moved him, as expertly as they had beaten tattoos on him with their clubs, beyond simple survival toward contemplation. Thus his true enemy became his own thoughts: he remembered his son, that wary, observant boy who had a strange gift for stillness, and could just sit and watch for hours without saying a word, and then, when quizzed, spit back all and everything that had passed before his eyes, no matter how insignificant.

He thought of his wife, the most beautiful gal he'd ever seen in his life, and how he'd fallen crazy in love with her that first time he'd seen her at the USO in Cape Girardeau in 1944, after coming back from Saipan and going on that bond tour in his fancy uniform, a designated hero of America meant to inspire people.

That's what came back the most to haunt him, and that's when he hurt the most. It was easy to be a hero when you had nothing to look forward to, and the only thing you had to believe in was the United States Marine Corps. But then, in love, he had to go back to another terrible battle, and he remembered the leaden sorrow he had felt, because for the first time in his life, the world had seemed so full of possibility.

But he went back. He had to. It's what he did, it's who he was.

> *Well, Lord, I woke up this mornin',*
> *man, I feelin' bad.*
> *Wah—babe, I was feelin' bad,*
> *I was thinkin' 'bout the good times,*
> *Lord, I once have had.*

They were singing to beat the devil down, or to beat the hopelessness from their own spirits as they chopped and chopped.

They are singing for me, Earl thought.

The camp was surprisingly elaborate, like a government installation, a series of barracks behind a barbed-wire fence, and, inside it, another square of barbed wire, and inside that, a single barracks.

At each corner of the inner square, a two-story tower stood, and Earl could see the machine guns mounted in them. He saw how flexible they were: they commanded the entire compound, and with .30-caliber water-cooleds capable of sustained fire, and with the barracks beneath them simple jerry-built structures of wood, no place was safe from their wrath, given the physics of the ballistics. If it were necessary, the guns could hose down the compound in a matter of seconds, minutes at the most, and all inside the barracks would be dead. There was no cover from the guns; they controlled all.

They entered the first compound, and it was almost a community. Not all the men were at work, but some hung back, cleaning barracks, scrubbing floors, hanging laundry, doing all the administrative work that would keep such an institution going. In a separate shed, he could see women cooking at big vats, preparing food for the men, all of it under the eyes of guards, who patrolled under the drill instructor hats, watching intently for too much fraternization. Just beyond the wire there seemed something like a free community, or a trustee community, where in relative freedom a few older men lounged and chatted laughingly with each other. That had to be the famous 'ho-town. Yet they all stopped to stare as this strange little convoy approached them: a white man in the stripes of a convict. Surely they'd heard rumors or knew of the white boy locked in the coffin, but hadn't really believed it. Here he was at last, in the flesh, a white boy, chained and being led by the tough boys in the hats.

Then they reached the inner compound. Earl could see Bigboy in there, surrounded by his ass-lickers, watching him approach with something not quite glee but certainly smugness.

The gates were opened after an elaborate ritual with the locks, so that no gate was opened completely. They stepped in, it was locked behind them, then the last gate was opened.

"Welcome to the Ape House," said Bigboy. "Jack, you're going to like it here."

Earl just saw another barracks building, with barred windows and a row of crude shitters outside, the wood all dilapidated and every which way, as if some invisible burden of woe had bent the place down over the years. Its roof was wood and it was painted the pale green of institutions everywhere.

"Let me tell you, Jack, who your new roomies are going to be. They are the worst of the worst. They aren't just killers, they're the crazy, wild Negroes, the angriest, the most violent. You have multiple murderers in there, you have all the riffraff in the state that everybody wanted to hang but couldn't quite, because maybe they only killed another Negro and not a white man. But in there, Jack Bogash, in there there isn't any hope and there is no future."

Some laughter came from the guards around Bigboy.

"You won't last a night in there. You're going into a hell so deep no white man can come out alive, or maybe would even want to."

Bigboy brought his dark-glassed eyes so close to Earl's, Earl could see his own scraggly self reflected in them, big as life.

"You are the answer to their hopes and dreams, Jack Bogash, you are. There's a blue-gum nigger in there named Moon, and he's the meanest black bastard who ever walked the face of the earth, and they say he's endowed like a horse. Tonight is the best night in Moon's life. Moon is going to shine tonight, Jack. So Jack, what's it going to be? Are you coming clean, Jack, you telling us your real name? Or you going into the Ape House?"

"My name is Jack Bogash," Earl said.

19

SAM knew people; people knew Sam. That was one of his gifts; he had made friends wherever he'd been.

So now, feeling he'd pretty much used up his congressman's assistant's assistant's good will and energy, he turned to the colonel of the artillery battalion he'd served in during the war, the same man who had pinned the Bronze Star on Sam for blowing up the German armored column.

But Russell K. Parsons was a brigadier general now, and he worked in that strange new building that was so singular it inspired awe, a skyscraper on the ground, broken down into five units, called by its geometric shape the Pentagon.

A phone call got through easily enough; the general headed something called the Army Logistics Command, designed to hustle toothpaste and tin cups and condoms and Lucky Strikes and packs and Garand rifles over to Korea or wherever.

"Well, Sam," said the general, "I'll be damned, how are you."

"Sir, I am fine," said Sam, realizing again that the colonel, now the general, was three years younger than he was.

The two chatted; Sam had been a damned good artillery officer and the general had been happy to have him in his command. It was citizen soldiers like Sam, the then colonel often said, who won the war, not the few West Pointers such as himself salted through the ranks.

But of course the general knew this was not a social call, and got quickly enough to the point.

"Don't suppose you're calling me to set up a get-together for the families, are you, Sam?"

"No, sir. I probably couldn't stand your kids and I know you couldn't stand mine."

"Well then, designate your target, set your coordinates and open fire."

"Sir—"

"Sam, you really should call me Russell. Frankly, as an elected official you probably outrank me now."

Sam said nothing about being turned out at the polls last time; he just played the role.

"Sir, I could never call you by your first name. You were God to us, and I'm comfortable that way."

"Well, then ask God for a favor and possibly God will look with pleasure upon it. It's nothing to do with manna from heaven."

"Only information from the Pentagon."

"Why, that's more valuable than manna from heaven, and probably harder to come by."

"Even for a general?"

"Sam, in this place, they send brigadiers for sandwiches. I'm lucky to have a job."

So Sam finally got to it.

"The 2809th," said General Parsons, "a medical research unit."

"Yes, sir."

"Major David Stone?"

"Major Stone, M.D." Sam left out the detail that the man was dead. It wouldn't do to suggest that he already knew quite a bit.

"All right, Sam. I will have a sergeant look into it, and if that doesn't get it done, I'll send a captain. If that fails, some poor colonel is going to be working for you and not even know why."

It took a few days—anguished, of course, but Sam couldn't call to press, for he knew that would be a mistake—but finally the general got back to him.

"Now, explain to me why you need this information again?" There was an edge to his voice that Sam picked up on right away, even as he launched into his new cover story about a lawsuit against the state of Mississippi regarding the wrongful death of a man in the vicinity of the state penal farm at Thebes, for which he was trying to assemble information by people who had been there. A doctor who had served in the war and was by all means an outsider would certainly be considered objective, and would be highly regarded for a deposition.

"Well, I'll have to disappoint you there. Sam, Dr. Stone died, in 1945, at that duty station."

"I see."

"Yes."

"Sir, is it known of what cause?"

"No."

"No, it's not known, or no, you don't know."

"It's not known," said the general, a certain distance coming into his voice.

"Is something wrong, sir?"

"Sam, this thing isn't well documented. In fact, it's unusually poorly documented."

"I see, sir."

"Well, possibly you don't. In fact, I did have to send a sergeant, a captain and finally a colonel on this errand, and even that didn't work. So finally I went to Records myself, and of course it turned out I was at the Point with the OIC. We'd played football there together in the early thirties."

"Yes, sir."

"So he looked. He himself, a full bird colonel, he looked. Sam, we got David Stone's personnel file out of the storage room."

"Is it classified?"

"Sam, it's more than classified. It's nonexistent."

"I don't—"

"The jacket is there, but inside there's nothing. The contents of the file have been physically removed. That's highly irregular."

"There was no reference, no note, no explanation or anything?"

"Not a thing."

"Could such a thing simply be lost?"

"Possibly. But not probably."

"So what do you think?"

"Someone took it. It was physically removed."

"Who on earth has it?"

"Someone else."

"I don't—"

"Someone else in the government. Someone with a lot of power. Some agency or bureau or board or committee that can get things done."

"I see."

"Sam, I would run, not walk, away from this thing.

ASAP, as we say. If they can do this—make a file not exist where by all legal authority it is mandated to exist—then they can hurt you badly. You're in dangerous waters."

20

THEY led Earl in, and in the jamb of the door, the guards unlocked his chains.

As the men bent with the ancient keys and he felt the locks yield and the sudden weightlessness as the chains that had been his companions for so long disappeared, Bigboy leaned in close.

"You're on the levee tomorrow," said Bigboy. "And the day after that. And all the days after that 'til you either come clean or you kill yourself or your new pals in here kill you. You know what? It doesn't really make a shit's worth of difference to me. It does to the warden, who gets paid to worry about such things, but it doesn't to me."

He stepped back, and the door was opened, and the two men propelled Earl inward with a shove.

He entered a different world.

He knew it immediately from the smell. It was the smell of ancient sweat and blood, hammered into the wood. He knew from the darkness, because no details swam into his vision, but only indistinct impressions, mainly of rows of bunks, most full of men, and an open space at one end, near to him, where some men played cards.

But he knew mostly from the eyes.

At least thirty sets drilled into him. He could feel their weight. In the Marines, he'd felt such a thing when he moved to a new outfit, and the men he would be responsible for watched him out of fear or curiosity or in defiance or to test him. That was all right; that was human. That was recognizable.

What he felt now was fury. The eyes spoke eloquently. They were narrowed but intent, close to warriors' concentration, tracking his every movement, the details, committing them to memory, and most of all expressing hate. He could feel the mass will of obliteration upon him, unleashed, unbroken, unmitigated. These weren't the Negro eyes as white people experienced them, obedient, ready to please, hoping for a compliment or a tip. Earl had never seen eyes like these.

But as he looked he saw some eyes past caring. It became clear that sick men were in here too, or mentals or the feeble-headed, for a certain segment of the population was apart and it was men in strange states. One stood, arms clasped about himself, jabbering madly. Another rocked back and forth, shaking his head, a spume of drool running down his chin. Still another was lashed crudely to his bed, and thrashed, though with the diminished energy of the exhausted, against his bonds. One was stark naked, standing frozen in the corner.

Earl looked away; it would not do to stare.

It was fine for them to stare, and stare they did, as all the cards being played were set down, and the Negroes just looked at him. There was no greeting, no acknowledgment, no anything, only the sullen looks of an anger so pure and deep and old it was beyond reckoning.

Tentatively, he walked the rows of bunks, until he found one that was empty.

He unrolled the mattress, which had no sheets and only a thin stretch of blanket and a rough pillow, and sat.

"Dat my place," a voice came out of the darkness.

Without speaking or looking Earl rose and found another bunk like the one he'd tried, and he sat there.

"Dat be mine," came a voice.

He rose again, this time to laughter. Three more times he tried and each time a voice warned him off, until it became clear that none of the bunks were for him.

So he walked to the wall, and slid down it, and commenced to sit, staring at nothing, unmoving, willing himself so quiet and still it seemed he approached animal death.

But he was not ignored.

He heard the talking, the laughing, the joy of their voices. They were happy. This was damned interesting to them. They'd never seen a goddamn thing like this, a white boy among them. Put here without protection or explanation.

He waited. He knew they would come sooner or later, and he knew there would be more than one.

Finally, two young men rose from the card table, and sauntered over. They stood over him, but he did not look up at them.

"Hey," one finally said, "you. White boy."

Earl at last looked up. They were splendid young men, muscular and lean with an athlete's grace and light dancing in their eyes. They wore the striped prison pants, but just undershirts, and their complex arrays of muscles gleamed off shoulders and arms.

"Dat's my spot," said one. "You can't be there."

Earl got up, moved a few feet, then sat down again.

"Hey, now he gots *my* place. Damn! He don't git nothing."

"Must be dumb. Hey, boy, you dumb? You be in Marcus's spot."

Earl didn't say a thing. He just sat there, giving no signal of response, as if he were made of stone.

They walked over again.

"See, boy, you done be in Marcus's spot. So you gots to move. You understand."

Earl stood up.

He looked them square in the eyes.

"Moved twice now. Figure I'll stay here a spell, fellows, if it's okay with you. If it ain't, well then, it ain't."

He smiled a little dry smile.

"Hey," said the one, "who you think you be talkin' to? Huh? You think this here be funny? You think you come in an' take a man's spot and it be *funny*? So you smile a bit? Huh, white boy?"

Earl just looked into nothingness.

"See," said Marcus, "we gots to make you understand how it *be* in here. It be *different*. You ain't no boss, you see that?"

Earl looked at nothing.

"I don't think this here fellow done be too smart," said the one. "He don't seem to be listening wif both ears."

"He don't look so smart to me. Hey, you got cigarettes?"

Earl said nothing.

"*You*. I'm talking to you. You got cigarettes?"

"Not for you," said Earl.

"See, here's what it is. What it is, you be paying us cigarettes. Every day. You git us a pack of cigs, and then we be your *friends*. Then we look after you, you got it? See, that's the way it is in here, okay. So you be handin' over some cigarettes."

"I said," Earl repeated mildly, "I don't have no cigarettes."

"Whoa," said Marcus. "Then we got us a *problem*. You know, a *situation*. He can't pay, what we goin' do?"

A hand flicked out, and snapped Earl hard in the shoulders. He could feel the strength in the sting.

"*That* git his attention," said Marcus.

Two hands flashed out with good speed and propelled Earl hard against the wall, rattling his teeth. The two young black men stepped in close to him. Their eyes had drained of any mischief and were now dull and swollen, the pupils dilated large as saucers in anticipation of what was coming next. They were fixing to beat him hard, Earl knew.

"What you staring at?" one asked.

"Don't think the man *like* us," said the other.

"You got some problem, boy? Huh, you don't understand what we sayin'?"

"Boy, I think I'm going to have to teach you some *manners,* yes suh, so you know how it *be* in this here place. What you think about—"

"*All right!*"

It was a rumbling voice. A figure stepped from the shadows. He was an immense man, jet black, with huge biceps that loomed immensely on his large frame. He had almost no neck at all, and his eyes burned furiously. Earl could see a crescent scar running down one side of his face, like a quarter moon, and knew instinctively that this was Moon himself.

"Don't y'all be hassling this here poor boy," said Moon, smiling. His immense strength had the effect of pushing them back and away.

He turned to Earl.

"If he be in here, he be our brother. He be one of us,

yes sir. I can tell a good man when I sees one, and I know this here be one of ours, yessir. Son, what's your name?"

"Jack," said Earl.

"Jack? Jack, well, y'all meet *Jack,* our new brother, new to our world, and welcome to it. Jack, I am called Moon. Brother, I offer you my hand—"

He stretched out a big hand, as if pushed forward by the smile that lit his face in welcome.

Earl hit him in the throat. He hit him so hard even a man of his size was stunned, and gave up a pace, and then Earl drove the same fist hard into the center of the body, and heard the gasp as in reflex the air was pushed from Moon's lungs, and then he turned.

Earl lunged and before Marcus could get his fists up he hit him a three-punch combination, two to the head with a shot to the solar plexus between, which set the young man to his butt, retching.

That left the third who moved in on boxer's feet, bobbing behind his fists as if he knew what he was doing. He didn't. Earl fired a punch through his guard that broke his nose, slipped a weak comeback punch, drove inside for a body tattoo of five or six speed jabs, and when he dropped his hands to cover up there, Earl teed off on the side of the head.

In ten seconds, everybody was down. In that same ten seconds, everybody else was up, staring, some tensed for action but unsure, some falling back to avoid the riot, some protecting their poker winnings, but most waiting for the first man to make a move so they'd know what to do.

"Y'all listen now," Earl addressed them. "This here big fella, he wasn't no friend of mine. I know how these places work, so don't you be trying no shit like that on me. Y'all ain't my friends, not a one of you. You move softly behind me, and I will be on you hard. You move fast around me, you be behind me, I know you fixin' to kill me, that simple. So I get you first and fastest. You think you can take me in a group? Tell you what, you're probably right. But I will kill one man in the group before I go. Maybe it'll be you. Anything you pay me I will pay back with interest. That is the goddamn rule I live by, so don't you be gettin' bold on me. If you mess with me, I will hurt you so bad you'll be beggin' for Bigboy to save you."

Then he walked to the nearest bunk, flipped somebody's effects off the mattress.

"This here's my bunk. Nobody comes near it without making noise. I sleep real light, so don't think you can git me while I'm out. I won't never be out, not so's you know it. You want to git through this, you leave me be. You want to die young in this shithole, you come against me. I will finish you and not think twice about it."

21

Not even Connie could help.

Connie Longacre was forty-four and Sam's secret confederate in the adventure of his life. She was married to Polk County's richest man, Rance Longacre, whom she'd wed in 1930 when he was a glamorous naval aviator in Pensacola, headed for the fleet, and looked so dashing in his white uniform, so heroic. But Rance, as it turned out (this was Connie's bitterest lesson) wasn't particularly heroic; he was always the lesser of the men he was around except for the natural lubrication of the immense ranch and beef cattle empire he had inherited and which would produce more income than anyone could spend into perpetuity. For example, he didn't have a particularly distinguished war, serving on an admiral's staff far from the battle zone, where most of the county men had come back with medals if they came back at all, Sam with a Bronze Star and Earl, of course, with the Medal of Honor. The one thing Rance was really good at was staying buzzed twenty-four hours a day. He slept drunk, he awoke drunk, and there wasn't a second during the day when his Scotch glass wasn't within easy reach.

Connie tried other avenues, but her one son, Stephen, was more like his father than his mother, handsome and reckless and ready for trouble wherever and whenever he could find it. He was currently spending his father's money at a heartbreaking rate in New Orleans while attempting to stay married, through his many infidelities and other indiscretions, to one of Louisiana's most beautiful and socially connected young ladies, equally as wild as he, equally, it seemed, as hellbent on her own destruction.

So Connie, bent in her own unexpressed agony over the tragedy of a husband who would never accomplish anything and a son who would die too young, turned to the one civilized man she could find, a strong, fair, just man, who worked like a dog and said true things no matter the cost. Connie would have gone out of her mind if she'd never discovered Sam, who under his bushy eyebrows and his appearance of brusque annoyance, seemed to understand the deeper mechanisms of the universe in a way Rance couldn't and Stephen wouldn't. Sam had been to Princeton and Yale law, he had stood under the clock at the Biltmore and seen shows on Broadway, and secretly read novels behind everybody's back. He had a dutiful Arkansas wife who produced babies and biscuits and looked great at political functions, but felt numb around Sam, as Sam did around her, and so this whatever it was between Sam and Connie magically just happened.

It wasn't quite an affair. No one ever touched, and Connie, who was still quite beautiful, with perfectly formed features, a delicate mouth, and a shock of blond hair, always seemed too perfect to kiss, much less do anything more primal to or with. One didn't fuck a Connie Longacre; one simply enjoyed the privilege of her company, which was good enough for Sam.

So what they had was more a comfort, a sense that each would trust the other and that they really were betraying no one in the technical sense, if in the philosophic sense they were madly, endlessly in love and would remain so until they died.

Thus it was only to Connie that Sam could confess his anguish, which by this time was considerable.

"Here I sit," he said, "going to my office, and only God knows what is going on with Earl. Oh, Jesus, I keep lying to Junie and to my wife and to the state police and it is just eating me up."

"Sam, did Earl give you a date?"

"No, that's the damn thing. He was unconditional. Do not, he said, do not on any account contact the authorities."

"Well, he is a very capable man."

"Yes, but when he said that, he had no idea what he was up against. He thought it was a corrupt tinhorn sheriff in a dead old country town. I see now that it's something much bigger, much better protected, much more connected. Maybe even Earl is overmatched."

"Sam, the entire Japanese naval infantry didn't overmatch Earl."

"No, you're right. But—"

"Sam, Earl has natural gifts. He has a genius for action and force. It's beyond what normal people have, as we both know it. God decided to give him a great talent, and he has always used it in duty in dangerous places. His instincts would be much better than yours or mine in this situation."

"I know. But I just can't do nothing. I've done all the goddamned secondary research I can around here. I either have to go to Jackson and raise hell with the governor or I have to face the fact that I am no damned good."

"Sam, I won't hear you talk that way. You are a great man and you will lead this county to the justice and the peace its people, all its people, deserve. But you have to yield to Earl's instincts on this one. If he wants it to go a certain way—"

"It's just been so long that—"

"Sam, maybe it's this. Earl knew if he got captured and he knew people would think about coming to his aid, that hope, that belief, would poison him. It would destroy him. He had to be free of that delusion. He had to know nobody was coming, because only then would he have the freedom to do the necessary as he saw fit. So you should honor his requirements. He knew what he was doing."

This had never occurred to Sam, but as he turned it over in his mind, he saw that once again Connie had had an insight into men's minds that would have evaded him no matter how hard he studied it.

"Earl can't rely on anything," Connie said. "It is death to him to have to rely. He learned to take care of himself the hard way, in that terrible family, with that terrible father, so he prefers to pass through life unaided, trusting only himself for serious matters. That is why heroes are always so tragic, in the end. They are alone."

"You may be on to something."

"That is his nobility and also his doom. But possibly not this time."

"Still," said Sam, "I just can't sit here."

"Then you must do something productive. You must use this time. You must figure out what Earl would have you do if he were here and in full control of his faculties. In that way, you obey his wishes but you also honor his traditions."

Again, the woman had something. Sam stole a sideways glance at her—they were sitting on a park bench in Fort Smith, where they met every Tuesday at 4:00 P.M., for a picnic supper, far from prying eyes and able to enjoy each other, without the pretense of being mated to others.

Sam now and then had a terrible dream: that she would leave Rance and he would leave Mary, leave it all behind, Arkansas, the families, the expectations, the ambitions, the traditions: just go. Go to Paris or something. Connie dreamed of being a novelist; she could work on a book. He could—well, what? Well, nothing. That was why it would never happen. That was the problem: the only thing he had ever wanted to do was put criminals behind bars and run a county and be a force in the Democratic party.

"I don't know what," Sam finally said. "The government has the files."

"The files?"

"This doctor. He died at the prison in 1945, and it's classified. That may have something to do with all this, but I don't know. It's a dead end."

"Hmmm," she said. "You don't know where he's from?"

"Who?"

"The doctor."

Sam tried to recall.

"No."

"Well, you have his name. He's a doctor. Presumably a researcher, right? His files may be classified, but he had a life, Sam. A wife, children, a home. He left memories, clues, things of that nature."

"How on earth would I—"

But then he remembered Neal Greenberg.

"I knew a fellow at Princeton," he said, "named Neal Greenberg. Very decent guy, very smart. He went on to medical school and he's now on the staff of the American Medical Association."

"And so?"

"And so, I could call him. I'm guessing there'd be records and that he could find them."

"Yes."

"Yes, and then I could go investigate him. See his widow if he has a widow, his survivors if he has them. And . . ."

He trailed off.

"It's not much, is it?" he said.

"No," she said, with a wise Connie-smile, "but it's *something*."

22

"Let me 'splain how it works," the section boss said. "You work hard or I beat you with a stick 'til you bleed. You unnerstan' that?"

Earl didn't say a thing.

The man was on a horse, above him, as they stood on the levee at 7:00 in the morning, after a long tramp out. On the one side of them the land had been cleared, and a channel ran through it, irrigating it. On the other, jungle.

"Now, you think you tough? You beat up some colored boys last night? Well, whoop-tee-do on all that shit. You give me lip and I will beat you with a stick until you dead. You unnerstan' that?"

Again, Earl had no remarks for the man, who wore a Stetson and sunglasses, and had a Thompson submachine gun with a drum draped across the front of his saddle, his right hand cupped on the grip. Around that same wrist, on a leather tether, he wore a supple polished stick, maybe eighteen inches long, just long enough to build up some real speed for inflicting painful bruises or breaking bones.

"You do not want to give me no lip, or I will make it hard on you. Harder than you can imagine."

His flat gray eyes ate Earl up. He was just loving this, Earl could tell, as Bigboy had loved it, too.

"You want to run? Ha! That's my most favoritist thing. I love it when they run. If I see you, I give you to Mabel Louise. Mabel Louise take you for her own, boy. You understand?"

He patted Mabel Louise: Mabel Louise was his pet name for the big submachine gun. Earl could see the man had a fondness for the weapon and loved to strike heroic poses with it. He bet when he shit the gun Mabel Louise was not far away.

"And if you git away before I can let Mabel Louise loose on you, guess who gits you then? You see them hounds?"

He gestured over his shoulder. A pack of twelve hounds bayed and yapped on chains held by a struggling dog master.

"Them hounds ain't like no hounds you ever saw. Them is blue-tick hounds. They be smart and mean. You know what? Ever damned night, I goes to the kennel and beats 'em bad with rawhide soaked in nigger sweat. Yes sir, so they know the smell of a nigger, yes they do, and what they want more than anything is to get them teeths into a black boy and pay him back fo' all the agony his smell done caused them. So they goddamn hates niggers. And to them anybody working in the hole is a nigger. So you think you gon' make a break, I'll let them blue-ticks loose on you. They tear you apart. They like to tear niggers apart, and you just another nigger, you got that?"

Earl didn't even look up. The newly drained swamp section beneath the levee spread for a dozen acres or so. A channel had been dredged through it—by hand, no doubt, and Earl didn't doubt whose hands—so that the water had drained and pumped out and been channeled back to the Yaxahatchee. The land revealed by the water's fall was muddy still, treacherous and slippery; but worse, it was full of stumps and vines and rocks and the refuse of the swamp, all that had laid under the surface of the black water since time immemorial. It was the special province of the convicts of the Ape House to clear this land.

"So you git down there," the section boss said, "and I will be watching you. You git down there and you put your back into it, or goddammit, you will feel my stick upon your flesh."

They were not chained together. The footing in the newly drained section was too treacherous for that, and one man falling could bring down a whole line. But they were not free, either. Their legs were loosely chained, with enough play to let them walk in short steps but never enough to let them run, and the chains were forever becoming entangled in the vegetation or the rocks on which they worked. Similarly, their wrists were tethered by a good twelve inches of chain, which gave them the freedom to work, but not much else.

Meanwhile, five men on horseback patrolled from the sanctity of the levee, each with a Winchester pump gun. At any given moment, considerable firepower could be rained upon the men in the drained section, so rebellion was unthinkable.

"Men *down*," came a cry, and that was the order to commence.

But the section boss leaned low to him, and muttered something just for him.

"You know what Bigboy say. You want to be treated like a white man, you come clean. You tell 'em what they wants to know. Otherwise, you just another nigger and I own your bony ass and this is what you got till the world comes to a end."

Earl slid en masse with the other convicts down the slick side to the levee, and immediately the mud gripped him. Just walking through it was exhausting.

Earl saw also that the sick ones, the crazed ones, they were here too. Men on horses nudged them, some chattering madly to themselves, others gripping themselves against a phantom cold, still others so full of anger they could hardly see down into the muddy flat. Earl could hardly stand to watch. Because many of them didn't know their names, they'd been painted with big numbers, easy for a guard to read from afar.

"You, white boy," the section boss sung out, "you git with them other fellows on that there trunk. You lean into it now, or by God I'll whup the whole goddamn group of you."

Earl trudged toward the clot of men who circled a half fallen cyprus tree. They were digging at its roots, chopping at it, hacking away at it with shovels, trying to free it from the mud that insisted so feverishly that it stay put.

Earl found a spot in the circle, and began to beat at the mud surrounding the tree. His shovel blade didn't bite deep without a maximum driving effort, and the load it freed, saturated in the water, was achingly heavy. Though he was strong, it took only minutes for his lower back to begin to knot up in pain.

The sun rose, until it pressed against them with the insistence of a liquid, fierce and miserable. Mosquitoes buzzed around, and he could hear them in his ears as they drew close to feast on him. His sweat ran in torrents down his face. The exhaustion rose up through him and blurred his efforts, making him slow and stupid.

Someone poked him.

"Git wif' da rhythm, white boy. You be messin' us all up."

Then he felt it. It was something deep and unknowable by the ways in which his mind worked, but somehow nevertheless nurturing. The men had fallen into a syncopation, not planned but brilliantly improvised, finding a way of coming up and coming down in concert that enabled each man to deposit his pain in the will of the collective and thereby, strangely, alleviate it just enough to survive it.

Whang-chop, *whang*-chop, *whang*-chop.

The shovel rode up like an ax, found equipoise in the air, then descended with a bomb's inevitability, exploding into the mud, sending spatters everywhere, but you were so immersed in the rhapsody of it you didn't feel it, and you didn't feel it when with one foot you just drove the blade in that much deeper, and then there was a pause, perfectly timed, and the mud was lifted out, not with the small of the back but from the thrust of the thighs, and a glob of earth came free and was tossed.

Whang-chop, *whang*-chop.

At a certain moment, and without a leader so directing, a thinner man ceased his shoveling and began to slither his way up the bent trunk, his weight adding on. He bounced up and down.

"Damn, she goin'," came a cry, and exactly as that cry called out, the little man's weight was enough to send the tree toppling forward, its roots now pulled naked and grasping from their bed of swamp bottom.

The men didn't pause to watch what happened next. A squad of specialists with axes would now alight on the fallen tree and hack it to pieces, and then another would pull the wood over to the levee and haul it up, piece by piece, 'til a wagon would come by and it could be loaded on that and carted away for burning.

But there was no time to consider the process. In their own rhythm and by internal communications to which Earl was not alert, they moved to another giant obstruction, this time a stump of an oak rather than a tree itself, and began to struggle again. There was a sense of prehistoric hunting to it, and it made Earl think of some picture he'd seen in a book somewhere in a past that was the other side of the Marine Corps and the war in the Pacific and so hardly real at all: but the picture, in some kind of child's book, showed men clustered around the flanks of some great hairy elephant beast caught in a pit, and they were stabbing at it with spears made of sticks and chipped stones. So it was with the men of the Ape House and this great oak stump; they circled it and tried to kill it and it defied them by not dying, and the more they struck it and dug at its roots, the more it resisted them. The battle was well fought, for the purchase on the ground was hard, and each man fell in his ordeal a dozen times and slammed knees into the knobs of root or cut themselves against its rough skin, or, as in Earl's case especially, felt their hands pucker with blisters against the raw hardness of the shovel.

On and on it went, without reference to time or temperature, though one passed slowly and the other rose fiercely. Nothing, really, had been as bad as this, not the coffin, not Iwo, not Tarawa in the water, not Guadalcanal the two nights of the great human wave attacks, not the screaming fury of his father as he beat him. For those things at least constituted in themselves, by their very structure, the possibility of ending. He would die or survive, he would grow old and leave, whatever. Not with this: this was just *it* forever, the torment of the crushing physical labor without help under the watch of the men with sunglasses and guns and no pity at all.

"Now you know what a nigger feel, white boy," somebody muttered at him. "You gots to be crazy to do this shit you got a choice. Us, we ain' got no choice."

"You shut up," someone else said. "Moon catch you talkin' to the white boy, he skin you."

And now and then Earl's prickly sensitivities for such things picked up the heaviness of eyes upon him. He looked up, then, risking the syncopation of the shovel rhythm, and thought once he caught a glimpse of the great Moon staring at him from among the ax-wielders, but then he lost him, as he had to get back on the rhythm.

A thousand years passed, or possibly a million. But at a point in time when Earl thought he'd die from it, he heard some new phenomenon of sound—jingling, shuffling, bells and animals linked together—and looked up to the levee where his supervisors watched, and there discovered a man arriving in a wagon pulled by two homely, wretched old mules.

The man was scrawny, with one of those ageless black faces that had seen so much woe and survived so much it could have watched life on earth for anywhere between forty and seventy years.

"Fish here, boys," the man sang from his wagon, "old goddamn Fish come to you."

No signal was needed. The arrival of Fish meant some sort of lunch break, and the men turned from their labor and sloughed through the sludge to the levee and began the hard, slick climb upward, each helping the men around him, though no one helped Earl, and he didn't get up till nearly everyone else did, which put him last in the line that formed at the end of the wagon.

As they filed by, each man took a swig of water from

a tin cup chained to a water can, then dropped it and reached as Fish handed each what appeared to be a piece of biscuit dipped in gravy or grease of some kind, which they took over to the edge of the levee and consumed in repose, if only for a few minutes. That was lunch, but it struck Earl as something of a feast.

But when he got there, Fish looked at him coldly.

"This here the line for colored," he said.

The guards, who'd dismounted and were eating better fare, laughed. Some of the convicts laughed.

"You go find the white line, boy," said Fish.

"Come on, old man," said Earl. "I am hungry."

Earl grabbed the cup and brought it to the spigot, but Fish tilted the water can, and it fell to the ground with a thump, its fluid spilling out in the dust.

"Ain't fo' no white man," said Fish. "You gots to go to a special white place."

"Where would that be?"

"I don't know. The white peoples didn't tell me!"

Everybody laughed.

Earl looked at the empty water can in its puddle of sodden dust. It seemed the saddest thing he'd ever seen. His throat felt cracked and dry, his lips wooden. He moved on to the bin with the biscuits but when he reached for one, old Fish handed him a special one. It was smeared with some kind of animal shit.

"This here be fo' you, suh. This here be *special*. Go on, you eat that, boy, you tell me how you be likin' it."

"Just give me a biscuit."

"Oh, you be de boss now. Suh," he yelled back at the section boss, "is this here a new boss?"

"No, it ain't, Fish. It's just another nigger. You don't owe him nothing, not the time of day or nothing."

With a clatter, Fish kicked the tin of biscuits to the

ground, where they bounced down the slope of the levee and settled in the thick, brackish ooze at its foot.

"There yo' dinner, boy. Seconds, even, 'cause you be *special*, you hear? Ain't no one else got seconds."

Earl felt like snapping the little man's neck. He could have done it, too, in less than a second, for he still had some strength left. But what was the point?

Earl pulled away, hungry and thirsty, but he would not beg, out of a mule-headedness that was not heroic in the least but only crazy. He went stoically to where the convict crew lay along the levee, all gobbling their biscuits, some lounging extravagantly, yammering among themselves. There was no place for him, nor did he expect one, but simply crouched at the edge, eyes fixed on nothing.

Whack!

A jolt of pain struck him in the small of the back, and he jackknifed up, his feet slid out from under him, and he tumbled down in a cloud of dust into the mud at the bottom of the levee.

"Whoo-eee, y'all see that white boy *jump!* Didn't know them boys could jump like that!"

It was old Fish, scrawny and demonic, his face knitted up in a glee that only half hid his anger. It was the toe of his sharp boot, delivered with a great deal of springy force, that had just nailed Earl.

Earl almost cursed and called him the ugliest word for a black man that he knew and headed up the hill to beat on him for a while, but then caught himself. That's what you'd do in the world if a man kicked you in the back. He wasn't in the world; he was in Thebes. He looked and saw a bunch of convicts staring at him.

"You go git him, white boy! Yassuh, go git him, see what it gits you."

Suddenly the section boss was next to Fish, on his horse, his tommy gun pointing at Earl.

"What's going on, Fish?"

"This here man said you be a old bastard, boss," lied Fish with a grin that showed only a few teeth behind his cracked old lips. "So I done fixed his ass good."

He stared at Earl with malevolent yellowed eyes.

"That true, convict?" asked the section boss.

Earl shook his head.

Suddenly, the boss man fired his tommy gun. It was a ten-round burst, and it kicked into the mud next to Earl, a neat stitch of lead that popped ten geysers in a single second. The roar of the gun raced through the air, rebounded off the far trees where the river lay, and came back in rolling echo. All the Negro boys lounging on the levee flinched and cowered at the noise. The shots were meant to make Earl shiver and collapse in terror. But Earl had been shot at before, and so he simply winced at the noise, wiped the mud spatters off his face, and said, "You want me to show you how to run that gun, let me know. Otherwise, you might hurt somebody."

The boss's eyes flared with rage; clearly he had a petty vanity about his Thompson skills, and it was evidently part of his legend among the men, and a source of his power. He expected respect, admiration and fear from the men he commanded.

He reined his horse around, drew it steady, and, one-handed, fired another deafening burst, this time spattering up geysers on Earl's other side.

But Earl stood still.

Then he said, "I don't believe Bigboy wants me dead yet, so if you put one into me, he will whip on your ass for a month of Tuesdays. So as far as I am concerned, you are just wasting ammunition to no good point."

"You must want a taste of the stick, boy!"

"You want to come down here and give it to me, you come ahead."

"Your evil tongue will win you no favors here, boy. I swear on that."

He reined his horse over a bit, and turned to the men.

"Since y'all find this so amusing, I'm going to cancel the water break at three, goddammit, and you c'n work straight through till dark. You got any problems, you tell it to the white boy. Now, go on, back to work!"

"*Men down*," came the cry, and the men groaned as they rose and headed back down into the mud.

Earl headed back to the stump, and around him the black convicts sloshed and pushed along as well. At one point, someone bumped into him, and he went down briefly, but he rose, thinking it was going to be a fight or something. Instead, something was pressed into his hand by an unseen body, and he looked down and saw that it was a half-eaten biscuit. He stuffed it into his mouth, ground it with his teeth, and felt the pleasure of solid food.

Then it was back on the stump and back on the shovel.

> *Be my woman, gal, I be your man,*
> *By my woman, gal, I be your man,*
> *Every day is Sunday's dollar in your hand,*
> *In your hand, Lordy, in your hand,*
> *Every day is Sunday's dollar, in your hand.*

That was Rosie. Rosie was their dream, their love, their inspiration. Rosie got them through the long afternoon hours, otherwise unmarked by time or incident.

A man killed a snake.

A guard hit a loafer with a stick, or maybe he wasn't a loafer, maybe he was just sick.

The boss cursed out a lazy nigger.

The men just worked, that was all, without rest, without speeding up or slowing down, just abiding by the harsh rules imposed and finding instinctive ways beyond it, with the help of Rosie.

> *When she walks, she reels and rocks behind,*
> *When she walks, she reels and rocks behind,*
> *Ain't that enough to worry a convict's mind,*
> *Ain't that enough to worry a convict's mind.*

And they loved her for worrying their minds, for when they worried about Rosie, they didn't think about the boss with his stick and gun, they didn't think about the blue ticks hungering for their flesh, they didn't worry about the strutting clown prince Fish, who sucked up to the guards and wore his petty gift of stature like a crown, and they didn't think about the heat, the mud, the sun, the mosquitoes, they didn't think about a tomorrow and a tomorrow and a tomorrow of that same hard thing without end.

Earl slipped twice in the mud, and once hit his knee on a rock hard enough to bruise. He felt his hands pulping up in pain, swelling, and glanced at his palms, which were seared raw with his own blood.

"You, white boy, you keep on a-shoveling, you don't need to be looking at them purty hands, 'cause they ain't so purty now," the section boss called.

"You keep working, white boy," a voice crooned to him, "or they beat you silly and then they beat us just fo' the fun of it."

Earl took the advice to heart, and gave himself to the

shovel, and never again that whole afternoon did he take a break or look away; he just gave himself to the rhythm of the labor, and like the men around him, tried to close it out.

Only one oddness struck him; he looked up late in the afternoon for the glinting of light on a lens far off. Sometimes early in the war the Japs gave away their positions that way, and the brief flash would be answered with a long belt of .30-caliber machine gun fire or a mortar barrage. So he knew: someone was watching from far away, with binoculars, steadily and professionally.

Section Boss worked them hard that day, as he would all days, and after dark they shuffled back to the Ape House. There were no showers or mercies or softnesses waiting for them there, either. They stripped and ran naked through hoses held by white guards, that was the shower, and then pulled the same foul clothes on. The food was cold grits, coffee, a biscuit, some beans ladled out in the cookhouse, on tin plates, gobbled quickly under the watch of men with guns. They ate with their hands, squatting in the yard, then went back to soak the tin plates in a cauldron of boiling water.

Then they went back to the Ape House, and the card players took up the game and the talkers started up reveries about 'ho-towns they'd visited, and the crazies and the sick ones retreated to their corner of hell to gibber irrationally, and Earl pulled his bunk against the corner and slept lightly.

The next morning at 4:00 it started all over again, the same thing, exactly, and on and on it went, the hot mornings, the jabbering torture of the monkey Fish, the baleful stares of Moon, the visits in song of Rosie and the escape she brought. On and on. Over and over. There was nothing else, except now and then he'd catch the flash of light off lenses. Whoever was watching from afar was making a consistent, scientific job of it. Meanwhile, he lost track of the time. A week, a month, a year? It felt the same.

And then one day as they were climbing from the pit, a weariness on their bones so powerful they could hardly speak of it, somebody brought himself close to Earl. It was a man who'd never acknowledged him, one of the card players, but he whispered something fierce, and then slid away, and nobody had seen him do it.

He whispered, "They gon' cut you tonight, white boy. Moon and his fellas. Cut you to death."

23

Sam stared at the photo. The man was extraordinarily handsome, and if one had the inclination to imbue beauty with more substantive virtues, he was possibly noble.

The late David Stone, M.D., Ph.D., Maj., United States Army Medical Corps, stared back at Sam from his formal studio setting, tinted vaguely sepia after the fashion of 1943, when the shot had been taken. He wore his uniform proudly, with the entwined staff and serpent of the medical corps glinting on his lapels next to a block of ribbons that testified to a career that mattered. He wore a pencil-thin moustache, and had pearly teeth, his hair pomaded back neatly. He looked like a philosopher prince of some sort.

"He was a very good man," said the widow Stone, sitting across from him in her apartment, which overlooked a rolling splurge of meadow, pond and tree called Druid Hill Park in Baltimore, eight stories below.

She was a lovely woman, too. There was something aquiline in her facial features, and her eyes were darkness embodied, but lively, merry, so intelligent. They were eyes made for laughter, but not raucous yuks; rather, for the laughter of wit, of erudition, of the bon mot.

He could see them as a married couple, how they fit together, how well they set each other off, what a center to a set they'd be, with his dashing nobility, her brilliance and beauty. It seemed so Eastern somehow, something Sam had glimpsed in his time in New Jersey and New Haven, a brilliant world, but one sealed off; you couldn't get into it without fabulous talent or fabulous success or fabulous family. Lacking all three, and moreover aware that he lacked something more—a capacity to dazzle seemed to be it—he knew he'd never move in such a society. He wanted to prosecute rapists and bank robbers in a little county in western Arkansas. No Eastern woman could understand such a thing, and he was hopeless when it came to articulating it. Only a Connie Longacre, stuck there in her tragic marriage, could understand, after much hard study.

"Harvard, as I understand it?" he asked.

"Oh, yes, second generation. David's father was a doctor before him on New York's Park Avenue. Society, that sort of thing, and with it all the expectations that David lived up to without even breaking a sweat. He had a moral investment in life, if I may say. So David did his undergraduate school at New Haven, then Harvard for medical school, just like his father. Then, after a few years of residency and a fellowship, he came here, to

Baltimore, and got his advanced degree in public health at Johns Hopkins."

"You'll have to forgive me, ma'am, I'm just a humble country lawyer. It would seem he could have gone anywhere in the world with those credentials and had a very nice life. An opulent life. Even while doing good practicing medicine. Yet he went into public health, which, if I'm not mistaken, is not the most remunerative of fields. And if I'm not mistaken, he spent the early thirties in Africa and Asia."

"That is correct, Mr. Vincent. David wasn't interested in money. As I say, he was a moral man. He was in some way obsessed with goodness, with progress, with doing well for the world. The money was nothing. He'd grown up with it, he had a private income, a small one, so possibly he took it for granted, and simply earning money for the sake of earning money held no magic for him. I had some money, too, from my family. We wanted interesting and useful lives, not big houses. This apartment was fine for us. We never wanted a spread in the valley."

It was a four- or five-bedroom apartment in what had to be the city's best building, a castle overlooking a deer park. What Sam experienced was some sort of tabernacle to a life of the intellect, of stimulation of imagination and eye and mind: it was a book-lined warren, with eclectic furniture and a medical library as large as some small college's, Sam guessed. But there was also literature and poetry on the shelves, and modern art on the walls, and crazed sculptures here and there, and a great many African and Asian artifacts and pieces, as well as a riot of textures and colors from various forms of textile art. The view of the park, Sam had noted, was magnificent.

"You must have been so happy," Sam said.

"Yes. But it was hard. David was a man of work, of

duty. He wanted to bring mercy into the world. He wanted to cure the great tropical diseases, yellow fever, malaria, rickets, all the terrible ulcerations and cataracts of the eye, the lack of nutrition and sanitation. He wanted to make all those faraway dark places light and clean and full of healthy babies and smiling mothers. I can't say I was as idealistic as he was, and it cost us. It cost us a child, a family. After we lost the first one, I couldn't have any more. Not that you asked, and not that I give up such information to any person that comes along. But you have to know how hard it can be to live with a saint."

"I'm very sorry for your hardships, ma'am. I truly am."

"Now, you wanted to talk about the war? That was your original line of questioning?"

"Yes, ma'am. I represent a client who is suing the State of Mississippi over the death of a Negro at a prison farm called Thebes in 1948. But Thebes was the site of the research station which the late Dr. Stone directed when he was a major in the—" he made a show of checking notes, though he knew it by heart—"the medical corps, in that unit, the 2809th Tropical Disease Research Unit."

"Yes, that is what it was."

"And as you might expect, the state of Mississippi isn't being particularly helpful. It's not much interested in being sued. So I'm hoping to uncover testimony that shows that the situation in Thebes under Army control was quite benign and it turned somewhat ugly when the prison reverted to state control, under a civilian warden, and such things could occur too often."

"I would very much like to help. I'm a great believer, along with dear Mrs. Roosevelt, in the plight of the American Negro. It is a shame on the bosom of our country."

"I agree, ma'am, and possibly the work I'm involved in"—Sam half-hated himself for the nobility he was pretending to, particularly in the presence of the widow of a man who was genuinely noble—"will help advance that cause."

"You are a man of stern belief, Mr. Vincent."

"No, ma'am. Your husband was a man of stern belief. I'm just a country lawyer, taking a deposition. May I ask, how did he die, if it's not too indelicate a subject?"

"It was a disease. He wanted to destroy it; it destroyed him."

"I'm so sorry."

"No need to apologize. It was a mighty enemy, and he lost a noble battle. I think of Hector and Achilles. He was Hector. Heroic, but sadly human, at war with one of God's most favored killing machines. He'd never been dipped in immortality. It ravaged him and he died, that's all. Some bug stung him, some dying patient breathed on him, some germ crept into his water or food. It's very tragic. He could have done so much more than he got to do. He wanted to help so much."

"I take it the Department of the Army was very aggressive in setting up this project."

"As you might imagine, tropical diseases weren't of much interest in this country until the war came along. Then our boys started suffering from them in the Pacific. So of course it all changed, and David was suddenly very popular. He was commissioned directly, given a budget and an agenda. I'm not sure why Mississippi was chosen as opposed to Florida, the Everglades or something, which at least would have been close to a sophisticated city, Miami. But for some reason, he had to go to God's Little Acre, Mississippi. I gather its impenetrability was part of its allure. The conditions were primitive in that part of the state. It was much like being in an African jungle. And you couldn't fly there or drive there; just getting in was arduous enough. But he loved the work, and he was very optimistic about his research."

"I'm sorry, but wasn't there a road? I mean, couldn't you have flown to New Orleans, traveled to Pascagoula, then driven up the road parallel to the river?"

"Well, there was, until the Army Engineers destroyed it."

"They destroyed it?"

"They cut it off. I suppose it had to do with security. Possibly they were worried about German or Japanese spies, or inquiring newspaper men, or whatever. But they went to a great deal of trouble to isolate it."

This was new. The people in the area believed the road had just been destroyed naturally. But now the government was destroying it, to protect whatever Dr. Stone was working on.

Sam wrote down this development.

"Do you know, exactly, what it was he was studying?"

"You know, I haven't a head for medicine. I believe it was malarial virus work of some sort. He may have explained it to me at one point or other, but if I understood it then, I honestly can't say I do today."

"Did he ever specify the exact nature of the work? I mean, was he treating patients? Was he examining blood? Was he looking for cures and running a medicine test of some sort?"

"As I understand it, they had volunteers who agreed to be infected with various strains so that their progress could be monitored and cures tried. The whole point was to do it quickly, to arrive at some kind of cure or medical protocol years in advance of the normal techniques. It was very accelerated, that I know."

"Would they have used prisoners?"

"I'm sure they were volunteers, Mr. Vincent. It would

be very dangerous work, and you couldn't possibly *force* a man to risk his health, his body, his life like that, now could you?"

"No, ma'am. Well, then, would he have sent back photographs of any sort? I'm looking for a way to document the changes at Thebes Penal Farm."

"No, Mr. Vincent. David was not a photographer, I'm afraid. He was caught up entirely in his work."

"I see."

"Now," she said, "there were letters. Lots of letters."

Sam swallowed and hoped he didn't give away both his surprise and his idiocy for not having come up with this possibility on his own. He finally said, "I suppose you've got them?"

"Of course, Mr. Vincent."

"Would it be all right if—"

"Of course," she said.

24

IN the dark, men breathed heavily as they snored through sleep painfully earned. Some farted away the pressures of a bean-rich diet, some moaned in pain or dread, and occasionally someone cried out from the unconscious but far more pleasant other world for a Rosie or a Mama or an Alberta.

But even in this darkness there were gradients in the shadings, as there always were in any darkness. That deeper patch over there, was it the shape of a man,

prowling, hunting? Or was it a discoloration on the
wall, the play of obscure shadow? That small ticking
sound: the ancient timbers settling yet again, another
tiny degree? Or a man opening a secret pocketknife to
do some powerful cutting?

He watched, waiting for movement, waiting for some
indication of assault, trying to control his breathing.

Earl had slipped from his bed an hour after lights out,
and oozed with a sniper's patience slowly along the floor
an inch or so at a time, until he crouched a few feet from
the mattress where he'd been sleeping these past nights.
He was in his underwear but had his heavy work boots
on. He tried to be soundless as he cocked his legs for a
spring and readied himself for a fight.

He even had a weapon, for he could not fight in the
dark without one. It was a knot of branch, secreted into
his pants late in the day, heavy for clubbing, pointed and
broken for stabbing.

But what if they didn't come tonight?

If they didn't, he'd lose the sleep and he'd never gain
it back; the work in the hole was grinding him down in-
exorably, and he could feel his strength ebbing. And
with his strength, his will was going.

He'd been thinking about one thing: escape.

But it seemed impossible.

The problem wasn't the fences or the guns or even
the swamp; he could slide under the fence, he could
evade the guns, he could navigate the swamp. He'd already figured two ways to escape the barracks at night.
No, the problem was those goddamn dogs, who'd hunt
him down long before he could reach the only fair
chance at escape, which was the river. Before, he'd been
able to plan, to build traps and switchbacks to throw
the hounds off. No chance of that here: he'd be blind in

the swamp, and the dogs would be on him in no time.

Yet that wasn't the worst. He knew the worst: it was that each day he was here, he lost a little strength, a little spirit, a little hope. He had to move soon or he'd never move. It was too much. It was horrible. In the war, at least you had responsibilities and comrades to get you through, to share the ordeal and lend you their strength. Here he had nothing: no Negro would have a thing to do with him, and Bigboy and his bullies wanted him dead, and this braying monster Section Boss wanted him dead slowly. Only the warden was keeping him alive, and for how long? Eventually the warden would conclude that enough time had passed, and that if Earl were indeed the agent he believed him to be, his agency would come looking for him to make a big stink. Absent that proof of Earl's importance, the warden would conclude he was just what he said he was: a nobody. And being a potential embarrassment, he'd be easy enough to dispose of. Who would say a thing?

He tried to keep his mind sharp. He couldn't. He kept sliding off into blurry reverie. He remembered so many nights like this in the war, particularly early on, on jungle-rich Guadal, where the Japs crept in through the shadowy trees and left a man or two with his throat slit every night. Earl had caught one once about to finish him after he'd finished another man in the gun pit, and Earl had kicked him in the balls, then beat him to death with an entrenching tool. It was not a pleasant memory, and as it stole over him now, waiting, he felt a sense of shame. He remembered the glee with which he'd whacked and whacked at the small, squirming yellow man, and the strange notes that came from his enemy's constricted throat, and the exultation when it was over, and he was blood-smeared, exhausted but alive for one more tropical sunrise and one more shot at survival.

He tried not to move his head, or let the pain stinging in his tensed legs get to him. He scanned without motion; his eyes simply rotated left and right, scoping the abstractions for a sense of movement, listening for a sound.

But nothing came. It was going to be a—

They were fast and quiet. They were as good as the Japs. They rose soundlessly from nowhere and only passed through a tiny smear of light from a dim moon beyond the window to alert him, and they were on his bunk in split seconds; they made no noise at all, like expert jungle killers, men well experienced in mortal confrontations and well studied in the leverage of force against flesh. He watched their arms blur as they struck again and again into the hump of knotted clothing that was a laundry bag he'd stolen in the dark.

In the next second, they realized they were stabbing at somebody's sweaty underwear, not a man, and in the next second after that, he was on them.

Earl was without mercy. He was not in a universe where mercy was allowable. Mercy equaled death. Yet even as far gone as he was toward savagery, he was not comfortable with what happened next, though he was its sole author. As he lunged, he swung the limb with the force of an ax, wishing for more weight up top. But it didn't matter, for his timing was exquisite and he struck one of his antagonists—too dark to tell which one—full in the face with it and felt the satisfying shudder up the shaft of the club and the length of his arms to signify a solid wallop. That man, stunned, loosened and slipped, gasping, his two hands flying to his injured face, which now must have worn a broken nose, a shattered cheek and a mouthful of broken teeth. He was out of the fight.

Earl was quick on the rebound, knowing he'd never

get a full swing off again; instead, from the full extension of the first blow, he came driving back this time with the sharp point of his weapon, driving it hard into something soft and moist, a neck he presumed, that belonged to the second man. He drove this shaft like a piston, back and forth in cruel, savage strokes, at the same time shoving his body with all its strength against his antagonist's, and yet also keeping that now-screaming man between himself and the other who was charging around to cut him.

Earl separated from the second bleeder to meet the rush of the knife man. He countered the blade with the stick, catching the last man's lunge, and spared himself a deep stab. But he knew also that he had not hurt the second man enough to put him out of the fight, and if the two of them got to him, and the fight went to the floor, as most fights do, they'd crush him beneath them, grapple him still, and gut him.

The other blade probed again, this time glancing off Earl's parry and slicing a bad wound across his forearm. The blood spurted, but there wasn't any pain, for his system was too aboil with blood chemicals to register hurt. He got a short stroke of the haft into the face of the other fighter, driving him back, and then the second man recovered enough to get him in a driving bear hug and slam him into a bunk, spilling two screaming sleepers from it.

Lanterns were lit somewhere, and in the pitching darkness, Earl saw that it was big Moon himself who had him crushed, while another man retrieved the knife to close on Earl. So Earl squirmed and improvised. With his boot he crushed Moon's instep, and when the giant screamed and loosened his grip, Earl head-butted him backward in the nose, breaking it. Then he spun, saw an opening, and nailed him with a hard jab to the lower side of the head, and felt the jaw he'd smashed snap and twitch; he'd broken it clean. He grabbed the injured heavyweight and pushed him in the direction of the knife fighter, deflecting him.

But not for long. The knife boy knew his stuff. He evaded Moon deftly, stayed balanced and without panic, went to a trapping backhand grip on his cutter, and his eyes were empty of emotion but full of skill. He was fast as he danced at Earl, and the knife then came at Earl's face so fast even a man as fast as Earl couldn't completely avoid it, and it sliced along the line of his skull, opening a squirting gash. But the point missed his eyes, which had been the idea behind the thrust, and Earl didn't panic when he was hurt as so many do. He closed faster than the man withdrew, knowing the closer he was the more he cut the power of the stabber. And before that one could get the knife back into play, Earl tattooed him with a left-right-left-right combo to the center of the body, knowing the satisfaction of punches well delivered. The other buckled and stepped back, and with hazy eyes flailed at Earl with the knife, which Earl evaded easily enough, and when the blade had passed, hit him a haymaker over the jaw, taking the consciousness away from him. He twisted down in a heap.

The lanterns were fully on now. Moon was alone, his jaw disfigured, a great foam of redness spread across the heaving blackness of his chest from the many gougings Earl had applied with the back end of his club.

"Come on, big man. Let's finish it," Earl shouted in full rage, blood and sweat streaming off him. He had surrendered fully to the warrior's madness. He wanted to kill and crush his antagonist, but Moon, rather than stepping forward, stepped back, raising a hand. He slinked away, trying to stem the blood from his wound. He was done for that night.

Earl staggered slightly, as the pains his adrenaline had kept him from feeling now announced their presence. His hands hurt the most and his knuckles were garlanded in red. He opened and closed his fists, feeling the pain as fire, hot and raw. But no bones were broken. When he turned he saw horror on the faces of the lantern-lit Negroes who stared at him as if he were some kind of rough beast, newly born among them. Then he realized he was bathed in blood.

He touched his head where the long slice had been opened up, and his fingers came away red. He looked at his left arm, where the other cut was. Both oozed. He went to his own laundry cache and pulled out a clean undershirt, broke the seams with his teeth and quickly improvised cotton bandages around them to stanch the blood flow. He knew he had not been hurt mortally but that the less blood he lost the faster he'd recover. Too bad there wasn't fishing line about; he'd sew himself up. Then he heard the commotion.

"Mama! Mama! I ain't goin' to de Screamin' House! Mama, don't let dem take me to de Screamin' House! Lord, Lord, ain't goin' to de Screamin' House."

He saw that it was the knife fighter, now conscious, now aware he was dying. Knocked out by Earl's blow, he had managed to twist on his blade. He had buried it in his thigh, and the blood ran so swiftly and puddled so hugely that it seemed clear he would bleed out. Around him stood men watching, seemingly frozen in the drama of his exsanguination.

"*Oh, God!*" he screamed, waving his hands futilely, "don't let me die like this. Please God, don't let them take me to de Screamin' House."

No one seemed able to help. Memories danced through Earl's mind from the war: young men, blood, the shock of loss, the disbelief that oneself could be so badly hurt so quickly, the numbness of the survivors, their tentativeness. It was all too familiar.

Earl pulled himself up off the floor and went to and kneeled by the man.

"You deep cut, son," he said.

"Don't let dem take me, boss. Please to the Lord, no."

"You hold on tight now. The less you scream and move, the less blood you lose."

Earl bent closer. It was a butcher knife with an old, worn haft.

"I'm going to pull it out, son. Goin' to hurt like Jesus."

"Help me, boss."

Earl called, "Some you other fellows, you come here. Give this man something to hold on to. Someone else, you go get a cool cloth from the pump and wet his face. He has to be calm or he is a goner."

The men shambled to do what he wanted.

When they had him secured, Earl leaned his strength against the meaty thigh with the wooden grip buried in a well of bubbly red, winked at the man—a boy, he now saw, just as so many of them had been in the war—and drew it out. The boy shuddered in the pain, though he didn't scream.

Immediately the blood flow increased.

"Ya'll git me a cord or a rope or something. We have to tie off that artery."

Someone went to improvise one, but the blood came so fast, Earl was afraid it was too late. Gently, he pried the wound open.

"Git a light down here so I can see!"

The lantern was lowered and Earl could make out the pulsing, severed artery. He had no clamp at all, so he reached in and plucked the little spurting tube between his two fingers and closed it.

"He's got to stay still like this 'til medical help comes."

"Won't be nothing 'til the morning."

"Well, if we can hold him still and keep him calm, now that I got this hose shut down, he may make it."

"Fo' what?" somebody asked. "Come back here?"

"You got a point, man. But still, I say keep this young man alive for better times. Whyn't ya'll do some of that singing you're so damn good at. Maybe that'll keep him with us an extra minute or two till the doc comes."

The men began to sing.

25

Well, sweetheart, it isn't pretty and it's primitive, but after Africa and Asia, it's certainly comforting to be in one's own country, although Mississippi has a long way to go before it joins the rest of the U.S.A.

Sam sat in a leather chair in a study. He had before him a cup of coffee and a pile of letters on the thin paper that marked the V-mail of the war, a large sheet folded many ways to make it a small and efficient package for delivery. VICTORY it said at the top of every fold.

This was the earliest one, marked January 9, 1943.

"It's so odd," the doctor went on,

you expect Mississippi to be hot and swampy and to see men in chain gangs working in dust and heat. You expect to run into Walker Evans images everywhere. Now Let Us Praise Famous Men. Well, it's not at all like that. It is squalid, of course, and underdeveloped, but it's both cold and wet and of course dreary as well. Everything is muddy and the forest or jungle or whatever it is is impenetrable. I certainly can see why they put this prison here on this old plantation site; the question is, why did they put the plantation here in the first place?

Sam was a thorough, disciplined man. He read each letter completely, occasionally taking notes on his yellow pad. He skipped nothing, he tried to prejudge nothing, and he willed himself to pay no attention to the emotional content of the letters, which was none of his business.

Yet that of course, particularly in the early going, was the only thing he could notice. As a couple, Dr. and Mrs. Stone seemed so . . . well, damned perfect. He had censored his own men's letters during the same time period, as he moved his artillery unit across up Italy, then over to England, then to invade France and roll toward Germany. He therefore had a reference point, but quickly found it of no use. For while the average soldier's letters were full of sentences like, "You tell Luke he still owes me that $300, and I am not forgetting it when we finally win this thing" and "Who is this Bob you keep writing about. Shirley I am sleeping in cold dogshit every night and these German fellows are trying to blow me up and I DO NOT appreciate hearing about Bob taking you to the church supper." But the Stones were like a couple in a movie: "Miss you darling, dearest, and am so proud of the work you are doing at the U.S.O." "Thanks, sweetness, for that last wonderful letter, and it doesn't surprise me that flower club politics are so rough. All politics are rough, from the Medical Corps to the flower club. You *will* become treasurer in the next election, I am sure of it."

Unable to help himself, Sam wrote the words "emotional authenticity lacking" on his yellow pad, unsure himself quite what he meant.

Occasionally, he'd look up when the sentiments grew too cloying and Hollywoodesque, pinch the bridge of his nose, take another sip of coffee, and glance around the study, with its wall of photographs taken in obscure foreign places where the great humanitarian had gone in his quest for a disease-free universe. The photos were the same and seemed in bright color, even though they were black and white: the great man, in a white coat or a pith helmet, standing among a coterie of little people of differently hued skin and differently configured wardrobes, enjoying their adoration and his own sense of centrality. His wife was in some of the photos as well, always a beautiful woman of classical posture and self-possession, the memsahib of a dozen or more native cultures. The little people were brown, black, yellow, in a variety of fabulously interesting garb: feathers, loincloths, ceremonial gowns, animal skins, black pajamas, sometimes in just the pale dowdy uniform of colonialist lackeys in some empire's far-flung bureaucracy. Among the pictures, of course, were the testimonials, some even in English. They spoke of the same thing: the doctor's commitment, the doctor's love of people, especially children, the doctor's courage. It was a fabulous cavalcade, and it made Sam himself feel a little banal and worthless. He'd blown up some German tanks and put some bad fellows in a little county in nowhere, U.S.A., in prison or in the electric chair. What was that in comparison to a life lived so grandly, so heroically?

"Would you care for more coffee, Mr. Vincent?"

"Yes, ma'am. I was just looking at the photos and tributes on the wall. I wish I'd known the doctor during his lifetime. It would have been an honor and a privilege."

A dreamy look of assent flew across the woman's face, which itself was her reply, and off she fled to get more coffee.

"The engineers have at last finished the levee," the doctor wrote, "and we can therefore count on uninterrupted work. No more floods, no more lost documents and protocols, no more horror stories terrifying the 'natives' around here."

Hmmm. Army engineers had built a levee to protect the doctor's project from flood damage? This in the middle of the war—July 6, 1943, Sam was in Sicily then—when engineers were in high demand in the world's combat theaters. That suggested how important official Washington considered his project or how much private influence a mere major could wield even in the military, if he were charming, famous, charismatic, well connected. Sam remembered the crumbly bridges his guns had traveled as they crossed that rocky island, and how he'd lost one, and two men, both maimed for life, when in some nameless village the truss bridge built by the Romans had given way, and collapse had ensued. They could have used more engineers in the Sicily of 1943.

"My spirits are high, darling, and we are making progress. I must say even the 'volunteers' are taking this in good cheer. They want to do their part too! Everybody wants to win the war, so they can go back to their loved ones proud of what they've done to put Herr Hitler and Tojo-san out of business!"

Sam wondered about those innocent quote marks around "volunteers"; to a sophisticated man such as Dr. Stone, punctuation could express a whole range of subtle irony and camouflaged meaning; was it some reflection of ambivalence on his part, a whisper of cynicism, a subconscious projection of contempt?

It all began to change by the spring of 1944. Evidently the early days of great progress had run into a wall and, medically, whatever it was the doctor was working on now resisted his efforts.

Darling, I'm afraid I won't see you next weekend as I had promised. There's so much to do here and so little time. Now that the invasion is imminent, I'm losing personnel to go to Europe. It seems I've slipped a little in the priority department. It's as if they expect miracles, and when I can't produce them overnight, they lose confidence in me and the project. It's so damned unfair, but then, I keep reminding myself, that is the way the military works. It's very much like it was at the Hopkins with batches of us competing for attention, and first this project and then that looks the most rewarding and gets the lion's share of the funding. But I soldier on, darling, and will see you as soon as possible. Love and kisses, your ever-loyal David.

David canceled his next leave, too; that was August of 1944, and in December, he was even sharper.

Darling, I love you truly, but I cannot in good conscience have you coming even to New Orleans. There has been a shift in the direction our program is taking us, and I feel I must be here constantly to supervise our reconfiguration. Moreover, in these momentous times, darling, we must discipline ourselves and give all to the immense task at hand, especially when the end is so near and we are so close to victory and to a return to our way of life. To have you taking up valuable railroad space to see someone as insignificant as me is simply wrong; best give that seat to the war widow, the kid on last pass before hitting some godforsaken Pacific atoll, the fellow on compassionate leave over a sick and dying mother. Meanwhile, in my way, I struggle on, fighting for what I believe and doing my damndest to eradicate the ancient enemy.

Sam thought he was getting a little florid and overmelodramatic; the woman's passage to New Orleans by December of 1944 certainly wouldn't have counted a bean's worth against the war effort. Again it felt emotionally inauthentic, as if something were wrong.

In the next letter, Sam realized what was wrong: the guy had a screw loose. He was nuts.

Yes, we are making good progress in our new direction, but it's hard, in a way. He was our ancient enemy, who has stalked us for years. He's been a wary adversary. Now we try to make him work for us, and yet he's still the enemy. It's like collaborating suddenly with a Nazi, very depressing but I'm sure very necessary. So I still wrestle him, though now I try to wrestle him to our side. Am I tarnished for my vanity, for my belief I can master him? Perhaps. But then I realize, I don't matter, the only thing that matters is continuing the struggle, and what others might think of me, well, that too is meaningless against the larger, more insistent drama of the crusade. Darling, when I think of your sweet pureness in this world that is so filled with filth, perversion, decadence, weakness, cowardice, it sickens me. It is not right. Darling, you are too good for this world.

What was going on with the doctor? Was he delirious? Was he losing control? Nowhere in all the previous correspondence had such an insane note been struck; it was as if the doctor were no longer himself and no longer writing these letters. Some other had taken over, some Being. And what was this mysterious "change in direction" in the project? Whatever, that certainly seemed to be upsetting the doctor. Was it driving him insane, as he tried to reconcile his "goodness" with whatever the new aims were?

There was a long lapse in the letters, at least six month's worth. By June of 1945, the doctor's mind was really scrambled:

Am I God? I think not. I never wanted to be God! But science makes us God, or at least gods: what are we to do? I sought to learn the truth, to help, and that humble mission was enough for me. Yet THEY sought me out, and let me have my way. They made me a GOD! They gave me the POWER! What is life and death to a GOD? I smote what was evil, wherever I could find it. I found it in my own heart and there I smote it most grievously, but in doing that, I smote myself. In dying, I learned I was not GOD, I was but a man. I am so sorry we lost the baby all those years ago. I'm so sorry I wasn't there when it happened. I am so sorry what was going on through the microscope was more real to me than what was going on in my own house. I am so sorry about all I did before you. Darling, forgive me. I never meant to be GOD.

There were but two other letters. The penultimate was from the War Department.

Mrs. David Stone, 12 Druid Hill Park Drive, Apartment 854, Baltimore, Maryland.

Dear Mrs. Stone, the War Department regrets to inform you that your husband, David M. Stone, MAJ., U.S. Army Medical Corps, died of complications after a short illness June 23, 1945, at his post at the medical research facility at Thebes, Miss.

Major Stone did a great deal to assist his country in the pursuit of final victory and we are saddened that he did not make it through the conflict.

Yours Very Warmly,

George C. Marshall
Chairman, Joint Chiefs of Staff
United States Army
Washington, D.C.

But the last V-letter arrived after the death notice; presumably Dr. Stone had written it as he faced death full in the face on his last night.

It only said: "The darkness."

"Such a shame," she said.

He was not sure when the woman had entered. She stood across from him now, pale and beautiful as death, as he put down the last letter.

"Ma'am, I'm very sorry."

"Was this of any help?"

"Well, uh, I'm not certain. It contains certain leads I may be able to follow up on. Time will tell."

"He tried so hard. He fought so valiantly. He was such a hero."

"Ma'am, toward the end, he seemed to be . . . well, not quite himself. Do you have any idea what was going on? And there was something about a 'change in direction' in the research. Do you know what that could be?"

"I presume the disease was working on his mind. I wrote him letter after letter begging him to slow down, to relax, to go on leave. I wrote the War Department, the Medical Corps, everyone I could think of, or knew. I could feel him getting dangerously mixed up. As for the change he mentioned, I honestly couldn't say. He didn't share things like that with me."

" 'The darkness.' What could that have been?"

"I don't know."

"What was done with the body?"

"It was shipped back in a closed coffin. He was buried here in a small, somber ceremony."

"Here?"

"Here in Baltimore."

"He's in Baltimore?"

"Yes, Mr. Vincent. At Green Mount Cemetery. But what would this have to do with your case? After all, you represent a man suing the State of Mississippi for a wrongful death well after the end of the war."

Sam didn't even have an answer: he was thinking, *I have to get that body autopsied.*

26

WHETHER the boy died right away or later was unknown. In any event, he had been more or less in survivable condition by the time the guards arrived at 4:00 A.M. and he was hauled off, though not, he was assured, to the Screaming House.

Earl thought he'd make it. The cut wasn't deep, but arterial, and he'd spent the last two hours with his fingers in the boy's thigh, pinching off the blood flow, while the boy moaned for his mama over and over again. The other men had gotten him calmed with their strength and their music.

But he died, anyway.

As for Moon, the same hidden convict grapevine conveyed the news that his jaw was broken and he'd been wired up as best as possible, but he had to be shipped via the prison launch to Pascagoula, where a surgeon would repair his jaw and he'd be in a maximum security ward while his jaw healed. He'd be back in a few weeks or so.

It was another day on the levee. Earl worked hard, though at a strange angle, because he didn't want to stress his own wound, which had not been stitched closed as it should be but instead bound up with linens. He knew a sudden twist or jump and the blood would start spurting again. It wasn't arterial, so he wouldn't bleed out fast. He'd just get weaker and weaker.

The sun was a monster's eye that day. It was a huge, angry thing, and it poured out its fiery radiance, and it sucked the energy and the will off them all. The flies, the skeeters. The heavy work, the poor food, the never-enough water. Section Boss sneering at Earl up top his horse, but now, since he'd kept himself alive much longer than anybody had expected, keeping a wary distance. They were afraid of Earl now, the guards. Earl liked that. Somewhere deep inside himself, he liked that a lot.

The rain came at 3:00. It slashed down from heaven with such vengeance that even Section Boss, now in a hunter's poncho, understood that it was pointless to work, a rare concession to the elements. He commanded the convicts out of the soupy hole and up to the levee, where they could at least sit this one out.

Earl sat, as usual, alone. But he had a strange sense that men were closer to him than before.

"You, white boy. You box? You musta boxed, boy. You gots fast hands." The voice came from directly behind him, but nobody was looking at him.

"Did some fighting in the service," Earl said, in response to the first question anyone had asked other than Moon or one of his young thugs.

"I worked corners and cuts for a coupla years. You gots fast hands and can slip a punch. Nice jab combo."

"You pick things up," was all Earl allowed himself to say.

"You so smart, buckra, how come you done made a big mistake? You be dumb as any nigger, ask me."

"What mistake is that?"

"You shoulda kilt Moon. He down, he out of the fight. You should have pulled that blade out of that no'count Junior and come over and gutted Moon."

"He'd said he was through."

"You is dumb, buckra. You is *dumb*. That boy gonna come back with one thing on he mind. He goin' kill you. You done messed up his old haid twicet, he gots to kill you. You best kill him first night he gits back, else he kills you deader 'n a motherfucker."

It was solid advice, Earl knew. Moon wasn't the sort of man who'd learn a lesson. He'd get through his pain and fury in the prison ward in Pascagoula, wired up without anesthetic, and he'd lay in silent pain for a week or two or three, in the darkness, and all that time he'd nurture his hatred for Earl, he'd think on it and polish it and lick it shiny, until there was no other thing in his mind, no other thing at all. That was the way a fellow like Moon worked.

So: Earl had to kill him.

Or: Earl had to prepare to die.

Or: Earl had to escape.

None of the possibilities were inspirational to him. Instead, he just tried to fight the despair by snatching a quiet moment in the warm, hard rain, feeling slightly cleansed for the moment. He looked around: fronds of palmetto pulsed out of the green undergrowth, and before him, down the levee slope and in the hole, though the ground had turned even muddier and more desperate, the vegetation was green and glisteny. It was like a Guadalcanal in Mississippi, where the beauty of the wild place stood in contrast to the squalor of the savagery. That was the now. That was the present. That he could enjoy.

"Hey," he said to the man who had spoken to him,

"tell me something. The Screaming House Junior was yelling about. What would that be?"

"You don't want to go there, white boy. Take my word on that."

"It's the end of the line?"

"You see them bedbug-crazy boys down 'end of the barracks? Look, they standing over there."

Earl glanced quickly through the rain, to a small knot of gibbering crazies who were shunned and stood apart from the others. He recognized a few: the fellow who talked to himself, the fellow who gripped his own arms so tightly you thought he'd squeeze himself to death, the gentleman with the fused spine who looked as though an iron bolt had been sunk through the center of his spindly old body. Each had a bright red number painted on his shirt so that he could be recognized.

"Them boys should be in a hospital someplace."

"Ain't no hospitals here. Only the Screaming House. You ain't been here long enough, but when one gits so bad he can't work, they comes git him in the night. They takes him off to the Screaming House. We calls it that. No man never seen it. It's off to the west a bit. Fish claims it's cool there, and clean. But off goes a crazy boy and you can hear him in the night, the wind is right, the weather calm. You can hear him screaming. He scream and scream and scream. These country niggers let a place like that grow on their minds, think it's some kind of torture place. Think these guards got a special torture place."

"What happens?"

"The screaming stops. That boy don't never come back. Nobody never comes back from the Screaming House."

"I will avoid that place if I can," said Earl. "What they sick from?"

"Don't know, white boy. Some say it's bad blood. Some say it's the fevers of the river. Some say it's the shots they give us when the doctor look us over every three-fo' months."

"What kind of doctor would let men like that fry in the sun?"

"The white kind," said the man, simply, and that seemed to end the conversation.

Earl noticed the rain had stopped just as suddenly as it had started, and now shed of his poncho, his tommy-gun named Mabel Louise gleaming from frequent cleanings, Section Boss rode the levee road commanding the convicts back into the hole.

"Git 'er goin', you lazy niggers. Work to be done. You too, white boy, you git on down there and don't you think you be slackin' none. I catch you leaning, I'm going to beat your hide with my stick, boy."

Earl rose, feeling the endless pains cut at him. His respite was over. The hole beckoned, with its sucking mud and stubborn, iron-hard cyprus stumps and its endless tangles of bramble and thorn, its mosquitoes, its snakes.

"You do what Section Boss says, or I be on you ass, white boy, and maybe, heh heh, I be *in* yo' ass!"

It was Fish, who'd jingled up on his mule-drawn cart unnoticed during the rain.

"You tell him, Fish!" came the cry from the guards.

"Yassuh, boss. Talked to ol' Moon afore he done left. Moon, before he guts you, he goin' *fuck* you! Yassuh, he be goin' do dat. Up the ass! Make you his sweet bitch. So you die a bitch! Ha, lawdy, lawdy, don't that beat it all! Make you wear lipstick! You be a fancy lady!"

The homosexual content of the jibes annoyed the hell out of Earl. Things like that weren't right. Shouldn't be said out loud. He'd once caught two Marines doing something sexual out near the shitters on one island rest camp and immediately transferred them out of the unit, to different regiments. His fear on this one went deep, for some reason.

"Hoo, don't think the white person like to know he goin' be Miss Katharine Hepburn for old Moon when he gets back! Hey, white boy, iffn' you can take out the garbage and wear nylons, maybe Moon *marry* yo' pale bootie!"

Earl lost himself in his work, trying not to feel humiliated and debased by this new tack of Fish, who clearly had a way of getting under the skin.

As Earl used his hoe to chop at the root of an old tree, Fish was making Lana Turner smooching sounds, full of the suggestion of tongue and spit, to raucous laughter from the guards, particularly Section Boss.

Earl tried to erase the contaminated image from his brain, but couldn't. Himself being held down and stripped buck naked while Moon, behind him, had his way. It was a shame he couldn't live with. It would kill him, that's all. He feared it, for some reason, deep in his brain, beyond all logic and clarity.

That would kill me, he knew.

I'd rather be gut shot and die slow than live with that in my mind.

He chopped and dug and dug and chopped. The heat and the sun came back. He was in a dream of fear, trying to see only what was before him. It had one salutary effect, and that was that the afternoon seemed to pass more quickly than ever before, and soon enough the twilight was on them, and the cry came down the line, "Convicts, out of the hole and form up."

As Earl came out, he saw something new. It was a car.

It was the first car he'd seen at the prison.

It was a black Hudson sedan, gleamy and creamy in the twilight. And standing next to it, like a general attended by his staff, was Earl's main antagonist, Bigboy himself, examining the world through his MacArthur sunglasses. Two minions hung by him; Section Boss, even farther down the line of hierarchy, had dismounted and assumed a submissive position.

Earl felt Bigboy's eyes on him through the dark lenses. But he didn't dwell on it. He simply clambered up the slippery slope, took his hoe to the toolshed where a trustee stacked it, and looked for his exile's place at the end of the formation.

But suddenly two men were beside him and a third behind him. In the next second, they collided upon him, his chains were drawn tight, two more added to secure his arms to his body with no clearance whatsoever, and he was dragged in his mincing, humiliating walk before the great man.

"You still alive, Jack Bogart? You know what?" said Bigboy, "you made me some money. These section guards swore you wouldn't last a night. You've lasted twelve. You've killed a man, even if it was only a lowly Negro. You've made friends and influenced people. I had money riding on you, and I've come out to collect."

Whap!

Someone hit him hard upside the head.

"You look at Mr. Bigboy when he be talkin' to you, son. That's how we do it here."

"You are a sight, I will allow, Brother Jack," Bigboy went on. "Cut and beaten, you still fight on. From what I hear, it only gets worse. Everybody is saying old Moon has special plans for you. Why do I think you aren't going to enjoy what Moon intends? Seems to me a hero like you can't lose his dignity, or he's nothing. That true, Jack Bogart?"

Whap!

Another openhanded strike to the back of the skull.

"Cat got your tongue, boy? Answer the guard sergeant."

"My name is Jack Bogash," Earl said. "It ain't no Jack Bogart, like that movie fellow. I am a truck driver from—"

Whap!

The boys commenced to beat on him, for their amusement, for a few minutes. Even Section Boss, emboldened by Earl's chains and pain, came over and got a few licks in. One of the blows opened the cut across Earl's body, and he felt the blood begin to seep out of his shirt.

"Enough," said Bigboy. "Get him up and in the back of the car. Jack Bogart, you're going for a ride."

TRAMMELED by his chains and pinned by the beef of guards on either side, and with a sawed-off Winchester pump rammed in his ribs for good measure, Earl rode through the penal farm. Once he even glimpsed the river beyond, pale and flat and broad, like some highway out of town. But soon the vegetation thickened and darkened again, and the tropics took over; they came to a gate.

"Yes, sir," said Bigboy in the front seat as the driver ran out to unlock the gate and pivot it open, "you listen hard to what the man is going to say to you. You won't get another shot at redemption. We don't sell redemption here. We're not in the salvation trade. We're punishers. We make the evil pay for their sins, that's our specialty, but on account of my deep and abiding affection for heroic types, I have arranged something special for you, along temptation lines. We shall see how tough you are. Pain doesn't frighten you, Mr. Hero, nor does the fear of death or degradation. We'll offer you what the devil offered Jesus Christ himself, which is the whole world."

He chuckled softly in the fading light.

The car purred along a narrow jungle path and soon encountered a strangely tidy building nestled among the loblollies and the palmettos, white and trim, well built along strict government guidelines. It had a very 1943 feel to it; it reminded Earl of the jungle headquarters the Seabees would throw up so efficiently on back islands away from the battle zone, where staff and intelligence matters were considered in comfort.

Earl was dragged out, further confused by a mechanical hum arising from somewhere. It was the sound of generators, well insulated, churning away, another cue familiar from the Pacific in wartime.

In he went, to an utter astonishment: coolness.

The place was air-conditioned.

The temperature must have been seventy-two degrees. He blinked in low darkness, and the two hulking guards took him down a shiny corridor. Doors off it opened to what appeared to be ward rooms, and one was opened just enough so that he saw a black man in an oxygen tent, clearly close to death. They reached the end of the corridor and an office which, entered, proved to be clean and modern along military lines, with a medicine cabinet, a sink, a shelf of jars, a pile of clean towels, many sterilized packets of either pills or small instruments and an examining table.

Two men in white coats over otherwise nondescript clothes awaited him.

"You keep still, Bogart," the senior guard said. "You let these fellows work on you or I will do some serious thumping on your haid that you will not enjoy one damned bit."

Earl was placed on the table. Quickly, the technicians snipped off his foul clothes and washed him with the smoothness of medical orderlies, which he now saw they must be. They were impersonal, efficient, uninterested. They disinfected his wounds, and quickly sewed them up. He winced each time the needle perforated his torn skin, but the two orderlies were not at all put off by his pain.

Then the hypodermic needle came out. Earl flinched involuntarily as the technician drew some fluid into the shaft of the thing, then walked around, prepped his arm, and slid it in with a sting. Something about the needle was more hurtful than all the beatings he'd gotten.

"Waste of that fine medicine on this sorry specimen, you ask me," one of the guards said.

"No one is asking you, Rufus," said the orderly snootily, claiming his hierarchical superiority over the fellow, whom Earl knew to be called Clete.

"Okay, now get lost," said the other orderly to the guards. "We'll take him from here."

The guards obeyed, angry to be shown up by the two lesser but somehow higher ranking men.

"Here now, this'll relax you," said the technician, and quickly gave Earl another shot.

"Just a little tranquilizer, sweetie. Keep you calm and collected. Now you just sit here a bit."

Earl waited. Whatever it was hit him hard; it softened him, and the world seemed to fall ever so slightly out of focus. He blinked, almost passed out, and felt a great calmness, almost a sleepiness, pour through him.

"There you are, sunshine," said the technician, coming back. "My, aren't we relaxed now. Okay, you come with us now."

Though still chained, Earl was wrapped in a cotton bathrobe, and the two men led him through another door. He was trying to track details, but they wouldn't stay tracked as his mind seemed to slip in and out.

Was this a hospital? There was a hospital smell somehow, but at the same time he felt no sense of bustle or movement or urgency. That was certainly missing from the hospital sense of the place. He couldn't figure it out.

The last door led to a room oddly lit. He sat on a chair and the two orderlies stood by.

"Doctor will see you shortly, stud boy. You just sit tight now."

Earl couldn't sit any other way. He felt himself on the edge of consciousness.

Earl sat there.

The door opened and a man slid in, and even through the strange condition of his mind, Earl right away recognized the doctor who had given him the shots after his time in the coffin.

"Do you want a cigarette, friend?"

Earl nodded.

A cigarette was placed in his chained hands, and he put it to his lips. Quickly it was lit, and that first drag was like paradise, biting through his drugged blur.

"You know, it doesn't have to be like this," the man said.

Earl said nothing.

"You're a remarkable man. You're strong, tough, resilient, heroic. Nobody denies that. But you're fighting the jungle, and the jungle always wins. Surely you've figured that out."

Earl knew this to be a fact, but he didn't acknowledge it. He didn't say a word.

"Who are you? You can't be who you say you are.

You're too motivated, too clever, too experienced, too well trained. Are you some kind of federal agent? FBI, perhaps? Are you military intelligence? Are you something military? What is your interest? Whom do you represent? Why are you here?"

Earl was silent. He took a puff on the cigarette.

"You keep fighting. It's really amazing. You should be studied. I've seen heroes before, believe me, and most are ordinary men compelled by circumstances to the incredible. You are heroic every single day. Every single one. Amazing."

Earl paid him back in silence.

"All right," said the man. "I'm going to give you an out. I'm going to give you hope. You don't even have to tell us who you are, at least not until you want to, and you will want to, eventually. It's simple. You come over."

Earl said, "Come over?"

"Yes. You join us. We need good people. I can have you here in a second. You'll be fed, you'll sleep in clean sheets, you'll have a pleasant duty day. It'll seem all strange at first, even frightening. But you'll see that what we are doing is very necessary. It's work of the utmost importance, and it ennobles everyone associated with it. These poor Negro convicts, these ignorant white trash guards, the brutality, the death, the seeming wanton cruelty of Thebes, the shots they get: it's all justified. It's all for a higher good for our country and our way of life. You won't see that at first. But eventually you will. There'll come a time when you'll believe. Then we can let you go back to wherever you came from. And you won't be bitter; you'll be proud you've served your country."

Earl drew a last breath on the cigarette, then stubbed it out on the desk.

"No," said Earl. "Not a chance. Not a goddamned chance. I may die here, but I won't be a part of whatever terrible thing you're up to."

"A shame," said the doctor.

27

SAM could not lie. Sam was against lying. All kinds of mischief sprang from lying. It wasn't merely that it was wrong, but that it felt wrong. A tide of liar's phlegm overwhelmed your esophagus, your heart popped, your knees trembled. Sam hated lying and liars.

Sam lied.

He lied, he lied, he lied.

He hated himself for it and swore to God if he ever got out of this horrid sewer into which Davis Trugood and the Thebes State Penal Farm (Colored) had dragged him, he would never tell a lie again, not even a social one, like "Honey, you sure look pretty today."

But what bothered him more than even that was how well he had lied, how he had *learned* to lie over the course of this ordeal.

"Ma'am, I'm afraid I have some very good news and some very bad news," he had said to the widow Stone. "Your husband, David Stone, M.D., is heir to a not inconsiderable fortune. Ma'am, I'm not yet prepared to divulge financial details, but I would estimate that it is in the seven-figure range."

Even Stone's beautiful widow, smooth and polished

and cosmopolitan as she was, gulped slightly at this information.

"Yes, ma'am. It seems his father had a brother, a rogue in the family you might say, who went off on his own. This man, Daniel Stone, had a rambunctious, tumultuous life, he did indeed. Possibly your husband never mentioned him nor did his father, because I believe some time in the penitentiary was involved."

The widow had gasped again.

"But he died intestate and wealthy, through certain interests in the West involving industries not exactly on the up-and-up. After probate taxes, the estate is, as I say, considerable. Your husband was his last living relative. As heir to his estate, you are therefore the beneficiary."

"I see," said the widow. "But as you can see, I'm quite well off from my own family's estate. I see no reason whatsoever to enter into a protracted legal engagement to acquire money I don't have any need for."

Ach! Sam hated this! Character! A woman who could not be motivated by greed! Now there was a tough one.

"But madam," he said quickly, "think of the money not for you but to in some way commemorate your husband. Think of the David Stone Scholarship for Negroes at the Johns Hopkins School of Medicine. Think of the young doctors that would come out into the world, and how well they would reflect the best of the American Negro, the good they would do, the mercy they would bring to the world and their own people. Now would that not be a testament to the greatness of your husband?"

It was so amazing. This beautiful woman from the highest circles, with her knowledge of art and beauty, her social connections, her dead husband's brilliant reputation to sustain her, her many (he assumed) fractious suitors, was biting. Not for some free dough but for the narcissism of Doing Good and Feeling Good: put that before her and she was any tart in a bar looking for a sugar daddy.

He hated himself for manipulating her. He hated her for being so malleable. He hated it all.

"Ma'am, what I need to do is disinter your husband's body, don't you see? I need to ascertain beyond doubt that that is indeed him in Green Mount Cemetery, and that you are his legal widow, and with that we can swiftly accomplish the transfer of the funds. Think of the future."

And so it was that Sam now stood in the mortuary room of the Smallwood Brothers Funeral Home in downtown Baltimore, where a casket, still caked with dirt, had just arrived. He had the proper authorization, the proper paperwork, everything in its place, every *i* dotted and *t* crossed.

In her apartment the widow awaited his call.

He was used to death, of course, but not its ceremonies. For him it was a wartime thing, squalid and tragic; or an issue of small-beer west Arkansas murder, where a husband choked his wife blue and bulge-eyed out of rage at an infidelity she had not really committed, or a businessman neatly perforated the liver of his embezzling partner with a nickel-plated .32, or two wild country crackers cut each other dead in a ditch in a drunken waltz of anger and stupidity.

This was a dark, subdued place, without joy. It felt as if a heavy coating of oil had lubricated every surface, so that friction was impossible. Things moved slowly, with greasy decorum; it was more like a graduation than a mortal inquiry.

The funeral director supervised; the undertaker executed. It didn't take long.

"Mr. Vincent?"

"Yes."

"Sir, we have removed the decedent from his inner casket."

"Yes. And—"

"Sir, there appears to be a mix-up."

"Of what nature?"

"There's a discrepancy between the death certificate and the remains. Would you like to see? It's only over here."

"Frankly, sir, no. I will take on trust a report of your findings."

"Yes, sir," said the funeral director, one of the Smallwoods.

He was a man used to mortal circumstances, well schooled to represent dignity in the face of crushing grief. His solemnity was unbridgeable, but Sam knew something was up when he saw that dry tongue lick nervously across those dry lips.

"Sir, according to the death certificate, this is a forty-three-year-old white male. But the remains are those of a thirty-year-old Negro male. I don't know what to say."

"I don't either," Sam said.

"Worse, he appears to have perished of some grotesque disease. I can't say I've ever seen anything like it. Chancres, tumors, limbs eaten away. It is a true horror, sir. I would like to burn it—him—in the next minute or so. The fires are ready."

"Oh, Christ," said Sam.

28

THE sun blasted down as it usually did, and Fish showed up, as he usually did, with the water wagon drawn by the two old mules in the jingly tack. Earl hardly noticed. He was in a depression so deep and dark he could hardly breathe. He hacked at a stump with his hoe until he heard the call, "Men, out!"

He was slow clambering out of the hole for his place at the end of the line and a guard gave him a whack with a stick to speed him up.

"You slower than the niggers now, boy!" he said with a whoop, as he laid the flat of the club hard against Earl's kidneys, driving him in a spasm of pain to the ground.

"He used to be white," sang out Fish. "Haw, boss, now he all nigger. He mo' nigger than any nigger you got!"

Earl humbly made it to the rear of the line, wishing he could rub the new bruise with his hand but unable to reach it because of the chain. At a point his eyes lost focus and he went to a knee.

Whap!

Another blow. Since he had turned down the mystery

fellow in the mystery house, the word had gotten out among the guards. He was fair game. The process would intensify, then intensify some more. They would break him or kill him, and it seemed now not to matter. Maybe Moon would be his killer. Earl was the dead.

"You stand straight in line, nigger, or you don't git nothing," the guard sang. Section Boss, on his horse with Mabel Louise the Thompson gun dangling over the horn on a sling, patrolled back and forth, not far at all from Earl. He was a good horseman, and in a second, if he wished, he could use the power of the beast to crush Earl to nothingness. His closeness was ominous and full of anger. But he said nothing, and Earl didn't look up at him, for that would merely earn another whack.

The jungle always wins, the man had said.

It was true. The jungle does.

Earl tried not to give up hope. But, really, with the dogs, with his own declining strength, with the fury of the black men at his whiteness, he had nothing to hope for. Maybe Sam was—

No, he tried not to think of that. If he thought of that, it was the sign that he'd given up, that he was relying on the offices of others, and he couldn't have that in his mind if he were to survive. He had to do it on his own.

At last he got up to the water spigot, following even the sick and crazed inmates. He reached for the cup, feeling Fish's harsh eyes upon him, when a peculiar thing happened. He didn't reach the cup, but in the quickness of a blink, Fish intercepted his hand and probed his palm with a horny finger. Then it was over, as if it had never happened, and Earl looked up at Fish, who'd looked away and was smiling up at Section Boss now.

"Can I whack him one, Boss?" asked Fish, smiling broadly in that ass-kissing, shit-licking way of his.

Suddenly he drew back his hand as if to issue a mighty clout, and Earl flinched, drawing back. But Fish just laughed.

Earl grabbed the cup, greedily sucked down the half cup of water, and turned, and suddenly Fish was on him.

The old man had surprising strength. He'd leapt from the wagon and actually landed on Earl's back. His strong, wiry arms lashed across Earl's chest, drawing him in, and his legs locked around Earl's thighs.

Earl struggled but could not get at the little man and spun away, and then felt the thrust of a sexual pelvis grind against his rear end.

"I's Moon!" Fish was screaming, "I's fucking the white boy! Whooooo-eeee, look-a-me!"

The laughter rose raucously, the black man mounted on the larger, slower white, grinding into him in scabrous imitation of the sexual spasm, the white man, all tangled up in his chains, lurching, spinning, unable to get leverage to separate himself from the smaller tormentor.

"Go git him, Fish!" the guards yelled.

"You hump that Nancy!" they cried.

"You ride that boy just the way Moon goin' ride him."

It had to be funny in its pathetic way, for the inmates themselves started to laugh, and they generally wouldn't acknowledge the shameless way Fish played to the guards.

"Goin' fuck you, boy, yas I am, goin' fuck you *hard*, boy, have my way with you," Fish crooned amid the laughter, and Earl spun desperately, trying to shake the man off, trying to elbow him, but the chains would not permit his arms the freedom. He spun, dizzily, a clown being fucked by a monkey, raising dust from the dry levee until it floated like a fog while the men moved aside to let the comic spectacle go on.

"I say he lasts a minute."

"Hell, he gon' break that bronc. He gon' make him his, you bet!"

"You go, Fish, you go. Ride that horsie. Ride and fuck that horsie."

Earl spun to the edge of the levee, but then his foot stepped off it, and down the two tumbled, a bone-jarring spill that brought them crashing down the incline into the mud until they'd rammed hard against a stump.

And Fish was off him in a flash, dancing back up the incline. He stood up there, doing a little jig of triumph as Earl, muddy and humiliated, dragged himself from the soupy mixture of the drained swamp, breathing hard.

"Look at him," Fish crowed. "So high and mighty and look at him now."

"White boy Bogart," said Section Boss, "you is one whipped pussy, you is. You a dis*grace* to the white race. You is no longer a white man, no sir. I hearby drum you out of the white race. You nigger through and through."

Earl sank to his knees.

"*Men, down,*" came the call, and the convicts rose as one, much amused by the show, and headed down to join him. At the same time, a very merry Fish jumped aboard his wagon, gave a theatrical flourish to his audience, and turned to the mules to go on about his rounds.

But what nobody except Earl knew was what Fish had whispered in his ear as they lay in the mud down below, entangled for just a second.

"I can git you out of here. I knows the way."

29

SAM wished he could take the cab straight to Friendship Airport, plunk down some more of Davis Trugood's money, and fly to Little Rock aboard that big United DC-4. He wanted that desperately. It would be so much easier.

But the duty part of him, that nagging little monster inside that would not ever leave him in peace, would not permit such indulgence. Which is why he found himself, feeling like a condemned murderer, hunting for the courage to knock upon the widow Stone's door in the beautiful old apartment building outside Druid Hill Park.

He tried twice, three times, and then a fourth, knew he'd manage it on the fifth, but before he could find out if that were true or not, the door opened.

Dressed for a summer outing, purse in hand, she was stunned.

"Why, Mr. Vincent! What on earth are you doing here?"

"Ah, ma'am, I had—" he stammered.

"Oh dear. The news is bad?"

"I don't know what the news is. I really don't know what it is."

"You had better come in, then."

He followed her back to the living room and sat in the same chair he had sat in a day or so ago.

"So, Mr. Vincent?"

"Well, ma'am, straight out, you see, that isn't your husband in that casket."

At first it seemed she didn't understand. She blinked, twice, and swallowed, once, and then said, "I'm afraid I don't quite—"

"Ma'am, it's not him. It's a Negro male, much younger."

"Are you telling me my husband is alive?"

"No, ma'am. I am only telling you that he is not in his casket; someone else is. What that means, I don't know. Possibly it's a terrible mistake made by somebody at an Army mortuary back in nineteen forty-five. Possibly, it's—well, I can't even begin to imagine what it is."

"Good heavens."

"Ma'am, is there any—well, ma'am, I am by profession a prosecutor and I proceed by blunt methods. So if I may be blunt, is there anything in your husband's life or character that would suggest his capacity to become mixed up in something not quite aboveboard?"

"Excuse me?"

"Well, I'm just groping for explanations here, Mrs. Stone, and I—"

"Are you imputing that David Stone, the medical researcher and heroic savior to the world's beleaguered and benighted, that he is involved in some criminal activity?"

"No, ma'am, I'm—"

"Mr. Vincent, I may have to ask you to leave. This is very upsetting to me."

"Yes, ma'am. I'm just trying to get a fix on all this. I'm just trying to—"

"You're not here for the reasons you said, are you?"

"No, ma'am."

"That whole business about the fortune. That was all a lie, wasn't it?"

"Yes, ma'am."

"Sir, you are despicable."

"I do not deny that."

"Really, you have to leave. Immediately."

"Yes, ma'am. I'm sorry. This is so unfortunate."

"It's more than unfortunate, Mr. Vincent, if even that is your name, it may be criminal."

"Yes ma'am," he said.

"So tell me, finally, after it's all over: Why are you here?"

"In truth, I began working for another attorney in Chicago, and I was investigating the death or disappearance of a Negro man at what was your husband's medical station. Not during his tenure, but somewhat later. That is, recently. I journeyed down there, and barely escaped with my life. It's something of an American disgrace. And even as I speak to you, a good man who rescued me may be dead for his assistance. I have a private compact now with my conscience to find out what is going on in Thebes, Mississippi. I'm sorry I lied. I'm not in this for money or financial gain or anything. But I am very concerned about my friend, and until I find out about him, I am making it my business to learn everything about Thebes that I can. Your husband's name came into it from a governmental source in Washington, but all the files have disappeared. So I was working from this end."

"You think my husband was involved in the murder of a man?"

"No, ma'am, I don't. But I thought his involvement might lead me to someone who might lead me to someone who . . . well, that's the way we investigate."

"I see. This is very upsetting."

"Ma'am, if you wish, if you'd feel more comfortable, possibly you'd care to call your attorney. Possibly if you will let me continue this conversation, you'd feel more comfortable in his office instead of your home. I'm very sorry I misrepresented myself. It was unethical. But I'm under great pressure to get a fix on that place, in order to help my friend."

"My attorney won't be necessary, Mr. Vincent. I'm simply going to reassert that you must leave. My husband was a saint, a hero, a martyr. He died giving his life for his country. Were you in the war?"

"Yes, ma'am."

"Well, that's something."

"I was an artillery officer."

"So you shot cannons at Germans or Japanese. Well, my husband was in battle too, only he shot microscopic cannons at germs and parasites and worms. I will not let you defame him. Please, leave, or I shall have to call the police."

"Yes, ma'am."

Sam got up, wooden-faced, and walked to the door. He had certainly blown this one and would be fortunate to get out of Baltimore without getting arrested. But he had to try one last thing.

"Ma'am, you'll forgive me, but one question I have is that in one of the letters, your husband expressed sorrow over 'the baby'—"

"*Mr. Vincent!* How dare you! How *dare* you? I was

taught that people from the South are gracious, and yet you ask me the most personal questions imaginable. I will call the police if you don't please leave at once."

"I'm very sorry, ma'am."

"You should be *very* sorry. My husband was a great man and that was part of his greatness, his capacity to forgive. He had a terrible disappointment. I cannot have children. It is nobody's fault, so you may not believe anything ill of him. Do you understand? You cannot believe anything ill of my husband."

"Yes ma'am. I'm going to leave now."

But he didn't, and his crudeness produced a crude treasure. It was an old prosecutor's trick; he hated himself for using it. But it worked: to ask someone highborn a lowborn question, one notable for its lack of taste and sensitivity. It frequently shocked such people into tears, and before they realized they had lost control of their emotions, they blurted something out that no amount of torture could otherwise have produced.

"I cannot have children," she said, "because I contacted a virulent venereal disease in my early twenties; I was a month pregnant at the time. My husband worked feverishly to help me and save the child, but it couldn't be done. He blamed himself for my misfortune."

"Ma'am, I'm very sorry. It's none of my—Ma'am, I can't believe that *you* contracted something so—"

"I was raped, Mr. Vincent. One night, late. In Asia. It was very violent."

"I'm very sorry."

"The disease killed my baby, it killed all the babies I would have. It was the cruelty of the world, and a perfect example of the sort of tragedy that my husband gave up his life to prevent. Now please leave."

"Yes, ma'am."

30

Earl watched and waited, but there was no approach. He thought: maybe it's a trick. Maybe it was part of Fish's psychological war against him, just to whet his appetite and get his hopes up, then to let him down.

And he cursed himself for letting the little bastard get to him. He tried hard to pretend he didn't feel crushing disappointment when lights-off and lockdown hit at ten and the place settled into wheezing darkness. He waited in the dark, and the more he waited, the angrier he became, and he realized the fury was a form of medication against the despair he was beginning to feel.

You got yourself into a goddamn fix, partner, was what he couldn't admit feeling. But he knew he felt it just the same. For the first time in his life, he was very close to feeling beaten down and broken.

Sleep came roughly after too much time and too many pictures in his mind of other places and other lives he had lived and would never live again. But it came, and if he dreamed he didn't know it or remember it, because the next thing he felt, something bit him.

Goddamn!

It jerked him awake, some little insect or mouse where it shouldn't be, on the side that was down on the mattress. Now how the hell—

Another bolt of discomfort came, and his mind settled down enough to put two and two together properly: he realized it wasn't a bite so much as a poke, up against him from the other side of the mattress.

He leaned over his bunk and saw some kind of rod extended up from the floorboards, where it had poked him awake. There was somebody down there.

He slipped off the bunk and put his mouth to the crack in the floorboard.

"Yeah?"

"You crawl to the third window, eastern side."

And that was all.

Earl low-crawled, listening to the snores and the groans and the farts. He made it without a problem and wondered what was in store for him there. And then he felt the floor drop out, as one board was removed from beneath. He waited until another came out, and he had enough room to snake through.

"You come on," Fish whispered.

Fish rose and took him around back, so that he was invisible to the men in the closest tower with the searchlight that commandeered the Ape House, yet too far in the dark to be spotted by any of the other towers.

"We be okay here," said the old man. "The patrol don't come back this way fo' half a hour."

"You said you could get me out."

"Didn't say that. Said I knows the way out. Maybe you man enough to make it, maybe you ain't. Took five fellas out. Four be dead. One got out. That too much a risk fo' you? One in five. It ain't easy. Fact, it's the hardest goddamn thing you ever done, and I'm bettin' you been in the war something fierce. Harder than that even. You want me to go on? Or you want me to disappear and you can go back to waiting for Moon to slit your belly or Bigboy take you to the Whipping House."

"Why?" said Earl.

"Why what?"

"Why you get me out? You hate me. I'm the white boy. Everybody in this place hates me."

"You got that right. I was sent up here by white boys just like everybody else in here. And we do hate you. You done us so wrong and you ain't even got no idea. You took us over here in chains and we in chains still. You fuck our women and make 'em whores, and when we gets angry you be actin' all su-prised. You keep us poor and weak and set it up to crush the life out of us, and you pretend it be fo' our own good, 'cause we too stupid to be otherwise. So onliest thing fo' us be: yes suh; no suh! Yassuh, with a big coon-ass smile and bright white teeth. Y'all like our white teeth."

"Sorry I asked."

"I pick you 'cause of two things. I heard first off you kep' your fingers on Junior's artery, keep him from bleeding out. He was my sister's boy. So I owe you."

"You don't owe me nothing. I'd do that for any man."

"Way my haid work, I owe you. Second is, as I say, to do this thing it takes a bucket of guts. Not many have it. Even brave men, strong men, hard men, they don't have it. It's a motherfucker. It's a big old royal-ass motherfucker."

"I don't have that kind of stuff, old man."

"Oh, I'd bet you does. You just got to make me two promises, that's all."

"So what are they?"

"Tell you later. I get you out, I tell you."

"I ain't promising no promises I don't know about."

"You'll make these promises. All them other fellas done it, and one them out now, living high on the hog."

"Just tell me where this is going."

"It's simple. All you got to do is open this."

The old man handed him a brass lock, an almost antique thing that weighed nearly a pound. It was tighter than hell. Earl pulled and felt no give at all in the connection between the hasp and the lock body. He tried to examine it in the darkness, and felt for buttons or screws but touched only rivets. He tried to put his finger into the keyhole underneath it, and of course made no progress at all.

"I can't do it. Nobody could do it."

"Gimme," said Fish.

Earl handed it over, saw it disappear in the old man's hands. There seemed to be some fiddling, maybe a massaging, and in two seconds, the lock came sprung with a barely audible metallic snap.

"Jesus," said Earl. "You do that bare-handed?"

"You pick it," the old man said, displaying a pin about two inches long. "It take practice, but when you learn it, you can git her open in about two seconds."

"Yeah, fine, except where do I get the pick?"

"See, that's it. That's why I touched your hand. You got enough callus to carry it now. You couldn't done it till now."

Earl watched as the old man made the pin disappear into the ridge of callus that decorated his horny old palm. He turned and looked at his own hands and saw that yes, now they were ridged with a hard pad of deadened, accumulated skin, where healing skin had covered broken blisters but come out tough as leather gum. It was a dead zone, one of God's few kindnesses to those who worked hard with their hands.

"Gimme that paw, boy."

Earl put out his left hand and felt not pain but pressure. The pin punctured his hand and rode across the palm. There it was, tightly held.

"You got to practice. I give you the lock. You practice every night. You got to get the pin out, get it into the lock. You make a 'H.' You feel the softness of the tumblers. You get the two on the left, cross over, git the two on the right. Do it blindfolded. Do it at night. When the time comes, you won't be able to see what's going on."

"I'll be in a darkened cell?"

"No. You be at the bottom of the river. You be drowning. You make a mistake, white boy, and the hundred pounds of cement that lock chain to you keep you down there and you be drownded dead in thirty seconds."

EARL worked the lock every night in the dark. Out with the pin, a swift movement to the keyhole, no wasted motion, the insertion, then the delicacy of it all: feeling the tension in the tired spring-driven tumblers, trying to duplicate the pressure of a key against them, finding the right progression until at last the thing would pop.

The first night he never got it open.

You goddamn worthless scum, he called himself mercilessly the next day.

The second night he finally felt it move a bit and got close to getting it open.

The third night it came open by the second hour.

The fourth night by twenty minutes.

Only got to get another nineteen minutes and fifty-eight seconds off that time.

He worked and worked until at last a poke came in the night.

He slithered to the floorboards and out.

"You do it?"

"I got it down to thirty seconds now. We best do this thing soon, else these guards are going to beat me to death. Or Moon will be back."

"Moon be back day after tomorrow. He cut you first thing, white boy. Firstest thing. Ain't no nother possibility 'bout it. He cut you bad and deep, and fuck you bleeding. He want to be fucking you as you pass."

"Christ."

"You up to killing him first?"

"It ain't my style a bit."

"You pussy, boy."

"Done my share of killing. You don't know the killing I done. You got no idea. Nobody here does. But if I fight this guy, and even if I whip him, he's going to hurt me bad, and I can't do this thing, right?"

"That's right. So it's got to be tomorrow. Now I tell you the rest of it."

Earl braced himself.

"You tell Section Boss tomorrow first thing: You talk to Bigboy. You broken. You tell 'em what they want. Yeah, they gos, gits Bigboy. He drive up in his shiny new Hudson car."

"If I tell 'em who I am, they kill me."

"I knows. So here's what it be. When Bigboy drive up, you'll feel Tangle Eye gittin' close to you."

"Who's Tangle Eye?"

"Big yeller convict. One eye go strange. Tangle Eye. A ax man. Best ax man in Mississippi."

"Yeah?"

"You slip down. Tangle Eye, he give yo' wrist chain a whack right where it clip to the bracelet, right hand. Yo' hands free. But you hold that chain tight so nobody don't see it."

"Yeah."

"Now come the fun part. You be called up out de hole. You g'wan over to Bigboy, and when he smile at you you pop him hard. You pop him so bad you break out his teeth and his nose. You hit him bad."

"That is the fun part. Only problem: it gets me killed."

"No, it don't. It do git you beat. Gits you so beat you wish you dead. But they don't kill you. They don't even make you unconscious. They won't whack yo' haid. They bang yo' ribs, yo' gut, yo' kidneys, yo' legs. Have a good ol' time with them sticks."

"This don't sound like no fun at all."

"You want out?"

"Ain't there no other way?"

"This be the only way you beat them dogs. No other way. The dogs run you down if you try to bust out through the bayou or the piney woods. Dogs rip you up right good. So you listen here to the hard part."

"Go on."

"You got to *humiliate* Bigboy. Make him so mad he forget hisself. So he kill you just fo' his own pleasure. This is how they kill at Thebes. They take you to what they call the Drowning House."

"Lots of houses at Thebes."

"It's a city of houses, you got that right. At the Drowning House, they chain you to a cement block. It's locked with that lock you done been working with. Nightfall, they take you out on de river. They likes to hear 'em beg and cry and plead. Makes 'em feel powerful and strong. They gots a special boat. Boat got a door in the side. Git out there, the cement block goes over. You go with it."

Earl thought about this. He remembered the long walk in on Tarawa, with the Jap tracers skating over the surface of the water and the pack on his back dragging him down.

He shuddered involuntarily at the horror of the memory.

"You in the water. You got yo' thirty seconds. You get that lock off. Oh, one thing. I forgot to ask. You can swim, can't you? White boys swim good, I hears. I can swim good, 'cause I raised on the Mississip. Hey, why you think they call me Fish?"

"I can swim okay. Ain't no Johnny Weissmuller."

"Who?"

"You know, that Tar—. Never mind. Yeah, I can swim."

"You can't come to de surface fast, and break it and suck in the air. You gots to swim away underwater, come to the surface slow, be gentle when you gits to it. Otherwise they hear you, 'cept they havin' too much fun to notice usually. You swim in, real slow and quiet. Follow them to their shore, 'cause otherwise you be real mixed up. You swim to the wrong shore, I can't help you none. Got it?"

"Where do I go?"

"Swim upriver maybe quarter mile. Look for a flash. That'll be me with a old carbide lamp. You come ashore there. You rest up couple of days, I'll set you free with a compass. It's a straight run to the tracks twenty-five miles out, you hops a freight and back you go. I got some money fo' you. No dogs trackin' you, no mens with guns and trigger fingers all twitchy-like, nothin'. They think you daid. They seen you go into the dark river. They don't know nothing. You home free. They never come after you. You got that life of yours back and you do wif it whatever you want."

Earl could think of nothing to say.

"But even if we get that far, then you gots them two promises. You make them, or I swim you back out there and chain you to that rock again."

31

Sam got back in a mood of near suicidal grief. So much for that adventure. His peregrinations in Baltimore had destroyed the serenity of a good woman and he had learned almost nothing of use. Dutifully, he typed out a report and sent it off to Davis Trugood, along with a careful, thorough accounting of all expenses.

He called Connie, was bucked up by her to a small degree; he went to one of his son's baseball practices where the boy did well, and that buoyed him even more. But it all went away late in the afternoon, and not even a powerful bourbon could destroy the sense of a life wasted, a friend betrayed, all control slipping away from him.

He finally made his decision. At 10:00 A.M. the next day, he would call Colonel Jenks, the commandant of the Arkansas State Highway Patrol, and tell him everything. It was time at last to get official convening authorities involved in the situation, and if there were anything that could be done, it would be done. Then he would call Junie Swagger, whom he now avoided like a disease. He would tell her, own up to his idiotic responsibility for all this, and tell her that he was trying to obey Earl's mandates, but now too long had passed, and it was time to get this thing settled.

He awoke with a sense of mission, showered, shaved, put on his suit and tie, had breakfast with his wife and two of the boys and two of the girls, and went downtown to his little office. He climbed the steps and sat at the phone. He could not make himself call at 10:00 A.M., but by 10:15 he had screwed up the ambition. He reached for the phone, set it before him, and—

It rang.

He let it ring a bit, then picked it up.

"Sam Vincent."

"Sam, it's Melvin Jeffries."

Mel was the pharmacist in town. Sam had once declined to prosecute one of his children on a fool shoplifting charge, for which Mel had been eternally grateful. That boy, if Sam recalled correctly, was now up at Fayetteville, doing well.

"Mel, what can I do for you?"

"Well, Sam, nothing at all. I just thought you should know a couple of fellows were here."

Sam paused.

From Mississippi?

His breath dried to a little spurt.

"Which fellows?"

"G-men."

"G-men?" Sam said.

"Yes, sir. They had all sorts of questions 'bout you."

"FBI agents?"

"I think so, Sam. At least that was the impression I had, even if they didn't say. Men in suits, with badges, carrying guns."

"What did they want to know?"

He waited: all about your adventures in Mississippi? How you were an escaped prisoner from Thebes County. How they think you killed a woman. How your friend, Earl, came down there and you got him killed. How you violated the law and—

"Well, Sam, mainly it was your politics."

"What? My politics?"

"Yes."

"Why, I'm a Democrat like everybody else here in Arkansas. Why would they have to know my politics? I ran for the Democratic party. I hope to run for the Democratic party again in a year or so. I've been a Democrat my whole life. What business is my party affiliation to the federal government?"

"Not them kind of politics, Sam. More like, were you 'suspicious' or anything. You have any strange 'suspicious' ideas about politics? Were you sympathetic of unions? Did you listen to the Negro jazz music or classical music? What magazines you buy? What books you read? What was your sentiments about the Soviet Union? Did you ever speak favorably about Mr. Stalin? Were you upset we went to the aid of the Koreans? Did you speak agin' the atom bomb. Did you think it was a shame we didn't share that secret with our Russian allies? What was your opinion of communists in the pictures or on the radio? Seemed like they thought you were a red, is what I gathered."

Sam realized: they were investigators from the House Un-American Activities Committee.

"Well, what did you tell them?"

"You's a true blue American war hero and went after criminals hard as hell and kept the order and represented the state and that you had good judgment and character, but also a heart and a sense of discretion. You know how highly we think of you in this house, Sam, after what you did for Harrison."

"It's not right that they're asking these questions," Sam said.

"No, Sam, it ain't. But they're all over town this morning. I thought you should know."

"I see. Thank you so much, Mel. How's Harrison doing, by the way?"

"He's fine, Sam. He just pledged SAE."

"Well, that's terrific."

"You have a good day, Mr. Sam."

"I will," said Sam. He put down the phone, shaken. HUAC? Now how the hell? What the hell? Was it that somebody in Mississippi had complained? Or was it that—

The phone rang again.

This time it was Mary Fine, who ran Fine's Dry Cleaning. The same story: two government men, questions about politics, insinuations about a radical unreliability, stern, judgmental demeanors, disappointment. Something like that could ruin a fellow with public ambitions in a hurry.

Then it was the barber, the newspaper editor, and finally Harley Bean, the county Democratic chairman, who was also the mayor and the undertaker to most of Polk County.

"Sam, what the hell is goin' on? You must be the least red fella I ever heard tell of. Unless you consider sending Willis Beaudine up to Tucker for diddling that nigger gal."

"Some would say that's pretty red," said Sam.

"Well, Sam, I can't tell you your business, but if you're red I'm going to suggest we surrender to the commies, as they've already gotten too far."

"Well, Harley, you know I'm not red."

"Well, what is this all about?"

"They haven't reached me yet. Sure as hell, that's what they're here for."

"Well, Sam, you know I'd go to bat for you in any ball game in America. But when the FBI—"

"Did they say they was FBI?"

"Hmmm, Sam, now as I recollect I am not certain. I did have that impression, however. They just flashed badges and government IDs and on they went."

"I don't think they're FBI. I think they're House investigators. That means they're not bonded police agents, and if they're carrying concealed weapons they are doing so in violation of the laws of Arkansas."

"Well, Sam, nobody pays much attention to that law, anyhow. They certainly act like FBI. I'd get to the bottom of this, I was you. You know we have big plans to get you back in the prosecutor's office."

"Thank you, Harley."

Sam knew this was because he was a good prosecutor and a good Democrat, though the meaning of the second was in contravention to the meaning of the first; good Democrat meant he'd just naturally look in other directions when certain county contracts were let. That was the system. Sam accepted it because he knew he couldn't change it, and his willingness not to change it meant the party would elect him wholeheartedly, to make up for the nastiness of his loss to reformer Febus Bookins, who mainly used the office to reform his own bank account. Sam would never have done anything so crude; everybody knew he didn't care about money, but only about something called the law and something else called justice.

The worst was that night. One of his children, Tommy, eleven, came home in tears. He had been called out of class by two mean Yankees in suits, who'd questioned him about his father. They had scared him seriously, as they'd meant to, and the boy was shaken over it.

"There, there, Tommy," he said to the child, cradling him tenderly, "it's all a misunderstanding. Those men didn't mean any harm, and they'll be going away soon. I promise." That made the boy feel better, but not Sam, who went to bed in a purple rage and awoke the next day in a black rage. He hit his law books for two hours, made several calls, then sat back.

They finally arrived at the office at around eleven.

He was polite. He let them in.

"Sir, we're federal investigators, examining a case of national security."

They showed him credentials, which he did not examine carefully. They had badges and bulges under their coats, where shoulder holsters concealed revolvers.

They wore suits, hats and one wore glasses. They were big men, presumably ex-cops of some sort, from some Northern city. They were used to having their way, their badge frightening people into compliance. Detectives worked that way, good and bad.

"Now, what is this about, fellows?" Sam asked, being a good sport about it all.

"Well, now, sir, we're pleased you're cooperating with us. You'd be surprised how much hostility we run into. We've just got a few little matters to clear up, then we'll be back on our way to Washington. These are troubling times, you know. You'd be surprised where your enemies turn up, and how they wheedle their ways into high places."

"I do believe you, gents. You can count on me for cooperation, yes, sir."

"Mr. Vincent, let's see, you were—" and he summed up Sam's life pretty succinctly.

They wanted to impress on him how much they knew

about him already, what tiny corners and cracks of his life they'd already shined their light upon.

"Yes, sir," he said. "You've certainly been looking into me right thoroughly, I can tell. If the FBI thinks it's that important, I'm surely going to help out. Is this serious?"

"Well, Mr. Vincent, your name has come up in certain inquiries. Certain possibilities have been raised, may I say. We just want to discount them."

"Certainly. How can I assist you?"

"Well, sir, it seems you've been in Washington lately, and you've raised questions about a top secret project in the nineteen forties in Mississippi. It's not the sort of thing—"

"You folks from the FBI don't miss much, do you?"

"No, sir, we don't," said the other.

"Now, could you tell us why you have an interest in a highly secret government circumstance? I mean, it's a little out of the way for an Arkansas prosecutor."

"Yes, sir," said Sam, "I will be happy to answer that question. I don't want there to be any misunderstanding or any doubt about my loyalty. No, sir, I'd have thought winning a Bronze Star in the war would pretty much be it as far as proof of loyalty goes, but I guess you boys don't care much about that."

"Sir, your military record is not at issue. We have a national security mandate to—"

Sam lifted the newspaper off his desk.

There was a tape recorder, and it was recording.

"Would you speak a little louder, sir. I want to make sure I get this for the trial."

Little pause.

The two men looked at each other.

"It would be better for you if you cooperate, Mr. Vincent."

"See, that's what I's just about to say to you, sir. Isn't

that a laugh? You thought you were investigating *me.* Here it turns out I'm investigating *you*!"

"Mr. Vincent, where the hell do you think you are—"

"Impersonating a federal officer. That's two to five. First offense, the judge'd probably let you off with a warning, except I know all the judges, and I can guarantee you they won't."

"Look, here, Vincent, this—"

"I got you on tape acknowledging you're an FBI agent. But you aren't. You've been calling yourself federal investigators. You aren't even that. You're staff assistants at HUAC in D.C. You have no police powers, no right or authority to represent yourself as such, and no right to carry concealed firearms in this state. That's another two to five. Again, if you have friends, it could go away. But in Polk County, see, here's the funny thing, *I'm* the one with the friends."

The two looked at each other

"This is not helping your case," said one.

"This is not helping your case," said Sam.

"You wouldn't dare—"

"I would dare, gents. See, I don't like you. I don't like nosy men who come by and bully the uninformed and take advantage of the uneducated."

"We have subpoena powers, sir. We could call you as a—"

"You do *not* have subpoena powers. You can request a subpoena through a congressional liaison and, if authorized, a subpoena may be issued at the discretion of the Congress. You think it's automatic? Well, it's not. It's a question of who's got the juice to get it done. You say you can get me subpoenaed. I say I can get you fired and set it up so you won't ever work again in that town, or any other."

He looked at them. They looked at him.

He smiled. "Suppose I call my good friend Harry Etheridge, of the Sixth Congressional District? You do know Boss Harry, don't you? Believe you do; he's chairman of the Defense Appropriations Committee, which makes him quite a big fellow in your town. Well, guess what? He's from *our* town, originally, before he moved up to Fort Smith. He even has a summer place a few miles west of here. Now suppose I call Boss Harry and tell him two monkeys from Congressman Dies's committee are down here stirring up trouble, alleging that Boss Harry has communists in his own hometown. Think how embarrassing that would be for a patriot like Boss Harry, and how he would have to set that right. And what do you think Boss Harry would do if it turned out those same two boys were pretending to be FBI agents and frightening honest folks and picking on little boys in school?"

At last. A swallow. The one on the left licked his lips nervously, and then he swallowed too.

"I'm sure if we explained—"

"And I'm sure if I explained. Tell you what, let's find out, okay? Let's call Washington *right now* and see what Boss Harry says."

He picked the phone up off the hook, tapped the receiver a few times, until Mildred came on.

"Mildred, honey, it's Sam Vincent. Can you put me through to Washington, D.C., Boss Harry's number. No, no, not his office number, his *home* number. I don't want to have to go through Claude, I'd rather go through Betty. She'll get him on the phone in ten seconds. Yes, Davis 3080, that's right."

The two men looked at each other.

They both knew that an adversary like Harry Etheridge could make life difficult for them, and that their own guy, Martin Dies, didn't have enough juice to stand.

It was simple calculation on their part. Was Sam bluffing or *could* he get Boss Harry?

Clearly, the answer was not worth finding out.

"Now, see here, Mr. Vincent, there's no need to get upset. Why don't you put that phone down and we can have a little chat. I feel we've gotten off on the wrong foot."

Sam put the phone down.

"I'm listening," he said.

"We're not here to make any trouble. It's just been suggested to us confidentially by someone in authority that some inquiries you made weren't appreciated."

"What authority?"

"That is confidential."

"You tell me, goddammit, or you will spend five years in an Arkansas state penitentiary."

"It was from a security operative at an installation called Fort Dietrich, in Maryland."

"What?"

"Sir, I don't know what you've been into that got those people up there so alarmed. But you have been messing where you should not have been messing, and we were sent down here to make sure you stopped the messing. Now we've communicated that. Sorry if we did it too roughly. Why don't we just get on out of here, and let you go on about your business. We've delivered the message. That's all we're here for."

"Hmmm," said Sam. "I do believe even the questions have done me some harm."

"Well, sir, I suppose on our way out of town we could stop off at a couple of places and explain the whole thing is a big misunderstanding. Would that set it straight by you?"

"I suppose it might."

"Well, sir, then why don't we shake on it?"

He stood and offered his big hand.

"No, sir," said Sam. "Down here we take our etiquette seriously, and we only pay it out to those we respect. Y'all came into this town with blackness in your hearts, and now I'm chasing you out. You stop off on the way and clear my name as you say, and I won't have you arrested or have Boss Harry make a phone call to the chairman. That's all you get from me. Now please leave. I have business."

He sat down as they passed from his office and his life.

He thought: Fort Dietrich, in Maryland. What the hell is that one all about?

The phone rang.

"Hello?"

"Sam, why'd you hang up on me?"

"Well, uh—" It was Mildred, the operator.

"Well, anyhow, you gave me the wrong number. There ain't even a Davis exchange in Washington, D.C. If you want Boss Harry's number, I got that for you, Sam. You need to talk to Betty?"

"No, Mildred, I don't. Sorry."

"All right, Sam. Good-b—oh, wait, your light is flashing. Put the phone down."

He hung it up and it rang in seconds, as Mildred made the connection.

It was Junie Swagger.

"Sam, come quick," she said. "It's about Earl."

32

IN the gray dawn the prisoners jogged out to the levee between the horsemen who ran them like cattle.

"You boy, you keep up, goddammit."

"Jethro, yee-haw, watch that nigger on the left!"

"Ya'll keep together, goddammit."

The snap of whips flicking supersonically through the air stood out like rifle reports amid the general thunder of hooves, running men and yelling men. Now and then came the *whap* of a solid shot against flesh when some low man displeased some high one, and the sticks were used.

They reached the levee and formed up the line to get the tools out of the old toolshed, where a trustee with a key went to open the old lock and pay out the implements while another trustee ran the count.

"Fifty-six out, boss," came a cry.

"Fifty-six," Section Boss cried in reply, "you mark it good. Fifty-five black niggers and one white nigger!"

Earl stood in the line and Section Boss rode up to him, his horse veering ever so close to make Earl draw back.

But Earl knew the horseman wasn't going to come too close; he was scared of Earl.

Then Earl looked up.

"Section Boss, got to talk to you."

"Well, damn, boy, don't that beat it all."

"Please, Section Boss."

Section Boss backed up, steadied his horse, and climbed off. Immediately a couple of other riders came up to cover him, their sticks and whips at the ready, their freshly greased Winchester .351s close by in their saddle scabbards.

Earl approached humbly.

"Speak, boy."

"Sir, I can't take it no more. When Moon gets back, he going to do sumpin' awful to me, and it preys heavy on my mind. All these other men gonna laugh about it. Then he going kill me. I can't die in no prison for colored. Please, sir, you tell Guard Sergeant Bigboy I am a broken man at last."

"You see the error of your ways?"

"I do, boss. Surely I do. I will come clean, yes sir, and we can git this all straightened out. I can't take no more of this shit. I won't last another night."

"You punkin' out after all? And you'd be such a hero! You'd be such a tough boy!"

"Ain't no kind of tough, boss. Ain't no kind of hero. Ain't nothing but a man."

"You git back down in that hole!"

"Boss, I—"

"You git back down in that goddamn hole, boy, like I say, or I'll please myself to give you another thumping. I may tell Bigboy, I may not. I's looking forward to tonight. What I hear, Moon got some real plans for you. Moon gonna have fun tonight. Maybe we'll just let him and take you in tomorrow."

"Oh, boss, please don't do that."

"Git in that hole, boy, while I think this over."

Earl got back in the line, where his conversation with Section Boss had been noted.

"You finally goin' over to the man, buckra?"

"He done slept wif' niggers enuff. Yes suh, the white boy goin' on back."

"Moon still gonna hunt his ass down and do it up fine. If I know Moon, that's what's goin' to happen right swell."

So Earl had another morning in the hole, and at 10:00, when Fish showed up, he worked Earl over plenty hard, as he did all the time, mainly along male rape lines and the power of Moon and his boys against the weakness of the lone white man. He worked him over so hard Earl wondered if it were a dream or not, the whole fantasy of escape. Maybe it was something his crazed brain had heated up for him as a way of retreating from the reality of the place.

But though Fish mocked him blasphemously, to the amusement of both his white and his black audience, as Earl reached for the cup, the old man grabbed his hand to check for the pin with a quick probe of his fingers, found it, and threw a wink at Earl. That gave Earl some sustenance.

It was finally about four o'clock. The sun had pulled down in the sky and swelled up red, like some big fruit corpulent with its own close-to-rotted ripeness. It threw a golden glow across the land, and the wind had stilled. They saw it coming, all of them.

It was the new black Hudson Hornet that had carted out Bigboy in the first place. This was so unusual that all work stopped, and even the guards reined in their horses to watch the approach of the vehicle.

It was here under the guise of the distraction that a

powerful presence pressed against Earl; he looked to see a large man whom he had noted but who never spoke. Up close, the man's face revealed its mutilation, a crust of scar tissue lighter against his jet blackness, though all was touched golden by the sun. The man's eye, in that sea of frozen pain that was his ruined flesh, was askew and wandered its own dumb, blind way. This had to be Tangle Eye.

He nodded briskly to Earl, who made as if he'd slipped, went briefly to his knees and pulled the wrist chain taut across a trunk.

The blow was swift and perfect, and in the same second that it was delivered, Tangle Eye pulled away and headed back to his detail.

Earl saw that he'd not hit the link closest to the ring on the cuff, but the ring itself, the one point where the ancient steel was thinnest. Earl hadn't even felt the shudder or the sting of vibration, so perfectly placed was the blow and so completely sheared was the ring. Earl grabbed the now freed chain with his free hand and pulled it close. He was no longer tethered.

The car pulled up, and someone dashed out to open the rear door. His royal hugeness, Bigboy, sunglasses and drill instructor hat in place, perfect tie putting a point to his immensity, stepped daintily out, sniffed at the brackish air, then looked about until his eyes rested at last upon Earl.

"You, Bogart. You, up out of the hole."

"Yes, sir," cried Earl, "I am coming."

He got halfway and he turned.

"Ain't going to be with you no 'count trash no more, you bet!" he screamed. "I'm goin' back to the white world, thank you, Jesus."

The men regarded him furiously, as he climbed the rest of the way out, reached the levee, and with a shuffle and a shit-eating grin minced toward the big man.

"Take me from these low men, sir, for they are beasts of the field, and I am white."

Someone grabbed him roughly and brought him stumbling to Bigboy.

"So you want to talk, eh, Bogart. Finally seen the light, have you? You have been a stubborn cuss."

"My 'pologies, sir, but being among the colored is enough to set any white man straight."

The guards let him stand free.

"And one more thing, Mr. Guard Sergeant. You're a tub of white-trash monkey shit."

Bigboy's mouth fell open in astonishment, and Earl stepped back as his two companions moved in on him. They grabbed; he ducked and slipped, then banged the first one hard with a double jab to the jaw, feeling that bone shatter on the second hard blow.

The other man roundhoused him, and Earl dropped under the arc of the clumsy punch and nailed this one right in the heart. It took the fight out of him, and he went low fast, his face whiter than terror, his eyes big as fried eggs.

"No guns," Bigboy screamed, for guns were coming out all along the line.

"You, Bigboy, let's see how much tough you got in you," Earl yelled, drawing near.

"You're about to find out, partner. I have this dance saved up special for you," said the man, who had not a lick of fear anywhere in him and suddenly welcomed the assault as an amusement of great potential.

Somewhere the dogs started growling, their throats filling with sound as the excitement of battle violence filled their dog veins and brains.

Bigboy tossed aside his hat, pulled his big Colt hand-gun and tossed it. Last to come off were his sunglasses, which he neatly folded before tossing to another guard.

"I can rack him, boss," screamed Section Boss, who'd heaved near atop his mighty horse and unlimbered the Thompson gun from his saddlehorn.

"No, sir," said Bigboy, his fists circling with a pugilist's grace as he moved with surprising agility left, then right, dancing like a well-schooled heavy. "This here boy's been aching for a boxing lesson, and I'm going to give him one. You think us albinos are weak and red-eyed. Ho, boy, you goin' learn the truth."

Earl shot a left, which Bigboy flicked away, but in the next instant Earl drove a hard right into the big man's gut and met nothing but an impenetrable wall of muscle, skinning up his knuckles but doing the big fellow no apparent harm.

"My old man hit harder than that," he said, smiling.

Mine didn't, Earl thought, a little surprised at what a cool athlete this big monster was turning out to be.

Bigboy fired off a right that hit Earl above the eye. It was a fast, hard punch, an expert's punch, the punch of a man who'd worked both light and heavy bags for years. The big fellow had fast hands, too, but Earl shook it off, trying to show no pain, even if half-a-second's worth of bright lights skyrocketed off behind his eyes.

Earl circled on his toes, and so did the big man. Two jabs were thrown by each, and caught by each high on the arm, for bruises that would emerge in two days but not now. Then Earl fired a good shot off that struck the big man in the nose, crunching it. Blood gushed, but Bigboy merely dropped back a step, spat disdainfully into the ground, a goober of red-shot mucus, then set himself again and moved into the attack.

He was a body puncher. He was so slathered in muscle and so anesthetized by fury no blows could stop him.

He absorbed pain on his arms, kept his head hunched behind his big fists, then worked in close, unleashed a flurry of sharp jabs that flew to Earl's ribs and lit off hell. Earl fell back, his backward motion somewhat defusing the punches, then slipped the one blow thrown from the outside (meant to crescendo the flurry) and countered with a good hammer to the jaw. It would have KO'd a lesser man and rocked a greater man, but like the nose-buster, it merely made the Bigboy blink and spit, take a step back, then set himself and move in.

He would take pain to give pain. That was his strategy. It was crude but based on conviction: he knew he could dish out more than any man could give. He would emerge from his fights bruised and bloodied, but always the winner, on that principle alone.

Earl had a sudden fear: he would lose. The guy was a polished professional-level fighter, who could take a punch, who expected pain, who had the stamina of a platoon, and whose will to conquest was unquenchable. Plus he had good health and nourishment, six inches in height and six in reach, forty or fifty pounds in weight, and lots of gym workouts going for him. And pleasure. This was *fun* for him. He was loving this, loving the drama, the power, the savagery of it, as he must have hated the delicacy of the Earl problem and now could deal with it without frustration.

Earl took a couple of shots to the arm, ducked and moved in to pummel the gut, and took a glancing blow to the temple, which nevertheless opened a gash that soon issued copious amounts of red blood.

"No cut men in this ring, Bogart," sang the happy warrior. "No corner men, no bell, son, just you, me, until you drop, and son, that's coming up real soon now."

He smiled and closed, threw two hard rights, the last of which glanced off Earl's blocking arm and reached his ribs for a stinging shot that brought tears to Earl's eyes.

"Oh, felt that one, did you? More coming, convict."

He threw a punch that Earl countered, but Earl's return blow was somewhat blurred by the fatigue that now corrupted his body, and didn't land square enough to do any damage.

The big man dropped back, reached up and undid his tie and tossed it away, while he sucked oxygen.

Earl, in this moment of respite, realized that the drama was so intense that both audiences, black and white, had formed an auditorium around it. No one spoke, but they watched in utterly raptured fascination.

The big man ripped off his shirt, revealing an undershirt sopped in sweat that constrained muscles of unusual density and precision. He had a statuelike quality to him, marble wrapped in wet cotton. He wasn't fat at all, just big and solid as Wall Street.

The big man went back to his toes and came at Earl.

"We're going to finish it right soon, nigger," he said.

Earl went into his crouch, bobbed and weaved, dashed this way and that, as the big one sought to close. Earl now saw what he must do. Tire the man, wait for a guard to drop out of fatigue, then hit him hard and fast and dash back out of range. This was no ring, so there was plenty of room to move.

But in that same instant, Bigboy backed up, dropped his arms and yelled to his boys, "Get those dogs behind him. He's running too much. This ain't about running, it's about hitting."

Earl sensed that ordered activity unspooling behind him and knew his backing days were done. If he couldn't dance, he couldn't win, he knew, for the big man would corner him and pummel his arms. His arms would die, and then his body and then his head.

He heard the dogs screaming on their leashes as they were brought near. They smelled the blood and sweat in the air and knew that killing time was near. He felt them scuffling frantically behind him, and a sudden snapping yap sunk into his heel as one of them got a brief hold on him. He pulled his leg back and saw there were no options.

"Time is running out, boy. No place to run," Bigboy snarled, after lunging out another red goober and shaking the sweat off his brow.

He threw a fast punch that snapped off the crown of Earl's skull, opening another cut. Earl felt the blood spurt and blinked it out of his eyes, though some reached his lips and tasted of salt.

"Ooo, you didn't know how much speed I had on me, did you, convict? You think you're tough, you're the champ. Hey boy, you have *met* the champ."

He threw another rocket Earl's way, and Earl slipped it, hammered him quick twice over the ribs, bobbed out of reach and had some space to evade. But still Bigboy came on, no sign of weakness. His eyes were red, the irises open like headlights, and the sweat poured off him, but he was on his toes and his guard was well held, steady. Onward, inward he rushed, crouching, taking blows to deliver blows.

Earl saw he would lose. It was the law of boxing: good big man beats good small man. The physics decreed the outcome. He hadn't the weight, the strength, the endurance to stay with Bigboy, and if he was faster, it was only by a little.

He never saw the next one. He was too busy thinking, and not busy enough fighting. It clocked him above the jaw, flush to the side of the face, and the world jacked out of focus while someone banged kettledrums loudly in his ears. His eyes saw only white and he backed off, feeling grogginess spread through his lungs up his neck and ooze warmly through his brain. He almost went, and felt his consciousness slipping away, like bubbly water down a drain.

Bigboy came in to finish.

Earl hadn't been faking it.

It wasn't a trick.

He hadn't thought it out.

But Bigboy's vanity spelled his disaster, for he rode in on a cloud of arrogant confidence, sure that Earl was rocked. And Earl *was* rocked. But Earl came back faster than even a near pro like Bigboy could imagine, and when Earl cleared up, he saw just the flick of a sloppy opening revealed by a dropped left. Earl drove up through it, and landed his uppercut square on the underside of the astonished big man's jaw, a punch so hard it lifted all of Bigboy off the earth. When he returned to the planet, Bigboy's arms, getting no signal from the disconnected brain, briefly became cogitated and unknowing, and as they drifted, Earl somehow found the grit to close yet again and launch a left-right combination to the face that put Bigboy down.

He fell like an ox, hard and lifeless to the levee, and when he fell, a puff of dust was unleashed from the earth at his circumference, like rose petals of celebration, and he went so limp and flat he was dead gone from this world.

Earl now heard the cheers. Bless their goddamned black hearts, all the Negroes now cheered, defying their masters, and their joy was as powerful a pleasure as Earl had or would ever feel on this earth, even if it lasted but a second.

In the next instant, Section Boss hosed out a burst of .45s from his tommygun that whistled overhead, driving the convicts down and shutting them up. But Earl didn't notice that at all. For in that same second, the guard force was on him, six, eight of them, pounding him wherever they could get at him with clubs and saps and boots.

They beat him pretty badly.

"Not the head," someone was shouting, "Goddammit, not the head!"

Earl, in the blur of all his many injuries, saw that it was Bigboy shouting, for he had returned to the land of the living and the thinking, and he wanted Earl conscious.

Earl soon knew why.

Six men held him down, and it was Bigboy who kicked him hard in the ribs until they started to crack, screaming all the time, "You motherfucker, you motherfucker, you motherfucker!"

THEY drove through the night. Earl was in a swamp of pain, too much of it to specify location. His body was ripped, particularly from the stomping at the end, and in his head a gong pounded over and over.

"Sergeant Bigboy," he heard someone say, "you sure about this?"

"Goddamn sure," said Bigboy, his stone heart set on the course he had determined.

"But—"

"But nothing, goddammit. I am tired of this special boy screwing up my system. You see the niggers. He gives 'em hope. They get hope and we have problems."

Then his rage flared again and he stomped Earl's jaw.

"You *goddamn* boy, you! You *lucky* goddamn sonofabitch, no man ever knocked me down 'til you got in a lucky goddamn punch, *Goddamn you!*"

Earl was on the floor of the Hudson's rear seat, chained again, and many heavy boots pressed him still, the heaviest of all Bigboy's.

"Sir, all I am saying is—"

"That's enough, Caleb, damn your soul. He tried to escape. He drownded. Happens all the time at Thebes, and that's all anybody's got to know."

"Yes, sir."

Bigboy leaned down close.

"Breathe deep, Bogart. It's soon to be your last."

The big car at last stopped, and the men poured out. Earl was dragged forward. He smelled river in the air, and saw it, just through the tropically ragged line of trees, a broad band of sparkle, flat and calm and multi-faceted. A moon had risen, but not much; it was blood swollen, plump and fat just over the horizon, its power-ful cold blaze dancing atop the surface of the river.

But he had no time for sightseeing; in the next sec-onds he was dragged and shoved down a path through the jungly woods that took him to a ramshackle shack and a dock. An old scow sat moored to the dock, drift-ing this way and that in the currents.

They unlocked the shack door and shoved him in, roughly.

"Welcome to the Drowning House, Bogart."

He was thrown to the floor, and the work that fol-lowed was swift. It was a place of murder. He saw wooden forms, a manual cement mixer, sacks of cement as yet unmixed, various metal fixtures and chains, and a wall where old locks hung.

A grunting and a groaning sounded, as two of the heavier fellows bent and lifted a square cement block with an iron ring sunk deep into it aboard an old wheel-barrow, which one of the boys then wheeled toward him.

"I'll do it myself, goddammit," said Bigboy.

He kneeled and put a knee on Earl's bruised stomach and roughly took his chained legs and clamped them in irons. These in turn were looped with a length of chain, and it was held fast by a lock. Earl had an anxiety explosion and almost couldn't bear to check, but then forced himself to, and when he saw it squarely he knew it to be the lock he'd practiced on, which by some of Fish's magic had been replaced to its rightful spot on the wall where the locks hung in their neat order.

"Goin' have to get some new locks soon," somebody said.

But Bigboy leaned close, his face still screwed up in dementia.

"You see what fighting the Man gets you, Bogart? Do you see? You do not have the power to go against the Man! The Man rules. I am the Man, and if you go against me, you go against everything, and this is what it gets you. You think on that, Bogart, as the black water fills your lungs while you sink down to river bottom."

He rose, spent, and said, "Get him in the boat."

"You okay, boss?"

"I am fine. Get his goddamned ass in the boat."

Three of the staff controlled Earl as he was led to the boat, the chains around his wrists held tightly, while the wheelbarrow bearing its hundredweight followed behind.

They lowered him roughly into the scow, and it turned out they even had a system for getting the heavy weight aboard; it was not lifted off the barrow at all, but a plank had been set on an angle that matched up fine to a plank sited in the boat's hull, so that the thing could be wheeled down as if on a track. It took but some practiced effort, and down it went with just the gentlest thump as it arrived on the floor of the hull; the boat trembled only momentarily as the wheelbarrow was steered and manipulated toward its stern. The rest of the men jumped aboard, the engine was fired up, the lines cast off, and the boat began to nudge its way into the current.

A breeze blew. The moon had risen enough so that it was no longer red but now that pale, radiant bone-white, and it flickered off the stillness of the water. Its radiance did not quite blur the crazy quilt of stars and fancy patterns that filled the sky. It would have been a night of magic if it hadn't been a night of murder.

"This is usually where they start to cry," somebody said. "Boo hoo, it ain't fair, they got chilluns, they got a mammy and a ol' lady. Show some mercy, Mr. Boss, cut me a break, suh, yassuh, I be a good ol' nigger boy from now on, I be. You goin' cry, Bogart?"

Earl said nothing.

Someone kicked him.

"He thinks he's tough. He thinks he a hero. He ain't gonna give us the satisfaction, ain't that right, boy?"

Earl said nothing.

Now he had this last thing to do. The pin had been inserted horizontally into the callus along his left palm, so that he could still form a fist to fight with, and in forming a fist he was protecting it. But in the disorientation of battle, strangeness is mandatory, and no plan survives its first contact with the enemy. This means things fall apart all the time, and you adjust to them or die. So Earl now snaked a finger into his left palm, with a moment's prayer of a small request to God that the pin still be there, that it not have slithered out and be resting in the dust of the levee somewhere, and with it all his hopes and possibilities.

It was there.

"Sometimes they just beg hard," one of the guards said. "Other times they angry. Got to smack 'em down hard, and they fight 'til the end. You like that, Bogart? You goin' fight and spit and curse as you go down? You goin' to face the Maker with blasphemy on the tongue, white boy?"

"He won't cry," came the strong words of Bigboy, who even in the dark had his sunglasses on and his hat flat over his eyes to mute the swellings and discolorings where Earl's fists had imprinted them. "He won't curse or scream. He will face it straight on. He is a hero. Bogart, you are a hero. That's why you are so dangerous. You are a formidable foe, I give you that. That is why you must die. These other folks here, they are soft. They don't recognize what must be done to persevere. But I have the strength to face reality. I do. So I take the mantle of responsibility, and I see that what needs to be done is what gets done. Do you understand?"

Earl said nothing. The guy was stone crazy, that was all, and now as he executed Earl, he seemed to be demanding some kind of sentimentalized gesture of respect, of acknowledgment, warrior to warrior.

Earl finally said, "Pigman, you are a rank, stinking piece of pork, without no guts nor brains, who only got his way in the world by lucking into a place that needed pure-D crazy evil as its highest value. You will pay, I pledge you. Someone goin' to come out of this water—"

He was kicked hard in the kidneys.

"This is far enough," said Bigboy. "Dump him."

Earl was pushed to the rear of the boat. There two of the minions unlocked the old lock, ran the chain through the steel ring into the block on the barrow, then resecured the lock. It snapped closed with an oily click. The fellow doing this—Caleb, Earl saw—rose, and without a thought tossed the key into the river. Nobody said a thing, and there was no ceremony to it at all. They cut away his clothes until he was nude. Then someone lifted the wheelbarrow on its forward axis, and at a certain point, the cement block slid off with a mild splash, and in an instant had pulled its chain taut and Earl didn't bother to fight it, for what was the point? He jumped before the chain could pull him.

Off he went, following the block, down into the dark river.

DOWN, down, down.

Don't panic, he ordered himself, as he slipped through radiance and bubbles, the weight of the cement chained to his ankles immobile and unforgiving.

Down, down, down.

Then it stopped. The block settled into the river bottom thirty feet beneath the surface. Above, he could see the black hull riding the water, and watched as its screws began to churn up a wake, and it described a lazy U and headed to shore.

Don't panic, he told himself.

You've done this a hundred times.

He felt no oxygen starvation yet. Calmly, holding himself together, he cupped his hands, and his fingers felt for the pin. His fingers had inflated in the cold water and were stiff and numb and clumsy. His hands ached and bled still from the beating they had administered. But still there was some mobility left, and he felt the pin and worked at the tiny segment that was not buried, had it pinched tight between thumb and forefinger and began to work it out steadily, smoothly ever so—

But as his eyes adjusted to the underwater murk, something stunned him. It was a tree twisted strangely in the form of a man, like a submerged, crucified Christ, the moon glow having penetrated far enough to illuminate its ghastly pallor.

It was a man.

It was a man, still buoyant, still erect, still reaching

for a surface he'd never make, the chain that held him still tight. Earl turned his head, and saw not another man but what had once been a man, before age and rot and water had taken all that was human about him and left only skull and shards of meat and tatters of clothes, linked fragilely by threads of ligaments. He, too, reached upward for a surface his fingers would never break.

Earl was in a glade of corpses. They floated and bobbed in the subtle drift of current, in every state of decomposition, some hard bone, others molted flesh, some dressed, some naked. Oozy weeds twisted about them, and fish flashed in schools in the deepwater moonlight, negotiating the alleyways of a metropolis of corpses.

Get it back, he ordered himself, as his lungs at last began to sing for air, and he bent to his ankles to insert the pin in the lock, and jimmy it free, and rise, but his fingers remained clumsy and puffed.

Be calm, he commanded, which was fine, until the pin slipped away, and he watched in horror as his grasping fingers could not catch up to it, and it disappeared.

33

SAM tried to obey the law as he always did, but he could not this time. Especially beyond town, with just two-lane Route 8 and no twists or turns or traffic cops between himself and Board Camp, where the Swagger farm was, he punched the pedal and his Pontiac roared its merry way along, pulling up dust, scattering chickens, scaring children and birds, earning the curses of mommies who observed his thoughtless speed.

His heart was thumping, but it was pain he felt.

This would be it: news from farther south that Earl Swagger was gone. There could be no other news.

He tried to steel himself for the scene, as he'd seen it enough when a hero dies: the weeping wife, her face a ruin of mucus and tears, the numb child who cannot begin to imagine how his life has changed, and how he has just inherited a vision of the universe as a forever imperfect engine, a place with a hole in it that sucks out the good and permits the reigns of chaos and violence.

It seemed to take forever, but that, of course, is merely the lengthening of time by the release of blood chemicals under stress. In reality, less than fifteen minutes had passed.

The place looked the same, and he wished he'd been much better for Junie. In truth, so ashamed was he and so confused by the situation, that after passing along the money from Davis Trugood, he'd stayed away, for he could not bear to face the woman nor see the child.

There were no other cars, so she had not yet called the state police. Sam swore that at last he'd tell what he knew, what he had found out, and would get it going, whatever it would be, some form of war on Thebes.

He parked, dashed up the driveway, and didn't bother to knock.

He entered the house of mourning and saw Junie sitting on a sofa, a dazed look on her face.

"Junie, what is it? What did you hear about Earl?"

She looked up and smiled through her tears, and Sam thought he saw the delusions of madness on her face, as people act peculiarly in the arrival of a life's worth of black grief.

"Oh, Sam," she said.

"Earl? Please. What happened to Earl?"

He thought he'd have a heart attack.

Someone said, "Sam, why don't you set a spell and have some of Junie's nice lemonade," and Sam turned to see that it was Earl, even browner than before, brown as a man who'd spent two months laboring in the sun, and he held his son in his arms and was smiling.

34

As consciousness ebbed and the bubbles took over, a wraith or an eel or a large, slippery fish flashed before Earl's dulling, darkening eyes. He was aware of some kind of movement, and in the next second felt the full glory and pleasure of release.

Upward and reborn he coursed, seeing what all those down there had seen in their last seconds but could never reach and died dreaming of, and that was the surface.

He broke, feeling the rushing intake of cold sweet air, dipped beneath the current, surfaced again for more of the stuff. Even now he was not insane. He didn't gasp or gulp or shout, for somewhere was the boat, though those aboard would likely not be paying attention.

At that moment the old man broke the surface next to him.

"Can you swim with them chains?"

Earl nodded; there was enough play in the bonds to allow him to propel himself and his victory over death had filled him with energy and exuberance.

"We go slow. You stick with me. If you lose sight of me, you orient on that low star there and swim to it. We less than fifty yards out. You reach walking depth in less than twenty-five yards."

Earl nodded again, and the two set out. Earl had no problem staying with the smaller man as he undulated through the water in a limited but satisfactory version of the backstroke, and indeed, in a few minutes he realized the man near him was walking, not swimming. He let his feet drift downward until they reached mud, sank an inch or two, and then were on something solid. At that point he realized it intellectually as well as emotionally: again, he had survived.

They made it up the bank and over the levee which held the water back from the land. Earl scrambled up and over it, while reckoning they were downstream a couple of hundred yards from the Drowning House. The old man had cached a blanket here and retrieved it to wrap around Earl. That done, they found a path, more a deer track in the woods, and continued along it for a mile or so. Now and then something mean would cut at Earl's bare feet, but he felt no pain at all.

At last they reached their destination, which was an old duck blind left over from years ago, when whoever owned the original plantation that became Thebes took his autumn harvest from the sky. Earl slinked in, the old man behind.

"You okay, boy?"

"These goddamn chains."

"Gimme just a second."

The old man bent, pulled one of his amazing secret

pins out of some spot or other on that wiry old body, and quickly unlocked the cuffs and the ankle braces. Earl was free.

"You rest up here. I gots to get back. You be fine, here. No one knows a thing."

"Yes, sir."

The old man pulled over a cloth sack.

"Like I say, boy, some clothes. Dungarees, a work shirt, some old boots, a hat. You look like a tramp, but nobody be looking fo' you. There's also some biscuits and cornmeal. There's a compass. You want to follow the river and this old track here for about five miles till you come to a island in the river. At that place, you steer north by northwest through the piney woods. You cut railroad track in 'bout twenty miles. Long as you stay north by northwest and keep moving and don't panic, you goin' be okay. There's a freight runs up to Hattiesburg every day 'bout four o'clock. You hop that, take her into Hattiesburg, and from there you on your own. About fifty dollars hard cash should help, so it's in there too. Buy some clothes, a bus ticket. Be cool. Nobody looking fo' you, nobody know a thing. You a dead man, and ain't nobody looking fo' no dead man."

"I got it."

"The woods don't scare you none?"

"I can get through woods."

"Then you all set, white boy. You home free. Go back to freedom land. You done crossed the river of Jordan."

"Old man, why you doing this thing for me?"

"Way to beat these boys. Onliest way there is. All the time I'm looking fo' ways to beat them. It ain't much, but it's something."

"I can't say enough—"

"You hush on that. Now you gots two promises to live up to. Remember?"

"I do."

"You listen good and live up to both of them. That's what you owe Fish."

"I will."

"First is, you go to N'Awleans, my old town. You gets yourself two fine yeller Chinee gals and a bottle of bubbly and a room in a nice hotel and y'all have a time. And when you got mo' pussy than any man done got in a single night, you lay back and you drink a toast to old Fish. Fish done this so he could get pleasure thinking on that.

"Second is: you put this place out of your mind. Here we are the lost. We are in hell's farthest pasture. Ain't no getting out or coming back. Nobody care, nobody want to know. You go on, have a good life, and don't let what you done seen down here poison your mind. Don't let it do no clouding. You can't do nothing about it, so you forget it, or it wins. It kills you. You blows your brains out from sadness, thinkin' on the pain. Don't you no way think about coming back here to set things right. It can't happen, not now, not in ten years, not in twenty, maybe not never, and no point rapping yo' head bloody to find that out. I already knows."

Earl considered.

Then he said, "Well, old man, you're going to have to swim me back out that river and chain me down again, because I'm not keeping either of those promises. I am a married man with a young son, so I don't need two Chinese whores for fun. Sure would enjoy it, but it's not in the cards. And as for the other, I can't help you none there neither. For I will come back. And this time when I come, I ain't coming alone. This time I'll have some friends. And you know what else, old man?"

"No," said Fish.

"This time I'll have a whole lot of guns."

"Whoooeeeee," whistled the old man in the dark, enough moon glow creeping in to light his face. "Whoooeeeeee! That pale horse coming to Thebes at last! That pale horse coming."

The Old Men

35

S AM said, "We must tell people."

Davis Trugood said, "Nobody will care."

Sam said, "Then we will make them care."

Davis Trugood said, "All this is happening to Negroes. To many in the South and even to some in the North—possibly more than you would ever believe—the Negro is not fully human. They take the *Dred Scott* decision as gospel still. Allow me to quote: Mr. Justice Taney wrote that the Negroes were a 'subordinate and inferior class of beings [who] had been regarded as beings of an inferior order, and altogether unfit to associate with the white race, either in social or political relations; and so far inferior that they had no rights which the white man was bound to respect.' "

"It isn't eighteen fifty-seven anymore," said Sam.

"It is in much of Mississippi," said Davis Trugood. "It has never stopped being eighteen fifty-seven down there."

Sam screwed up his wily face. "You know a bit more about conditions down there than I might suspect, sir. More than you could have learned from my reports."

"All I know I know *from* your reports, Mr. Vincent. You are the author of my opinions."

"Then why do I reach different conclusions?"

"Because your template for interpretation is your own mind, which is tolerant and logical and orderly. But it is ill-equipped to deal with that which is not."

"You say you never argue, sir? You argue well."

"When I must, I can, I suppose. But the true expert on Thebes County has yet to speak."

Earl had sat listening to these two palaver for an hour now. His ribs were still heavily taped, as four of them were broken. He had serious internal injuries, a doctor thought, possibly as bad as a ruptured spleen. He still could not walk without pain, or move quickly. The doctor had put 134 new stitches in him, and had grown annoyed when Earl stuck to a stupid story about being the victim of a beating by gamblers.

"If you are the victim of a beating," he had said, "why then would your hands be swollen still, your knuckles ripped to hell and gone? You may have several broken fingers."

"If my fingers move, they must not be broke. As for the rest, those fellows must have drug me after I passed out," was all Earl had said.

"I should call the police," said the doctor.

"Sir, I can handle this."

"No getting back at these fellows then. It has to stop here, or I will call the police. You must learn the power of forgiveness."

"Yes, sir," Earl had said.

Now, both pairs of eyes turned on him. He was in Sam's office three days after his return, and Davis Trugood, alerted by telegraph in Chicago, had arrived as soon as the travel schedules allowed.

"I have something of an idea," said Earl. "I would like Mr. Sam to leave the room. I don't want him to hear of it."

"I will do no such thing," said Sam. "Earl, I am a party to this as much as you. I got you in. I will not leave."

"I do not want you knowing what horror I am capable of imagining. Your opinion of me will drop. That, and you may feel obligated to make a report to the police, or no longer be able to represent the law fairly."

"I don't like where this is going," Sam said. "Earl, you are a good man. You are a hero. You have your whole life to live. We need you as a witness. You need to speak of what you saw down there. You need to be the centerpiece in our campaign, not merely to make those responsible pay, but to change the thinking of the South. Other Southerners must know what some Southerners are capable of and what is being done in their name."

Earl said nothing, as Sam lectured him. Sam, as usual, had all the answers. But possibly to the wrong questions.

"Earl, listen to me," Sam continued. "And you, too, Mr. Trugood. I have thought this all out, and it is the only way. Earl, we depose you. With your medal and your reputation, your account has instant validity and importance. We can get people to listen to your story. I have the whole campaign mapped out. I know that we can get the support of progressive people in Mississippi and throughout the South, but I also know it must be blue ribbon. We must not mess about with radicals, socialists or communists, and we should have white and Negro clergy united on our side, but no Negroes of frightful disposition or unruly countenance. That is what is best. You are our secret weapon. Your vengeance will be your survival and testimony, if need be in a court of law, if need be in the court of public opinion."

Earl listened politely. Then he said, "First off, I do not want to be no singing clown in some kind of circus who is crybabying about all them awful things done to him. I don't like lights shining on me. But second off, and more important, here's what would happen after that. Nothing. Not a thing."

"See, that's my point too," said Mr. Trugood. "He sees it to the nub, Mr. Vincent."

"I cannot give up on the rule of law and the majesty of the courts," said Sam. "Even in a benighted zone like Mississippi."

Earl said, "You seem to think we have a choice. Your way isn't a choice at all. It's an impossibility."

Sam made a face of disapproval.

"Now, Earl—" he began.

Earl kept going.

"You know, I don't have a education like you two. I don't know enough words. But I am looking for a word now, and it means something like 'logical.' But logical in the way of institutions. The way institutions act with each other. They progress along certain lines that everybody knows, that makes a sense everybody agrees upon. What is that word, Mr. Sam? You would know it."

Sam narrowed his eyes, then spoke. "Earl, I believe the word you mean is 'rational.' "

"Yes, sir, that is it. That is the very one, right there."

"But where is this going?" asked Davis Trugood.

"I'm trying to be clear about what they've done down there, and why the ordinary remedies are doomed. You see what they've engineered? They've engineered a system that is unbreachable by what you would call a rational action, the action of men or systems who themselves are rational. They've thought about their enemies and how they'll come at them. Their whole campaign on me wasn't at all about me, but about who I represented. They thought I represented someone, and they had to work out a way to deal with that body. When they concluded I did not, it became clear they were going to kill me. But not until."

"Earl, possibly you are thinking too hard about this."

"No, Earl knows a thing or two," said Mr. Trugood.

"They are set up along one line and one line only: to survive any 'rational' attack on them. If any institution attempts to change them, they can defeat it. They will know in advance it is coming. The newspapers, the police investigators, the federal investigators, all that: it can't work because that is what they are the best at. That is what they expect. You yourself asked some questions in Washington, and for your troubles nearly had your career destroyed, Mr. Sam, by federal investigators."

"I may yet have it destroyed," said Sam. "And if we go where you're going, I may end up in prison."

"You can't do nothing rational and get them. They will always have the answer. They will go on and on and on. They'll always know in advance, they have connections, they are doing what everybody wants them to do, and clearly at some level there's some federal protection. So if you think newspaper campaigns and Negro ministers and blue-ribbon fellows are going to do a thing agin them, you are wrong, dead wrong. They're smarter than that, and they will win every goddamned time. You cannot do it on a rational basis."

Now it was Sam's turn to say nothing.

Earl turned to Mr. Trugood.

"Sir, I don't know why you're in this, but I'm going to tell you what must be done and we will see if you have the grit to see this one through."

"Go ahead, Mr. Swagger."

"They are invulnerable to rational assault. They are vulnerable to unrational assault."

"*Irrational*," said Sam.

"Irrational, then."

"And what does that mean?" said Mr. Trugood.

"It means something that can't happen. Something that isn't supposed to happen, not in this day and age, something that isn't in the cards."

"And that would be?"

"Men with guns in the night. Boys who know the place and can shoot a bit. It means fast, hard, complete, total surprise. Seven is the right number, I think. And I can get those men. I can. I know who they are and where they can be found, and I have the means to convince them to sign aboard. I can get 'em in, and lead 'em in a good night's work, and get 'em out. You know why this'll work, and nothing else? Because everything they done to fight the rational opens them up to the irrational. The isolation. The guns pointed in, not out. An installation that's out of communication and that has no reinforcements at hand and thinks its location far up a river in a jungle and a forest is all the protection it needs. Seven men, Mr. Trugood, with guns and some light equipment. I can get 'em in, lead 'em to do a night of man's work, and get 'em out. And the State of Mississippi won't cotton to it till three or four days later."

"Earl, are you going to break some men out of prison? Is that it?" said Sam.

"You don't quite get it, Mr. Sam. I am not meaning to break some men out. I am meaning to break them *all* out. I am meaning to break the prison. When the morning sun rises on Thebes, there ain't going to be no Thebes. None at all. None. I'm going in and shoot to kill those who stand against me, free the convicts, burn the buildings, and blow the levee and drown the place under twenty feet of black river. Nothing is left. It is gone, razed, destroyed, like Sodom and Gomorrah in the Good Book. It is finished. I can't say what happens next, other than that it will be different. I take on trust it will be better."

"Earl, that's insurrection you're talking. You could start a race war in the South."

"No, sir. Because it'll happen so fast and so totally that there won't be nothing left. The evidence is under water and mud. The few witnesses don't make no 'rational' sense. And the state don't want to shine no spotlights on Thebes. None at all. It don't want people peeking at what went on in Thebes. It will see the wisest reaction is to let Thebes stay dead in its tomb of river, and move on."

"Jesus, Earl," said Sam.

"I told you I didn't want you involved."

"We have now committed the felony of conspiracy to assault," said Sam.

"So be it," said Earl.

Sam shook his head.

Earl said, "Mr. Sam, when them German tanks were coming on, did you call the newspapers? Did you convene a panel? Did you file a suit? What did you do?"

"I calculated range and wind. As I recall, it was 2950 meters off by range finder, with a wind of more than 10 miles an hour to the west, a full-value wind we called it. We were already zeroed at 2000 meters, so I had to come up 73 clicks, and then come over 15 clicks to the right for wind deflection. I fired a salvo for double-checking my calculations, then I fired high explosive for effect. We blew them off the face of the earth," said Sam. "There was no other thing possible. But the state had decreed a general condition of war."

"Well, that is where we are," said Earl. "We are in a

general condition of war. Or, we turn tail and forget about it and go back to our lives and live happy ever after. And Thebes goes on and on, maybe for years. You can't fix it. You can't modify it. You can't reform it. You can't make it better or gentler. You can only do two things. You can wait for it to change, meaning you wait until the world changes, which it might do tomorrow or next year or next century or never. And all that time, that city of dead under the water gets more and more crowded, the Whipping House gets bloodier, the Screaming House gets louder. And we're the worst, because we knew about it and we didn't do a goddamn thing. Or we can blow it off the face of the earth. Those are the only two possibilities, realistically."

"You would take a force up that river?" said Mr. Trugood. "Or through that forest? It seems to me you'd be easily spotted and you'd have no surprise at all. Yet with only seven, you'd need surprise. I don't see—"

"I can do it. I know the way. It's a thing nobody ever thought of before."

He told them.

"When?" Trugood asked.

"It's now the dark of the moon almost. I want to go in the dark of the moon next month. I want it done fast, with good men. If I hustle and travel and palaver good, it can be set up and brought off that fast."

Sam listened and saw the possibility of it.

"Earl, you are bent on this thing."

"I am, Mr. Sam."

"And if I say 'no' and that I have to turn you in?"

"You will do what you have to do, and I will do what I have to."

"Can he do these things?" Mr. Trugood asked.

"Mr. Trugood, if Earl says he can, then he can," Sam said.

"Mr. Sam, are you with us?"

Sam said nothing for a bit. Finally, he realized what he had to say, and declared himself to be a man of the law. "I cannot go against the law," he said. "But you say to do nothing would be to go against a bigger law."

"That is the gist of it, sir."

"All right. Then I can then only say this: Earl, I cannot make up my mind in a single evening. I know you must begin to make your preparations. You will do that no matter what I say. So I will ruminate, examine, penetrate the mystery, lock up with the epistemology of it. Excuse the big word, but that is how I must proceed. If I find I cannot support you, Earl, you have to trust me to come to you and tell you. If it comes to it, I will have to go to the authorities. I may consider myself as having no choice, but I will face you square and tell you so eye-to-eye."

"Fair enough, I suppose," said Earl.

"In the meantime, you'll forgive me if I don't practice my small arms marksmanship. I have said I will find something out about that place. I have begun that effort, and in good faith and in obeyance of my decision, I will proceed. Again, fair enough?"

"Fair enough," said Earl.

"I wish you could join us enthusiastically," said Davis Trugood. "But I respect your honesty. As for me, I know my part. It is financial. You cannot fight a war without money."

36

It was cool and still in the minutes before dawn, and in that gray flush, only beginning to light some in the east, Earl sat on a shooting bench, enjoying a Lucky Strike. He was early, but he meant to be early.

Around him towered some magnificent Idaho mountains, but he could not see them yet. It was quiet, until at last he heard the sound of an automobile approaching, grinding its way uphill over the cinders of a road to this shooting range.

He watched as a humpbacked Chrysler from some year before the war pulled up next to his own rented Chevy, and a man got out. He was what some might call all hat and no cattle. He was a small man in a large hat. The glowing ember of a lit pipe illuminated his tough little face if you looked carefully, but as he made his preparations, he was all business. He opened the trunk of his car and took out a leather shooting box, which contained at least five pistols or revolvers, as well as a large amount of ammunition and various cleaning tools and chemicals and rags; it had a door flap that could be unlocked and locked in the upward position, and a spotting scope then attached, neatly moored to check targets. You saw them at bull's-eye matches.

He lugged this thing up just a bit to another bench, and there set it down. He noticed Earl.

"Howdy," he said.

"Howdy, sir."

"Looks to be a right fine day, don't it?"

"It does," said Earl.

The old man got himself set up. He opened the flap and connected the telescope. He pulled out the case's drawer to reveal the five guns which turned out, as Earl saw, to be all heavy revolvers manufactured either by Colt on the .41 frame or by Smith & Wesson on the N-frame. Then he removed several plastic boxes, removed the tops, and Earl saw neat rows of cartridges.

Next, out came a roll of paper targets and a staple gun.

"Cease-fire?" he asked.

"Yes, sir," said Earl.

The old man walked out on the range to a frame fifty yards gone, and quickly stapled the bull's-eyes to it. He returned to the bench and sat down behind it.

"Range hot?"

"Range hot it would be," Earl said.

The next thing out was a notebook where, with a scholar's intensity, he turned to a page where a good deal of data was already recorded, and reviewed it, almost as if he were checking over this morning's lecture before the students arrived.

So compelling was this immersion into the physics of it that he didn't look up for quite some time, now and again writing himself a note or underlining something that was already written, occasionally dealing with his briarwood pipe, which, like Sam's pipe, went out almost as often as it went on.

Finally, the sun came up enough for him to see the target and he removed a revolver—Earl saw it to be a Smith N-frame, with a four-inch barrel well engraved by an artist, and a highly carved, palm-filling ivory stock—opened the cylinder, and slid in six fat cartridges. Setting the gun down on the bench, he reached into his pocket and pulled out a wad of cotton.

"Say, friend, don't know if you mean to shoot yourself or just watch, but I'm going to protect what little hearing I've got left with this here cotton. Would you care to help yourself?"

"Sir, my ears already ring like hell and I hear about ten percent of what is said."

"That's the damage the guns will do. You should have protected your ears when you were young."

"Yes, sir," said Earl.

"Still, I'd use some if I were you."

Earl agreed, and went over to take a wad from the little man who, approached, was more eyebrow than hat as it turned out. That is, he was about fifty-five years old, with a face that looked like a walnut's meat if it has dried in the sun over a long period, but what was remarkable were the feathers or whatever the hell they were over his eyes. They were like caterpillars possibly, extravagant things on a face so dour and grim.

Earl stuffed in the cotton as he returned, and then watched.

The old man shot. Six times. Each time the revolver jumped off the bench rest he'd set it on, and the report was loud enough that its pain penetrated unpleasantly through Earl's cotton earplugs. The old man took no notice. He simply recorded remarks in his notebook with a great deal of patience and detail. He opened the cylinder and used the hand ejector to pump out the six spent shells, which he examined with a great deal of care, again taking notes.

It went on for two hours, with time off for the old man to remove one set of targets, measure them carefully and note them duly in his notebook and hang another.

Finally, at around 9:00, he was done, and it seemed that he had returned to planet Earth. He took his hat off and rubbed his hand through his hair, revealing also that the upper third of his forehead was stark white, as if it had been hidden behind the giant Stetson for years and years, his whole life perhaps. He then cleaned his guns methodically.

Then, at last, he turned.

"You are a patient fellow," he said to Earl.

"Yes, sir, Mr. Kaye, I am."

"So I see you know my name."

"I do, sir. I have heard great things about you. Not merely have I been reading your articles over the years, but a friend of mine, now passed, knew you well in the old days. Is that your .44 Special load you are running?"

"Yes, it is. I've got one of my own design Kaye 200 grain semiwadcutters atop varying amounts of Unique. She steps out."

"I could see the recoil."

"Oh, that," said Mr. Kaye. "I don't pay much attention to that. Recoil's for sissies to worry about. Are you a sissy, son?"

"Don't really know, sir."

"Well, I am seeing how much she'll take before the pressure signs start showing: you know, bulged primers, tight casing, that sort of thing. I'll probably blow up three or four guns before I get this one finished and get where I want to be. Now, you mentioned a friend, son. A friend of mine?"

"Yes," said Earl. "His name was D.A. Parker."

"D.A.! He is a good man! He is the best! He faced many an armed man in his time, and put most of them facedown in the dust. Say, how'd you know D.A.?"

"It was my privilege to serve with him in some dirty work in Hot Springs. It was a messy fracas. Cost that fine man his life."

Elmer Kaye's face knit up in some concern as he factored in this information.

Finally he said, "So you are a lawman? So you saw some of the kind of action D.A. saw. You have faced shots fired in anger."

"There, sir, and in the war before. And before that, in the Marine Corps. A bit in Nicaragua and some in China, against the Japs even before Pearl Harbor."

"Hmmm," grumped the old man. "You are a formidable fellow, then."

"I am one lucky fellow, truth is."

"But I'm betting your arrival here was no accident, not if you knew my name and heard D.A. Parker chat about me."

"That is true, Mr. Kaye."

"Well, what would it be, son? Daylight's wasting, and I've got work to do. Have three pieces due at *American Rifleman* by the end of the month."

"Well, sir, it's about a little trip. A hunting trip."

"I don't guide no more."

"I'd be the guide."

"Hmmm," said Elmer Kaye. "I have Africa penciled in for the fall, and Alaska in December. I'm in South America for a bit, but I don't think that's until February of fifty-two. I might have some time in January, if it tempts me."

"Sir, actually it'd be in three weeks, dark of the moon."

"Three weeks! Impossible."

"You might make an exception for the game I've got in mind."

"And that would be?"

"Two-legged. Heavily armed. Mean as a skunk. Shoot first, ask questions later. 'Bout fifty of 'em, some with machine guns."

Elmer leaned forward, his heavy eyebrows narrowed up in what looked like the beginning of formidable anger.

"Say, I don't think I like where this is going, friend. I'm not some gunman for hire. I am a friend of law enforcement, and have never committed a crime in my life, nor even thought for a second about doing so. You must have me figured for some other kind of fellow, and I don't care to hear more of it."

"I know how upstanding you are. That's why I thought you'd be interested. And I thought to get you to listen to me from here on in, I'd show you something they gave me after the war."

He reached into his pocket, removed the Medal of Honor and pushed it across to the old man.

"Where?"

"Iwo. Close-in work. Killed a mess of Japs in very short order. Wasn't happy about it, but they's killing people in my platoon."

"You *are* formidable. Then why on earth—?"

"These boys I'm gunning for need gunning, believe you me, Mr. Kaye. They live on death and pain. They hurt for fun. They run roughshod over all other forms of life, and laugh about it. They are as pure killers as any who walked the earth. And they think nobody can touch them. They are beyond the reach of the law, so isolated they will see all comers a-coming days in advance, and be ready for them. I want to touch them hard in three weeks. I want you and a few others like you to come a-hunting with me. I've got a fellow who'll even pay expenses. And although I can't guarantee what happens in the fight, I can guarantee that it's easy in and then easy out, and no law will ever track you down and hold you accountable. You'll get no credit and no profit from it, but you'll have a night of gunplay like no other on earth. If this sort of thing matters to you, you'll never have another chance like this one. Chances like this one are leaving the world as it gets more and more modern. I'm giving you a night in Dodge City, where I bet in your heart of hearts you've always wished to be. And you can see what that super .44 you're working up can do. Now what do you say?"

The old man fixed him square with his intense eyes.

"Okay, son. You've piqued my interest. Now tell me all about it."

An hour later, Elmer Kaye said yes. How could he say anything else? You don't get but one offer like Earl's in a lifetime.

37

HE had a professorial mien, with rimless glasses, a fedora, a tweed sports coat, the tie tied perfect and tight. He was about fifty himself, with the worn face of a man who's been a lot of places and seen a lot of things. Earl watched as he assumed the classic kneeling position and fired.

It was a Winchester Model 70, scoped, and far down-range, a small part of Idaho lit up behind a target. He cocked the rifle effortlessly and fired again, then three more times, in about thirty seconds.

Then he consulted the spotting scope.

"A nice group, Mr. O'Brian?"

The old man looked up, startled. He was used to coming out here by himself, and his eyes examined Earl quickly, reached a judgment, and he decided to answer.

"Not bad," he said. "Everybody insists you can't get tight groups with a .270, but that's because they don't make bullets carefully enough for it. Fellow in town makes these one at a time for me, weighs 'em out and throws out the ones that are off-weight by just a tenth grain or so. It looks to me like I'm within an inch down-range."

"Great shooting from the kneeling."

"You're a position shooter, are you, sir? A rifleman?"

"I did some shooting in the service, sir. Never worked at it, never was no champion. But in the war, when I shot at someone who was or was planning to shoot at me or my fellows, he usually stayed shot."

"God bless you for your service."

"You want me to spot for you, sir?"

"Well, you're not here to spot for me. You've got some kind of proposition, else you wouldn't have driven all the way out from Lewiston. Are you starting a new magazine? I get fellows trying to get me to write for this new book or that one all the time. But I am staying at *Outdoor Life* and that's all there is to it. I have a nice arrangement with them, and the gun companies and the ammunition factories are supportive of my efforts."

"Well, sir, actually, I don't think there's no writing in what I'm here to talk about. You wouldn't want to write about it. What I'm looking for is a rifleman. He's got to hit six one-hundred-yard shots in about five seconds, as I've figured it out, and it'll be dark of the moon."

"Impossible."

"The targets will be well designated."

"Well, in that case, any competent marksman could do that. If you were in the service you would be able to come up with dozens of fellows capable of that."

"It helps that he's an older fellow."

"Now why would that be?"

"He's had his children or decided not to. He's lain with a few women."

"Sir, I have lain with only one, and she is to this day my wife and I am a lucky man for it."

"Yes, sir. But the man I'm looking for has also seen enough things to know there's not much to miss if he passes on. He won't fall apart when things get tight. He's got discipline, talent, solidity, and a sense of values. He ain't in it for the money. He's in it for the shooting and the rightness of it. And if he gets killed, he died doing something he was born to do, and that'll hold him together in the tough moments. And there's one other thing: I've seen enough young men die in the war. I hope to never see it again. Old fellows have some living behind them, so they won't be bitter if it happens."

"Then it's dangerous. I'm sure you're offering a great deal of money."

"Expenses. But the fee in other ways is high."

"And what would those other ways be?"

"Experience. You won't get a chance to do this one again, and you're lucky as hell that you're getting it at all."

"It sounds illegal."

"It may be. However, it is righteous."

"All right, you tell me what it is you're offering. In plain language."

"Kills. You'll get a passel of kills out of it. I'm gambling that an old rifleman like you has it in him to wonder, deep down, how he'd do if the animal on the other end of the scope could shoot back at him. Your kind of rugged fellow must wonder about that all the time."

Jack O'Brian's lack of an answer told Earl he'd hit the right note.

"I have no desire to kill men," he said. "Except that the ultimate usage of the gun is in the hands of a warrior. Not a hunter, but a warrior, defending his tribe. I'm wise enough to know that, and maybe it's something I hold against myself."

"I can't guarantee you you won't catch a cold from a bullet. It sometimes happens to the best of us. But I can guarantee you the following: easy in, easy out. One night, this would be in three weeks, the total involvement of time being about a week. No police interest. You go home free and clear, and your odds are good, with surprise on our side."

"Who are you?" O'Brian then asked.

Earl told him, and got out the medal, and told him some more. Then he handed him a sheet of paper with some names and numbers on them.

"You might know a few of these men. They are old shooters."

"I know at least three of them. I shot against them at the Nationals. This fellow was squadded two down from me, I believe."

"I served with each in the war. If you'd like to call them and ask them any question you have about me, that would be fine."

"I may just do that. Now tell me what this is."

Earl told him.

Jack O'Brian said yes, with only one proviso.

"I would only ask that the one man who not be requested to join us is a knotty, stubborn, senile, cantankerous bastard named Elmer Kaye. I cannot be in the same room as Elmer Kaye."

"Can you be in the same house?" said Earl, then gave him the bad news.

38

THE world's oldest gunman slept in his rocker on the porch, in a blanket wrapped up against the cold, except of course there was no cold, only a memory of it.

Outside it was Montana everywhere you looked. Beyond the far meadows some blue mountains rose out of mist, but so many miles off no details could be tracked. In his chair the old man slept as soundly as the dead. In repose his features softened some. He had an egg-shaped face like a dream granddad and not much hair left. He was pink, as so many men in their seventies become. Though swaddled in the wool, he clearly had stumpy arms and a stumpy body, and short legs. And, like many men of his generation, he was dressed formally, for to face the world, even in sleep, without a tie was to admit that one was a no 'count. But without a hat was even worse, and though he dozed, his round head was crowned in ten gallons' worth of imposing black Stetson.

Earl wondered if he were indeed dead, but every few

minutes or so he'd let out with some low, growly sound from who knew where? He'd stir, shiver, twitch, but only for a second; then it was back to dreamland.

"Mr. Swagger," his granddaughter said, as she brought him another cup of coffee, "I'm sure grandpap wouldn't mind if you nudged him awake."

"Thank you, young lady, but I feel Mr. Ed has earned his sleep, and I'll not be taking any of it from him."

She was a pretty girl, possibly twenty, with the kind of pugnacious jaw that suggested that under her sugar lay considerable spice. Earl marked her down as a fire-cracker, even as she twinkled at him.

"I swear, he sleeps the day away most of the time. He needs an eight-hour nap so he'll be fresh for his twelve-hour-night sleep."

"He's running down some."

"Just a bit. If he comes to in a good mood, he'll still be a one-man fire station."

"That's what I'm betting on."

"I'm sure he will. He so likes his visitors."

Earl waited an hour, then two. He smoked three or four Luckies, but mostly he just sat patiently.

Finally, well past the noon hour, the old man stirred with more gumption than ever before, seemed to spit and cough and struggle a bit with his breathing, and came out of his sleep as a man comes out of the water that's just tried to kill him.

"Huh? Wha? Umph, er, ah, whoa, what the—?"

He blinked, spluttered, shook his head, and looked about.

"Sally? Sally, honey?"

"Yes, Grandpap," came the cry from within.

"I must have dozed."

"Just a bit. Are you ready for some lunch?"

"Yes, please."

"Say hello to your visitor."

The old man looked over at Earl.

"Howdy," he said. "Care for some lunch? The girl makes a fine tomato soup."

"It's only Campbell's out of a can," Sally called from inside.

"That would be fine, sir."

That said, the old man sat back and quietly contemplated the meadows for a while. Earl did nothing to hurry him along, figuring that Ed McGriffin would take his own sweet time about things.

The girl, Sally, brought a tray, with a bowl of tomato soup, a few saltines and a glass of Coca-Cola with ice. The old man crunched up the crackers into the soup— Earl saw that his fingers were still clever and firm—and commenced to eat with considerable gusto. Earl had a bowl of soup too, though he passed on the crackers.

When the eating was done, Mr. Ed belched, and Sally came to take the trays away. Then he said, "I now have to pee. You can wait another few minutes, can't you, sir?"

"I sure can."

"Well, I have to say, you're a patient fellow. You don't believe in speeding things along, do you?"

"Things will happen or not, and whether you speed them up don't matter much, I've noticed," Earl said.

"True enough," said the old man. Earl helped him rise and watched as he found his legs, and then stomped inside. A few minutes later he returned.

"Now I won't have to pee for at least another seven, or maybe even eight, minutes. Well, go ahead, then. Speak your piece. I get fellows up here all the time, want to hear about the old days or want me to dictate stories to some magazine or other. That what you want, young fellow? I do have to levy a small fee, you understand. Milk money."

"No, sir," said Earl. "I think I'm up on what you've done. I do have an offer, however." And he told him who he was, who he knew, and what he wanted.

When he was done, the old man sighed. Then he said, "You say it's up a river. Now, how the hell is an old coot like me going to get up a river? I can't sit still in a boat, I have to pee every three seconds, I can't run, much less climb stairs or dig a hole. I can't even paint a house no more, and I made my living painting houses."

"But you can still shoot, I'd bet. As good as ever."

"Probably," the old man said. "I'd say it's like riding a bicycle. Once you learn, you don't never forget."

"Can you still throw five glass balls in the air, draw and hit all five double-action before they hit the ground?"

"Before they hit the ground? Hell, boy, I can hit them before they reach apogee. Maybe now the fifth ball would be in descent when I pinged it, but none of them would touch the planet whole again."

"That's what I thought. And five shots in a two-inch group at twenty-five feet in less than four-fifths a second?"

"I reckon. If not that exact, close enough so's no one would note the difference without electric timing gear. Say, seven-eighths a second. I always could shoot a Smith .38 right dandy."

"I'd imagine practice had a bit to do with it."

"It's better to be talented than to be a hard worker. But to be a talented hard worker, that's the best combo, son."

"Many a man has said you are the best revolver shooter who ever lived, bar none."

"That may be so. I try not to dwell on it now that the end of the journey has been glimpsed."

"Do you wish you'd been around in the days when

the Earps and the Clantons ruled, when Billy and Bat and Wild Bill were the fancy Dans? You'd have been better than them all."

"And then I'd be famous? Someone might have made a movie about me and gotten it all wrong, and then cheated me out of my money. So I've done all right, I suppose. But yes, now and then, a little part of me wishes that just once I'd gone up against a bad man for all the stakes. Now you offer me a chance, but it's too late. Maybe five years ago. Three even. But as you can see, I'm not vigorous no more."

"Well, here's the funny part. Everything I told you was true, and we are going to go in come dark of moon and set it right. And you will be able to go along if you so choose."

"Son, I—"

"Mr. McGriffin, I have a way. It's a new way, ain't nobody hardly never thought of before. I'll get you into that town no more tuckered than if you'd taken a Sunday walk in the park. High and dry, too. And I'll match you against some bad boys who think that their guns are the loudest. You will prevail. You may not survive, but you will prevail. And if you do survive, I'll get you back just as high and dry as I got you in. And you'll be on your way, and you'll be able to consider your life as complete. You will have done all the things a man of the gun can do, including the most important: using that gun in service to justice."

"Mr. Swagger, I'd never call a man who won the Medal of Honor a liar, but unless they build a railroad track into that swamp in less than three weeks, I'm stuck here."

So Earl told him.

"Well, you've figured it out right pretty."

"You've figured it out right pretty but for one thing,"

came the voice of the girl. She walked into the porch from the living room, where she'd evidently been sitting, and listening. "That one thing is me."

"Ma'am?" said Earl.

"Now Sally," said old Ed, "don't get your back up."

"Sir," Sally said to Earl, her features bunched and her eyes forceful, "if you think I'm going to let this fine old fellow travel all that way by himself, you must have left your head in Buffalo Bend, or wherever it is you come from. He only has me in this world, and I only have him, and if he's going on some fool trip of adventure, you'd best believe I'm coming too, and I won't hear another word or there'll be trouble. I may look frail but I pack a punch."

"Sweetie," said Earl, "you'd be stuck down in a farmhouse with a bunch of old fellows, none of whom has a tenth the grace and manners of your grandpap here. I can't think it would be pleasant."

"And who'll cook for this geezer crusade?"

"Ma'am, it'll mostly be beans and franks."

"Well, I know ten ways to cook beans and ten ways to cook franks, and someone has to mulch grandpap's food and make sure he don't wander off. I will go with grandpap or grandpap will go nowhere, and that is the truth. And you had better adjust to that now, or you will be an unhappy fellow for some time to come."

"When Sally speaks, what she declares is usually what happens," said McGriffin.

Earl shook his head.

"You won't have a fun time. It ain't a party."

"I can handle myself," she said, and as she was Ed McGriffin's granddaughter, Earl knew she spoke the truth.

39

It was a snitch who told Bigboy first, and he just laughed. But then another snitch told him, and this time it wasn't so much fun. The third time he heard, it began to sound ominous. So naturally he went to see the warden, who had the keenest insights into Negro psychology of anyone in the world, to have a chat.

"Warden, it's the niggers. You know how you've always said they let us rule them because they have no hope of anything else, and so in the end they come to think such an arrangement is necessary and even right, to save them from themselves."

"Yes, Bigboy, I believe I do. Our enemy is hope and belief. We must crush them because that is our duty. But if they grow, they can grow in wild ways, and bring down the most intricate and stable of edifices."

"There's a disease spreading."

"Yes?"

The two men were in the warden's office on the first floor of the ghastly old house just inside the prison walls. Bigboy actually hated this place, for its smell of rot and corruption, of damask crackling toward dust and wood turning to mush, was faintly sickening. He never understood why a brilliant man like the warden took such pleasure in it. It could have been torn down and the state persuaded to build a more modern structure quite easily. The warden had powerful allies in Jackson, men who knew what he was doing and approved of it heartily. They would want him to be happy, for he was their bulwark, their champion, against the coming of change.

But the warden loved this old place. It held a secret meaning to him that even Bigboy, intelligent in practical ways, could not imagine. So Bigboy sat in the office, sipping port to the flicker of lamps and candles, on a warm summer night, where servants waited just outside of visibility. If you closed your eyes it was 1856 or so, before the convulsion of the War of the Rebellion, when the South stood at the apex of its civilization. Bigboy, not a native Southerner, nevertheless felt the powerful pull the era had for such as the warden and the men who supported him in Jackson. That past was as alive as their gardens, and just as alluring; if it could not be preserved, its memory could nevertheless be preserved, if not enshrined.

"It's the disease of hope," said Bigboy. "They're stirring as they've not stirred before. They have a dream. They have a possibility. They see change coming."

"And what is this hope?"

"It's obscure. I do not know the meaning of it. But I know it's being whispered nigger to nigger, and the whole farm is alive with it. Where it came from, I do not know."

"That is disturbing. Did you know that before the Sepoy Mutiny in India in 1857, chapati cakes were distributed. No one knows how or where or by whom, or what it signified, but it held some inchoate meaning to the natives, and these simple disks of unleavened dough were passed hand to hand to hand. It was an omen, and the British were blind to it. Then came the mutiny, and years of slaughter and rapine. Race war, really, though no one will call it that. The world ended. Or, rather, *a* world ended. Thousands and thousands of lives later, the British reestablished control, but not really. It was all different, and they never had confidence again. Possibly that was the beginning of the fall of the British empire even before they were half done building it, and look at India now. Improved? I think not. The wogs run everything, and everything is running down toward savagery and chaos, as it must when an uncivilized mind assumes charge. Are they better now that they are free of the English? Hardly, and it will get worse. In such a way, will the Negro be better off when he is free of the white man? Of course not. He'll be worse off. There'll be nothing to check his natural tendencies, his infantile but potent sexuality, his commitment to appetite, to instant gratification, his inability to imagine a world of permanence, because he was raised in tropical innocence for a million years, and at some deep conceptual level lacks the imagination to foresee a time without heat and rain and verdant greenery, which is where all his troubles come from. Worse than that, however, is his lust for the white woman, and the progeny that ensues: children with Negro bodies and appetites, with Negro fury, with Negro violence, but as guided by secret white cunning? That is a world I care not to live in, Sergeant Bigboy, and have dedicated my life to preventing. The Negro and the white must never cohabit; only anarchy can follow."

This was a cherished rumination on the part of the warden, and Bigboy had heard it many a time before, but it was delivered with such force, he dared not interrupt.

"My, my, how I *do* go on. You come with a report, I give you a lecture. And you are gentleman enough not to correct me and hold me on track. So, back to this magic message, this hope. How is it expressed?"

"In the following idiom," Bigboy reported. "The words are 'pale horse coming.' They are muttering it among themselves."

"Well, what an unusual turn of phrase," said the warden.

"Mr. Warden, would you know what it means? You know so much, I thought sure you'd know it."

" 'Pale horse coming.' Has a biblical feel to it, doesn't it?"

"It does, Mr. Warden. Is it from the Bible?"

"Possibly. Let me think. But if I tell you what it might mean, that knowledge will corrupt you and taint your own thinking. I prefer before I comment to hear exactly what *you* think it means, Sergeant Bigboy. You are a man of immense sagacity, and your instincts should be trusted. Please tell me. Before we let any fancy learning intrude and occlude things for all time."

"Sir, I think it refers to that fellow, that white fellow, Bogash, we called him Bogart, who was killed trying to escape."

"Yes?"

"He was a tough one. He was a hero. He was an impressive enough boy in his own right, who stood up to 'em in their own jungle and fought them down, all of them. Then he stood up hard to us. In the primitiveness of their minds, they might come to believe he's a messenger from God. Some kind of angel. And as Christ returned from the dead, Mr. Warden, so it seems to me that they could allow themselves to think that he would return from the dead."

"I take it that is not possible."

"It is not."

"Your report was sketchy on details."

"I guarantee you he will not be returning from the dead. Not in three days, not in three years, not in three millennia, not in three *million* years. I guarantee it."

"I trust you. And I think you may be right. The word 'pale' does have religious connotations. We first find it in the Revelation of Saint John, Chapter Six, Verse Eight: 'Behold a pale horse: and his name that sat on him was Death, and Hell followed with him.' "

"Yes."

" 'Pale,' of course, is a logical association with death, for it reflects the pallor of the flesh when having passed, denied of warm blood, marbleizing, calcifying as it breaks down. It's cold, really, and paleness is a feature of the cold. Snow is white, it is pale, it is cold. A pale sky is a chilled sky. We find paleness as death in many places in the western imagination associated with death. Then there's 'and Hell followed them'; yes, I can see how that connection to the Bible would satisfy these desperate, evil men, for they believe that when that pale horse comes, death rides upon it, and in concert horse and rider bring hell to us here in our humble institution. So sayeth Saint John the Revelator."

Bigboy nodded. The warden took another sip of port. There was no stopping him once he got going.

"Mr. Warden, begging your pardon, but do you think a Mississippi nigger here at Thebes would be reading much Saint John?"

"No, indeed, but that is the miracle of the way images move through literature, memory and the imagination. They wouldn't know Revelations from shoofly pie, but they will have met people who have had, and will have communicated not so much the information as the idea. So 'pale' as an expression of death delivered will have forceful meaning to them, even if they know not why."

"Yes, Mr. Warden."

"Keats too was absorbed in paleness as death, but he saw it in the form of extremely competent men, very gifted, capable men. 'I saw pale kings and warriors, too,' he writes, 'pale warriors, death-pale were they all;/They cried 'La Belle Dame sans Merci / hath thee in thrall!' Now what is the meaning of 'La Belle Dame sans Merci,' and what is this thrall she holds over the pale warriors?"

Bigboy had about as much chance of answering this question as he did of flying to Mars. But he understood that it was rhetorical, and so he said nothing.

"Well," the warden answered his own question, "though interpretations vary, I would say the beautiful lady without mercy is that hideous cow, duty. She demands that we give up all for her, she has no mercy on us. In thrall to her we fight, in thrall to her we die. So in this meaning of the phrase, he seems to be predicting the arrival of men of duty, with guns, who want to kill us all, and bring hell to our little part of the earth."

"So you would take this very seriously?"

"Very. Very, indeed."

"Then I will find out where it came from, what it relates to. It will not be pleasant work. You may hear the screams in the night."

"I've learned to sleep through screams in the night. It is necessary sometimes. Our fortunes, our lives, may depend on those screams. Sergeant Bigboy, do what has to be done. Do it fast, do it without mercy. I will not be like the British, slaughtered in my bed because I didn't read the signs. Find out what is going on.

"Meanwhile, I will notify the doctor that we suspect mischief afoot. If he feels threatened, he will conjure the highest powers of the state in self-protection. Our mission is to protect his mission; that is what gives all this nobility as well as necessity."

40

IT was a long flight. It was hard to find a cab. The city was rundown, seedy, like the worst parts of Little Rock, but it had crests of low mountains running through it. The local businesses seemed mostly to be pawn and doughnut shops, though car washes were numerous as well, and restaurants serving what Mexicans ate. But mainly: doughnuts. It was the cake doughnut capital of the universe, Earl thought.

But eventually, he got there, an even more run-down section of town, and he stepped out of the cab, felt the blast of heat, the movement of pedestrian traffic. He glanced about: palms stood, but they were far from the majestic ones he'd seen in the Pacific; these were bent down, brown at the edges, and looked as if they'd breathed in too much automobile exhaust for anybody's good. You could catch cancer from a palm like the sorry specimen that grew crookedly in a patch of dry dirt out here in the flats of an unlovely place called the San Fernando Valley, where Hy Hooper had his gun shop.

In the window it said: HOME OF THE .357 ATOMIC!

Earl shook his head. Instinctively he didn't like California generally, and Los Angeles specifically, its brown hills, its sense of thickness filling the air, like they were burning rubber somewhere nearby, the arid little neighborhoods of bungalow amid burned-out shrubbery, its heat, but most of all: its showiness.

This was where they made the pictures, and Earl didn't like the pictures a bit, except for that John Wayne fellow or one or two other cowboy-style heroes. He could never remember their names. But there was something sinister about the picture business, and it seemed to have been reflected all through the Los Angeles he'd just traveled, and here it was again: THE .357 ATOMIC! What the hell would that be but some slightly jacked-up .357 Magnum, which had been around since '35, but now some slick boy was trying to make it showy by connecting it with the atom bomb!

Yet this is where he had to go. Grudgingly, carrying his valise, straightening his fedora, he stepped in. He found himself in what might be called more showiness yet: a cavern of guns.

There were guns everywhere. Unlike other gun stores, where the guns were in display cabinets, in this one they lay there, but not only there; hundreds, it seemed, had been mounted on the walls, and as Earl looked up, he saw that the guns rose to and spangled the ceiling as well. The low firmament was filled with cheap break-top .32s and .38s from the first part of the century, most of them looking unshootable and unsafe.

"Sort of takes your breath away, doesn't it?" asked the man behind the counter, who was florid and heavy-set, with his hair slicked back. He had a cowboy belt on, much carved, with an elaborate silver buckle, and his khakis were cowboy-style as was his shirt, which had some kind of floral inscriptions on the chest. He wore a white Stetson and had a car-salesman's smile to him.

"Quite a few guns, I'd say," said Earl.

"And you'd be Earl Swagger, I'm guessing. You look like someone who could handle one of these things."

"Yes sir, I am. Mr. Hooper?"

"I am that, sir. Please, it's an honor to shake the hand of a Medal of Honor winner."

He reached and Earl complied.

"You'd be surprised who drops by here once in a while. Why, just the other day I had a nice chat with Marsh Williams. You know him?"

"Fellow that designed the carbine?"

"Designed in *prison* no less. How's that for genius. He was up for manslaughter in North Caroline. To keep his mind free he concentrated on guns, which he knew well, and that way he figured out a way to get a semiauto into a much tinier amount of space than anything before. Six million M-1 carbines later, he's a national hero. They say they're going to do a picture about Marsh, with Jimmy Stewart."

"Won't that be a thing," said Earl.

"Did you carry a carbine, Mr. Swagger?"

"No, Mr. Hooper. I was a tommy gun man. We did a lot of up-close work, and I liked the thump of the Thompson. I didn't mind a little extra weight for the extra thump. But you can bet a lot of our boys did. It was a right handy little number."

Earl would keep his actual opinion of the carbine to himself.

"Then, Mr. John Wayne. I'm trying to get him to carry our .357 Atomic in his next Western picture. That'd really move them off the shelves. But you didn't come to talk about picture stars, did you, Mr. Swagger?"

"Only the one I wrote you about, Mr. Hooper."

"Well, like I told you on the phone, I know him well, and he's a fine young man. He's a wonderful young man, though he has a touch of that Irish melancholy to him. But I called him, and gave him the invite, and maybe he'll show and maybe he won't."

The youngest of the old men, but also the oldest, was late, of course. But not by much. Earl watched him arrive. He pulled up in some bright English sports car, red as blood, gleaming and slick. He wore sunglasses, a cowboy hat, an elaborate gentleman cowboy rig of buckskin coat and pressed dungarees, a white shirt with pearl buttons and a string tie, and finally a pair of handmade, three-hundred-dollar boots. He looked like somebody playing at being a grown-up and the grown-up he was playing at being was Hoot Gibson.

He came in shyly, and Earl could sense reticence in him. He wasn't one of those fellows, like Hooper here, who grew larger in the presence of others. He grew smaller, waiflike, lost.

"Well, Audie," said Hy Hooper, "I'm glad you dropped by. This fellow's come a long way to meet you. He's one of your own kind."

Even in his sunglasses, Audie Ryan wouldn't look at Earl. The older, larger man's presence seemed to have him unhinged a bit. There was quite a war going on between the California fancy cowboy swagger of his style, and the pale, diffident boy it concealed. Finally, he took off his glasses, and Earl saw almost a gal's eyes, soft and gentle and sensitive and a face startling in its beauty.

Hard to believe this little perfect angel was the most decorated soldier of the Second World War and had killed close to three hundred Germans, at least fifty of whom he got with a .50-caliber machine gun atop a burning tank destroyer as they came in to wipe out his unit and break out into our lines. He killed them all, and single-handedly drove back the tanks in support, and was given the Medal of Honor for that day's work, which was only one of many good days he'd had across Europe.

"Major Ryan," said Earl, "I'm Earl Swagger, sir. It's an honor to meet you."

Audie Ryan smiled shyly, embarrassed. He almost giggled to be reminded of the rank at which he left the Army in 1946.

"Gee, Sarge," he said, "nobody's called me 'Major' in five years. It's just Audie. And I didn't do anything you didn't do, Sarge, from what I hear, so the honor's just as much mine as it is yours."

"I think we were both lucky bastards," said Earl, "and the real heroes didn't make it back."

"If I had a drink, I'd drink to that, as that's the truest thing I've heard in months."

He had a soft accent from his native Texas, in whose northwest corner he'd grown up hardscrabble and poor, where it was his rifle alone that put meat on the table for a large, fatherless family. He learned to shoot well and early, and in the war his hunter's skills had paid their dividends.

"So, Sarge, Hy tells me you've got some sort of proposition or something?"

"That's right," said Earl.

"Say, fellows," said Hy Hooper, "why don't you step on back and use the office."

He led them back, and in the little room the heads of various beasts killed the world over stared at him. It reminded Earl of his father's study; his father had been a mighty hunter, too.

"You haven't got the buffalo back yet, Hy?" Audie asked.

"No, it takes a bit. I got back from Africa some weeks ago," Hy explained to Earl. "Took some fine trophies, including an eighty-four-inch horn-spread Cape Buffalo."

"Wow," said Earl.

"Yep, proudest moment of my life, and listen to me talking about what *I'm* proud of in the presence of two men who've won the Medal of Honor. I ought to be skinned alive. I'm butting out. You go ahead. There's Scotch and bourbon in the desk."

He scurried out.

Audie Ryan, still a little nervous, poured himself a finger of bourbon and offered it to Earl.

"I gave it up soon after the war," said Earl.

"I should give it up. But if I don't, I see Germans," Audie said, downing the brown fluid and quickly replenishing it.

"I still see the Japs everywhere."

"It never goes away, does it?"

"No, it doesn't. And everybody forgets."

"What I hate most of all is, they think they want to know about it. And they ask about it. But it turns out they really don't want to know about it. What they want to do is tell *you* about it. They know more'n you."

"I get that, too. It does grow heavy on the shoulder."

"This town is the worst. This picture business was probably a mistake, but since I can't hardly read, and these people think I'm a cutie pie, I guess it's what I'm stuck doing. It's a stinking business, though. Everybody lies, everybody just wants to git ahead, they'll do any damn thing. New York people run everything, and they talk so fast you can't hardly understand them. But you get along with them or you don't work. And so much waiting. I may get a big picture made by John Huston. You ever hear of him, Sarge?"

"Can't say I have."

"Maybe it's that other one, John Ford. Always get them two mixed up, which could hurt me bad. Whichever, it's a war picture. But the Civil War, based on some old book. Of course, they can't *really* show a war. They make it all pretty and heroic."

"That it sure wasn't."

"So anyhow, don't suppose you care much about the picture business, Sarge, do you?"

"The truth is, it seems silly. A man who's done what you've done, out here with these showy people."

"The truth is, it is silly. The truth is, I am sick to death of it all right, but stuck to it forever, I suppose. So if you have something to propose, I am all ears. I need a vacation from my vacation."

"Well, Major Ryan—"

"Audie. Everybody calls me Audie. The Mexican boys who fill up the tank on my MG call me Audie."

"Audie, then. Well, Audie, can't say why you'd say yes to this here thing. It may be sillier than the picture shows. It may even get you killed, and it don't make no sense at all. I don't even know why I'm doing it, except somehow something's got to be set right and nobody nohow no way is interested in doing it. It's gun work, maybe heavy, and you and I both know that you can do everything right and take no chances at all in that game, and still some little piece of metal's going to bounce off a doorknob and park between your eyes."

"I do. Meanwhile, some guy who never takes cover doesn't get a scratch."

"That's it."

"Well, at least I could git some sleep then. You have trouble sleeping, Sarge?"

"Every goddamned night. First year I's back, I almost blowed a hole in my head. Held the gun up to it, pulled the trigger, and the gun went snap. I'd forgotten to jack a shell into the chamber. Never forgot that in my life since, so I guess my number wasn't up that day."

"I think about it every goddamn night. A few drinks, get the fancy Peacemaker out that Colt's gave me when I toured the plant one time, spin the cylinder a few times, and then at least I wouldn't think about Lattie and Joe and what happened to them. I'd be with them. So go on, tell me."

Earl told him. Told it all, start to finish, up to whom he'd recruited and who he still meant to see, how it would be done, when it would be done.

"Old men," Audie noted.

"All of 'em 'cept you."

"I can see why."

"That's right. Don't care to see any more young fellows die. These boys have all laid with their women and had their kids and written their articles and gotten ever last thing to be got out of life. If they pass, so be it. But it would a shame if you did."

"Ah, well," said Audie.

"They can all shoot, so they don't have to be trained. I can't waste no time on training. But I need one other fellow who's been in action, and who won't panic if we run into heavy automatic fire. They need to look and see someone cool and collected. I also need someone fast as I have it figured out. Who can get from place to place as needed. I can get each boy where he's supposed to be and get him started, but if it gets heavy at some place, I need someone sharp to bounce over there fast."

Audie poured himself another drink.

"As I said," Earl went on, "you'd be a fool to do this. You can stay in this town and make these pictures and lay with all these starlet gals and be the toast of America. Have a house with a pool, a fancy sports car, wear them expensive boots. Don't know why you'd risk that."

A faraway look played over Audie's delicate features. He sat back beneath a buck's princely head, in his grown-up cowboy outfit, and his eyes focused on something not there. Earl knew where he was. Back in the little ruined towns and the snowy fields, up the heartbreaking, back-breaking ridges and hills, fording the cold, cold rivers, sleeping in mud and shit, hunting men in gray who hunted back.

"Oh, boy," he finally said, "it sure beats waiting around for some New York fellow to call you and say you got the picture."

"Maybe at least it'll give you some new nightmares," said Earl.

"Hey, I like that," said Audie. "Sarge, you know. Yep, sign me up. I need new nightmares to replace the old ones."

BUT that wasn't Earl's only stop in Los Angeles. He had one more, a brick warehouse building back over the low rims of hills in a part of town near to, but not officially part of, Hollywood. The cabbie dropped him and volunteered to stay, because he knew Earl'd never find another one in this godforsaken patch of nowhere. Earl thanked the guy, and said he didn't think it would take too long.

In he stepped, to air-conditioning, and to a grim foyer of a greenish unpleasant place, where a girl was behind a desk, and behind her many men in ties but not coats worked phones hard.

Earl had called ahead; he was expected.

"Mr. Swagger?"

"That's it."

His fellow was his own age, with the beaten look of too many disappointments. Thinning hair, glasses, no tan, grubby fingernails from a lot of ballpoint work.

Earl sat at his desk in the bull pen.

"Now I can make you quite a deal. You've hit it just right."

"That's what I understand."

"The studios have switched over to newer stock. Modern stuff, easier to care for, no disintegration."

"I see."

"So right now there's a glut of the old stuff. Our market is usually TV stations who'll run this stuff for kids, fill out their programming. They call them old-time movies. Ever hear of Johnny Coons, Uncle Johnny, in Chicago? That's all he does, and he banks a fortune."

"No, sir."

"You're from the South."

"Yes, sir. My people would like old-time cowboy pictures, is my belief. None of this new stuff. They don't care about new stars. They want the old."

"Well, sir, I can put a package together for you, probably for under a thousand? Is that the budget area you're looking for? I'm not sure how much your chain has to spend."

"I was thinking more like half that."

"Five. I can work with five. I'll throw some extra in, because I like you."

"You're a fine man."

"Not really. Okay, let's see, I think I could do Hoppy. Lots of Hoppy. Hoppy's still big in the South, I'd bet. Hoppy's moving to TV and so nobody's going to pay to see him on-screen when they can see him on the television. You like Hoppy? *Hoppy Sees a Ghost. Hoppy and the Riders of the Purple Sage. Hoppy and the Indians. Hoppy and the Mystery of the Bar X Ranch.*"

"I like Hoppy. Hoppy is fine."

"If you want to go back further, I have Hoot Gibson, Tom Mix, Buck Jones, John Wayne as Sandy the Singing Cowboy, though he can't carry a tune to save his life. What about Gene Autry?"

"Gene can sing."

"Yes, he can. Also, I've got some old William S. Hart. Have you ever heard of him? A little before your time, I'd guess."

" 'Fraid so."

"Well, sir, you'd like it. Your audience might see it as a novelty. Real 'pure' stuff, you know. Not fancy like it later became."

"Yes, sir. Throw that in, too."

A deal was struck. Earl bought the exclusive rights to exhibit a package of one hundred prewar Western movies, for less than five hundred dollars in an area of Arkansas, Mississippi and Louisiana. The films themselves were part of that deal and would be shipped to the address Earl specified. It was understood that if he wanted to show them on the television, he'd have to pay a further royalty.

"Doubt I'll be showing them on television," he said, signing on the dotted line. "Ain't no television yet where I operate."

"Take advantage of that while you can, sir. The television will change the face of our business, I guarantee you."

"I believe you are right."

After the papers were dispatched, and the check written and handed over, his representative had a grand statement to sum it all up: "Sir, you are the inheritor of the myth of the American West. You should be very proud."

"I hope I can live up to it," Earl said.

41

SAM sat in the medical school library at Fayetteville. He was completely puzzled. He was still studying the fabulous career of the fabulous David Stone, M.D., M.S., Ph.D., Maj., U.S.A.M.C., beloved humanitarian, disease battler the world over, and he was wondering: Where is the research?

Perhaps he had misunderstood. Perhaps Dr. Stone wasn't a researcher. Perhaps Sam didn't quite connect with the protocols of a complex, high-level medical career such as the late or possibly late doctor had enjoyed.

But for whatever reason, the man simply had ceased to exist after 1936, at least on paper. Before then, as the mountain of books before him on the table of the reading room testified, he'd been everywhere, stunning the world with the brilliance of his research. He was in the *Journal of the American Medical Association* four times, he was twice in the *New England Journal of Medicine,* he was twice in *Lancet,* the British medical publication, and he was once each in a series of regional medical publications or publications devoted to specific diseases or specialties, such as blood, eyes, upper respiratory, virology and so forth and so on. Judging by the letters his pieces always generated, he was a brilliant researcher.

And then . . . silence.

And this was well before he entered the Army, before whatever happened to him or he happened to in Mississippi.

Well, it was not quite silence. It was the doctor who disappeared, that is to say, the research physician in desperate small countries the world over. That man vanished. The Dr. Stone everybody knew and loved did not disappear at all; if anything, he had flourished, and if anything, the glory wall in his widow's apartment only told the half of it.

In the popular press, he continued to thrive, and the *Reader's Guide* yielded citations in the *Washington Times-Herald*, the *Baltimore Sun*, the *Los Angeles Times*, *P.M.*, *Collier's* and *Newsweek*. He even got a 1938 spread in *Life*, where in his pith helmet, with his beautiful wife by his side, he was in the slums of Bangkok in a country called Siam surrounded by beautiful and not so beautiful little yellow people. The story described how he'd advised the Red Cross on a clinic and spent six months there working with the poorest of the poor, the most wretched of the wretched, all in the name of humanity and science. But details were scanty.

And none of this, moreover, had a thing to do with some installation in the wilds of Maryland about which, in all his learnings, Sam had not uncovered a single thing. What was done at Ft. Dietrich to have them so interested in what was done at Thebes State Penal Farm (Colored)? There was no evidence of a thing.

Sam had a headache and a dead end.

He couldn't call the widow who now hated and despised him, particularly since she'd blurted out her hideous secret (he knew how the human heart worked), and he'd exhaustively worked the War Department, the Medical Corps, the American Medical Association and the American Virology Association, having burned out those bridges, or having them burned out by those industrious boys from HUAC.

Where could he go?

He realized he had but one course open, and it was a tedious one. He had to try and find the names of Stone's 1928 Harvard Medical School graduating class. Then he had to call them. Every one of them. Sooner or later, he'd find one who had known Stone well, or so it seemed. Sooner or later, he'd find one who'd talk. Sooner or later. But he realized there were only a few weeks left till the dark of the moon, so he hoped it would be sooner rather than later.

He wished he believed in what he was doing a little more fervently.

42

THE two men sat at the back table in the dark cavern known as Pablo's Cantino, in the city of El Paso, another long flight from the last destination.

Earl watched them. How they ate expressed their deep personalities. One was feisty, quick, full of aggression, hungry for sensation. He devoured his food. To him, life was a picnic of Mexican vittles, a profusion of spices to be sampled for flavor, then devoured. More controlled, the other man sat glumly, picking at his plate, a giant of control and taciturnity; he looked like a minister at an orgy.

"Fellas," said Earl.

"Well, goddamn, Sergeant Swagger, didn't know you'd be bringing my old friend Bill along," said the feisty fellow, who was a former border patrol officer named Charlie Hatchison. He was wiry, peppery, loud, and couldn't sit still. His sharp eyes darted everywhere on constant patrol, and it was a problem for him to keep a smirk off his face, for what one sensed most immediately about Charlie Hatchison was the pleasure he took in being Charlie Hatchison.

"Bill's quite a feller," he went on maniacally, "and if it's action upcoming, damned if I don't want to stick close to old Bill, on account he'll git me through it, right, Bill?" Charlie was a needler. He liked to prick at people. Everybody was a challenge to him, and he was always looking for ways to bring people down a notch or two.

Bill Jennings was his opposite, lanky and solemn. His face was like a melted puddle of bronze, hardened, then tempered. It never changed expression, not even slightly. It was the dullest face anybody had ever seen. To most men, that epic mug with its message of violence contained was enough. People surrendered to him in legendary numbers, and that exactly was the bone of contention between the two men. Charlie Hatchison, in a life on the border in the twenties and thirties, had killed seventeen men in gunfights, and had savored every one of them. Bill Jennings, an author and renowned fast gun, who'd performed revolver tricks on *What's My Line?,* had killed no one. Charlie was not famous, though he'd won the national bull's-eye competition four times in the thirties, and Bill Jennings was, though he'd never won a thing.

"Yes, sir," said Charlie, "see heah, if'n I git in a jam,

you know, why I just pull out a copy of Bill's book *Second Place Is No Place,* and I look up my situation in the index, flip to the pages listed, and damnation, hellfire and brimstone, it'll tell me what to do!"

It was quite a show. Charlie liked being noticed. He expected to be at the center of attention, and when he wasn't he grew surly and restless.

Finally, Bill spoke, though quite slowly.

"Y'all probably think I *put* that burr up Charlie's butt. Fact is, he's *born* that way. Passing strange, but that's how it is. Pay him no mind, and he'll quieten eventually."

Charlie laughed.

"You can't git Bill's goat, 'cause he done *strangled* the goat some years back. You can call him *anything* and he just looks at you with them dead eyes and you feel the Lord's presence, beckoning you forward to them pearly gates."

It was true. Bill Jennings looked like death in the tall grass, with that lanky frame, those long arms and big hands and that eerie calm, while Charlie looked like a traveling salesman for a snake-oil company.

"Hell, he *is* deadly. Why, between us we killed seventeen men," Charlie laughed.

"What I am offering the two of you," said Earl, "is something hard to come by. It's what you want. It's the best thing for gunmen, and the world is changing so much it's going to be gone soon, or at least gone in the way I'm offering it. I'm talking about action."

"I will drink to action," said Charlie, throwing up a tequila and downing it neat. "Gittin' close to the worm," he said, indicating the gross object that floated in the bottle.

"It's all changing," said Earl. "If you have to put a man down in the line of duty, you got lawyers and bureaucrats and newspaper reporters barking at you, you got those in the community calling you trigger-happy, you ain't a hero no more, you're some kind of outcast. And you got reports. You got endless paperwork and talks with the prosecutors and justifying and interpreting and figuring it all out."

"That is true," said Bill Jennings.

"Bill, haw!, you wouldn't know if it was true or not. You done fought more with your face than with your gun hand!"

Bill's face remained placid, overly affected by gravity, all its many lines vertical, his eyes dull as mud. If a flicker of distaste flashed through them, only Earl noticed; or maybe it was a trick of light.

"I never filed no reports on the seventeen I got," said Charlie. "Some was Mex, and of course you never would bother with paper on them. But even the white boys, like that Perry Jefferson, I done perforated him like a piece of cheese with my Browning 5 with the duck-bill spreader all loaded up with blue whistlers, wooo-eeee, what a mess, but he's as white as white can be, and nobody gave no two shits about him, 'cause he's bootlegger trash from Dallas, carrying heavy guns with him ever which way. Sent him to his maker and was proud of it. Bill, now you tell the hero sergeant here 'bout your best action and the aftermath."

Bill ate a tamale.

"Well," said Earl, "let me tell you what I have going. Then you decide if you're in or not."

"I'm in," said Charlie. "Tell you that right now. Bill's in too, 'cause he don't never want it said Charlie H. done something he's afraid to do. His book might not sell no more."

"Bill, you're still serving law enforcement. What I'm setting up is technically against the law."

"Never let the law git in the way of a good fight, right, Bill?" said Charlie. "Hell, on the border we'd cross and gun them bad boys who's gunning for us. It was them or us in them wide-open days, and we's serving justice first, survival second and the law maybe dead last."

"Bill, I—"

"Hell, just say your piece," said Bill.

So Earl just said it. Said it all, as he had with the others, while Charlie, if he listened at all, paid more attention to setting the worm in the bottle free, and Bill ate another tamale.

"That's it," said Earl. "So now it's your play."

"You know what, Earl," said Charlie, "truth is I never had much use for your colored folk. That's how I feel. So don't look for me to hold no hands and do no holy-rolling. But you're offering something money can't buy, and that's kills. I got me seventeen and figure on notching up my gun a few more times before I pass. So if I don't got to lollygaggle no niggers, but just do some serious gun work, count me in, like I said."

Earl turned to Bill, knowing that the big man had a lot to lose on this job, but was rewarded with a nod, almost imperceptible. Bill of course would remain silent on his motives, his dreams, his aspirations. Palaver wasn't for him. You'd just have to tell him where and when, and if he said he'd make the party, by God, the party he would make.

Earl finished with his last details.

"I'll give each of you five hundred dollars in cash. With that I want you to finance your travel and your guns. You travel to Tallahassee on September 5 and buy the newspaper. In the personals, there'll be an ad selling a nineteen thirty-two Ford motorcar for six hundred dollars."

"Hell, Earl, nobody pay six hundred dollars for a nineteen thirty-two Ford."

"Well, exactly. So you call that number, and I'll tell you where you come to the next day."

"Ah."

"You travel separately. You don't swagger or make friends or buy drinks or let no one buy you drinks. You dress for hunting, not fighting."

"Bring our guns?"

"No. Certainly nothing duty-issued where your serial number is recorded, or anything that can be identified as yours. Also, nothing military. Bring sporting arms only. I'd go to the pawnshop and pick me up a good rifle, say a lever gun, and a pair of .38s or .357s. If you want to shoot .45 or you have an old Luger or something, that's fine. But don't bring nothing you'd be afraid to leave in a swamp. Don't bring Billy the Kid's Lightning, if you happen to own it."

"Hell, I got so many old guns I don't need to go to no pawnshop. I must have three hundred of the goddamn things," said Charlie.

"You travel low-key without no fuss. You're hunters, traveling to the field. Got that?"

"Got it."

"We'll be there just a while. Then we'll move, have our fun, and move out, all in a single night, fast and mean and loud. Then you never talk about this no more. Is that agreed?"

"It is," said Charlie, and Bill nodded, again imperceptibly.

Earl slid the two envelopes over, and each was quietly slipped away.

"That's fine."

"Y'all drink a toast with me now," said Charlie.

"Believe I will," Bill finally said.

"I'm on the wagon. I'll drink this here Coca-Cola, if you don't mind."

"Suit yourself," said Charlie, throwing himself another shot of tequila, then throwing one to Bill.

The three glasses came up.

"Learned this one in France," said Charlie. "It seems to fit right nice here in Pablo's. Haw! *Vive la guerre, vive la mort, vive le mercenaire!*"

43

THE warden sent a man to Sheriff Leon Gattis, requesting that worthy's fastest presence. The sheriff, who'd essentially been created by the warden, came apace.

He tied his horse at the rail outside the great house within the old brick wall. He tried not to look at the ruin of the Whipping House off in a grove of palmettos and palms, for he knew the purpose of it and it filled him with unease. In fact, the prison itself made him a mite nervous. That WORK MAKES YOU FREE arched over the entrance; what was that? It was familiar somehow, but the sheriff couldn't place it. Then that place called the Screaming House, off by the river, where the convicts said you went, you screamed, and you never came back again. The sheriff shuddered ever so slightly.

Also, the Negro women lined up to get into the Store for their week's ration of food and goods were not a welcoming sight. The women were surly, hangdog, defeated. They hadn't the sass of your average colored gal; none of them looked to be much fun in the hay, and that was generally where your nigger gal outshined her white counterpart. These gals looked hungry and scurvy, like someone had just let them down off the rack after applying the cattail ten or twenty times. They had no light in their eyes, no laughter in their primitive souls, though one or two, the sheriff could not help but notice, had nice sets of jugs wobbling loose under their sack dresses.

A trustee, old nigra-style, admitted the sheriff, who stomped his boots clean before entering the great house. Inside, he hit that same wall of ancient smell: dust, rot, the damp cool of mildew, a significant temperature reduction, the whole thing out of a South that only existed in the movies and there with no exactness to it. Daylight at least meant there was no need for candles or lanterns, which turned the place even ghostlier. The old trustee, moving as if his spine were fused into a solid pole and each step a pain, took him to the warden's office, knocked, opened and admitted him.

There the great man sat, alone at his desk, working hard. He held up a hand in pause, as if to suggest his concentration was so mighty it could not be breached, and thereby held the sheriff frozen at the door. A big clock ticktocked as the second hand loafed along. Books, portraits of old gentlemen of fine breeding, Southern pastoral scenes in oil, a rack of fine rifles, the state flag of Mississippi all filled the place with color and detail.

Finally, with a flourish, the warden finished up whatever it was he was writing with a fountain pen, pressed a roller across the pages to dry the ink, then carefully removed the document to a desk drawer and permitted himself to look up.

"Why, Sheriff Leon, how kind of you to join me upon such short notice."

There was no chance in hell that the sheriff would not obey a summons *immediately*, but it was the warden's preference to proceed by the old Southern ways of politeness. He was a polite man, as if he believed that politeness, chivalry, the rules of society, were all that separated him and his kind from the niggers.

"Yes, sir, it is my pleasure."

"Do sit down. Join me in a glass of sherry?"

"Sir, may I be frank?"

"Of course, Sheriff Leon."

"Sherry would not be to my likin'. My people never had no sherry, and so I never grew a taste for it."

"I have some fine sour mash bourbon."

"Sir, that would make this old dog a happy dog indeed."

"And I'll join you, Leon, if you don't mind."

"Yes, sir. I'd be proud if you would."

The ceremony of the drinks, quite elaborate, unfolded, and in a few minutes each man had returned to his respective seat, though now each was armed with two fingers of neat brown fluid.

"That is a fine batch," said the sheriff, after a taste.

"It is indeed," said the warden.

"Now, how may I be of assistance?"

"I have read your report over and over, Leon, about the Arkansas lawyer who escaped."

"Yes, sir."

"You recommended that the situation be looked into?"

"Yes, sir."

"In my wisdom, I thought it wise to let sleeping dogs lie. That is to say, my thought was that as he had not seen our institution he only had a confused picture of what he would have dismissed as 'typical Southern methods,' unlikely to bestir the world at large. There was furthermore the issue of the fellow involved with

him, whom we felt we had to learn more about. Alas, he
is no longer with us."

"Yes, sir."

"Now, Leon, that was my judgment. Leon, it was the
wrong judgment. I am not averse to acknowledging my
failures. You were right, Leon, I was wrong."

"Sir, you ain't hardly ever wrong about nothing. You
done got this county and your prison set up just fine,
and we all the better off fo' it, with good jobs, money in
the bank, bread and vittles on the table, and a solid future. You have done things down here that have—"

The warden let Leon lick his boots for several moments, though he didn't much enjoy it. But finally, when
the fellow was done groveling, he continued.

"Now, Leon, I will tell you very confidentially that
something is astir among the convicts. They are muttering about a deliverance. In their primitive minds, God is
gathering the righteous to strike, riding in on a pale
horse of retribution. Do you know a thing about it?"

"No, sir. Not a thing."

"Of course not. I do not believe this has a thing to do
with that lawyer. I cannot in my mind work out a chain
which would in some way not merely involve him, but
more to the point, permit the knowledge of his engagement to return here and boil up my black wards. It
doesn't make sense at all, does it?"

"No, sir, it don't. But—"

"Yes?"

"But, well, wouldn't it be safer, just in case—?"

"Exactly, Leon. Exactly. You read my mind and you
help me correct my misjudgment. We must make certain
we are not under threat. We have our responsibilities. I
have a great charge which must be protected. We have
the doctor to think about, our country, our society. I

have some latitude in these matters, and know that if one acts, one must act decisively."

"I know a fella in N'Awleens who's very clever at gizmos. The gangsters there and throughout the South used him, and though many knew of him, he was never caught, on the simple reason that whatever acts he engineered by their very nature precluded much in the way of investigation. Hell, how do you investigate a hole in the damn ground?"

"How, indeed? The answer is, you don't."

"I have the contacts. I could arrange a package be delivered up to Arkansas. It would not be sent from Mississippi at all, and would have nothing to do with Mississippi, much less Thebes. It would look like any other package."

"Hmmm, well thought out."

"When it is opened by this here lawyer, they won't be nothing left but smoke and bonemeal floating in the air, and there'll be a new crater in the middle of Arkansas. This fellow could do that up right good."

"Yes, I like that," said the warden. "That would settle matters nicely, indeed. That would make all of us happy, and I would feel that my responsibilities—Leon, you have no idea the world of weight I carry on my shoulders—would have been well lived up to."

"I'll do it, warden. You are a great man, and I feel ever so good when I can serve you."

"There is a great man here, Leon, but it isn't me. I am but a humble servant. The great man is that doctor who works by the river, where he is saving our country."

44

SAILORS everywhere. Earl did not like sailors. It was nothing personal. It was just that the Navy was always the daddy to the Marine Corps, and was always lording it over the Corps. That unease of relationship came through especially during the war in the Pacific, where Earl believed that no island was bombed or shelled enough before the Marines had to land on it, no ship got in close enough to get the wounded to safety fast enough, no supplies arrived soon enough, and on and on and on, a whole symphony of grudges.

So Earl did not like Pensacola, for it was full of sailors. They were everywhere, and now and then jets roared overhead or old prop jobs blew by in low formation, for Pensacola was a Navy town, as Navy a town as existed anywhere, and its particular form of the Navy was naval aviation.

So he bit down on his distaste and went about his business, though it was hard, for in the years before the war, there'd been too many occasions when he and his pals and sailors had found the fit in this or that port city bar too tight, and fists had flown. He'd learned as much about fighting there as he had under the mentorship of the old sergeants who'd coached him when he was fighting for the service in the late thirties in the Pacific fleet.

Earl knew he wouldn't get into any fights because he no longer went into bars. Where he went instead was into a bank, where he deposited a large sum and opened a checking account under the name John R. Bogash. Then he went to a real estate agency, and there had an earnest conversation with an agent.

He was, the story he made up went, looking for a quiet place where he could park a while with his very sick father, so that that old man's passing could be comfortable in the warmth and sun, rather than in the chill of up North. The father had been in the Navy, and it always cheered him to see the boys in their white uniforms parading down the street; and he liked airplanes, and as he sat on his porch waiting for the end, it would do him good to see the trim Navy aircraft practicing their skills overhead.

Did Earl want seaside?

Earl did not want seaside. Too much traffic seaside. People going to the beach and all. Someplace in the country would be nice, possibly with some room, for the dying old man was fond of his dogs, too, and wanted to be with his and watch them roam.

Well, the real estate agent made some calls, and soon enough he located a series of farms that were available. So off they went. This was always wrong, and that was always wrong, as they ranged ever farther northward, almost to the Alabama line, and the agent thought he'd lose his client to a competitor from Brewton, up in 'bama. But Earl eventually took a particular shine to a certain place, which lay at the end of a mile of dirt road, its fields fallow, its barn in need of paint, its general maintenance feeble.

The agent was somewhat baffled as to why Earl made such a big deal about the size of the near field, for he hadn't got the impression much from Earl that that was necessary. But Earl looked hard at the field, then peered at the location of the place on the map. But it was far and private and exactly what Earl had in mind, and so a check changed hands and in two days, when the check cleared, Earl took over the lease for the next six months.

"Hope you and your daddy are happy out here, Mr. Bogash," said the agent.

"This place'll make Daddy right happy, I guarantee it," Earl said.

That done, he spent the next few days setting up. This involved, of course, notifying the phone company to get the phone hooked up, but once that was done, it was mainly rounding up supplies, but never overbuying in a single store. Though if you looked, you might have been surprised to find that in each of ten gun stores in northwest Florida, and in Alabama, in towns such as Brewton and Bluff Spring and Atmore, then all the way over to Crestview and Milton, then as far west as the larger city of Mobile, which had three gun stores and pawnshops, and as far up as Greenville, five boxes of .38–44 high-velocity police cartridges had been sold. The fellows would bring their own rifle ammo, but Earl had to provide for himself, so in each of the stores he picked up something for the long gun he'd determined to carry, which was a .348 Winchester Model 71 that would punch through nearly anything solid. It was the biggest of the American big-game cartridges, and the strongest lever action ever made, and the bruise it left in his shoulder was nothing to the hole it left in what he'd be shooting at.

In each of the same number of grocery stores, he purchased like-size amounts of Coca-Cola, coffee beans, hamburger meat, cans of green beans, mustard, ketchup, buns, steaks, roasts and chucks, plus plenty of bread and milk were taken up, to say nothing of detergent, soap, toothpaste, toothbrushes, and of course toilet paper. Elsewhere, in department stores: sheets, blankets, pillows. You'd have had to travel a wide circle to catch on to the fact that somebody was caching up for the arrival of a group. Then he made his most astonishing purchase: at a war surplus store in Pensacola, he bought two cases of canteens. Not American, however; rather, these were Italian, from World War I, and they resembled wine bottles. Each had been well maintained, and each had a canvas cover with a strap.

He worked for a couple of days laying in these supplies and setting up the place for the few days in a week or so when it would be occupied. He had other tasks: he called Los Angeles and arranged for shipment of his cowboy pictures. He also studied maps of the state, the next state, and of course the next state after that, which was Mississippi. He tried to think of everything. Was he missing something? Had he forgotten a detail? He had good men, a plan, and had kept a careful running account of all this for Mr. Trugood, whose advance he hoarded shrewdly and paid out of with a great deal of misery. He couldn't think of a thing, but he had a nagging suspicion there was a hole in his thinking. What the hell was it?

But it never came to him, and finally, he had but two last jobs to do. The first was easy: it was sending a cash payment and a letter to the classified ad section of the Pensacola *Journal Times*, specifying that a certain ad should be run on a certain day. That was the ad that would alert all the arriving boys to his number, so he could get them directions to come on out. But the last was tricky.

He wrote a letter, addressed to a fellow in government service in Pensacola. He waited. There was nothing to do but wait by the phone for it to ring, and he thought it would, for the man he'd written to was extremely dutiful about obligations. It could have taken a week; it took a day. Earl answered. They had a brief chat, and agreed to meet the day following in a bar in downtown Pensacola.

Instead of his slacks and a sports shirt, Earl put on his suit, Brylcreemed his hair, KiWied his shoes, tied his tie tight, and tried to look as prosperous and solid as possible.

He then drove by back roads to Pensacola proper, and there he located the naval station. A uniformed shore patrolman stood sentry outside the gate that Earl had figured on, and Earl of course had his usual irritated reaction to such a fellow. They'd been the bane of his young life, but this one simply sat in his little house in his dress whites, saluting and letting folks in and out.

Then Earl saw the man he'd written to and who had called him. He was in civilian clothes and drove a '50 Dodge convertible, jet black, but even so dressed everything about him looked military: the closeness of his haircut, the stern set of his mouth, and the precision of his head to his body, and the squareness of his shoulders and the erectness of his posture.

Earl followed him from five car-lengths back in his own car, the point being just security. He wanted to make certain nobody was following him. And nobody was.

The officer pulled up to the bar he had chosen at exactly the moment he had said he would, and he walked inside.

Earl lingered outside and made sure the meeting was unobserved, and then he headed in as well.

He entered, blinked in the darkness, and saw the

man. He didn't know him well, and the man, when he recognized Earl, didn't smile. He put down his glass, stood, and briefly assumed a position of ramrod posture, a military gesture in an old run-down honky-tonk on the bad side of town.

The last time Earl had seen him was October of 1942. On that day, he was bleeding from two bullet wounds in the cockpit of a Grumman Wildcat that the Japs had just shot down. The plane was on fire and the Japs were still shooting at it. Earl shot at the Japs, driving them back, and raced under a screen of covering fire to the plane, which incidentally was about to blow up, said to him, when he got there, exactly what he now said in the bar, nine years later: "Sonny, this ain't no way to meet new friends."

"Howdy, Gunny Swagger," said the officer. "Jesus Christ, nice to see you. I know you got out a first sarge, but you'll always be 'gunny' to me."

"Well, sir," said Earl, taking the firm grip and paying it back with one just as firm, "it don't matter, 'cause now it's just plain old Earl. And you may not be so happy when you hear what I got cooked up."

"Knowing you, gunny, I'll bet it's a wowzer."

Earl smiled.

"It is, Admiral. It is."

45

SAM came home ragged and spent. He was not in the best of moods. He gathered up his mail, poured himself a bourbon, and retired alone to his dark study. Throughout the house, he could hear the echo of kids, which had once filled him with joy. Tonight, it just made his headache greater and his depression heavier.

He'd spent hours on the phone, tracking fellows from the Harvard Medical School class of '28, and all that he could find were well established now, deep in prosperous practices or inhabiting prestigious professorships, which meant of course that they were too busy or too important to come to the phone, and when they did, they were usually so pompous and self-adoring that it took a great deal of nudging and apple-polishing to get anywhere with them. And when he finally got someplace, it was no place.

Some, but by no means all, remembered David Stone, and an even smaller subset of that group were willing to share any insight into him, and even those who did, it quickly turned out, knew only the David Stone that Sam began with: brilliant researcher, selfless humanitarian, hard worker, charmer. Married a beautiful woman. Came from a great family. Never had kids, no, but he was too busy on the frontiers of medicine, doing good in the world. Did something important for the Army during the war. A real tragedy, his loss. There seemed to be something of a physicians' benevolent protective society in play by informal fiat, by which one doctor agreed never to say anything negative about another doctor.

The David Stone that Sam had uncovered—a man with secrets, a man obsessed with cleansing the world, a man who in his most intimate letters to his wife was strangely inauthentic, a man with a nervous disposition that might be regarded as clinical madness—only existed in Sam's knowledge, but there was no other public acknowledgment of such a personality.

So Sam had the hideous weight on his shoulders that he was simply wasting his time and the money that Davis Trugood would have to pony up for the phone bills of so many long-distance calls. And Sam *had* to charge him, for he was very low on funds, and no other even small cases were coming to him, as if the men from HUAC, though vanquished and driven off, had still besmirched him in the county imagination.

So Sam also kept busy living up to his civic responsibilities during this period, to keep himself before the public eye, though his heart was no longer in it. He attended town council meetings and Democratic party meetings (essentially the same, and Sam always wondered why the hell they just didn't combine them) and continued as a deacon of the church and as recording secretary of the P.T.A. and made the rounds on the Negro churches because he didn't want to lose that vote, and encouraged the newspaper to continue its chronicles of the various malfeasances of the hapless Feebus Bookins, his scandalous replacement.

And of course he worried.

This was his natural condition. He had given Earl a conditional blessing, and thought he meant it. But a certain part of him was not convinced, and that part of him continued its campaign of undermining all that he enjoyed and poisoning his life.

It is not right.

It was not right. You cannot lead armed men against legally sanctioned civil authority and commit violence. That is murder, it is insurrection, it is a form of treason. It does not matter how corrupt and despicable your antagonists are; if you do that, you become them, and once you become them, you have lost your soul.

He picked up his mail, found the usual accumulation of bills, circulars and advertisements, then came across something new. It was a personal letter from one Harold E. Perkins, of Washington, D.C.

Sam searched his memory. The search revealed no record of a Harold E. Perkins, which Sam took to mean either he was losing IQ points fast in his quest, or that Harold E. Perkins was a complete stranger writing for money.

Sam opened the envelope, found a small, handwritten note card.

"Dear Mr. Vincent," it began,

I don't know if you remember me, but I am, or was formerly, the member of Congressman Etheridge's staff that his chief aide Mel Brasher sent to look for information on a David Stone, M.D., for you. I ascertained that none was available via Army Medical Service.

Since then I've left the congressman's employ and am now working for the Department of Atomic Energy in a clerk's capacity while going to George Washington University Law School at night.

I write you because of a small item I encountered in my duties of no import to anyone but which I thought you should hear about. I was examining records of nuclear material shipments from the Los Alamos Plutonium Laboratory to a facility in Maryland, called Fort Dietrich. I have no information on Ft. Dietrich, or what was being done there in conjunction with plutonium experiments, but I note that the information was cc-ed to a doctor at Thebes State Penal Farm, Thebes, Mississippi. I don't remember the name, but it was definitely not Dr. Stone. I only noticed it because for some reason the word 'Thebes' leaped out at me, being somewhat unusual. The more I thought about it, the more I thought you should know about it.

I would like to ask a counter favor, if you don't mind. I think Mr. Brasher got the wrong idea about me owing to certain events in the men's room, in which the Capitol Police apprehended me. I never really had a chance to explain the misunderstanding. I wonder if you'd drop him a line, telling him how much I've helped you out. Thanks so much.

Harold E. Perkins.

Sam turned this new information over in his head. Fort Dietrich again! What on earth was going on at this obscure post in Maryland that now involved some form of nuclear materials from Los Alamos, and why on earth would all of this be reported to an unknown doctor in Thebes, Mississippi?

"Daddy?"

It was Caroline, his seven-year-old daughter, an adorable child who had her mother's blond hair and freckles and her father's serious intelligence, but also, from neither of them, a sense of humor and amazement.

"Honey, Daddy's busy now," he said, too cruelly and too quickly.

"But the man said you had to sign," she said.

"What?"

"The present. Someone sent you a present."

"Oh, Lord," said Sam. "Who in hell would send me a present?"

"It's from New Orleans. From the Scott's Department Store."

"Hmmm," said Sam.

He rose wearily and followed his daughter out through a roomful of children, some his own, some his neighbors'. A delivery man stood patiently in the doorway, with a package under his arm and a clipboard with a form on it.

"Can I help you, sir?"

"Mr. Samuel Vincent, sir? That would be you?"

"Yes, sir."

"Well, sir, I have a package on special delivery for you all the way from New Orleans's finest department store. Someone must think highly of you."

"Not likely," said Sam, quickly signing the form. Outside he saw the delivery truck, brown, part of the famous fleet of such trucks that worked faster and better than the U.S. mail.

"Very good, sir," said the man. "Here it is, and enjoy it."

"Thanks."

The children were excited. To them, packages were automatically a festive occasion, associated with celebrations such as Christmas or a birthday. Happiness was a package.

Sam carried the thing to the dining room table. Whatever it was, it was solid weight, about three pounds, with no rattle or gurgle in it, no sense of anything cloth or paper. Possibly a paperweight or possibly a set of old books, though it didn't seem big enough for that.

He examined it, and nothing surprised him. It was professionally wrapped, with his address typed cleanly on the address label and the return address denoted the store he knew to be one of New Orleans's most prosperous.

He tore the package open, and the brown paper revealed festive colored paper, merry and gay.

"It *is* a present," said Caroline. "Oh, Daddy, open it!"

"Sweetie, I'm sure it's just a business gift. Don't get your hopes up. It isn't going to be a new doll."

"Doll! Doll! Doll!" Terry, his youngest at three, began to cry. She loved presents. She loved dolls and prissy frilly things, and was still a sweet baby, still her daddy's favorite.

"Bet it's a ball glove," said Billy, who was clearly projecting his own desires on it, for at six all he wanted was a ball glove like his two big brothers.

"Billy, it's a pewter mug from the State Prosecutor's Association or some such," Sam said dourly, as he pulled off the wrapped paper, tore off the ribbons, and got the thing free to reveal a white paper box ensnared by a final gold ribbon, which could possibly hold a selection of books or shot glasses or a telescope or pair of binoculars.

"It's candy," Caroline concluded, and she had a formidable sweet tooth, so that would please her immensely. "Chocolate candy, with strawberries inside."

"Could be candy, we'll soon see," Sam said and pulled the ribbon loose.

"I bet it's jelly."

"No, it's a dolly, I know it's a dolly."

"It's a plastic airplane, betcha. Daddy, hurry. *Hurry, Daddy!*"

"*Hurry up,* please, *Daddy!*"

But Daddy couldn't hurry. Daddy had the ribbon half off the box, and he froze. He froze dead still and his face lost its color and its joy. It was frozen into a mask and he himself seemed frozen in the odd position. He had the ribbon pulled tight, just almost to the breaking point, but he was holding it as if it were the rope to a boat or something in danger of floating away, and with his other hand he kept the package pinned to the table. He could feel an unusual tension in the ribbon, a tension that should not be there. But that alone wasn't the source of his sudden desperation. It was an odor that seemed to float up from the package, just a trace, but enough to re-create a whole world for him, and that terrified him.

"Caroline," he said very carefully, "I want you—"

"Hurry, Daddy, so I can have a—"

"*Caroline!*"

His voice stunned them.

"Caroline, honey, get these kids out of here. Get them across the street. Do it now, sweetie, do it now."

"Daddy, I—"

"Sweetie, do what Daddy tells you, and don't let anybody come in here, do you understand? If Mommy shows up, keep her from coming in. And tell Mrs. Jackson to call the fire department and the police, and please, please, baby, do it right away!"

46

THE Whipping House was never quiet now. This is how Bigboy investigated: with the calm, methodical, unemotional application of whip to skin. The speed was supersonic, the devastation cruel and specific. He could open a nick, or a slice or a gash or a hack. He could make the whip tease like a feather or bite like a lion, but he preferred what lay in between, in escalating degrees, increment by increment, with enough downtime and not too much blood loss so that the boy could understand with perfect logic and clarity that which was happening to him, that which would happen and, finally, that there was no other inevitability save the will of the whip man.

In the Whipping House, the whip man whipped. When a boy passed out, he was cut down, revived, treated tenderly, his wounds dressed, and just when it seemed he was out of his agony and removed to a more benevolent universe, he was hung again, and whipped again, harder, taken farther into pain, but not quite all the way to death.

Nobody died without talking, for that is the way of a

good whip man. The whip man knows. The whip man is brilliant, cunning, and has all the attributes of a chess player or a counterintelligence officer or a gifted businessman. He has an intuition for the psychology of weakness, he can anticipate, he knows just how close to the line he can come each time, and each time he cuts that distance in half. And there is always another half to be achieved, always. He can string you along for hours or days, take you through lifetimes of pain, so that nothing else has ever existed for you, and the only mercy is a dream of death which he is too wise to give you easily.

In this way, Ephram gave up Milton, and then Milton gave up Robertson. Robertson tried to kill himself by biting on his tongue, piercing it in hopes of drowning in lungs a-burst with his own blood, greedily swallowed to avoid further destruction, but the whip man was too smart, and saved him, for an especially long time on the rack, with the play of lash and light and sweat across the darkness of the night, until ultimately Robertson broke and gave up Theo, who broke fast to give up Broke Tooth, who gave up One Eye, who gave up Elijah.

It was a pagan scene, with the fires bright, and the sweat shiny on the bodies of the hung man and the whip man in their intimate squalor, and the singing in the air of the lash and the crack as it struck, each crack a detonation in the flesh that transmuted in a nanosecond to the deep brain where pain is registered.

Bigboy worked Elijah hard, for Elijah was the rare enough hero and would give no man up, and Elijah fought him all through the whip man's night, filling the Whipping House with pain. But finally Elijah broke. They all broke. There was no other possibility.

Elijah gave up 22 and 22 gave up Albert, but there was a hitch.

In the case of Albert, the man was discovered in bed, his throat cut, a straight razor in his hand.

"He knowed he was next," said Caleb.

"No," said Bigboy. "Someone else knew he was next, and thought to cut the chain off before it led to him. And left the razor there to confuse us. But we will find him."

A day was lost in that barracks, as each convict was interrogated by rough means, until at last one Yellow Ed gave up Mr. Clarence, and Mr. Clarence broke and ran, in the old days just exactly the ticket out in the amount of time it took a guard to pump his Winchester '07 to his shoulder and ship off a .351. But nobody shot Mr. Clarence. The dogs ran him to earth, and he too went off to interrogation. The nights of the Whipping House continued.

FISH knew he eventually would be found out. Knowing this, he had two choices. The first would be to hand himself into the warden and Bigboy, explain that he was indeed the originator of the phrase "pale horse coming," and then tell exactly what it meant and why in his foolishness he had told it to but one man. That was his sin: hubris. He had no ability to keep his tongue from wagging, and for that his brothers were paying in flesh.

He would tell all: about the white boy Bogart's secret survival, and his pledge to return in the night with men and guns, and pay out retribution in spades.

But if he did that, Fish knew also that the warden and Bigboy would take specific security precautions against exactly what it was the white boy Bogart had planned. That would doom Bogart's attempt, that would get Bogart killed. The assault on Thebes would come to nothing; Thebes, like an evil city of the ancient times, would go on and on and on. It was like a Rome, and no force could bring it down except time's slow track.

The other course demanded more belief. It was harder. It was hardest of all, because it could be construed by his own self as the cowardly way. That was to say nothing, and let Bigboy work his way through the convict population, hunting the disease of hope, until at last, depending on the courage of those who fell under his lash, it reached himself. This way played for time, and in that time the gamble was the white man Bogart would assemble his forces and smite the evil, wipe them off the face of the earth, and that he, Fish, would be here to see it. It was a coward's way, for the first path surely guaranteed that he would himself get the lash, for even if the warden and Bigboy believed he was telling the truth, they'd take him to the last drop of blood to ascertain if what he said was truth. He would avoid that, but he would live with the screams of the whipped in the Whipping House, that anguish that floated every night damp and heated on the gentle breezes, so that all could hear and all could fear.

That is, if Bogart the white boy came. For many a man speaks powerfully when full of wrath, and makes great promises of what will come. Yes, and just as many a man forgets his pledge in the light of day after a woman's soft caress or the numbing blur and comfort of whiskey, or the purr of a satisfied child cuddling with its daddy, and the warmth of a blazing hearth. These things, and a million or so others, will make cowards out of most men, who will not give them up to come back to muddy hell and set things right. They forget quickly, their memories erode, and after all, the men of Thebes were lost already. Maybe the white boy Bogart would be like that. What white boy, after all, would risk his neck to save a passel of niggers? Never happened before, maybe never would after.

But goddamning himself to hell, Fish decided at long last, after many a bitter and sleepless and scream-filled night, to believe in the white boy. That fellow had something, for sure. Something in the way his eyes blazed with death's promise, and he took all this righteously, as if personal. He would ride that pale horse back with God's mighty scythe and cut down the wicked of Thebes. That's what Fish concluded. It was his only faith.

So he would give the white boy Bogart another week. He would give him till dark of the moon. Then he would stop the hurting and the dying by taking it on himself. Until that time, he would be hard of heart while yessin' and shuckin' and smilin' and crawlin' before the white demons. He hoped it earned him one thing: not a dispensation from hell, for he knew that was where he was going, but only the knowledge that certain others would be arriving at that destination first, or at least soon after.

THROUGH these long nights of screaming, the warden slept soundly. He had taught himself from long practice not to be affected by the grim necessities of power. Power is what it must do, and if it lacks the will to do it, it will not remain power much longer. That is the rule of history, as written by the Romans and the Spanish and the British. He had made peace with it.

He slept soundly, for he knew that whatever had to be done, he was a truly good man.

47

I⊤ seemed to take forever. Sam stood there, transfixed, caught up in the utter fragility of it. His fingers, not ideally distributed against the tension of the ribbon, nevertheless held it taut, and with his other hand he pinned the cardboard box flat. He had very little room to move, not without disturbing his hands and somehow altering the tension on the ribbon which, if he had figured this thing out correctly, could release the firing pin of what had to be an M1 Pull Firing Device, or something similar, which would allow the spring-driven striker to plunge forward against whatever primer was in the package, and the whole thing would go ka-boom. End of house. End, more to the point, of Sam.

He tried to recollect the thing. The M1s were ubiquitous in the war, standard equipment for rigging booby traps in defensive positions, but common to any artillery or mortar unit as well. For if you were in danger of being overrun and didn't want your guns to fall into enemy hands, you could unscrew the fuse of a shell, screw in the M1, pull out the safety pins (two of them), and run a cord from the big ring at the end of the device to your position under cover. One pull on that ring, and the dance began and ended one second later with that big ka-boom. No guns for the Germans to turn against us, as they were wont to do.

Sam forced himself to concentrate. In that way, he drove from his imagination the fear and the discomfort. The discomfort, however, was not so easily vanquished. It refused to obey his will and insisted on manifesting itself in the cramps that had begun to spread through his awkwardly splayed fingers, in the itchy sweat catching in his hairline, in the sudden weight of his glasses, which had slipped down his nose and were pinching his nostrils and clotting his breathing, in the needles that had begun to prickle in his feet as the blood collected there, and in the dryness of throat and mouth as his throat grew raspy. It seemed as if the atoms of his clothes were increasing in density and acquiring weight, until they were pressing against his skin and constricting his chest.

He heard the sirens. He was aware, somewhere, of great activity. It had to be outside, and soon the familiar pulsing red illumination of fire and police department emergency lights came flashing through the windows. If a crowd gathered—as why would it not?—he heard that too, that low human buzz of a species drawn hypnotically to drama, hungry to see and feel another's tragedy.

Yet no one appeared.

He waited and waited. The seconds seemed to liquefy and elongate, like drops falling off a window sill, fighting gravity till the last, until a final gossamer broke and off they plunged, slowly, slowly to obliteration.

Goddammit. when will they get here?

When will somebody get here?

The sweat now ran lazily down his face, irritating

under normal circumstances, insanely bothersome under these. He scrunched his brow to stop it, and failed; it cascaded down, and his knees knocked, and his heart thudded.

He imagined that at any second the pin could slip that final millionth of an inch from where it now prevented the striker from plunging, and one hundredth of a second later there would be no Sam, only a crater in the block where Sam used to live.

At last a door opened.

"Mr. Sam?" came a timid voice from outside.

Sam recognized it as Sheriff Harry Debaugh.

"Harry! Thank God you're here."

"What you got in there, Mr. Sam?"

"I think it's a sixty-millimeter mortar shell with a detonating thing screwed into the fuse. Pull it all the way out, it goes off. I started, and, well, anyway, I stopped just as I felt the pressure of a spring. So now I am hung up but good. I can't move. If I relax, I think it'll go."

"What should we do, Mr. Sam?"

He didn't know! He had no idea!

"Well, call Camp Chaffee and surely they have an explosive ordnance disposal team with equipment. That would be one thing." Why do I have to think of these things myself? They should be on the way *now!* "Or try, let's see, Little Rock would have a bomb squad. Maybe they could get here faster. I don't think the state police boys up at Fayetteville could get here in time. Harry, I could drop this at any second, goddammit. My hands are cramping up something fierce."

"Sam, you hold tight. I'll make them calls."

Another geologic epoch crawled by. One-celled animals evolved into fishes and plants and dinosaurs and then snakes and bugs and dogs and birds and monkeys and finally men came into the picture. Cave-dwellers arrived and departed, and then the Greeks, the Romans, the Dark Ages, the Renaissance, the French Revolution, the terrible nineteenth century with its Civil War, and then, fifty-one full years and two major wars into this one, Harry again piped up.

"Sam, it's going to take at least an hour. The Army people have to git together. I've rung up state police and they'll escort 'em in, sirens an' all, but, dammit, I don't think it'll be no sooner."

Sam knew he couldn't last that long. He had another twenty minutes at most before his fingers reached muscle failure, and then the ribbon would slip and it would be over.

"Sam, you sure? I mean, it could just be a bottle of bourbon."

"*No!* Goddammit, I smelled Cosmoline. In arms depots, small arms and ammo are stored in a penetrating grease called Cosmoline. Its smell sinks into everything. This shell must have been wrapped up in excelsior from the place where it was stored. I *smelled* it as I was pulling the ribbon. That's why I stopped."

"Sam, you hold on now. No need gittin' upset."

I am one tenth of a second from being blown to smithereens, but I AM NOT UPSET.

"Listen, Harry. I can't hold this position much longer. What I need is a cool young volunteer. Someone who can cut the cardboard away so that we can see what we have. Then maybe I can improvise a way to defuse the thing."

"Sam, I can't order no man to—"

"I said *volunteer,* dammit!"

"All right, Sam, hold your water. I'll ask."

Harry disappeared, and again Sam stood alone in the living room. He glanced around as the seconds pulled their long tails by. He could see a wedding picture of himself and his wife on a shelf, he could see a radio, he could see a picture taken at Hot Springs and one in Miami, the whole family, all those kids who would now grow up without a father. He could see plaques from Kiwanis and Rotary and the Masons and the Chamber of Commerce. He could see books from the Book-of-the-Month Club and *Life* magazines and *Time* magazines piled up in the magazine rack, but no damn television, as he wouldn't have one in the house. He could see . . . he could see his whole damned life and how little it came to, how much nothing it was.

God, if I get out of this one, I swear I'll do SOME-THING. Don't know what, but something.

He knew who it was from, of course. It could have come from but one source.

Goddamn them, they got me. I thought I got away clean, but they got me. They reached into Arkansas, into my house, into the bosom of my family, where my children gathered, and they got me and they would have killed them all.

The bitterness was so intense he almost yanked the ribbon that last quarter inch just to release it. But he didn't.

Oh, Lord, he thought, *just let me survive this and get my licks in.*

And then Harry was back. Sam sensed him sliding nervously up to the house and lingering there in the lee of the door, breathing hard.

"Sam?" he finally said, and his tone carried the whole story.

"Yeah?"

"Sam, nobody would do it. It's too tricky. I can see the point, too, can't you? I mean, either your thing is going to go off or it's just a bottle of Pepsi-Cola and we can all laugh about it, that's all. And if it's the first, getting another man killed, I mean, what the hell good does it do? One's enough, by my reckoning. I wish Earl were here. He could do it."

"Well, Earl isn't here, dammit, and we will just have to deal with that."

"How do you feel, Sam?"

"This palaver is no help at all. But my hands hurt like hell, my arms are weakening, my lower back is cramping and my knees are shaking. Oh, and my vision is blurring."

"Sam, I . . ."

"Yes, Harry?"

"Sam, I can't stay here. A mortar shell goes off this close to me and I'm cooked too, along with you. I'm sorry, Sam. You see what it is, don't you? Either them Army boys are going to get here or not, and either there's a mortar shell in there or there ain't. My being here, it don't matter."

"All right, Harry."

"Do you want me to say anything to your wife and kids?"

"Only what they know. That I loved them, that I wish I was a better man for them. Now get the hell out of here, Harry, and get busy on your praying."

But Harry wasn't listening.

Some sort of ruckus came up outside, a welter of noise and emotion, hard to make out, though indistinct sentence fragments came around the corner and into the room where Sam so delicately stood, the ribbon taut, the pains scaling his arms and legs, the sweat running down his face into his bushy eyebrows.

"You can't—"

"I told—"

"Sheriff, we tried—"

"She wouldn't listen—"

"Now, Mrs. Longacre," cooed the sheriff, "this is a very dangerous—"

"Goddamn you," came the clear, hard tones of Connie Longacre, "you get out of my way, Harry Debaugh, or I will sic such a crew of lawyers on you, you will wish you had never ever set foot on this planet from whatever coward's rocket ship you arrived on."

And with that, she stepped around the door, the sheriff and two deputies in pursuit, but unable to stand against her force of will.

Connie was beautiful. She had blond hair and soft skin and a nose like an ax blade. She could have used more chin, and eyes of blue or green instead of sea gray, and she could have dressed more like the woman she was instead of in jeans and boots and a sweater, but she was still such a heartbreaking vision Sam almost started to cry.

"Connie, for God's sakes, get out of here. This is—"

"Sam, I tried to stop her."

"Mrs. Longacre, this is a crime scene, and you are not authorized."

"Ma'am, your husband—"

"You shut up, all of you. I've heard enough. You run away, you little man, and pray I can help Sam or my husband, Rance, will be very angry."

"Sam, I—" began the sheriff.

"Sam, what is all this nonsense?"

"Connie, please, this thing could go off at any moment."

"Mrs. Longacre, won't you please come this way and—"

"*Don't you touch me!*" she screamed, and the two deputies jerked backward. The sheriff yielded, then surrendered.

"All right, Sam," she said, approaching as steadily as a three-masted schooner under nine sheets and a full breeze, "what the hell have we got going on here?"

"Connie, I cannot—"

"I am not going to go sit in the car, Sam, while you blow up, so you had better tell me what to do and tell me now!"

CONNIE cut slowly, with perfect concentration. The surgical shears were sharp, and she cut in smooth strokes, unfaltering, unperturbed, unhurried, as if she'd worked with bombs her entire life. She had most of the back end of the box off now.

"What do you see?"

"Just a second."

With a deft snip, the scissors closed their last. She set them down gingerly, then with her pale and elegant but steady hands, removed the rear of the box.

The smell of Cosmoline immediately flooded the room.

"How disgusting," she said.

"It's government gun grease."

"There seems to be wads of paper or something."

"Can you get them out so you can see?"

"I can try. How are you doing, darling?"

"I'm fine. Never been better. I may start to dance any second I'm so happy."

"There, there, darling. We'll have a nice martini when this is over, and then touch fingers and go back to our happy marriages."

"Connie, for God's sakes—"

"All right, I'm pulling it out, just wait."

Using the scissors' tips as pincers, she eased out a wad of crumpled newspaper, then another, and then another.

"Now I can see our boy," she reported.

"And?"

"Hmmm. Yes, yes, what a naughty boy he is, too. He's about eight inches tall with a set of stubby little fins at the end of a shaft at his bottom. His body is egg-shaped, greenish, with striations around the middle. The end is conical, but there's some kind of gizmo there, a sort of pipe coming out of it. I can't see for sure, but it looks like a nest of wires at the top."

"Can you see if any of those wires leads out of the box, through a hole or something?"

"It's too dark, darling. Do you have a flashlight or anything?"

"Yeah, right here, in my pocket, I'll just put this down and get it."

"Sam, don't be a smart aleck, even if you're about to be turned into Swiss cheese."

"There's a flashlight somewhere, but oh, Christ, I don't know where it is. Get a lamp."

"Mary will be so upset."

But Connie went to an end table, seized a lamp from it, and ripped off its shade. Carefully holding it so the cord ran free, she brought it over to the package on the dining room table and snapped it on. The harsh, shadeless light made Sam flinch, and he did not need to flinch, for he almost let the ribbon go.

But Connie was peering in intently at what the light revealed.

"It does appear there's a cord tied neatly through the ring at the tip of the pipe, and a taut line runs up to the box and—" she lifted her eyes to follow the cord—"and, yes, darling, it does seem to be stoutly attached to the ribbon you are holding so tightly."

"All right. This is what you have to do. You have to reach in there and very delicately unscrew the fuse from the warhead."

"I don't know if I can get my hands in there. It's very tight. If I bump, the thing may go off, right?"

"I can't think of anything else. I've got a fairly firm grip for now."

But that was a lie. Even as he spoke it seemed the fire in his fingers rose another ten degrees. Connie's presence let him block the agonies that assailed him, but now that magic was wearing off.

"Oh, where are those goddamn Army boys?"

"Just like an army. There's never one around when you need it."

"Connie, this isn't going to work. We aren't going to make it."

"Sam, we *are* going to make it. Tell me what to do and stop wasting your breath."

"Connie, I—"

His fingers twitched. It felt like he was hanging off a ledge on their strength alone, and now, one by one, they were dying.

"Connie, please go."

"Could we block it?"

"What?"

"Block it. The striker will fall, but if it strikes something else, then there won't be a boom, isn't that right?"

"Can you see in there? Is there a gap?"

Connie held the blazing bulb close again, and looked carefully.

"There should be a hole where they removed a safety pin as part of the arming process."

"Yes, I see."

"Listen, these things are made of cheap pan metal. They're not well made at all. Maybe with something you could scrape around the edge of that hole, enlarge it enough to get something in there to grind away at the hole and enlarge it enough to get something in there."

Connie didn't say a word. She opened the surgical shears, inserted the point ever so delicately into the tiny opening for the safety pin.

"You've got a good grip."

"Yes, ma'am."

Not quite true. But as good as he could manage, given the pain in his hand.

"So long, been good to know you," said Connie, and Sam felt the subtle change in the string when a kind of pressure was applied somewhere far down the system.

He looked at her. Her eyes were wide, and the harsh light illuminated the beauty of her face like a lamp on a statue in Italy. Her face was completely focused, completely calm. She wasn't even breathing hard. He yearned to kiss her.

A sharp pain cut through his arm.

"Ah," he said. "I'm checking out. I'm losing it. Go on, get out of here, I can't hold it, my hand is dead."

"Just a second, darling?"

"It's failing. It's failing," he screamed, for he tried to find his will to compress his aching fingers, but he'd been on this drill for so long, it seemed his whole life, and there was no strength left.

"Please, Connie, please, run."

"Just a second, darling. I almost have it. Now if only there was something I could guide into that hole."

She looked about.

There wasn't time.

"Oh, Connie," said Sam. "Please."

"Stop being noble. It's annoying." She reached into the box. "Maybe if—"

It was gone. It was over. He had failed.

"Connie, I love you."

"Of course you do, darling," Connie said, and his fingers at last failed, and the cord slipped and the pin worked its last tiny bit free and the striker was released, its captured tension in its coiled spring allowed to thrust forward toward freedom, and with a powerful snap it drove ahead.

Sam closed his eyes, knowing it didn't matter, for in the next tenth of a second he and Connie would simply cease to exist in their form and instead be rendered— well, he had seen enough deaths by high explosive.

But it didn't go off.

"Jesus!" he said, flexing his fingers to restore the circulation as he fell to his knees.

He looked at Connie. Her face was gray, her eyes blank, her lips tense, fine beads of sweat upon her brow. Then he realized what she had inserted into the hole to keep the striker from the primer.

It was her finger.

He raced around the table, took up the scissors and began to cut the box away, until at last he had the destructive device free. He could see it now: her smallest thinnest finger, inserted into the crudely enlarged safety-pin hole in the pipelike pull-fire gizmo.

"Okay," he said, "I'm going to gently unscrew the device from the fuse well."

"Sam, you say the sweetest things."

Holding the mortar shell by its warhead against his hip, and with the other hand securing the device, he began the slow process of unwinding the shell from its trigger. It fought him at first, and then he started when some moist warmth clotted up against his fingers and he realized it was her blood. But he unsteadily cranked a tenth of a turn by a tenth of a turn until after what seemed hours the shell itself separated from the firing device. As he set the shell down, something fell to the ground, like a quarter. He saw that it was an artillery shell primer, the necessary ingredient in assuring the explosion.

"Hold your hand up now to stop the bleeding."

Connie lifted her hand, its finger wedged cruelly in the opening of the pull-fire tube. More blood poured down, matting redly in the fiber of her gray sweater. He held her tightly, unsure what to do next. He wasn't clear if he could just pull it off, or possibly that would maim her finger all the more. He thought maybe he should get her to the faucet and run cold water, but the two of them were on the floor, and she was nestled against him, and it was as close as she'd ever be to him, and he was strangely happy.

"Oh, God," he said, "you are so brave. Jesus Christ, you are so brave. Oh, Connie, leave him, and I'll leave Sally and—"

"Oh, stop it," she said. "That would just make a big mess. If you want to be helpful, why don't you find my purse and get me a cigarette and then make me a nice drink."

Then she noticed they were no longer alone.

"Sam, there's a man from Mars over there."

Indeed, the Martian lumbered over to them. He was some sort of giant robot, stiffly encumbered in armor, his body a bulk of pure iron, his face an iron mask with a tiny viewing hole. He wore immense mittens of steel braid.

"Say, what part of Mars are you from?" Connie asked.

The Martian shucked off his huge mittens and removed his mask and revealed himself to be merely "Sergeant Rutledge, U.S. Army, ma'am," and in seconds everybody else was in there, including police officers, the heroic Harry Debaugh, a medical technician and two more partially disrobed bomb guys, pulling a huge metal box on wheels behind them.

"Look at all these party crashers," said Connie.

But Sam was thinking: damn, damn, damn, another second and I could have kissed her.

48

EARL looked at the telegram and wished it hadn't come. It sat, as yet unopened, on the table on the porch. It actually had arrived yesterday, and Earl could not bring himself to open it. It could only be from Sam. Sam had promised him he'd tell him man-to-man if he'd decided against the plan. Maybe Sam couldn't come, so Sam had sent a telegram. Earl imagined it said, At midnight, unless I hear from you, I will inform state police. Regards.

Sam, really, was not a man of war. Sam was a civilian. He thought like a civilian, he reacted like a civilian, he had a civilian's fears and doubts. Earl was a soldier. Earl killed people. That was a difference in the way the two minds worked that Earl could not bridge.

He should never have told Sam. He should never have come back. He should have done it on his own.

Earl sat on the porch of the farmhouse in Florida. He could see the empty barn, the rolling fields, and the long dirt road and in the distance the forest cut with palmetto plants, and above it all a blaze of sun.

There was nothing to do but wait; the boys would

begin to show up tomorrow or the next day, and dark of the moon was but four days off. To make himself useful, he was working with the .38–44 high-velocity cartridges, taking each one from its nest of fifty, and with an awl drilling a hole in the center of the semiwadcutter bullet, so that the bullet would rupture when it went through flesh, on the principle of the dumdum bullet. Illegal to do so in battle, but battle was a different phenomenon. This was a holy war, where the odds would be seven against Thebes. So it was allowed.

Earl worked steadily, trying to keep his mind clear, trying not to worry. He went over his own private operational plan, trying mentally to take it apart, to see it afresh, to figure on the unintended consequence. He knew that the confidence that he had thought of everything was the true sign of danger.

Then he saw the car.

It was a long way off. It pulled up the road, yanking a screen of dust behind it. Under the newspaper next to him on the table was a Colt .357 Trooper, loaded with the dumdums. Earl could get at it fast, but hoped he didn't have to.

But soon enough it was recognizable, and Earl put aside his thoughts of the gun. It was the Cadillac limousine that Mr. Trugood seemed to travel the country in.

Earl sat back, still dumdumming cartridges, until the car arrived, and a fellow popped out obsequiously to spring the door for the august Mr. Trugood.

Earl stood and beheld. The man was resplendent in cream linen, with a blue shirt and a yellow tie and a nice straw Panama, with a yellow band to match the tie.

"Hello, sir," said Earl, rising.

"Mr. Earl. You don't seem happy to see me."

"Come on up and get yourself out of that heat."

The man came up, following Earl into the squalid living room. He looked about with distaste.

"It's certainly not elegant, is it? Well, that's what sixty dollars a month rents these days."

"These boys won't even notice. They'll be too busy buzzing among themselves about cartridges and gun actions."

"Earl, you're still not happy that I'm here."

"Sir, I don't want no one down here to see you and identify you. If this thing goes wrong, I want to be the only man with the whole picture. I don't want it coming back at you."

"Yes, and you also don't want a rich fellow in a fancy car suddenly getting all the natives excited in this backwash, wouldn't that be equally true?"

"It would."

"Well, we traveled back roads, and after Montgomery I have not been out of the vehicle. Fair enough?"

"Yes, sir. Since you are paying, you are always welcome."

"Earl, I've come about the plan."

"Yes, sir?"

"Earl, I have to say this. I think there's a mistake."

"Since you're paying all the bills, Mr. Trugood, then if you think there's a mistake, I'll listen hard to it and try and get it fixed."

"Excellent."

"I've been butting against it myself. I'm trying to see it fresh. Maybe you've seen something I ain't yet."

"It's not the plan, not really. It's the bigger picture."

Earl squinted. What was this bird up to?

"Sir?"

"You're a Marine. You make your attack, you move on. That's it, right?"

It was so true Earl simply nodded.

"Yes. Well, what about them?" said Davis Trugood.

"Them?"

"The Negroes. When you're done, you'll have two-hundred-odd convicts and thirty-five odd townspeople stuck upriver miles from civilization. You've drowned the prison under twenty feet of black water. What happens to those folks, Earl?"

Earl thought it over a bit. Finally, he said, "You have a point. But in the war if we'd thought of that stuff, then we'd never have made the first invasion. We'd still be in our boats off Guadalcanal."

"Of course. I understand that. That is how you think. That is fine. I accept that. Only it cannot stand as is."

"What are you saying?"

"I will do that part."

Earl squinted.

"I don't think that's so good an idea, Mr. Trugood. You yourself said you're best behind a desk. Now suddenly you want to be up there where there's lead flying all over the place and things can get messy. No plan survives contact with the enemy, and I guarantee you that'll happen. Some of these boys may catch one, and I may even catch one. I don't want you catching one. You didn't sign up for that kind of work."

"Believe me, sergeant, I am no hero. I will do nothing heroic. I have no intention of going in harm's way. I'll retreat happily to my desk and wait for a call from you telling me all's well. But I must get a craft up there, something big enough to take all who want to escape away in the morning."

"If you take a craft up there, you will tip off the boys at Thebes exactly what we've got cooking in our little pot. So there would be no point in going. So why go at all? You can't have it two ways. You go in hard and trust what comes will be better, or you don't go in. That I know."

"Seemingly immutable, isn't it?"

"It is."

"So I thought it out. I thought it out, and I came up with something. You've heard of the Trojan Horse?"

It touched something in Earl from long ago. Couldn't quite get it straight, but sure enough he had it filed away for future usage back there among the point of impact of a .30–06 with a quarter value wind drift and the proper way to regulate the rate of fire on the gas pipe under a Browning Automatic Rifle barrel.

"Some old thing. Some big wooden horse, raiders was inside. The boys in the city, they thought it was a gift. Now me, I'd have burned it right there on the plain. That's how a sergeant thinks. But them boys brought it in, and that night the raiders slipped out and started slitting throats."

"That's it exactly."

"I don't think you're going to have a horse built, though."

"No, sir. Not at all."

"What will you build then?"

"I've worked this out neatly. It'll be a barge full of prefabricated housing materials. To build a church. A minister is starting up a flock for the lost Negroes of the swamp. Now the boys won't like that, but they won't quite know what to do. What they don't know is that anyone will see that the beams and the steeples and the roofing triangles can be quickly assembled into rafts. That way, there's an escape."

Earl considered. He didn't like it. But then, he wasn't paying for it, so in a sense it didn't matter what he didn't like.

"You sound so set I can't see much point in trying to talk you out of it. I have to tell you, in the morning, my boys ain't going to be hanging around to help folks put rafts together out of church parts. Our plan stays the same. We hit hard and burn the place and shoot any and all armed men. We free the prisoners, we blow the levee, and we're out of there at first light. My men ain't the kind to be helping old ladies get aboard rafts. You understand that?"

"Totally. It is time the Negro race learned to fend for itself. Surely someone among them will grasp the possibility. I'll simply have the barge towed upriver, moored, and the boatman will leave. I'm simply providing an opportunity. It helps me sleep the night."

"Then if it don't have nothing to do with my people, you will do what you have to do."

"Good, Earl. You understand that."

"I do."

"So I will be off. I have to get to Pascagoula, set all this up. That is all."

Earl didn't like it a bit. Any little thing out of the norm would send the Thebes boys out scurrying. All they had to do was put more men on night patrol, erect the smallest little fortifications, set up flare patterns or wire, and the whole thing got shaky.

"You go ahead then."

"Earl, I have to say one thing. I'm very proud of what we're doing. It's the right thing. I'm so glad you found men who would fight for this cause."

"Sir, you put that out of your mind. These boys ain't fighting for no cause at all. Most of 'em don't care much for the Negroes, if they thought about it a bit, which I doubt they done. They're doing it because it's their nature. They're gunmen. Some have been in it, some haven't, but they've all got to go to the dark valley one time or one more time and see what kind of fellows they are. That's all they care about. They ain't no Holy Rollers. They're bitter, tough old birds, and if you make 'em into something they ain't, you will be powerfully disappointed."

"I expect all righteous armies are like that."

"Wouldn't know about that, sir. To me, armies are just men doing what they think is right and proper, for whatever reason."

"So be it."

He shook Earl's hand, and walked off.

Earl went back to the porch and watched him go away.

Finally, it was time.

He opened up the telegram from Sam, held it in his hand for a second before unfolding it.

Hope you're with me, Mr. Sam. Lord, I hope you're with me.

It said:

UP 73. STOP. CORRECT FOR WIND 15 RIGHT.
STOP. FIRE FOR EFFECT. STOP.
SAM.

Earl smiled. For whatever reason, Sam had come around. That meant but one thing: blow them off the face of the earth.

Dark of the moon, Earl thought, I will do just that.

49

FINALLY, Moon.

Of course, Moon.

Who but Moon?

Moon was given up by Charles who was given up by Noah who was given up by Vonzell who was given up by Roosevelt who was given up by Titus who was given up by Raymond who was given up by George Washington Carver who was given up by Orpheus who was given up by Three Finger.

"You must be prepared for Moon, Sergeant Bigboy," the warden counseled. Yes, Moon was different than the rest, and Moon demanded special consideration, so Bigboy had gone to the world's greatest authority on the male Negro miscreant, classification, behavior, psychology and complexity: the warden, who knew everything about them.

"Moon is a monster, and he is a hero," the warden lectured. "Moon is all the nobility of the Negro race, its courage, its endurance, its cleverness, its strength, its physicality. Yet he is also all its flaws, its seething, never vanquished anger, its innocence about the complex, its inability to concentrate on one goal, its refusal to put today's small pleasures aside for next year's bigger pay-off, its ready will to violence of no point, its omnivorous sexual hunger above all else, its insane refusal to consider consequences. Moon is all these things and more."

"Yes, sir," said Bigboy, awed as always at the man's wisdom.

"You've seen the records," said the warden. "Moon has been a pimp, a gambler, a boxer, a confidence man. He has beaten men to death for money, and he ran a string of high yellers in Jackson. He has had money. He has drunken wine and bubbly champagne. He has won immense amounts betting on the ponies. He has had fine clothes, an automobile, an army of go-fers and factotums. He has raped, pillaged, burned, pirated, done evil by violence, cut men to death with knives. And all before he was twenty-two, at which point he shot and killed a Negro gangster named Jelly Belly Long, but the bullet traveled through Jelly Belly and struck a white child named Rufus, who had been down in the dark part of town with his holy-rolling mother, preaching the word to the fallen Negroes of Jackson's bitterest streets. Nobody cared about Jelly Belly; but the death of Rufus just barely avoided getting Moon lynched or tarred and feathered, and only because the judge was a noted radical did he allow for Moon's lack of intent toward the boy Rufus, and so put Moon away for life plus two hundred and made him, shortly, by the natural order of things, the new king of Parchman Farms. There he killed three guards, five convicts, escaped twice, once for six months, and that at last had him removed to Thebes and the Ape House."

"Yes, I had heard the stories, sir."

"So if you take Moon, you must take him hard and

well. You must tell him at the start who his master is, and strip him of hope, which is the root of courage."

"Yes, sir. But if I get him before the whip, I will break him."

"I know you will, son."

So, at last, Moon.

Taking him down was hard. The guards went in during the dead of night with twice the usual detail. They beat him in his bunk while others with shotguns held his boys off. Bleeding, chained and dazed, he was dragged to the black vehicle and taken to the Whipping House.

Twice he awakened and mutinied, breaking a man's jaw, caving in three ribs of another before he was subdued by another blizzard of blows. But his rebelliousness only put off the inevitable, and the inevitable had at last arrived. He was alone with Bigboy.

Moon was chained to the post, and it was early in the morning with a gray dawn beginning to edge its way into the day. Candles had burned low.

"I expect you'll fight me pretty hard, Moon," said Bigboy, who had stripped to his skin so that his muscles, every bit as sculpted and magnificent as Moon's, gleamed.

"You can't bust me, boss," said Moon. "Ain't got no bust in me. Yo' arm goin' tire afore I sing yo' song."

"Now Moon, if I remember, it's been a time since you tasted the lash."

"Ain't never tasted no whippin', boss."

"Of course not. Then, why now? And to what point? This would be so easy. You tell me who whispered to you the magic words 'pale horse coming.' Then you sit back, have a nice Pepsi-Cola, and I'll find that boy. I will have a talk with him. Then I will know what I am charged to know and it will be all fine here at the Farm."

"Ain't tellin' you nuffin', boss man. You think you

can beat it out of Moon, you go ahead. Moon done been beat before."

"But Moon, not by a whip man. I am a whip man. I can do things with a whip that will amaze you."

Bigboy thought of the massive muscle-ripple expanse of Moon's broad back as his new canvas. He would need all his strength. He would be pressed to the maximum, forced to find new creativities of torture.

"Let's try this for a start," said Bigboy. "Tell me what you think."

He unfurled the whip, gave it a crack like a gunshot as its tip broke the sound barrier, then unleashed five fast snaps like darts at five nerve points on Moon's broad back.

Moon jacked hard at each bite, for at the nerves the man is most vulnerable, and pain rocketed to his brain.

"How was that, Moon? Help me here? Was it much?"

"My ol' daddy done hit me harder than that, boss."

"Tell me, Moon, did he hit harder than this?"

THE Whipping House filled the air with screams that night, and the night after and the night after. It was an epic battle, if a bit one-sided. The whip man punished, the convict endured. On and on it went, the agonized screams floating like an unholy vapor, seeming to hang in all the air and casting upon it all a pall. Evil things were being done; everybody knew it.

At the Store, the black women of Thebes were especially surly. They could smell the blood floating in the heavy jungle air. They stood in their line with their tickets to get their pound of bacon, their five pounds of flour, their pound of coffee, and no one said a word. Usually, this was the best part of the week, for it was release from the muddy, grueling sameness of Thebes, the despair, the fear of men in the night with dogs. But no more. The women languished, silent, untouchable. Admitted, they did their business and left, for the long walk back through the piney woods. They never looked back; they traveled alone, and swiftly.

But perhaps the ordeal was hardest of all on Fish. Not that you would have noticed. Fish went about his ways, merrier, it seemed, than ever. He stopped in the kitchen house for the day's supply of lunches for the field hands, filled up his water can, and then rode about the fields with his wagon and his two mules, jingling wherever he went, bringing palaver, a note of cheer, a desperate hunger to entertain.

Nobody was in a mood to be entertained. Too many had gone in the night, screamed their nights away, and never returned. The guards were testy too, for they too had known something was up, that the pale horse was said to be coming, that their empire, so stable, so beautifully constructed, so munificent, was possibly in jeopardy. This led to an outbreak of twitchy-finger-itis, a disease that primarily afflicts men with guns in charge of men without them, where every shadow is seen to be a threat, every comment a promise of violence to come. Three men were shot, one fatally, over behaviors that in other circumstances would have been dismissed with a laugh, or at most with a smack or two upside the head.

The warden, who had the only working telephone in the prison, worked it hard every day. He called his network of snitches up and down the river, the politicians he owned in Jackson and Pascagoula, the sheriffs throughout the piney woods. He was reassured that the word was the same.

"Bigboy," he said at their nightly meeting, just before his bedtime and Bigboy's session with the recalcitrant

Moon, "there is nothing going on. Not a damn thing. If anybody seeks to move against us, they must come up the river or through the piney woods. I have instructed all to be wary of groups of armed men assembling here or there. They are on the lookout. All is clear. No one can come move against us without coming *to* us, pale horse or not. Only God could deposit men on our doorsteps without us hearing about it three days in advance."

"Paratroopers," said Bigboy, more given to tactical considerations. "They could 'chute in."

But the warden surprised him; he'd thought of this one too.

"I think not, Sergeant. That would involve a goodly expenditure, training, almost certainly some sort of government intervention at some level. Our people in the government who support this endeavor would find out about it, and it could not be done in secret. Who would support financially such an enterprise? No, we have no fears from the sky, at least not from a force large enough to do us any harm. No one coming in here without our knowing about it three days ahead."

"Yes, sir," said Bigboy, much assured. Then he went off to his assignation with Moon, and the warden went sleepily to bed.

Fish was having a nightmare. In the nightmare he was underwater, amid the field of dead Negroes chained to the concrete blocks of their own doom. He clawed for the surface, but he was held down. He pulled amid bubbles and sparkle in the water, his lungs all but exploding, his consciousness ebbing away. He could see faces just above the surface, all white, all laughing. Bigboy was there, just enjoying it so much, a nigger drowning slowly just beyond the surface. Fish saw his own dying face reflected in the darkness of Bigboy's sunglasses, where so much woe had been mirrored. The warden, too: not laughing, but intent, in that preoccupied way of his, as if relating things to things as was his tendency, always seeing the methodical connection, the link, the pattern in all things, pedantic, prosaic, a mechanic in the art and science of keeping the Negro down. He saw Section Boss with that goddamned motherfucker gun he carried everywhere, just guffawing away. He saw Moon, too. Moon, however, was a white man, though big and just as carved up by his adventures in the Jackson underworld, and Moon was laughing at little old Fish, the fixer, the smuggler, the bringer and taker, dying under the water. And he saw the white boy, Bogart, his savior. He was laughing because he was not coming to save Fish or any of them. That was the biggest joke of all.

Fish jerked awake.

He looked around on his pallet. He saw nothing in the darkness, no movement, nothing. He slept in his own room, as a senior trustee in the trustees' quarters, where the men like him who had responsible prison jobs and good incomes from illegal activities by which they could pay off the guards lived in relative comfort, far from the squalor of the field barracks or the Ape House.

Something was different.

He looked out through a barless window at the swamp, slightly agleam in the shimmery light of a shrinking moon. He saw water shining, the shadows of the bent trees, the snaky limbs and twisted fronds. Frogs, maybe a coyote, small mammals, 'gators: they slithered around out there. The crickets sounded.

What was different?

Then he had it.

There was no screaming.

Moon had been broken.

50

THE old bastards were making Earl crazy. He wanted to shoot them all. They were like old ladies, bickering among themselves, forming allegiances, then selling each other out in a trice and forming new ones. But also holding ancient, ruinous grudges, beyond any notions of forgiveness or grace. No Marine unit could have functioned with so much inner strife, but for these old fellows bitterness was one of the great joys of life. What was the point of being old if you couldn't hate your brothers?

Elmer hated Jack. This had to do with a philosophical issue, to be sure: Elmer was a believer in the theory of the big, slow bullet, while Jack only cared for small, fast bullets. But it was more than that, and if one had switched to the other argument, the other would counterswitch just to be not on the same side. Basically, each felt entitled to the leadership of what might be called the gun world. Each was a king. Each had a magazine that published his comments and research, each had a retinue of followers (who hated each other too, even more than the two old rulers), each had connections with certain gun manufacturers (Jack with Winchester, whose products he used exclusively, Elmer with Smith & Wesson, likewise). Each said nasty things about the other whenever it was possible. Each acted with arrogance and majesty. Each had killed over six hundred wild game animals, and while Elmer had once busted broncs and was very cowboy in his way, Jack saw himself as an aristocrat or even an intellectual of the rifle, and had no popular gifts and no interest in them. Elmer could spin a yarn, Jack could deliver a lecture. Each held to his positions as fiercely as rival party chairmen, which of course they were.

But at least Jack and Elmer didn't fight directly. Theirs was more of an oblique thing, the soft comment made just in earshot, the stony frigidity that expressed itself in formal politeness too ostentatious to be real.

"Morning, Mr. O'Brian."

"Mr. Kaye."

"What's that pipe tobacco, sir?"

"Why, Briarwood. With a touch of gingerroot."

"Oh, say, I'll bet that's a nice flavor. Favor rougher stuff than that, I do, but as they say, each to his own."

"Yes, Mr. Kaye. Each to his own."

As for direct confrontations, that was a specialty of the border patrolman and ex–pistol champion Charlie Hatchison. The other five men and Earl were at least unified in one thing: their hatred of Charlie.

Charlie was addicted to aggression. He never tired of telling the others he had killed seventeen men, and if asked, he'd speak all night on the details of each victory, the weight and design of the bullet, its placement in the flesh, whether the opponent died quickly, well shot, or, alas in the case of a poor Wehrmacht *soldat* whom the old bastard had pretty much simply executed, slowly, crying for *vasser* and *mama*. Charlie never tired of that one.

"You should have seen the look on that poor boy's face when my .38 punctured his lung. Never seen nothing like it. It was as if he'd been poleaxed. But he doesn't fall. Now here's the interesting thing. He sits down, very formally, by God, as if he's afraid he's going to dirty up his trousers and get in trouble with God or something. Ha! Never saw nothing like it. On the border, you shoot a Mex, he just goes all floppy, crybabying to his god-damned Catholic God or whatever them beaner people b'lieve in, but this German feller, he managed to kick off real slow like."

That was Charlie is a gentle mood. In the more common pugnacious mood he'd strut around looking for a fight, and it didn't matter to him if it were verbal or physical. His special target was the other border patrolman, the gigantic, taciturn Bill Jennings, another damned writer (all these boys was writers!) for the guns and hunting books, and Charlie loved to needle Bill.

"Bill, you sure you're what you call a human being? Don't say nothing. Don't even kill nothing. You just go around with that mug of yours, bluffing folks to surrender."

"Maybe it's his reputation," said Elmer.

"Hell, just 'cause he was on a television show drawing and shooting a Ping-Pong ball don't mean he's got no reputation, except maybe with that phony-baloney host. I mean a man-killing reputation."

"They say he's the fastest man with a gun ever."

"Hell, he looks like a goddamned mummy. He ain't faster than that old man over there, that is, if you can wake him."

It was true. Ed McGriffin showed up with his lovely little granddaughter Sally in tow, and she made his meals individually, presquashing everything and soaking it in milk so the old boy could get it down. And somehow, she slipped into making all the meals, and the men just let her, including Earl, who was amazed at her energy, her matter-of-factness and her endurance for no guff at all. She chased that damn Charlie out of there at least three times, suspecting, rightly, that he had something unseemly up his sleeve.

Meanwhile, old Ed just sat in a rocker on the front porch, sometimes rocking, sometimes dozing, with a nice pleasant look on his old face. He wore a tie every day and a three-piece suit, and carried with him a gigantic hat that dwarfed his almost hairless, egg-shaped head.

"That old man forgot more about shooting than you'll ever learn in a dozen lifetimes, Charlie," said Elmer.

"Maybe he does, but what the hell good it do anybody if he sleeps all the time? Earl, wasn't you being a mite over optimistic when you invited that geezer?"

"That old man invented fast, Charlie."

"Ah! Earl, you done read too many of those True West books. You b'lieve all that hokum."

"Charlie, Earl would know a thing or two," Elmer said. "He killed what you killed thirty times over. Only, he don't yammer on it all day long. They don't give out them big medals to no 'counts, that I know."

"I don't doubt but that Earl had a good day or two in the war. I'm talking about a lifetime of warring. I'm talking about living by the gun with the gun, with the gun's quickness, for over thirty years. That would be me. Y'all boys just talked on it and figured on it and wrote it up like you done it. Hell, I was *there*! I done it."

At that there came a wet, slurpy sound, and it was old Ed, gobbling down whatever damp stuff his system manufactured while he dozed, but now he'd come awake.

"Charlie, if you shot as much as you talked, there wouldn't be no Mexes left, nor no desperadoes. Yet we have a job agin' desperadoes, so clearly you ain't nothing but turkey poop."

"Grandpap, don't you talk like that!" scolded pretty little Sally. "You'd be mighty embarrassed to face your maker if words like that were the last to cross your lips before you passed. You'd have a powerful lot of explaining to do."

"You listen to that purt' gal," said Charlie, who had a carnal streak in him as well and was known to place himself so that he could get a good, uninterrupted look at the young woman. " 'Cause you don't want to check out with no blasphemy on your tongue."

"And as for you, Charlie Hatchison," said Sally, "why, you can say any damn thing you care to, for no amount of amening and dear Lording and holding back on the blasphemy is going to keep you from frying up all bubbly crisp in Hell like a chicken leg, and that's a fact!"

Everybody laughed, for Charlie was pure unrepentant sinner man. Everybody laughed, that is, except for Jack O'Brian, busy reading some flashy new book like Plutarch's dialogues or Marcus Aurelius's commentaries, who merely huffed majestically from across the room, as if his dignity had been ruffled by all the snippy spatting, and he felt so annoyed he had petitioned to make his feeling known.

FINALLY, the last of them showed, late and a little bedraggled. Audie Ryan climbed out of his MG sports car with a busted lip, a black eye and patches of scab on his knuckles. His fancy cowboy duds were all messed up.

"Audie, where you been, boy?" asked Charlie Hatchison. "You look like you got the worst part of it."

"Don't know why boys in bars always decide I need to be taken down a notch or two. I just wanted a damned beer. But twice, once in New Mexico, once in Tennessee, I had a bully wanted to smack me around some. Boys, don't ever get your picture on the cover of *Life* magazine. All kinds of mischief can spring from it!"

So, somehow, Charlie knew Audie, from some killers' Valhalla in the San Fernando Valley or possibly in north Texas. But the others crowded 'round to shake hands with the famous young man, and he seemed to fit in right away, among men he'd not have to explain a thing to.

He opened up the trunk of the car, pulled out his small leather suitcase and a machine gun.

"Wow! Audie, what the hell is that gun? You are loaded for bear."

"I traded a long-barreled Luger for this from some tank sergeant in France after the war," said the Texan. "Figured it might come in handy, and looks like I may be right."

"What the hell is it, Audie?"

"I think it's what they call a *Strumgewehr*. Model of nineteen forty-four. They call it an attack rifle."

"Them Germans," Charlie said. "They had a goddamn name for everything."

Audie pulled the thing out. It was ugly like no gun any of them had ever seen, stamped from black metal, its furniture of plastic, its magazine a curved thing like a banana, extending from the well beyond the trigger guard. The whole gizmo had a pungent whiff of some alien future to it.

"Looks like a goddamned ray gun," Elmer said. "What's it shoot, atoms?"

"No, sir," said Audie. "Some kind of short little bullet."

"It shoots a 7.92 short," said Charlie. "If they'd have had them early enough, we'd be holding this conversation in German."

"It's a lot handier than a carbine or my old Thompson," said Audie. "And it's pretty accurate, and it's got more punch. It's like a combination of a carbine and a tommy."

"Goddamned no 'count little bullets," said Elmer.

"The bullets aren't particularly small, Mr. Kaye," said Jack O'Brian. "Those are .324s. But the case is quite short, so it never develops rifle velocity. You could say it combines the best parts of a carbine and a Thompson, or you could say it combines the worst parts: too heavy, not enough punch. And I hope you have a lot of ammo for it, young man."

"Well, some."

"Little damn bullets," said Elmer.

"Yeah, Elmer, but when he hits you with it, it's like a hose. You get three in one second, six in two. That'll do the damned job," argued Charlie, contrary as always.

"If Mr. Jack O'Brian has his way, that's what we'd all end up carrying. Little goddamn guns with little goddamn bullets. I'll stick with my .44s, thanks very much, if it's all the same."

"Mr. Kaye, you are a cantankerous, obstinate, obdurate sonofabitch."

"Can someone please translate that into English?" said Elmer grumpily. "My Latin's a little rusty."

"I think I got the 'sonofabitch' part just right."

But before the two oldsters could square off, Audie defused the situation by piping up with, "Is that Ed Mc-Griffin?" He had spied the old man sleeping softly on the porch through all this blabbing.

"Yeah, but don't wake him!"

"Howdy there," Audie sang to young Sally.

"Well, howdy yourself," she replied.

"Oh, I think it's lovey-dovey at first sight!" said Elmer. "I think we got us a thang goin' on here."

Earl watched the two young people with an interest that surprised him. He hadn't thought that out, and he didn't want some romance gumming up the works here. Shit. It annoyed him, he didn't know why.

But Audie said quickly, "No, sir, I am just payin' my proper respects is all. Ma'am, pleased to meet you. My name is Audie Ryan."

"I saw you in a cowboy picture," she said.

"I hate them pictures," Audie said. "You have to wear girly makeup, and most of the men are kind of flower-sniffing, if you know what I mean. It ain't no work for a Texan."

"Pays good though, don't it, Audie?"

"Hell, I just use the money for booze, more guns and a fancy car or two. Ain't nothing big about it."

"I thought the picture was pretty good," she said. "Cowboy and all. Lots of cowboys."

"Well, girlie," said Charlie, "if that's your taste, you are definitely hanging out at the right medicine lodge. This here is the last corral, and we are, by God, the last cowboys. And we are riding out to our last big gun affray. After us, it's all gone."

"Yee haw," said Elmer. "That is the goddamned truth."

"I'd drink to that!"

Even Bill Jennings, silent as the sphinx, let a smile crease the lower portion of the battered Hoplite shield he carried around as a face.

"Well, while you all are drinking and telling each other how big and brave you are, and welcoming this here fellow, I'm out there trying to find some new way to fancy up franks and beans. So you just go on, you heroes!"

Sally stormed out, and the old men, and the new young one, hastened after, to avoid her wrath.

51

As he said he would, Davis Trugood drove straight through the night and arrived the next day in Pascagoula. The old city lay balmy in the soft breezes off the bay, and Davis stopped just outside of town, rented a room in a tourist home, took a nice shower, put on a new suit of white linen, a fresh spruce white shirt and a nice yellow tie. Meanwhile, his driver buffed up his shoes to a fine shine.

At 3:00 P.M., they drove into Pascagoula, but he wasn't looking for a place to have a church prefabricated under crash conditions, as he had told Earl. In fact, had Earl and Sam seen what happened next, it would have boggled their minds no end at all. For with no hesitation whatsoever, Mr. Trugood's driver headed them downtown and swiftly found the town hall on Pascagoula Street, where a crowd had gathered and some sort of festivity was soon to commence. The driver guided the large black car to the curbside, where indeed a red carpet lay, its destination the stairway into that ancient, distinguished building.

Davis Trugood stepped out.

Flashbulbs popped.

Applause arose.

A tide of well-wishers engulfed the man, pumping his hand, welcoming him back, assuring him that everything was as he had planned.

There, standing proudly on the steps of the city hall, was the mayor, the assistant mayor, the chief of police, the president of the city council, three aldermen, two distinguished-looking gentlemen from the governor's office in Jackson, ready to make excuses that the governor himself was not there to grace the proceedings with his presence.

Davis, accompanied by two smartly dressed police officers, was taken to the confab at the top of the stairs, where handshakes were exchanged all around.

Microphones were brought out, and quickly the mayor took over as master of ceremonies.

"May I say, Mr. Davis Trugood, we are so happy to see you back on this wonderful day, which promises so much for our fair city, for its out-of-work ship chandlers and carpenters, for the entire region of southeast Mississippi, for all our citizens, for our nation forever."

More clapping and, smiling broadly, Davis Trugood acknowledged the applause.

"These have been hard times," the mayor continued. "With the war over and the Navy shrinking, Pascagoula ain't the shipbuilding town it once was, and so our proud city has done seen itself on the decline. We have lost population to our northern neighbors. Our most talented young people have gone off to seek a better life in the North . . ." and of course it went on in that vein for quite some time, as the mayor was not one to speak succinctly when he could speak at length.

A few other officials got their moment of glory, each to speak an equally fine piece complimenting each other, the great city of Pascagoula, the great state of Mississippi and the future.

Finally, the mayor nodded, and an open limousine pulled up. The mayor ushered Mr. Trugood into its backseat, and, escorted by police motorcyclists and several other official cars, the small parade negotiated the few blocks to the waterfront where, outside a large building, another crowd awaited.

The ceremony was repeated, though much attenuated this time through, and at last, Davis Trugood was allowed to speak.

"Mr. Mayor," he said. "I am happy to be here on this historic day, and I am so happy to have a small part in revitalizing this beautiful old town. I should tell you how this came to pass. In the North, where I do my business, where certain things are taken for granted, where I have prospered, we count upon one thing: the immutability of earth. Earth there is solid. It is unmoving, unyielding and permanent. You may dig into it, build upon it, mold it, channel it, sculpt it, landscape it. But here, earth is shaky. It is soupy, tangential, marginal stuff, which may not be trusted. The history of your region is a tragedy of rivers taking their revenge. Well, sir, it occurred to me that I would take my revenge on the river. Yes, sir, I would find a way to defeat the river, at least in a small way, and seize from it its most disturbing violence, the violence it does to our dearly departed, those who gave so much to establish us here in what we call civilization."

The applause was nice.

"And so I have researched and invested heavily in this new factory. I have hired over fifty of your best artisans and I have provided them with the best materials. From quality lumber to quality caulking to quality joinery, and at a surprisingly modest price, for I am a kind man and wish not to make a profit but to assuage the anguish of grieving. I will, from this base, ship throughout the riverine southland, reaching into swamp and forest and creek and quay, and in that way, I will reduce the ache of pain that a man feels when not only is his home or farm devastated by water but his progenitors are so destroyed. Therefore, I give you the Trugood Waterproofed Casket Company."

The applause was slapped dryly against the gulf breeze and the smell of the river was everywhere.

"The new Trugood waterproof coffin is impervious to the ravages of the river. Your loved ones' mortal remains will remain exactly as they were when they passed. Your rural poor will no longer have to consign the dead to the uncertainty of the water table, nor to store them aboveground in stone mausoleums that we understand to be baking ovens that do as much damage as the water, only faster.

"Therefore, today we begin to ship to the immediate region." Of course, there was no need to point out that this commercial enterprise, well financed by Mr. Trugood, was hastened to accomplishment by numerous gifts, loans, presents, and promises he had given the good politicians of Pascagoula and surrounding counties.

"Today we ship to the Biloxi Bayou. We ship up the Pear River. We ship into Louisiana and into Alabama. We ship upriver even, so that our wares may even meet the benighted and isolated souls of counties such as George and Greene and even the farthest and most desolate, Thebes. Yes, friends, we consider this day the start of our revenge on the dark waters of Mississippi and all the grief and pain they have brought to our families."

52

SAM had removed his family to St. Louis, where they lived with his wife's mother, far from the retaliatory powers of the men of Thebes. He had become furtive, unsettled, paranoid. He knew he was on somebody's kill list. He couldn't even enjoy any time with the heroic Connie, whose finger had been stitched up and set (it was broken by the force of the descending striker), during which time she, of course, had made wisecracks and flirted with the young doctor. Sam had rented as cheaply and anonymously as possible a combination apartment-office in an undistinguished neighborhood of Little Rock, near the Air Force base, amid a sea of transients, where he could now but wait for Earl to strike in the dark of the moon and remove the threat against him and return his life to him.

So he returned to his quest, though the dark of the moon was but a few days off. He had determined to find out the secret of David Stone, M.D., and if, lacking gun skills, experience, and the type of mind to close with and shoot to death the men of Thebes, then he had decided that this last thing, small as it was, and perhaps as meaningless as it was, would be his last contribution.

If no doctor would help him, he would try lawyers. Reasoning that students at Harvard law and Harvard medical might share dormitory space, and having far more contacts in that world, he began to examine the Harvard law class of 1928, helped by the good auspices of a former governor of Arkansas, who was himself Harvard law of 1918. Thus he fought his telephone war, alone in his office in Little Rock, armed with numbers and charts of connections; in this way, he tracked men through corporate boards and municipal judicial systems, through great law firms, through directorships of huge organizations, and through the professorates of many great law schools.

It was among the last that he finally achieved just the faintest possibility of a breakthrough. He was talking to a Professor Reginald Duprey, of Madison, Wisconsin, and the University of Wisconsin Law School.

"Well, Mister—what was it?"

"Vincent. Samuel Vincent, sir."

"Mr. Vincent, you know, I didn't know anybody in the medical school except my poor brother."

Sam knew that from his examinations of the Harvard medical graduates there was no Dr. Duprey carried in the graduating class of '28, or '29 or '30 for that matter.

"I see," he said noncommittally.

"Jerry was a little wild. He made some mistakes. He was smart, don't get me wrong, but I think Dad pushed him into medicine, and he wasn't suited for medicine."

"Dad was a doctor?"

"Dad was a lawyer *and* a doctor. There are a few. We were to be one of each. I did what I was told, but Jerry finally blew out his third year. He was so close. But he got caught cheating on a test. It was a family scandal. Jerry's in Texas now. He's a high school biology teacher. I haven't heard from him in years."

"Do you have an address?"

"Yes."

Sam took it, and eventually reached Jerry Duprey in New Braunfels, not that it did any good, for at first Jerry denied knowing anything about his brother, then he denied having been at Harvard or even having heard of Harvard, and finally he denied ever having heard of a Dr. David Stone. But Sam had been a prosecutor long enough to know the little gulp that announced the presence of a lie or two, when a tide of phlegm clogs the throat as the liar improvises awkwardly.

So he knew Jerry Duprey knew a thing or two. He drove a full day to New Braunfels, a leafy town south of Austin, and called upon Mr. Duprey at New Braunfels High School. There, it was clear, he was a beloved figure, not only a popular teacher but the basketball coach, the chess team sponsor, the faculty advisor to the weekly *New Braunfelian* and the college counselor.

Jerry made him wait, and when he finally admitted him to the little office, was quite nervous.

"Sir," Sam explained, "I am not here to bring you any trouble. I am not here about any aspect of your past except that you might have a line on a man named David Stone. I don't even care where or when you met him, and this is not a deposition. It has no legal meaning whatsoever. I'm just asking a favor."

Duprey sat, caught in his own private agony. Finally he said, "I have built a good life down here. I am sorry for what happened and for my failures in the other life and for my father's rage and my brother's contempt. But I am proud of what I have done down here and the kids I have helped and I do not mean to lose that."

"I absolutely represent no threat to you. I will take no notes. I will declare under oath that I have never met you. This is not in regard to a legal matter and no court case is in the offering, nor any testimony of any kind. Give me the benefit of your memories, and I will never see you again."

"It was very long ago and I have forgotten much."

"Yet you did, in fact, know him."

"He was a friend. Briefly. I don't know why. Insanely ambitious, very hard worker. Maybe he scented in me what he was, and that is a son bending under a mantle of family expectations. In my case, it broke me; in his, I suppose, it made him a saint."

"He was a saint?"

"In that, unlike the others, he was not interested in money. He had a genuine interest in doing good. I think his rebellion against his father was different than mine. Mine was to destroy the life my father had planned for me, which not incidentally killed my father and estranged my brother. David's was to be everything his father wasn't; that is, not a society gynecologist, but a great researcher. Not a Jewish outsider trying to make it in the cosmopolitan town, and proud when he did, but someone known far and wide for his goodness. He was obsessed with 'goodness,' somehow."

"He sounds dangerous."

"See, that's your cynicism. You're a prosecutor; you think everyone is guilty of something, even if only in their minds. But I don't think David was like that. He took great pleasure in his goodness, almost sensuous pleasure."

"I see. Well, he lived a hero's life, he died a hero's death. But there are some things about him I thought maybe you'd have some insight into."

"Insight? Boy, that's a word you don't hear much in New Braunfels. Sure, yeah, try me."

"Ah, I visited his home and his widow. And found that he had secrets. Odd that he should have secrets, such a good man. Do you have a comment? I also found that the body reported to be his after his death in nineteen forty-five was not. It was some other man's."

The man's stony face met Sam's. In a time, he said, "You know, he was a good man. Why are you doing this?"

It was Sam's first true inkling that he was onto something.

"It's not about him. It's about what happened to him in the war. I have to find out his involvement in something in the war that may have led to something going on now."

"But you can't tell me what?"

"I have confidences to keep, too."

"Then you certainly understand that I must keep mine as well, if only out of respect to the dead."

"Well then, what about the fact that his wife was infected with syphilis in the mid thirties, and could have no children. Now, again you'll think it's my cynicism, but suppose she got that disease from him in the first place, he knew it but could not face her knowing of a secret life. So he had her raped, so that the syphilis was thought to come from the rapists. Does that strike you as a possibility?"

"Good Lord, man, have you no decency?"

"His subsequent actions are consistent with incredible shame. He suffered what can only be termed a serious attack of nerves, maybe even a breakdown, immediately prior to what was called his death. But it gets stranger yet. There still seems to be, at some high level, some sort of government involvement in the program that he founded in Mississippi. And someone is extremely interested in keeping it secret. It's a fine kettle of fish this saint has gotten himself into."

Jerry Duprey just shook his head.

"And finally this. He published for years, very aggressively, very dynamically, very brilliantly, in a number of prestigious medical journals. Then, in 1936, nothing. That would have to be about the time his wife was raped and lost the capacity to have children. He ceased to exist. Yet he didn't die until 1945. Or so it's alleged. But whatever, he ceased publishing. Do you know why?"

"Well, you are a clever man, aren't you, Mr. Vincent? You have uncovered a great deal. Is it that important? He meant well, he did well, he really did help the world. The sick, the poor, the victimized. He believed in them. Yes, I suppose he had some human appetites. Who doesn't? Don't you?"

Sam thought of the woman he loved more than his wife, with whom he would never sleep nor live, who would leave, eventually, and he would then wallow in his bitter destiny.

"Of course I do. But I'm not here to judge him. That's for someone else. Not me. And one last thing. Can you think of anything that might connect him to the Plutonium Laboratory at Los Alamos, or some issue of nuclear medicine, and thence to a government installation in Maryland called Fort Dietrich? I know that seems—"

"You've been seeing too many movies."

"I haven't seen a movie since nineteen forty-six."

"As for the other three questions, I happen to know the answer to all of them. It's really the same answer. But I'm not going to give it to you. Because I don't like your certitude. You are a man who has never made a mistake, and it annoys me, a man who's made many mistakes."

"Sir, take it from me, I have made some lulus."

"Well, then, I will give you one clue, for your lulus. One clue alone. If you are as smart as you seem, you will have no trouble figuring it out and all your questions will be solved."

"Fair enough."

"Maybe when he finally decided where his career had to go, he could no longer publish under his own name. For certain reasons. So maybe he published under another name."

"That's very interesting," said Sam, and thought immediately of that letter from Harold E. Perkins, about a bill of lading being cc-ed to another doctor in Thebes, Mississippi, years after the alleged death of David Stone whose name he could not remember but who he knew was not named Stone.

"I only know this because he was the one guy from Harvard who kept in touch with me and dropped me a card or two every year. He even offered to loan me some dough when I was kicked out. He *was* good, you know."

"I believe that."

"So he made a joke about what he was doing, and what it linked up to in his private personality that I knew about when I was close to him, and what he had to do to preserve the name of the 'good doctor' he had become."

Sam's eyes bored into him intently, the old prosecutor's trick. It had no effect. Jerry Duprey told him because Jerry Duprey wanted to, and for no other reason.

"His middle name was Goodwin. Remember that, Mr. Vincent. His middle name was Goodwin."

53

D ARK of the moon was just a few days off. The most important thing, Earl knew, was to let them get used to each other, or as used to each other as such a confabulation of ornery, egotistical old cusses could manage. Audie seemed to settle them down, though each little clique sought him out to join up. But Audie was too much his own man, and Earl was happy to see the youngest man avoid the pitfalls of siding with one or the other, and instead work hard to keep on the best of terms with them all. He was also, though he could find no words to express this, happy to see that no little puppy love thing sprung up between Sally and Audie.

So for two more days, it was more like a convention of old fools than it was any kind of gunfight preparation. They joshed and bickered and needled, and Charlie Hatchison got them all mad at him with his aggression, and Bill Jennings dominated by the steel countenance of his majestic face, and Elmer and Jack sniffed arrogantly around each other, and Ed snoozed gently on the porch, ate the food his granddaughter prepared, and had a pleasant if vague smile for them all. But if he seemed not to know exactly where he was, Earl knew that to be an illusion; he knew exactly where he was and what was set. He was simply saving up his energy.

On the night after the next, Earl finally had to take over and to begin to guide them. He did this by means of a meeting called for 8:00, after the evening meal, when all were most relaxed and before any had gotten too drunk.

Earl had played it quiet till now. He knew these old boys were stars in their own little worlds, and didn't need a sudden tyrant to bark at them and treat them like shit. They needed guidance more than leadership.

"Okay, fellows," he said. "I'd like to talk this thing out for all to hear and so that all can comment. Is that fair? Are you ready for that?"

"Earl," said Charlie, "these boys are too old to retain any information you give 'em. They're all so close to senile, there ain't no point. Just shove 'em in the right direction and tell 'em to shoot, and that's about all as you're going to get out of 'em."

"You speak for yourself, you dry old goat," said Elmer. "I got plenty piss left in my liver, and no dried-up old Texas stringbean Mexican-killer is going to speak for me."

"Well, yippie ki yi!" yelped Jack. "Mr. Kaye has gotten his back up."

"Now fellows," crooned Audie. "Let's just settle down and listen. You too, Charlie."

"Charlie thinks when he puts his butt on the toilet it's candy that comes out," said Jack O'Brian, from behind his harsh spectacles. "But so do all of you. I'm the only man of whom it's true."

"Jack, whyn't you go fiddle with them biddy-little bullets you like so much?"

"All right, all right," said Earl, as the bickering

threatened to break out and overwhelm them all. "Now look here and see what we got before us."

He pulled a sheet off something he'd brought to the head of the room and mounted on a couple of chairs, and of course it was a map.

But it was a map like no map they'd ever seen before. It was a high altitude photo reconnaissance map, complete to the tiniest detail of vegetation and architecture. "This is it. Thebes Penal Farm for Colored, as seen from thirty thousand feet by a Banshee photo jet nose camera. Got me a friend who's a high mucky-muck in naval aviation circles, and he pulled this one out of the hat for me.

"Look at it. It's got all the roads, all the distances; it's got all the buildings; you can even make out some of the paths in the woods. You can see the curve of the river embracing it. You can follow the roads. You can, and I know you are all good compass men, take your readings from this map so that when you are on the ground you can orient fast and night-navigate better than the boys who've been there ten years. That's the way they fight wars these days, and that's the way we'll fight this one."

The old men were at last silent. There it was before them, the sweep of the river, the Big House, the Store, the Whipping House, the Screaming House, the prison compound with the four towers around the Ape House, the road out to the levee project, the levee itself holding back the water, the Drowning House, with its scow moored to the dock. Earl could even see the little blasphemy of the coffin out back of the Whipping House.

"These people are heavily armed," he began. "This will be a gunfight, like I promised. You will prevail on your coolness, experience and shooting skills. These boys have never faced men who can shoot as well as you, have your determination and spirit. That's why I ain't training you or running any drills as I would with young fellows."

"And you don't want any of these old farts shitting up their pants," said Charlie.

"Thank you, Charlie, for your observation."

"That looks like a mighty big setup," said Elmer.

"It is. But like I say, seven men can take it. Seven against Thebes and it's finished. You each will have an assignment, and it'll happen smooth and easy, I swear to you."

"Earl, put me where I can get the most kills," sang Charlie. "Got seventeen. Want more. Three things a man can't have too much of: wives, guns or kills. In a pinch, I could do without the first."

"You ain't laid with a damn woman in fifty years," said Elmer.

"I'll put you where the shootin' will be fiercest, Charlie. You will have your goddamn snootful of action by the time this is all over. Anyhow, fifty guards, by my count, all armed with Winchester 07 self-loaders shooting a .351 Winchester round and Colt revolvers. I saw one Thompson and maybe a half-dozen Model '97 Winchester 12-gauges. They're housed in a barracks behind the Whipping House. We've got to seal them there. That's one big problem. The other big problem is the four Browning water-cooled machine guns in the four towers, and in each there will be a two-man night crew with spotlights. If those guns get into play, they're simply going to make matchsticks out of the barracks and kill all the Negroes. That's their point. They're Warden's insurance policy. They keep the boys good at night, 'cause he can kill 'em all in the snap of a finger.

"So do you see it yet?"

There was silence. Then it was Jack, the intellectual, who spoke.

"I see it."

"Tell them."

"The weakness is that everything is geared to keep the prisoners *in*. It's not to keep us *out*."

"That's it exactly. The forest and the swamp, and the long dark river: that's what they're counting on for their protection. And that's why I can get teams in there and up close without detection, and strike fast and hard. We have to trap them in their buildings. We don't want them roaming about, because then we're hunting targets all around us, and they're hunting us. If we got them in their buildings, we win, easy.

"So this is it: first off, our Irish invasion. Mr. Ryan and Mr. O'Brian will land here"—he put a marker pin on the map—"move across the fields in darkness, and hit the towers. That is your job. I'll give you a compass reading, and track you a path in away from populated buildings. You won't have no problems. You will get into one of the towers, take it over, and from that vantage point, Jack, you will pick off the other gunners. Then, Jack, you will remain in the tower as a kind of backup. You will scope the action, and wherever you see targets, you will deal with them."

"Got it," said Jack.

"Audie, over here is 'ho town, as they call it. It's where the women who work the prison kitchen and laundry live, and they's known to take in visitors from the guards at night. You have to clear that. Can you do it with that German gun?"

"Think I might," said Audie.

"Meanwhile, Elmer and Bill are going to be at the guards' barracks. They are going to do that one fast, in the second after Jack and Audie go into action. When he finishes his job, old Charlie will join them. I will come over from the Whipping House, which is my special place. We will hit them, and hit them hard, and burn them out. Most of the guards will be in the barracks, which is where the armory and the kennels are, and we want to hit them before they can release them god-damned dogs. If they don't give it up, they will go down hard. We may have to burn 'em out.

"Now Charlie, here's your play. You will be in the woods, 'bout a mile out. That's where the sheriff's deputies are quartered. You're going to light that place up and shoot any men that don't surrender. Then you join up with Elmer, Bill and I and work on the guards' barracks. Then the four of us join Jack and Audie, take over the compound and let the prisoners go. Then y'all head for the river, where you will deal with any remaining guards, but by that time, with the Negroes free and the place burning, most will have gone. You head for the levee. Audie, you got military demolitions skills?"

"I had to destroy some bridges, Earl. I learned how to blow things up right nice."

"I worked on engineering projects in my youth," said Jack. "I can blow up anything."

"Well, that's something I didn't know," said Earl. "It sure comes in handy. It ain't a bridge you're blowing. It's just dirt. You blow the levee and head back onto the river. While you're doing that, I will head down the road to the Screaming House. There is some business there I have to take care of. I will meet you all in the morning by the river.

"Now let me tell you who to watch for special. They got one man there I will honestly tell you I fear. Kill him, and the job is ninety-five percent over, for he is the guts and strength of Thebes. His name is Bigboy; he runs the place. Guard sergeant. Big white boy, so white he glows. He's an albino, but that doesn't make him weak and scared. It makes him tough as hell and twice as determined. He will rally his men, he will bring fire, he will fight a hard fight. So I am warning you, he is not to be trusted. See a big white man glowing in the dark, strong as a bull, he's the one you drop first, you hear?"

"If I bring his head, Earl," said Charlie, "will you give me a nickel and a piece of bubble gum?"

"Mr. Earl?"

It was Sally, sitting next to the old man.

"Yes, sweetie?"

"Grandpap wants to know his job."

"Grandpap will be in the town. I will get grandpap in the town and he will set up at a little bar they have there. That will draw a bunch of deputies, I know. He will deal with them. In fact, that'll be the start of the whole thing. When the deputies come to arrest Mr. Ed., Mr. Ed will take care of them."

Mr. Ed listened politely. Then he whispered something to Sally.

"How many?" she repeated, louder.

"Five, I'd say."

Agitated, the old man whispered something again to Sally.

"Grandpap says that since he'll have six bullets, what's he supposed to do with the extra?"

After the laughter died down, Jack had a question.

"Earl, if everything goes to plan—"

"It won't."

"I know. And I know that all evidence we leave behind us goes under the river, so there's nothing to trace anybody by."

"That's right."

"But my question is, we're supposed to burn all these buildings down. Are we supposed to carry torches?

Can't see running through the dark with torches while hillbillies are shooting at me."

"That's a very good question. My answer is: Who wants to watch a cowboy picture?"

There was silence.

"I have Hoppy, lots of Hoppy. I have Sandy the singing cowboy, and Buck and Hoot and even some William S.? Who's interested?"

Again there was no answer.

"Well, look here," he said, and pulled out an Italian canteen.

"Know what this could be? A World War I canteen. But it ain't full of water. No sir, it's full of chopped-up cowboy picture."

Stupefaction reigned.

"Come out on the porch with me."

They followed him out.

"Old-time movies were made on a kind of celluloid coated with a chemical called silver nitrate. The nitrate's fine; the celluloid is unstable, particularly as it grows older. Hell, it's explosively incendiary, which is why if you look, most projection booths are more like bank vaults than rooms. I got each canteen loaded up with bits and pieces of chopped-up movie film, and I rigged a kind of primitive match fuse."

He unscrewed the lid and unfolded a cord wedged in the spout.

"You just pull on this thing, and toss it fast. Don't be holding it."

He pulled the cord and deep inside the canteen, a match pulled against a striker board, lit, began to burn excelsior packed loosely about it, and in two seconds, by which time Earl had lobbed it, burned through a cardboard tube.

"Jesus Christ!" somebody said.

The canteen burst not into flames so much as into hell; the incineration spurted outward not in an explosion but in a kind of blossom, burning so white-hot and fierce it hurt the eyes of those who looked at it and they had to twist away.

"Burn through anything. Melts the canteen in a tenth of a second. Burns for a solid five minutes, white-hot like that, and spreads and oozes all about, blazing like a blowtorch, setting the world aflame. Burns under water, burns in the wind, just burns and burns until it's gone."

"I always say," said Charlie, "nothing like a good cowboy picture."

54

SAM sat in the medical library at the University of Texas at Austin, just a few miles up the road from New Braunfels, and watched a life swim into existence. The first spottings were tentative, in obscure journals.

"Certain predispositions toward distribution in an Asian strain of *Treponema pallidum*" by D. Goodwin, M.D., was the first, from a 1936 issue of the *Journal of Canadian General Medicine*. Then, quickly, a second: "*Treponema pallidum*: some Malaysian adaptations." This was from *Lancet,* the British medical journal.

In both cases, the identity of the contributor was a minimal amount of information. "D. Goodwin is a medical researcher" was all it said.

But D. Goodwin, M.D., flourished, if David Stone, M.D., disappeared. D. Goodwin, M.D., was like some kind of mounted knight in combat immemorial against *Treponema pallidum,* whatever that was, the world over. Where it appeared, he appeared to rush off and study it.

"Burma: A new strain of *Treponema pallidum.*"

"*Treponema pallidum*: variations on the lower Indian subcontinent."

"Influence of temporal variation on distribution patterns of *Treponema pallidum* in sub-Saharan Africa."

D. Goodwin, M.D., wouldn't stop working, wouldn't stop writing. He had given his life over to this illusive spray of germs or whatever they were, which seemed to cast such a long shadow through the world, and which seemed to exist everywhere.

By 1941, he had published thirty-one papers; then the war came.

But D. Goodwin, M.D., was intractable.

He even found time to publish while running the 2809th Tropical Disease Research Unit.

"Prevalence of *Treponema pallidum* among southern rural Negroes, Mississippi, 1943" appeared in the *Harvard Medical Journal,* though now the ID of the author simply read "is a serving officer of the Army Medical Corps."

Then "Similarities between varieties of southern rural *Treponema pallidum* and certain strains in Borneo"; this in the *Journal of Medicine* of the University of Chicago.

Sam sat in a great room. He scanned the articles, but it was mostly Greek to him. He was at a large table outside the stacks, and the place was crowded with students, all working intently, their eyes firmly fixed on the future. Outside, the famous tower of the University of Texas stood guard.

Then the documents ran out. There were none after 1946.

He looked around. He felt he was in a sacred place.

He turned, and two seats away from him a young woman pored intently through something called *Aspects of Brain Chemistry* with almost desperate intensity.

Yet there was something vaguely approachable about her.

"Miss," he whispered, "are you a medical student?"

She looked up, fixed him with a pretty American smile. She had freckles.

"Sir," she said, sweetly, "actually, I'm a nursing student. Second year."

"Oh, I see. Well, possibly you could help me just a second."

He slid his card over, and she looked at it.

"I am in way deep over my head. I am researching the career of a doctor involved in some litigation, and I came down here to take some depositions."

"A Texas doctor?"

"No, ma'am. Actually, I guess a Baltimore doctor."

That seemed to relieve the young lady considerably. She did not want to get into anything involving a Texas doctor.

"He's published a lot in medical journals, public health journals, you know, and it's mostly gibberish to me. Can't make out heads nor tails."

"I see."

"See, there's this one thing, don't know if it's a disease, or what, that appears in all his work. And there might be some connection with nuclear medicine. Atomic rays, that sort of thing? Are you familiar with that?"

"Well, sir, experiments are underway to use atomic power to cause genes to mutate to specific purpose. I don't know much about it, but it's evidently one of the great benefits of the atomic bomb research."

"Hmmm," said Sam. "I wonder how that would apply to our subject. Are you familiar with the term? It's called, ah, *Treponema pallidum*. Would you know what—?"

But the horror rose on her pretty young face, and she started to scream, and campus security got there within seconds, and they dragged Sam off before he could do any real damage, and held him until the Austin vice detectives got there.

55

ALL the talk is done now. The old enmities have run out of steam, the gossip on the misfortune of others has lost its lure, the fascinations of the technical have been discussed until they've been drained of all meaning. Bourbon has been drunk. Gunfights, famous and obscure, valorous and pathetic, have been gone over again and again; great pistoleros have been analyzed, respected or dismissed. Heroes have been saluted, cowards shunned.

There is nothing left.

Even Earl feels it.

Men about to go into battle acquire a certain pallor. They may be salty old dogs, such as these boys, or innocent kids, such as his Marines, but they know death is very close at hand and that there's no guessing what lies in the immediate straight-ahead. It settles them, it drains them, it stills them.

Still, they must turn to something.

And you can learn a lot about a man in what he turns to. The very good turn to the Bible. The very carnal turn to images of the flesh, in the thousands of sepia-toned male magazines of the war, with their starlets cupping ice-cream scoop breasts, or their skirts a-fling, showing luscious, stocking-kissed gams with fancy undergarment riggings. The prosaic turn to facts, memorizing the operational orders, studying maps and weather reports and even current charts. The physical turn to action: they must unleash themselves in basketball or wrestling or just plain horsing around.

The warriors turn to guns.

WE are in the revolver kingdom. Those brilliantly crafted devices, the hallmark of unnamed genius engineers of Hartford, Connecticut, and Springfield, Massachusetts, dominate both the law enforcement and the civilian imagination.

So there sits Elmer Kaye, the dean of the revolver boys. Elmer has cleaned his guns before and will again, but tonight he cleans them with a new cold knowledge. Meanwhile, outside on a calm night, a silvery moon edges toward extinction and battle.

Elmer will fight with his guns, and has decided to ignore Earl's injunction to use guns that can be abandoned easily and lead authorities nowhere. Better to love and trust what you fight with, and worry about the consequences later, than to go into the fight with a gun you don't trust, which lets you down and gets you killed.

So he's running a rod through the four inches of his big-framed Smith & Wesson .44 1950 model, a plug-ugly thing made grotesque by the thickness of the barrel combined with a hood for the hand-ejector rod, which gives it the look of a cartoon gun, as Donald Duck would carry, not a real one, that Elmer Kaye would carry. It wears ivory stocks from the Gun Re-Blue Company with the visage of an eagle on both sides, and the thickness of that grip will cushion Elmer's hand from the heavy recoil of his specially loaded "improved" .44 cartridges, with a dose of new powder and his own design of semiwadcutter bullet. The gun will buck hard when fired, but whatever that bullet hits, it will knock down and keep down. Elmer's already cleaned the other he'll carry, a Colt Police Positive as a hideout gun in a shoulder holster (it's delicate and ladylike, and he doesn't want Jack O'Brian to see it and tease him) and a Colt Single Action, that is, an old cowboy-style revolver, also in .44 Special, with a specially hand-honed action, so that cocking and shooting it is like squashing your fingers around a stick of butter.

Old Ed McGriffin is also a Smith & Wesson man. Been one his whole damned life. Set all his records, did all his exhibitions, trained many a policeman and Boy Scout, all with Smiths. Ed has two hand-honed mid-framed .38s with graceful six-inch barrels. He's fired each at least ten thousand times, and he knows them as well as any man can know a gun. His pretty niece, Sally, cleans them for him, but he watches, and once again his eyes are sharp and focused, as if he's willed himself back from the place of content and memories, for what she is doing is important. She scrubs out each cylinder, she ramrods the barrel, she uses a piece of screen to peel the impacted lead out of the barrels. She knows the guns, too; she's been cleaning them for Grandpap since she was eight.

Jack O'Brian isn't a handgunner, not really. His weapon of choice will of course be a Winchester Model 70 in his beloved .270, which is accurate as hell, especially with the loads he's prepared for it. But he knows he has to have a handgun, and the one he chooses he can't let Elmer see, for Elmer will tease him, because it represents exactly the opposite of his public position on these matters. He doesn't mind being a hypocrite if it'll keep him alive. So he cleans it furtively, up in his room.

It's a Colt New Service, in .45 Long Colt. It's a giant's gun, the biggest Colt ever made, its frame spreading the hand wide on it, its trigger-pull taut, even its hammer-pull a little tense. It's ugly, humpbacked, with its check-ered wood grips, a Pachmayr grip adapter to swell out the gap between grip and trigger guard. But it's the pre-eminent man-stopper; in fact, many knowledgeable New York detectives carry such a piece, but with its bar-rel cut down to two inches. They know that if they have to put a man down, they have to put him down fast and solid, and Jack has done his research.

It shoots gigantic shells that seem like ostrich eggs in their heaviness and density. Jack deposits each into the gaping chambers in the cylinder, then gently locks the cylinder shut. The gun trembles when he does so and, loaded, the whole weapon feels charged with electricity, with stored energy. Immense and sagacious, it waits to speak.

Bill, taciturn and controlled in all things, is the same in this. He does not have relationships with his guns and they do not speak to his imagination, nor is his ego ex-pressed through them. They are totally and completely tools to him. He has three, all Smiths, all .357 Magnums, which he'll load with the .38–44 super-high-velocity 158-grainers that Earl has provided. His actions have been honed, but what's odd about his revolvers that marks them as different from the others are the grips. He can't use the standard Smith magna grip, not even with a Pachmayr or a Tyler adapter to fill out the curve behind the trigger. Bill's hands are simply too big. Bill has huge hands, long arms loaded with fast twitch muscles, and at six feet four inches enough lanky body to make sleeping in a normal bed or walking through a normal door an exercise in patience. But the hands are the secret to his gun work, because in them, the guns can be manipulated with extraordinary effect, if he can get a good grip. Thus his Smiths wear a somewhat magnified set of stocks, swollen, though polished smooth, seemingly without art to them at all. They simply look like the noses of bowling pins or some such, but they are big enough to extend his fingers and make contact with his palm all the way around, and place the pad of his forefinger against the curve of the trigger, so that his strong forearms can provide the muscle for that steady, straight-back pull that is the core of all great revolver work.

Equally odd is his holster. Unlike the others, who'll wear Lawrence or El Paso Saddlery gear with a Western flavor to it, in basket-weave or floral carving, and fancy leather rigs for undershoulder carry for their backup pieces, Bill's holster is a simple pocket of leather, smooth and black, his trigger guard exposed. With the big grip, the smooth, small holster, his incredible hand size and reflexes, Bill can draw and fire faster than most people can see. He has even been on the TV, where he held a Ping-Pong ball on the back of his gun hand, drew and fired (a blank) so fast that his muzzle blast sent the plastic ball flying across the studio, setting an audience alight with glee.

Charlie goes the Colt way. Charlie uses a Police Positive Special with a King's sighting rib along the top of the four-inch barrel. It's got a slim, now yellowed ivory stock, with his initials "CH" carved vividly into it, and the gun has been honed and tweaked. But he's a devotee, it turns out, of the famous Colt shooter John J. "Fitz" Fitzpatrick, who believed that trigger guards slowed up draws. So Charlie has followed his mentor's mandates and had the front two-thirds of the trigger guard removed so that, under duress, he may seize the gun and his finger will fly directly to its trigger without having to curve, then straighten, to engage that part's sweep. Of course, if you don't know what you're doing with this outfit, you'll blow off your foot. Charlie knows what he's doing.

Charlie also has a couple of Colt Detective specials which he'll wear, one in a boot holster, the other in an underarm job. All of his guns shoot the .38–44 that Earl has provided, and Charlie knows that it'll take the fight out of a white man just as quickly as it'll do the same to a Mexican.

But Charlie's real killing instrument isn't his handgun at all, though he's done in a few possibly bad individuals that way. No, Charlie is a shotgunner, and for this job he's brought along the instrument that got him through many a tough night on the border. It's a Browning Auto-5, with an extended magazine, so that now it holds eight 12-gauge double-ought shells instead of five, and he refers to the shells as Blue Whistlers, for he's convinced that he can see them whistling through the air in fleets as he fires. But the best is that he's cut down the barrel to eighteen inches, and there, at the end of the new muzzle, screwed on what he calls his duck bill. It's a spreader. It's as if you squashed the bell of a horn till it was flat and its effect is to cause the shot cluster to sail down the barrel of the gun to spread horizontally rather than circularly, so that it exits the muzzle like a deadly spray of paint flung from a quickly flicked brush. It does the job very well on Mexicans, and a part of Charlie genuinely wants to know how it'll work on big ol' white boys.

Out on the prairie, alone, is the most haunted of

them. This is the young Audie Ryan. Audie has two Colts, but they're single-action revolvers, six-guns of the Old Western school, which he'll carry in custom-made black leather double buscadero holsters made for him by John Bohlin of Hollywood. You would think from this Audie is a cowboy; in the pictures, he's a cowboy.

Like so much of what's in the pictures, it's another lie. Audie wasn't raised on a ranch, though he's from Texas. His life had nothing of the West, or the range, or cattle or honor or horses or sidekicks to it. It was more out of Walker Evans's photography, those horrific images of the dispossessed, the thin-faced, the desperate hardscrabble Southern poor. Those are Audie's memories, sharecropping near Greenville in northwest Texas, after his no 'count old man lit out on them, and he and the boys had to rent themselves out early as sharecroppers, at twelve, just to keep a little food on the table and the sense of family, so instinctive, somehow alive. It was then that he began his hunting, and only alone in the hills with a beat-up old Winchester .22 single-shot—if he missed he went hungry—that he began to feel any sense of selfhood. A gun was at the center of it. Without the gun, he was a Texas redneck pretty boy with freckles and a girly name, who had to fight his way to and from school when he went. With the gun he felt the admiration of the family when he returned with rabbit or squirrel or pheasant or dove, each shot beautifully. He felt the most primitive thing a hunter feels: I have fed my family; I am a man.

So for him the war wasn't what it was to so many, a crushing obstacle erected across a promising life. It was an expression of all the lonely lessons he'd learned in the scruffy woods of northwest Texas, where the gun was the only means to manhood.

The two Colts are emblems of just how successful he

had been. In the war he had been a terror, a little, bitty speck of kid, almost without fear, who brought his talents for shooting and his instinct about the lay of the land to the fields of Europe, where, after the first day or two, everything just seemed to make sense, to fit together. His instincts were always right. He wasn't really frightened in the way a lot of the others were. He didn't really care if he got back or not; he had gotten off the goddamned farm where his goddamned father had left him; he had gotten off it, and how. When he fired, men dropped. When he shouted, men listened. Where he went, men followed, him hardly more than a child, with a soft, baby face, almost like a little girl, with small hands, but he was grit tough from the way he was raised, and even the Army food felt like a feast compared to the thin vittles of the rabbit split six ways he'd grown up on.

The two six-guns were presented to him by a very important man, Mr. Graham H. Anthony himself, the president of the Colt's Company, on the occasion of his tour of the plant in 1947. The folks there were all very nice to Audie, who didn't say much, and whose childish looks somewhat nonplussed them. Like so many others, they couldn't see in this polite, nearly mute young man of surpassing beauty the great hero who had killed close to three hundred of his country's enemies.

Audie loved the guns. Aware that if he were to prosper in Hollywood as a Western hero, he'd have to learn to shoot them and handle them, that's exactly what he did, even when he was living in Jimmy Cagney's pool house his first few years out there. He'd rise early and head out to the hills over the city and just practice, slowly at first. When the world didn't make a lot of sense, the guns always did. He drew fast, with both hands. He learned to slip fire, to Curly Bill spin, to fan, to hit aerial targets, to load and unload fast. It was amazing how much you could learn if you put your mind to it, particularly when it was men's work, with machines and techniques, not like this acting business, which was mainly about getting yourself seen, and "pretending" a certain thing, even if it wasn't true, and there were no rules at all.

So Audie, alone in the field, practiced a kind of warfare he had never fought, except in front of a camera: the Old West style, where the gun flew from his holster, clicked four times—C-O-L-T, the legend had it, as the hammer peened against Sam Colt's genius system of pins and screws and levers—and then fired with the satisfying detonation of a big .44.

With a gun in his hand, he knew he could do anything.

ALONE in his room, by design, Earl works the map again. He knows you can study a thing too hard, until you are so up close to it it makes no sense whatsoever. That is what he does not want to do.

His plan, he knows, is sound, if all the surprises work as they are set, and if the guards react as he expects they will react when confronted with strong, willful, armed men of extremely refined shooting ability and no mercy whatsoever. But he knows too that anything can go wrong at any time, and without radio communications, backup, a quick exit strategy, the whole thing can turn to catastrophe faster than a cat can blink.

But he can't do any more. A sergeant, in this instance, should be out and around, cajoling his boys, feeling their fears, trying to calm them. These old goats are too old and too salty for much in the way of sergeanting. So Earl leaves them alone to do as they may, for they will do as they may when the day arrives, ever so shortly.

Earl, like the rest of them, works on his guns.

Earl has two revolvers. He would have preferred a .45 Government Model automatic, for he carried one as a Marine for fifteen years and again in the fracas in Hot Springs. He knows the Government Model well, and can shoot fine with it. It's powerful, it reloads fast, it's reliable, just what the doctor ordered. But his whole sense of this thing is that it can't be a military operation. It's not commandos, raiders, a secret, private army. It's a posse of citizens who have taken it upon themselves to face what no one in authority has the courage to face. He thinks it's all right like that, if it can be all right at all, but now it's gone so far, it don't matter much whether it's all right or not. He's going to do it, goddamn, and live with it forever after.

Earl doesn't take a stand on American gun-making. He has a Colt and a Smith. His Smith is the Heavy Duty, on the .44 frame, to shoot the .34–44 high velocity, with the same stubby 4-inch barrel. The Colt is the Trooper, a beefed-up Official Police to shoot that same hard-recoiling .38–44. He's good and fast with both.

Now he, too, can do nothing but clean the guns, smoke his Lucky Strikes and watch the moon disappear.

56

THE phone call awoke the warden. He wasn't used to being alerted this early in the morning, and he had a moment of panic.

Was the pale horse here?

But no. It was his bedroom. It was his Big House. It was the cool of the morning, but already the place outside had come alive. His servant was close at hand. He felt no disturbance in the ecosystem of his great place, for he was exquisitely attuned to such small disturbances.

The warden blinked, felt his breath return to normal. He glanced around, took a drink of water from the pitcher next to his bed, then picked up the phone. Since there was only one other working telephone in all of Thebes County, he had no doubts as to who it was.

"Warden here."

"Sir."

Of course: the sheriff, Leon Gattis.

"Sheriff Leon, what is this about?"

"Mr. Warden, thought you should know. They've arrived."

"And, Sheriff, what would *they* be?"

"Why, sir, you know. Heh-heh, we had us quite a celebration when this all set itself up last spring. The *coffins*. The waterproof *coffins* that fellow done paid us to sell here to them bush Negroes."

The warden recollected. Yes, indeed, last spring, the big news was the coming of the waterproof coffin company to Pascagoula, and the Pascagoula County people were all happy, because it meant jobs, and it also meant many greased palms. One of the distribution points for the new product was set to be Thebes, and on account of that plan, the warden had taken an emolument of five hundred dollars, that is, five dollars per coffin, for there would be one hundred of them, as had the sheriff, because it was deemed proper and appropriate that on such issues, important personages in the county should get their beaks wet, to make certain that no unforeseen legal obstructions came in the way of men desiring to do business. The sheriff had spent his money on whores and bourbon in New Orleans, and the warden had shipped it to his broker in New York.

"Hmmm," said the warden.

Did he see conspiracy in all this? That would have to be a mighty conspiracy, for the coffin transaction was all set in place months before that Arkansas lawyer showed up, initiating this whole mad gyre of unease in his little empire. Who could engineer such a thing? No one alive, the warden knew.

"Sheriff," said the warden, "tell me how they came and who or what came with them?"

"Well, sir," said Leon, "they just came. They's here. I just got a call in from one of my boys. He seen 'em."

"Was there a fellow with them? Or a bill of lading? Or anything to make it official, as we would deem something official?"

"No, sir. Evidently, they's barged up in the night, and the boat what towed 'em got an early start back. The fog lifts, the sun rises, and there they be, a cargo of wooden boxes heaped atop a barge, which is moored by itself in the river."

"Leon, were you classically educated?"

"Sir?"

"No, of course not. Does the story of Troy mean anything to you? Or the story of a wooden horse in which men hid, and in the night broke out to raze a walled city otherwise impenetrable?"

"Hmmm. Might have heard something like that sometime, someplace."

"Leon, you set up a guard right now on that barge, and you keep watching it. I will meantime send my men downriver in the prison launch, they will board, and they will examine these coffins and see if any clever

Ulysses means to use them to engineer our destruction. And if that's so, we'll do what Priam never thought to do, and that's burn them on the spot."

"Yes, sir."

"Then, Leon, you comb the riverbank for tracks of men coming from that boat. Use those dogs you're so proud of. Find me my Ithacans, do you hear, Leon?"

"Yes, sir. Lord, yes, I do!"

LEON, of course, did what he was told, well and thoroughly and earnestly, and by the time Bigboy arrived in the prison launch he could report that no tracks had been found along the bank for miles in either direction, no dog smelled a trace of stranger, and that not a man or a thing had left the barge, which simply drifted listlessly against the current.

Bigboy, pulled from his third straight day from the surprisingly tough old man Fish, navigated the prison launch close enough and tied to it. He boarded it, he and three guards with weapons and a work detail of three large Negroes, who were happy to be spared the fields that day.

They set to work. The coffins were unstacked one by one, opened, and examined. It was a long afternoon's work, but of course it yielded nothing: no coffin had a human cargo, and all coffins were opened, turned, poked. Randomly, three were selected for destruction, and in pieces revealed themselves merely to be . . . wood, slathered with some sort of gummy water-resistant pine tar, held together by stout, well-driven nails; as the shipwrights of Pascagoula were among the best carpenters in the world.

Bigboy, having done his duty well, returned at the end of day and made his report.

"Sir," he said, "if a pale horse is coming, it doesn't have a thing to do with them wooden boxes, I guarantee you."

The warden duly noted this.

"I am sure you are right, Sergeant Bigboy."

57

THE cowboys are having a tea party. It's Sally's idea.

They sit out in the meadow on lawn chairs, all dressed for their fight, with legs daintily crossed, while the pretty young lady scurries before them, filling their teacups and offering scones and muffins, with dabs of jelly. To Sally it's a kind of farewell party, for the men will be leaving ever so soon, and she's enjoyed this all so much. She's moving about, dressed all old-timey, in a big old white cotton dress, fluffy with petticoats beneath, its frilly sleeves covering her pale arms, its full hem fluffing at the ground, so that she looks like some kind of schoolmarm in a cowboy picture.

It's been wonderful seeing Grandpap so happy again, among his friends, laughing and joshing with these colorful old fellows. Everybody is so nice, even if she suspicions that the one with the prominent nose and personality, Charlie, occasionally halts outside her room and tries to peek through the cracks of the door to catch a glimpse of young Sally in her boudoir. She can hear his dry, crackly, old breath. But he hasn't seen anything, she knows, because she has been very careful.

The men are wrapped in old-timey coats called dusters that give them the appearance of undertakers. These are full length canvas coats that reach to their boot heels. Under the dusters she can see something that might surprise many young women of her age but doesn't throw the granddaughter of Ed McGriffin a bit: that is, a lot of guns. A lot of revolvers in belts heavy with ammunition crossed this way and that across their bodies. The men clank a little when they walk, like old knights or something; they have a metallic seriousness to them, a density. Some wear chaps that exaggerate the flow of their legs. They wear their hats low over their eyes and don't speak much as they sit and wait, their gear—rifles mostly, though each has a pouch that appears jammed with something heavy—off to one side.

Only Grandpap doesn't wear a duster. He's too formal, still. He wears a three-piece suit and a black tie, knotted tight, and a high white Stetson, a fifteen-gallon hat, the boys joke. He's particularly twinkly today, and merry, in a way he hasn't been in ages. He's happy. They're all happy.

What is about to happen?

Sally isn't sure, and some of the old cowboys aren't either. They're to leave today, and somehow, some magical way, they're to get where they're going by tonight, unwrinkled and unchallenged by the journey. Sally has in her mind some idea of a bus, but she knows that can't be right, somehow. But Grandpap tells her it will be okay.

She pours more tea. The boys enjoy it. She offers Charlie a scone and he takes it, with a wink. Audie is quiet, seemingly in a dream land. Bill, with that granite face, is the same as always: imperturbable, silent, polite. Mr. Kaye and Mr. O'Brian are still squabbling, and take efforts to sit in directions so they are not facing each other. Mr. O'Brian, who fancies himself a man of high social standing, nibbles his biscuit discreetly, careful not to spill a crumb. Mr. Kaye, on the other hand, wolfs his down with gusto.

Where is Mr. Earl? Well, he's still on the phone. He got a call from someone called "Sam" just a minute ago, when everybody was heading out to the meadow for the tea party, and he's still on the phone, listening carefully, taking down information, nodding intently, as if some last bit of crucial information has arrived.

She heard him say, "I've heard of Fort Dietrich."

Finally, he too comes out. He's a tall, hard man, without much beauty to him, but he has that command quality that even Sally can feel, and he seems dark today, pressed by concern. He's not much for the tea and crumpets, and his duster is stiff because it carries so much ammunition in its pockets. She can see guns on his belt.

There's just a moment here that becomes weirdly still. The seven cowboys sit on lawn chairs in the bright sun, under a cloudless sky. They could be heading for a roundup, a showdown, some movie mission of the sort Sally has seen a thousand times on the screen. But it's different than a moment in a movie, for it's real, the guns have bullets, and whatever it is they're off to do, they're ready, even eager, if tense.

Then Sally hears it.

Engines.

Engines, low and from the south, where there are no roads. She is baffled, but none of the others are.

"Right on time," says Earl.

"Them Navy boys know what they're doing," says Mr. Kaye.

"Yes, sir, they surely do," says Earl. Then, to all of

them, "Okay fellows, time to load up. Y'all got your guns and your ammo and your maps and your compasses. I will see you in the river in a couple of hours and we will git this job done up right and finished."

Charlie Hatchison held up his teacup.

"A toast," he cried. "I celebrate us. We are the last of the cowboys, and this is the last goddamn gunfight at the OK Corral. Drink with me, boys!"

"Hear, hear," came the cheer, and the teacups came up and were drained.

Then Sally saw them.

She had never seen anything like them before.

There were three of them, low to the earth, bulbous craft of dark blue, squatty behind windshields that glittered in the sun, under three beating, whirling blades that suspended them from the sky. She thought somehow of insects; they looked like engorged blue-tail flies, buzzing malevolently, adroit in the air, graceful, somehow, in their insect clumsiness.

"Helicopters," said Elmer Kaye. "Damnation, ain't that a sight!"

It was a sight. Holding a tight formation, the three Navy whirlybirds vectored in on the party in the meadow, and Sally was stunned to realize that unlike airplanes, these flying machines could go straight down and straight up. Beating up a devilish roar, their spinning rotors whipping up a screen of dust and dirt so strong you couldn't look into it, so powerful you had to lean double to go against it. Napkins from the tea party flew this way and that, and a teacup or two was knocked atumble.

She heard Jack O'Brian scream over the noise to Earl, "Earl, you must know somebody big in Washington."

"Pulled a kid out of a Wildcat on Guadalcanal. He

ended up the chief of naval aviation, that's all. This is just a little training mission for these boys. They goin' to drop us and tomorrow they goin' to pick us up. Only thing is, we got to be there."

"We will," said Jack.

The men clambered aboard, three, two and two, and Sally watched as Earl helped her grandpap up the little step into the craft and got him seated. His face was boyish with astonishment and enthusiasm.

He waved at Sally as Earl conferred with the pilots, and then the thumbs-up was given.

Sally smiled, waved, and stripped off her dress. Earl's jaw dropped. What the hell?

He was rooted in stupefaction.

Her dress came off with a crackling of buttons popping, and in seconds it lay at her feet. She wore jeans, a tight khaki shirt with a bandanna, and pulled out a crushed piece of material which she unfolded quickly into a much battered cowboy hat. She picked up some kind of canvas kit and ran toward the helicopter.

Earl intercepted her in the hatchway.

"What the hell do you think you're doing?"

"I would not be the kind of gal who sits home, sir," she said. "What happens if one of these old fellows catches a damn bullet? Does he bleed out there? I have bandages, disinfectant and every other damn thing. I've patched plenty a bullet hole. Now stand out of my way, sir, or you and I will go at it, and as I said, I pack a punch."

"For Christ's sakes, you—"

But with a twitch of her strong pale arm, Sally wrenched free and squirted by him.

Her grandpap twinkled.

The roars accelerated and, suddenly lighter than gravity, the three helicopters rose vertically a hundred feet, then dipped their noses, oriented themselves to the northwest, and hurtled away, trailing a wall of noise as they went.

And then, as if they had not been there, they were gone.

IN an hour they were at their destination, for such are the miracles of the H-5 Sikorski. The navigators calculated well, charting a course over northwestern Florida, across the toe of Alabama, evading, of course, the city of Mobile, choosing an arc above the unpeopled zones of that state, and of Mississippi's southeast corner. Beneath, pine forest and swamp fly by, and the choppers head into the setting sun until by map and navigational reading they have arrived: there it is, a band of sluggish water, the Yaxahatchee, lost in silent quagmire two miles above the prison farm at Thebes and three above the town.

Each chopper works its further magic swiftly, for this is exactly what such craft are for, and this is exactly what they have trained on. Each bird approaches the river, and there pauses, as its blades beat rills into the water, as it hovers but five feet off the surface. An object sails from each hatch and lands with a splash that soon reveals itself to be more than a splash. In the commotion there's a sense of gassy pressure, and from each sense of commotion, again almost magically, there unfolds a yellow naval raft as it inflates. A chain ladder is lowered and, quickly, each cowboy clambers down, and then a few packages are dropped to the waiting men. The choppers alter their pitch, and with a yowl climb to three hundred feet and head back to where they came.

In the falling twilight, the three rafts begin their slow journey down the Yaxahatchee. As they pass the prison levee, one raft, with Audie and Jack, scuttles ashore. The two men pull it up, take a compass reading, identify land forms from the photo map, give the thumbs-up and head inland. They're headed for the guard towers at the Ape House.

A half mile down, past the prison launching facility where Earl was "murdered," the second raft pulls up. This one holds Bill and Charlie and Elmer, two of whom will infiltrate the Big House, the Store and the Whipping House from the north and one of which, cackling madly the whole time, will head north to the sheriff's station in the woods. That baby is his and his alone. Sally is with them. She'll stay close to Bill and Elmer, who will more or less be at the center of the action, and all of them will ultimately rally upon them.

Earl touches her hand.

"You do not have to do this."

"Yes, I do. Grandpap, you have yourself a nice time and be careful."

"I will, darling," says the old man.

Earl says, "Listen here, you men. You cannot be thinking about Sally in the fight. If you do, you will get killed. You do your job. Sally, you stay behind them, goddammit, and do not run into fire. If you lose contact, you break back to the river, which is due west of any place you'll be. Tomorrow morning, you look for us one way or the other. I will find you."

"There's no time, Mr. Earl," said Sally. "I will be fine."

She pulled off and fell in with the others, and Earl watched her go with something caught in his throat, or possibly his heart.

"Let's go, Mr. Ed," he said.

"Yep."

* * *

THE final raft pulls up close to town. Earl helps old Ed disembark and guides him up the town mainline toward the public house in the dark. The old boy is surprisingly spry tonight, almost gay. They pass through the dark, deserted town, almost a ghost burg.

A last few words pass between them.

"You okay, sir?"

"I am, Mr. Earl. Hale, hearty, fit as a fiddle. Feel as if I could lick my weight in wildcats today."

"You ain't forgot nothing?"

"No, sir. Wait till eleven. Then take up a position at the town bar. Them black fellows won't like it but that's what it's got to be. Soon enough some bad-boy deputies and maybe even a sheriff come along. They'll take their time, but sooner or later, they move agin' me. Tough boys, like to beat heads."

"That's them."

"Got a surprise for them."

"Yes, you do. I feel bad about your granddaughter."

"You try telling that one what to do. I never could."

"Well, I ain't had much luck either."

He left the old man, sitting quietly a few hundred yards from the bar, quite content and lively. Earl headed inland, toward the Whipping House.

EARL didn't see it. Nobody saw it. But that night, there was other action in Thebes. At about the time his men were wiggling into position, the mournful barge of coffins, floating ever so lazily against the current of the Yaxahatchee, stirred slightly. No coffin itself moved, for the coffins were empty, as Bigboy and his detail had ascertained.

But from the barge, or from a hollowed out space under the deck, a noise rose. It was the noise of wood on wood, as wood was unlimbered, almost like the wood in a wooden horse four thousand years earlier. A segment of the deck slid open.

The opening of this wood yielded, however, no party of mad Ithacan raiders, hell-bent on mayhem and city burning. Instead, uncranking as if from a long sleep, a more angular figure emerged, unsure, blinking, not especially confident but animated by a motivation no man could know. He rose, replaced the wooden grating on the deck, and looked around.

Thebes dozed peacefully under the black night sky.

It was his home.

Home again, home again, home again. After all these years.

Gingerly, he slipped over the side and waded toward shore. He pulled himself from the current just south of the city dock. It all was so familiar and yet so distant, as if he were recalling not a reality but a dream.

He headed inland, toward the Big House. It was his house, after all.

It was Davis Trugood; he had a gun.

58

SAM was done. He had solved the mystery; he had gotten the information to Earl, at the expense of his dignity, considerably shredded when he had been kicked out of Austin by the Austin Vice Squad, once he had convinced them he meant no harm and was entirely innocent, at least until the girl began screaming, of the meaning of *Treponema pallidum*. It was all a mistake.

I have done what I could do, thought Sam. I have done all I have said I would, and if it helps or not, that is beyond my control. Earl even knew what Fort Dietrich was, and had explained it all to Sam, and now, at last, it made some sense.

But he could not rest yet.

He had one last call to make, and checked his wallet to find the card with Davis Trugood, Esq.'s law firm number on it. But he could not. Who knew where it had gone? Sam lost things all the time. That was part of who he was.

But of course he recalled the august law firm's name, those hallowed syllables: Mosely, Vacannes & Destin.

From his hotel room in Waco, where he had taken refuge after the embarrassment in Austin and the strident suggestion that he leave town and only return after the world ended or Texas declared its independence, whichever came first, he called long-distance information to get the number.

"Sir, I have no listing for that firm."

Sam was taken aback.

Then he said, "I may not have pronounced it correctly." This always happened: Northern operators could not decipher the soup of what they thought was his corn-pone "accent," although his of course was the proper way of speaking and theirs the abomination. "Mosely, that would be MOSE-ly, VAY-Cans and DES-tin. I can spell—"

"Sir, I have no listing like that. I don't have anything even close to it."

"In the whole area?"

"In all of Chicagoland."

"I see," said Sam.

He hung up, most puzzled. His mind fulminated on this discovery. In a while he came up with something of a solution.

He had his notebook with him and quickly found the name of a federal prosecutor out of Little Rock who, if memory served, had logged much time in the parallel office in Cook County, that is, Chicago, Illinois.

Sam called, made swift contact with his old friend, and explained the peculiarity of the situation.

The man consulted *his* notebook and came up with a number. He told Sam to call in five minutes.

Sam did, and soon got, "Fifteenth Precinct, Detective Chicowitz."

"Ah, Detective, believe Charlie Hayworth just called on my behalf."

"Yes, sir. Mr. Vincent, that it?"

"Yes, sir."

"So run it by me."

Sam explained. He gave all the relevant data, and the detective said he'd call back.

That call took seventeen minutes; that's how good this cop was.

"Well, sir, there isn't a law firm called Mosely, Vacannes and Destin. Not in Chicago or in Evanston or Skokie or any of the outlying areas. However, I did find a listing for Bonverite Brothers, a firm in Chicago."

"Hmm," said Sam. "I don't follow. What does 'Bon—'"

"You said your fellow's name was Trugood, right? And all this has to do with something way down in Mississippi, where it's still Frenchy and dark?"

"Yes."

"Well, sir, the French for Trugood would be Bonverite. If you were a Cajun from down there, and you wanted to disguise your name but stay in contact with it, as many, many people changing names do, it's a pattern, then you'd come up with Trugood. See what I'm saying? That would be the closest thing in Chicago to Trugood."

Sam was dazzled.

"Now I checked the reverse directory. Here are four numbers leased to Bonverite."

He read them.

A litany of integers came back at Sam, woozily familiar.

"That's it!" Sam cried. "Yes, that's it! *That's* the number I called!"

"Well, it's been disconnected. Just recently."

"I see," said Sam. "What kind of firm is Bonverite?"

"It's an undertaking parlor. I checked with the boys. It's very prosperous. He has all the southside and uptown business. He buries a lot of people. He has a lot of money, does this Mr. Davis Bonverite."

"I see. Is there anything else I should—"

"Yes, sir. He's probably the richest of them in Chicago. He's probably got more than a couple of million dollars. He's quite successful for one of them."

"I don't—one of *them?*"

"Yes, sir. He's a Negro. Davis Bonverite runs his business at Cottage Grove and 139th on the South Side. Darktown. He's Chicago's richest colored man."

59

Not much of Fish is left.

Fish has hung from the chains for five days. For those five days, with all his cunning in full force, Bigboy has worked him hard with the whip.

There's no space on the old man's skin that hasn't been shredded. There isn't a nerve that hasn't been lashed raw. There's not a scab that hasn't tripled over, that is, scabbed, torn away, scabbed again, torn away again, and scabbed up again.

Fish hangs, his wrists broken, his hands dead crab claws, the weight of him fully on the shattered bones. His lips are cracked dry. He can't lick them because Bigboy has tied a bit between his teeth, jammed under the tongue, to prevent him from biting his tongue and drowning on his own blood to escape the pain. It's happened to Bigboy, but not recently, not since he got so smart.

Fish has tried to lose himself in the space of his own mind, to go there in madness and lose all contact with reality, and never come back. But he's too goddamned tough. He can't order himself to go mad, and his mind betrays him by refusing to break off with reality. It feels everything, it remembers everything.

"Fish, don't you die, goddamn you," the bare-chested Bigboy whispers, breathing hard into his shredded ear from ever so close. "You, me, we got business. You don't die till I say so. You don't die till you talk. You think you're close? I can spin you out like this for days yet to come."

Maybe so. Maybe not. Fish feels close to death. He knows his heart will give up of its own accord, strangled on the pain, crushed by the stench of his own shit and piss caked to him.

Besides hurting him, Bigboy has walked the other road: has offered him temptations. Bigboy always understood that Fish had the imagination to make him vulnerable to ideas of the future, to possibilities, to pleasures not palpably there.

"You can go free," he crooned one evil night. "You tell me, we take care of it, and you are out of here, old man. You spent your life here. This is the way out. This is the only way out, and I am the only one who can give you this. Think of it, old man. Back to N'Awleens with some jingle-jangle in the pocket. To sport with some high yellers and some slanty Chinee. Those girls know all the tricks. No tricks they don't know. You'd be at home. You'd be the old whoremaster, plump and well-fucked in his senior age."

Fish fought him on that one. He denied it, banished it, made it go away, thought of his own scabbed, scarred flesh, not of the women's. He fought him on all the temptations: freedom, sex, juju weed and Uncle Horse, wealth, pleasure, all offered in various stages between the whippings, so in his mind, he went from pleasure unimaginable to pain unfortunately too imaginable.

He howled and screamed and begged for mercy.

Mercy came in but one form, however.

"What does it mean, Fish? What does 'pale horse coming' mean? You have to tell me, you know. You will, in the end. The only question is when. Tell me, Fish. Save us both trouble, and the warden worry. Tell me, Fish, tell me now."

Fish did not and paid for his disobedience.

He paid, he paid, he paid.

And then he paid some more.

But he never opened his lips.

Now, at last, death dogged him. He could smell it, taste it, knew it was here at last for him.

Ha! That would be his victory.

But Bigboy wouldn't surrender.

"Even now, Fish, when you are so close to passing. Even now I can jack you with yet more pain, and I will, too. You know I will."

The old man tried to spit in his face, but could not, because of the bit in his mouth.

"Okay, Fish. Then here we go again. Now it gets bad again. Now it comes again."

He heard the man stride back. He heard him lift the whip from the table. He heard it unroll, then hiss as the whip man snarled it gently through the air, then made it snap and pop, so that the old man could actually feel the airwaves where the supersonic flick at the end pushed them aside.

"Fish, here it—"

From close by came the rattle of what could only be machine-gun fire. A few seconds later, more shots filled the air.

Bigboy dropped his whip and ran to the old man, pulled the bit out of his teeth.

"What is it?" he screamed urgently. "What is that? What is happening? Goddamn you, Fish, Goddamn you, *tell me!*"

Fish smiled.

"Pale horse be *here,* motherfucker," he said. "Pale horse done come for *you.*"

He laughed in the second that he died.

Dark of the Moon

60

THEY watched him. He was a stubby old fellow, and he sat in the flickering candlelight of the bar, and the two Negroes were behind the bar. They were nervous as hell. You could smell their fear.

But the old man seemed unperturbed, merry even, and that's what upset the deputies. He just sat there with a mellow grandpappy look on his face, in his three-piece black suit with his tie all neatly tied up in a bow, his huge Stetson down to his ears and he drank.

He drank, he drank, he drank.

"Don't know how a fellow swallow that much dadgum white lightning and stay sittin' up," said Opie.

"He must have the constitution of a horse," said Skeeter.

"He drink more, we don't have to whap him none a-tall. No sir, he'll just fall over blindy drunk."

"Yes, sir."

But that wasn't what had them so spooked. That wasn't why they'd sent their third member, Darius, to get the sheriff.

What spooked them was: Where'd he come from?

The old man was just there, sitting in the bar.

No boat had arrived, no horsemen had fought their way through the piney woods, no automobiles had suddenly come roaring up a suddenly cleared road. So where'd he come from? How'd he get there? Who was he? What was this all about?

"I say we go in there and thump him hard." This was Skeeter. Skeeter was the master of the billy club. Skeeter could beat a tattoo on your arm so fast that arm would be dead for a month. He could slap you upside the ear hard enough to kill, to stun, to daze, to annoy, all with the flick of a wrist. His club hung on a leather thong off his supple right wrist.

"Hmmm," grunted Opie.

"Just go in, do it. He's a old man. We cool him out, handcuff him, and then off he go to the station. That's all that is. And we git to the bottom."

Opie chewed this over. It seemed okay. But he didn't want to make the wrong decision.

"Pret' dadgum soon the sheriff be here. He'll know what to do. Meantime, this ol' boy just filling himself with rotgut, getting blurrier and blurrier. Let him drank himself to perdition, that be all. That's what the sheriff would want."

"I don't like it none."

"I don't like it none nohow neither," said Opie. "But that is what we going to do, dadgum it."

And dadgum it, that is what they did. In forty minutes or so, Sheriff Leon Gattis himself arrived, to find the scene the same. His two deputies were outside, peering in. Inside, the old man sat merrily by himself at the table, drinking jar after jar of white lightning, getting himself all lit up to hell and gone.

"Don't see how that boy is still standing," reported Opie. "All that corn shit he got in him."

"That ain't the problem. Whar'd he come from?" asked the sheriff.

"Don't know. He just come from nowhere, out of the air. Sheriff, I say we go in and thump him hard and brang him down. Then we git to the bottom of this."

Why was the sheriff reluctant? Why did he have an odd feeling in his gut? It was that the whole thing was so ghostly, somehow. It had the feeling of the remembered, or the previously glimpsed. He had already seen it, in a movie or a book or something. Very strange feeling.

The old cowboy sat there in the saloon. The funny part was, there wasn't a twitch of fear on him. He's either crazy or goddamned stupid as they come, and he didn't look neither. There was something bull-goose loony about the man, and the sheriff, at one time a New Orleans detective (a long, tragic story), had seen it on a few of the big-gun boys of the thirties. The Pretty Boy had it and the Babyface had it even more. Johnny D. had it best of all, that sense of masterly command, that sense of self-regard of the truly dangerous.

"Goddamn, Sheriff, he just a old man. A drunk old man. A *very* drunk old man."

Besides Skeeter and Opie and Darius, the sheriff had brought two more boys. That meant six.

"All right," he said. "We goin' do it this way. Ray, you go 'round back. Work in that way. Gun out. You stay just inside the doorway, cover that old geezer from the rear. That's just in case. The rest of us wait five minutes, then we go in and brace him good. Listen up, y'all. This boy look old and drunk, but to me, he also looks a little salty. He been around some. He may still be fast, some men don't never lose their quick. He may have some quick on him still. So you got your hands on your revolver grips so you're ready for your own quick, if it comes to that. It don't hurt none to be all set, all right?"

"Yes, sir," said the boys, and Ray peeled off for his back shot. Then it was only a question of waiting.

THEY didn't come slyer than old Ed McGriffin. He had a diamond ring on his pinky, given him by the president of Smith & Wesson in 1934, when he had set a world speed record, firing six times in four fifths of a second and hitting a man-size target in the gut thirty feet away in a group small enough to be covered with one hand. As he sat in the bar in Thebes, he held the jar in one hand, and slid his pinky underneath. It didn't take much grinding. Diamond always beats glass. In less than five seconds, he had drilled a hole in the bottom of the jar.

What commenced thereafter was a little old-salt theater. He plugged the hole with his finger, raised the glass to his mouth, let the foul stuff touch his lips, but did not admit it. Christ, it would blind a white man in three sips and put hair on his palms to boot. Then, he moved the jar to the edge of the table, let his finger slip off the hole and in that fashion bled out a gulp's worth of lightning. He'd done this through five jars now, and his left boot was sodden with the corn alcohol. Drop a match down there and he'd explode in flames. But otherwise he was just fine.

He picked up on the deputies right away. Subtle boys they wasn't, no, sir, not by a long shot. One, particularly idiotic, kept pressing his nose against the window, flattening it even further. He was the big dumb blond one. The other one was furtive, feral even; looked like a weasel, dark and skittery, with tiny teeth.

"Say there, Pops," called out old Mr. Ed. "Bring this old feller one more toot, okay?

The two elderly black men behind the bar eyed each other nervously. They didn't like this a bit. Not that they cared about crazy old white boys, but such a situation could get them in trouble with Sheriff Leon and his deputies, who tended toward extravagant solutions for simple problems. The place could get busted up bad; they could get busted up bad.

On the other hand, they were of a generation where disobedience to a commanding white person was unthinkable. It simply was not conceptualizable, so they greeted the paradox with utter sullenness and desperation.

One tottered over, filled the old boy's glass with the white lightning, of a very fine vintage: 2:00 P.M. that afternoon. He'd never seen a man, white or black, drink so. Should be blind, as the stuff was about 600 percent alcohol. It wasn't designed for refinement, but to hit with a sledgehammer after the first swallow and blot out a man's terrible pain for a whole night. This old geezer had had enough to blot out the whole damn prison farm's pain.

"Sir, the deputies in this here town don't cotton to no strangers. You could git yourself into a tub o' trouble."

"Oh, I'm the sort of fellow who gets along with everybody. If they show up, I'll buy 'em a drink, and we'll have a laugh or two about it. I've many an entertaining story and have traveled the world, so nothing in Mississippi frights me much. Whyn't you and the other grandpappy pull up chairs? Be pleased to buy each of you a slug of your own damned hooch."

"Sir, they wouldn't cotton to no Negroes and white mens sitting at the same table, neither."

"Now, don't that beat all. I say we're all on this earth

together, and the sooner we learn to git along, the better off we'll all be. Bet your damn blood is just as red as mine."

"Sir, I—"

But the door opened and five white men, large, armed and grim, entered.

"Willie, you knows it's well past curfew for Negroes here tonight," said the blond one.

"Sir, I *tried* to 'splain to the gintleman that—"

"Boys, boys, boys," said Mr. Ed, "it was me that *insisted* that these fine gents stay open and serving. Is there a fine? By God, boys, I will be *proud* to pay it up. Whyn't y'all take a load off and come over and share a tot. Mighty fine. Burns on the way down, and burns way down afterward. Fire in a bottle."

"Sir, I don't know what you think you're doing, but we have rules in this town."

"I'm sorry? Don't hear so good now."

"Rules, goddammit. We don't like strangers coming in and riling our colored folks. We don't like strangers buying liquor after hours in colored joints. We don't like curfew violators, outside Northern agitators, commies, Jews, Catholics, bleeding hearts nor other race traitors. We charged with keeping law and order down here in this powder keg, and goddamn we do it right dadgum good."

"Well, fellows, I sure ain't no commie. I actually may be Catholic, but it was so long ago, I don't remember. I certainly haven't been to confess—"

"Sheriff, the old bastard's funning on us. He ain't showing no respect at all. Let me clock him a good 'un." With that, the blond one flicked his wrist so his club came into his hand, and he smacked it hard against the palm of his other hand.

"I'm sure this old boy don't need no beating on his old head," said the sheriff. "Sir, you just stand up and raise your hand. We'll search you, we'll cuff you and take you off, and get to the bottom of all this."

"Sir, the bottom of all what? Here I sit, in a public place, drinking quietly. Surely that's no—"

Whap!

The young deputy pounded the table with his club, making the jar jump and rattle. The report of the percussion filled the air sharply, seeming to bring dust off the ancient rafters.

"You keep your goddamn mouth shut, pappy, when the boss here is talking. You in a heap o' trouble."

"Sir, we're done playin' here. You get on up and co-operate, or you will be a sorry pappy."

"Why, sir, I meant merely—"

"Goddamn *you, sir!*" the sheriff exploded, "this is not no time for palaver. You get yourself *up!*"

He loomed, eyes abulge, face grave, leaning forward in a stance of sheer aggression, his hands twitching.

"Okay, fellas," said Mr. Ed.

He rose.

His coat parted.

They saw his revolvers in two strapped-down holsters.

A long moment of silence came.

"Sir, you will with opposite hands remove them two guns or by God we will shoot you down like a diseased animal."

"See, I'm thinking you all the ones going to put down the guns."

"Who are you?"

"You no nevermind that. It ain't yours to know. You only have to know that the night of reckoning has done come."

"He is talking through his hat, sheriff. One old god-damned big-talking old geezer."

"Shut up, Opie. Them guns are tied down old-timey gun-boy style."

"Now fellows," said Ed, "here're the two things that can happen. First off, I'm thinking I want your guns out, opposite hand, on the table. Then you strip bare-ass naked, not no skivvies, but buck bare as the day you born. Then you go down, lie in the street while I figure what to do with you 'til the prison's burned flat then flooded over and all them Negro fellows you done been beatin' on are free and clear."

"It ain't never happening like that, old man."

"Then, boys, seems to me we are at where we were going the whole time. Palaver's over. Nothing left to say. You throw down and die like men or I will simply shoot and move on."

"You are a goddamned big-talking fool, old man."

Ed was done talking.

Opie drew first, and possibly a tenth of a second later the sheriff made his play.

It didn't matter.

Smooth is fast. Ed was so smooth and fast with both hands the revolvers were simply there, as if by will. It was not a physical act but a metaphysical one. His big hands flew, his fast-twitch muscles twitched, his dexterity was simply unrecognizable by human standards.

He fired five times in less than two-fifths of a second, the reports hung together like a single loud repercussion, as dust jerked from the old rafters above and the jars on the shelves rattled. This was well off his world-record speed, but it was fast enough by a far piece.

He knocked three down dead, Opie first (left ventricle), then Darius (throat), then a boy called Festus (solar plexus). They fell like tenpins bowled hard, with a thump to the floor, heaving more dust up as their heavy bodies yielded to gravity, each dying on the way down as the blood emptied from organs and spurted under arterial pressure into geysers. Skeeter fell slower, but fell just the same.

The sheriff had been shot last because he was slowest. He sat down, holding his gut.

"You have killed me, damn you, sir."

"I have, sir, for your evil ways."

At that point a small sound announced the presence of another gunman behind, as the deputy Ray stepped clear to fire. But Ed had heard him long ago back in there raging around like a bull, and simply pivoted his right gun hand under his arm and with circus-freak twistiness fired at the sound, after complex, nearly instantaneous deflection calculations in a brain that had fired several million revolver bullets in its time. The bump of Ray hitting the bar, then pulling jars down with him in a shower of shattering glass clatter, ended that drama quick enough. Ed didn't even look around.

"Who are you?" gasped the sheriff.

"We rode in from the river."

The sheriff's passing lacked movie drama. He simply slumped over, his eyes gazing forever into the eternal darkness. He didn't fall or scream or moan; he stopped breathing is all.

Mr. Ed turned. The two old Negroes were clasping each other in fear behind the bar.

"It's okay, fellows," he said. "Nobody here is going to hurt you no more."

"Ain't never seen no shooting like that."

"It is a night of fancy shooting. Now I am going to sit

on the porch a bit and watch all the fireworks. My suspicion is that you'd be well charged to wake up your people. This is the night it all changes in Thebes, and they've got work to do yet."

61

CHARLIE had worked well into the sheriff's station compound between the town and the prison. He was alone. The dogs slumbered or moped in their kennel, the only light that burned was in the lock-up fixed to the Big House. In the stable, the horses dozed.

It was a quiet Southern night. A soft zephyr of a breeze weaved through the piney woods all about, and the odor of the needles was clean and fragrant. Overhead, the stars, undimmed by moonlight, shone radiant and dazzling.

Charlie noted none of this. His mind didn't work that way. Instead, he visualized his course of action. How he would move, what he would do at each spot, what was important, what was not.

He was not a man without fear. But he enjoyed his fear. Perhaps it was even sexual, for he found himself with, among his guns and firebombs and pouches of shells, a rather large boner in his tight jeans. He took a moment to get it adjusted so it wouldn't hang him up one way or the other.

He crouched beside the lock-up, simply breathing, running a last equipment check, flexing and unflexing his muscles, wondering when to start. Earl had said midnight was a good guess, but that it couldn't be counted on. Depended on when the sheriff made his play in town. He had seen the sheriff, alerted by a deputy, mount up and head out with two other men about an hour ago. That was the only action, and it had settled down quickly enough here.

He waited, kept checking his watch. It was now close to 12:30.

Then he heard it. It was a fast crackle of shots—so fast it had to be Ed McGriffin shooting, for no man could shoot so fast. The sounds were soft and muted, but the wind carried them along. Behind him, in the kennels, he could hear the dogs stir. One or two seemed to pull themselves up and sniff the wind, alerted in that secret dog way to the presence of aggression and fear in the air.

Charlie knew it was time.

He rose and walked around the corner of the lock-up. A fellow came out of it. It was Pepper, the dog man, who usually worked a late shift in the lock-up, though that building was empty.

He saw Charlie.

Charlie saw him.

Pepper—Charlie of course did not know his name— was incapable of imagining an assault on this place. Though the man before him was strange, his assumption was that he was okay. He was fine. He was one of them.

"Howdy," he said.

"Howdy," said Charlie, and shot him in the throat.

Eighteen.

That report was loud enough and close enough to awaken most of the deputies who slept in the big pinewood station. Lights came on, and the sounds of men struggling reluctantly to consciousness swam from the open windows of the big place.

Meanwhile Pepper sat down slowly, with a stunned look on his face. Charlie, replacing the revolver to its speed-scabbard, a nifty tight holster made by a Mr. Chic Gaylord in New York City, smiled at him as he died. He seemed to bear him no animosity. It simply had had to be done.

The gun replaced, Charlie walked swiftly to the Big House, reached into his canvas pouch and pulled out the first of his firebombs. He quickly unscrewed the lid, and yanked the cord. Nothing happened. It didn't sputter to life at all.

"Damn," Charlie said, and threw it through the window into the room, where it came to rest on the floor. He drew, aimed with all his bull's-eye precision and quickly fired.

The firebomb detonated. It wasn't an explosion so much as a kind of burbling, though of intense white flame, not liquid. The flame was so bright Charlie blinked at flashbulbs popping off in his brain as if he were the president just arriving.

Somewhat dazzled, still blinking, he walked along the porch until he reached another window. He removed a firebomb, pulled the cord, and this time was rewarded with the fizz of fuse. He tossed it and it blew, but so close to him it scared him. It sloshed white flame through the room like a spilled pail of milk, and where the fire lit it caught and the room was ablaze in seconds.

Jesus. Charlie wanted exactly nothing to do with the firebombs from then on.

He crouched at the corner of the house, unlimbering the shotgun, that Browning Auto-5 with the duck-bill spreader, and clacked the bolt to hoist a 12-gauge blue whistler into the chamber.

Meanwhile, the fire, as it will, waged a swift campaign of destruction, as various hungry elements of it consolidated with other hungry elements, seeking fuel and oxygen, both plentiful in the pinewood building. The conflagration was close to instantaneous, though in fact it probably took fifteen to twenty seconds before the blaze was universal.

Nothing panics like flame.

Upstairs, the swifter deputies felt the heat scalding through the floorboards, smelled the swift accumulation of smoke as it rose through the stairwell and the heating shafts, and knew in an instant that they had to flee or die.

They fled.

They spilled out into the yard, coughing, screaming, utterly demoralized by the fire that was consuming their world so quickly, propelled onward by the screams of those above not so fortunate as to have arisen on the first report. Outside they fell to their knees, gasping for air, or they hugged each other in ardent premature celebration of their survival, or they squawked gibberish, conjecturing in mangled syntax and stunned stupefaction on what the hell was going on.

Charlie waited 'til no one else came out, and went to work with the Browning Auto-5. He worked left to right, fast, instinctive shooting, Blue Whistlers a-whistling. The gun bucked and spewed, lashing out in each shell a blast of eight .32-caliber pellets, which the spreader arranged in a horizontal dispersal pattern while Charlie regained control and moved on to the next.

He just gunned them down in a burst of semiautomatic fire, fast and stunning; it sounded like a sort of tommy gun. The shot patterns at that range were so powerful they didn't penetrate so much as eviscerate. Deputies were blown backward, illuminated by the light of the blazing building, amid sprays of severed limbs and ripped entrails and detached jaws and faces lost forever.

It was over in four seconds, and Charlie stood there, still locked into his combat crouch, in the rising heat of the flames, his face illuminated madly by their intense glow, the seething smell of gunpowder all around him, a litter of shot shells on the ground, the fallen men before him dead or dying, some twisting in torment, others gone still.

Nineteen.

Twenty.

Twenty-one.

Twenty-two.

Twenty-three.

Twenty-four.

Then he got shot in the left rib. The bullet cracked it, spewed left and not right, cut a track of a few inches, and exited his body, spinning, frontally.

He turned and threw his shotgun at his opponent on the porch, who was busy trying to cock a lever rifle. The flung shotgun conked him hard enough to knock him off stride, and Charlie drew his Colt and popped all six into him. Two would have been enough, three extravagant, but six did get the job done.

"You goddamn bastard, you shot me," he said.

He examined the wound. Man, did it hurt like hell. He'd never been hit before. Where the hell had that boy come from?

But Charlie wasn't the sort to panic at the sight of his own blood. Instead of fear he felt anger, hot and rough like steam. Who were these jazzbos to think they could shoot Charlie Hatchison?

He pulled a knife, cut off a swatch of bandanna, and plugged the exit wound. Wasn't pretty, but it should hold. The entry wound was so small it wasn't bleeding much. It just looked like a big pimple.

Charlie turned quickly, regaining his sense of mission. He retreived the empty shotgun, kneeled to swiftly reload his Colt, and edged around the perimeter of the house.

A man leaped from the second floor, landed hard. He was not a problem because he was aflame and ran around a bit, screaming, before he fell. A second man landed, not in flames. He hit too hard and possibly broke his ankle. He pulled himself up and began to hobble off, and Charlie shot him twice.

Twenty-six.

He waited another few minutes.

No other men came out.

The fire spread, and the whole structure blazed. It was like some mad pagan ritual celebrating the presence of the war god on earth, with the bodies of the sacrificed now browning like bacon in the heat of the fire.

Charlie was driven back.

Finally he knew it was done, but for a last thing.

He reholstered the revolver, drew six shotgun shells out of his duster pocket, readjusted his hat, threaded the shells into the gun, jacked the bolt, and walked to the kennels.

The dogs, driven insane by the fire, screamed and howled and threw themselves bloodily against their fence for freedom.

Swiftly, Charlie killed them all.

Then he headed for the stable. There, too, the horses bucked and whinnied. He opened the stalls on most and let them rush out into the night. He calmed the remaining animal, saddled it eventually, though the job was somewhat more difficult for the broken rib, and rode out to join the boys in the prison.

Behind him, the flames blazed brightly in the night.

62

EARL kicked in the door of the Whipping House. He had leaned his Winchester .348 against the building, for this would be close-in work, revolver work. He had a gun in each hand.

He wanted Bigboy. Lord, how he wanted him.

Instead he found a guard with a Winchester .351 self-loader, who popped off three shots, high; Earl dropped him with a square shot to the middle of the body from the Heavy Duty. The supervelocity .38 thumped a puff of dust off the man's chest, and he was dead before Earl could get to him.

He kicked in a door, found no one. He kicked in another, and saw two guards looking for targets outside. They spun, but only fast enough to die with the .38 high-velocities ripping through their chests instead of their backs.

He climbed the steps. He thumped up them, then stepped back. A man with a shotgun ducked out, thinking he had Earl pickled. But Earl fired with each gun and placed his shots an inch apart in the chest. The man rolled, bouncing, spraying teeth, down the stairs to land at Earl's feet, but Earl didn't notice, for he had taken just a bit of a break to slide twelve new shells into his two hot and smoky weapons.

"Bigboy," he shouted, "Goddammit, I am here for you! You come fight me."

But there was no answer.

Earl climbed the steps, but he knew that if there were guns on the upper floor of the old brick building, they'd be ready. So instead, he reached into his pouch and unscrewed the lid of a firebomb. He pulled the cord. Nothing happened. As he was short on them, he didn't feel right dumping it. He tried to force the matches back down the tube, and of course they ignited.

"Oh, Christ," he said, and if he didn't have such fast hands he would have barbecued himself to a char right there. But somehow in the two seconds that remained, he got the thing airborne down the hallway.

He heard the muffled pop as it detonated, and watched as the sudden glare reflected off the old brick walls. Presently a man in flames came running by him, but Earl paid him no mind. He could tell by the compact frame that the fellow could not have been Bigboy.

He stepped into the hallway, the end of which was bright aflame. The heat pulsated like the punches of a savvy fighter, but Earl turned sideways and cleared each room.

In the third one, he found old Fish.

It was the whipping room.

It was burning.

Fish hung, lips dried, head down, wrists broken from the twisted angle, his body in utter repose. The flesh was riven beyond any capacity to understand. The old man hung in a pool of his own blood, dark and jellified, mixed with waste. A cloud of flies buzzed about, taking small pieces of him for nourishment.

Such squalor cannot be imagined, though Earl had seen as much in the Pacific when a Jap was cooked to death by the flamethrowers or turned inside out by mortar shells.

Earl had no key to the padlocks that locked Fish in his chains, and the heat was rising.

"Old man, I did come," he said. "I came as soon as I could, and I am sorry I was not sooner."

The old man did not answer, of course. He had no last words of atonement or forgiveness, gave no pep talk or instructions. He was simply dead on chains, head pure weight slung forward and down, and the body could not be released for the simple dignity of burning supine; he would burn to ashes as he had died, hanging. Earl recognized it as Bigboy's work. No other man could have done such a thing.

"Bigboy!" he screamed, "where are you, goddammit!"

There was no answer.

The flames blossomed powerfully, sending a burst of energy down the hallway. The floorboards shuddered. Sparks filled the air and so did smoke, and in seconds there'd be no getting out.

Earl turned, to leave the old man hanging, knowing in seconds he'd be ashes. He never made it back to the Chinee girl and the high yeller of N'Awleens. He'd died, whipped slow, over time, by Bigboy.

Then he turned back, stupidly. Something strange yet powerful had occurred to him: no man should be consumed in fire while hanging in chains. Wasn't right, any way you look at it. It was dying a slave. Earl seized up a chain, put the muzzle of the .38 close to it, and fired. He was peppered with pieces of metal as the bullet chewed through the chain link, and the old man fell forward. Earl caught him, set him down gently, then moved to the other chain and sheared it with the same .38 high-velocity. He lifted the old man and made it to the door, where a guard stood with a shotgun.

"You! You supposed to be dead."

"Don't know where you got that idea," Earl said. The heat billowed powerfully, but the man opposing him was mad with rage, and Earl knew he was cooked. But then a shot came and hit the fellow square in the face and down he went.

Earl turned. There was no other man visible. Who had fired, God? But he made out the puncture hole in a window and knew from his memory of the orientation of the building that he lined up, three hundred or so yards off, with the compound tower. Jack O'Brian was on the job.

Still carrying the old man, Earl made it to the stairwell, as the part of the house behind him collapsed when the floor burned through, and the walls down there, without their internal support, gave way and caved in, so that the acrid dust of old brick mixed with the smoke and the sparks, making breathing a labor.

Earl set the old man's body down in a cool glade of trees some hundred yards or so from the blazing Whipping House. He knelt beside him. Of course he had no words, for words were not his specialty. He arranged the body in as neat a position as he could.

"I will make good on my promise to you," he told the body. "Except the part about the whores. But now I will burn this place to the ground, old man, and come the morning there won't be nothing left except ghosts and ashes. *Semper Fi*, old goat."

Some spark or piece of airborne grit must have gotten into his eyes. He knitted them in pain, and rose to continue the fight.

He ran across the yard, out of the light. But on the way he found one of the men he had shot coughing as he bled out, having crawled out of the building. Earl knelt.

"You!" the wounded man gasped, his words competing with the accordion groan of a sucking chest wound. "You's daid."

It was one of the boys from the boat who'd watched as Earl followed the block into the black water.

"I ain't, not a bit. Now tell me: Where the hell is that Bigboy?"

"Sir, I ain't seen him. He's alone with the old man, whipping on him. Whipped him every night, five nights running. Whipped him bad. Don't want to face my maker with sin on my mind."

"That ain't my department. Where's Bigboy?"

"He must have got out. Damn you, you have killed me."

"That is why I come. You die now, for you ain't no more use to me."

Earl turned.

Around him, flames rose. He looked. Elmer had already lit up the Store. In the distance, heavy shooting suggested Elmer and Bill had moved on to the guards' barracks.

Farther out, the steady crack of Jack's .270 suggested that the old man was doing his damage, steady as a rock.

Earl turned. The Big House itself hadn't been touched. Time now to go visit Mr. Warden.

WHO were they?

Bigboy had made it to the piney woods, and he watched the destruction of Thebes from afar. Shots rang out, men fell. Always, with the inevitability of sacks of corn dropped off a truck. These fellows could shoot, that was clear.

But it was more than just shooting. It was determination. There was no hesitation or reluctance; instead, as Bigboy was an expert in such matters and would quickly recognize, it was maximum force applied without conscience but with considerable skill.

Already the place was ablaze. The Store was gone; that meant all records, all debts, all supplies, all the things that sustained Thebes were ashes in the wind, as the flames ate through the wood structure and devoured it, and all that was inside.

The Big House still stood, but Bigboy had heard shots from within it. Somebody whacked the warden, you could count on that.

The world was ending.

Thebes was destroyed.

There would be no coming back from this night.

He had read the shots well and, leaving the old man hanging, had quickly come across two men shot through the head from afar, which convinced him that standing and fighting was a tragic mistake. So he bailed out a rear window, slithered across the yard toward the tree line, as shots rang out from everywhere. He meant to head to the guards' barracks, where he could rally his boys, distribute weapons from the strong room, and begin a defense. But he saw that that was too far gone; the point had been reached where all was lost, and the prudent thing was to survive for another day, conceding that these outriders would carry the night. On top of that, he had no weapons, no shirt, not a thing to fight with: except, of course, his whip.

He made it to the trees, and gathered himself. He had no compass and knew an ordeal lay ahead. But he calculated swiftly, saw that in two days hence, the prison launch would arrive up from Pascagoula, and he could forage for that amount of time at least, and emerge then, with a report and a future.

All that changed in a second.

That second came as the Whipping House itself ignited from within. The fire ate it with a vengeance. He could see it glow, smoke, throw spark and gas, and then almost explode, as flames reached the old wood roof and began to eat with a pig's gusto. In seconds the building was engaged totally, and seconds after that, one half of it collapsed in upon itself, throwing up a blast of dust and spark.

Then his eyes traveled to the other end of the house, and he saw a fellow coming out, carrying a man.

This was the first of them he had seen. He saw and read cowboy, for the man was sheathed in a duster and had a ten-gallon hat on, and had a cowboy's leanness and sinewy grit.

Bigboy tried to figure it out: Cowboy. Posse. Outriders. It had not occurred to him till that moment to contemplate his antagonists. That would come later; now was merely to survive. It amazed him nonetheless that this fellow was not law enforcement by uniform and not some kind of rogue Negro; he was just a goddamned cowboy from the last century or from the pictures, in on a night of helling and town-busting.

Then Bigboy realized who it was this cowboy carried. It was dead old Fish. He'd gone in and carried out Fish. That's when he knew who it had to be.

It was Bogart.

Bigboy had a moment of stupefaction. His lungs dried up even as his heart began to pound. He settled back, feeling extreme displeasure rocket through his body, as well as fear. His knees began to tremble, and his hands followed. He more or less fell apart, gagging on this reality, chewing it over for a few seconds.

How?

How the hell?

How on God's earth?

He searched his memory and again saw the man swallowed by the black river, sliding downward beneath its moon-riddled surface, trailing a wake of bubbles. No one ever comes back from that one.

Was he a ghost? Was he a conjurer's trick? Was he an illusion? Was Bigboy losing his mind? But Bigboy didn't have the kind of mind one can lose; it was too obdurate, too anchored in the realistic to be delicate enough to break free and float toward madness.

Then Bigboy realized he'd made a tremendous discovery. For if he had come across Bogart of a sudden face-to-face, he would have staggered into shock and the man could have dealt him a fatal blow while he stood there knock-kneed, sucking wind. But now he knew: Bogart was back again, somehow, and worrying about how or why had no point on this fiery evening.

It occurred to Bigboy that he would kill him again tonight. This time he would kill him right and proper and completely. He tried to think where such a thing could happen, where he would catch the man unexpected, and kill him with his whip. He would whip him to death as he had so many others, for that is what he was the best at. He did not want to fight him again with fists; the man was a hellion. The whip would be excellent: take his skin, take his will, take his eyes, take his hands, make him perish in pain so penetrating and absolute you beg for death, even when it's a long way off.

Then he understood what must happen and where he must go.

He turned and slid off into the piney woods, almost happy.

63

THE shots awakened Warden.

He jacked up in bed, hearing them crash all about. The flare of burning fires dappled his far wall, as a flame-orange glow suffused the room through the windows.

His first reaction was the phone, the only one to the outside. He could call Jackson, they could radio the nearest state police barracks in Hattiesburg and in . . .

But the phone was dead.

Then he felt the presence in the room.

He was not alone.

The other sat facing him in the dark.

"Hello, Cleon," came a voice from across the years.

"Davis! Davis, damn your soul!"

"I have come home."

"What are you doing? What is this monstrosity? What is happening?"

He saw his brother had a revolver, and his hand slid to his own under the pillow.

"Why, I've come back to destroy the plantation,

every Negro's dream. I've even managed to cajole some white boys into doing the dirty work for me."

"You are insane."

"Quite possibly. But insanity has its uses. It enabled me to succeed in a far-reaching plan and to accomplish the impossible. Remember, Cleon, how you used to humiliate the little pale nigger boy who was your brother? And now he's here with an army of gunslingers for a night of fire and brimstone."

"You were not a Negro, not ever. Were you a Negro, none of this need have happened, for you would have known your place and accepted it. You were mixed! We can have no mixing of the races, for that is the source of all evil and the end of us all, white people and Negro people."

"My, how you do go on."

"You are the worst of us. You are a murderer. Whatever you became it is because of Father. You owe all to him. Yet you killed him."

"I did, and would again. He killed my mother."

"It was an accident."

"It was the kind of accident that happens when a white man loses interest in the Negro woman who has borne him a son and seeks a younger, yellower gal. She fell down the stairs. She died in the servant's quarters, which you now call the Whipping House, though I believe if you check, you'll see that it's in flames and most of its occupants are dead."

"Do you have any idea what harm you do? This isn't just a prison. We are doing a mission for the nation. We are helping America! We have a charge from the government. I am providing a place for our great crusade. You cannot just come in and—"

"Let's have a look at you," said Davis. He lit a match, ignited the wick of a lamp, set the glass on it so that light filled the room. He saw that his brother was far too plump, that his hair had been dyed white, that he was somehow a different man. But he was the same man, too.

"Your journey must have been as remarkable as my own," Davis said. "No one here knows you as Cleon Bonverite. They just know you under whatever name you chose. They don't know you were born and raised here, that it was to be your inheritance. You left Thebes one man, and disappeared. Years later you returned, this time as another man, who had been appointed warden of the prison our father decreed into existence. You managed to become its supervisor. That was some trick."

"I had father's will and intelligence, just as you did. It wasn't easy. I've had no other life. Thus I recovered my own family inheritance. Thus Thebes survives, as Father wished."

"No more. It's already ashes, and all it stands for. It ends tonight. I swore I'd—"

"You were mixed. You should have been aborted at the start. You should not have been allowed! You have no right to live. Your mother's cunning whore ways got her swollen with the child that became you; so you are whore spawn. You think you deserve an entitlement; you do, the abortionist's scraper deep in the mother's belly, that's what you deserve. All our troubles in civilization are encompassed in mixing what cannot be mixed."

"Lord, how you hate me still."

"You should not exist! It's an atrocity! You combine the black man's rage and strength with the white man's cleverness and will, and you can bring nothing but tragedy and ruination into the world! You are not my brother. You are an abomination."

"I am what my father made me, as are you, Cleon."

"You burned him in his bed."

"He killed my mother."

"He did not kill your mother. Your father in his way loved your mother, which was his character flaw. He loved you, too, Davis, did you know that? Here's what you don't know, Davis: I killed your mother. I shoved her down the steps. She never saw me. I would have killed you, too, if you had not evaded me and burned Father that night. Oh, Davis, I killed a nigger whore, you killed your own father, who loved you. Don't you see the evil in your ways?"

"Then I punish you for Father, too. And I mourn him now."

"You are evil. You will bring it all down for nothing beyond your vanity. It is so wrong, Davis. It is so wrong."

Davis fired twice, Cleon but once. Davis's shots were truer. His brother lay back, breathing heavily as the blood seeped through the nightclothes.

"You killed me," said Cleon. "But I killed you, too. You at least will be wiped off the earth."

"Not quite," coughed Davis. "I have sons."

If Cleon heard or not, Davis would never know. For Cleon settled in a stillness that could only be death. Davis examined his wound and concluded it was fatal, possibly not in the next ten seconds, but certainly in the next ten minutes. He had seen many gunshot wounds in his time in Chicago's best undertaking parlor for Negroes. He rose, limping and leaking, and went to the window to see what he had wrought. He saw flame everywhere, rising in the night, the sky bright with the dance of fire. He had his mighty victory.

He turned and went to the lamp he had lit. He looked about his father's old bedroom. It was much the same but for his dead brother. A great tide of tragedy overcame him. Would it ever be over? Would we and they ever live together? He doubted it. He raised the lamp and threw it against the wall, where it broke, splattering flaming kerosene about. Quickly it spread against the old wood of the house.

He sat in the chair. The pain in his guts grew harsher, as did the heat in the room. When he could stand no more of each, he put the gun to his head and had a good laugh. This is what they came to. The Bonverites, that long line stretching back over a hundred years, men who had fought the land and made a plantation and prospered and passed prosperity down generation to generation. But other things were passed down, too, the Bonverite curse, which was its tendency toward violence, its impatience, its fury.

And so finally the two brothers, so smart, so educated, so dedicated, so thrifty and industrious, so gifted in their own ways, ending up in the bedroom of the house where each had been born, though one upstairs and one down.

He laughed.

It was perfect.

It was everything he had dreamed of.

He pulled the trigger.

EARL found them like that as he raced through the burning house. Both gone, both together. Who were they? But the flames drove him out and took them both.

64

ELMER lobbed a Hopalong Cassidy firebomb onto the roof of the Store and watched it detonate with a pop and spew a bouquet of flame across the shingles, where each lick caught and started its own fire.

But he had no time to contemplate fire.

He ran onward, beyond the Whipping House to a larger building that was the guards' headquarters. Three men prone outside testified that the affray had started already. That was Bill's steady, quiet work.

Elmer was close to a door, and so, with a large .44 in each hand, he kicked it in, and found a corridor full of half-dressed men, most in a state of panic and confusion, some with weapons, others not. Elmer fired with each gun, the powerful, amplified .44 slugs finding targets in the hallway. It was a killing time.

The .44s didn't just hit a man, they thumped him good. They thumped him so hard he didn't fall, he was bowled to the ground. Moreover, the muzzle blast was so tremendous it too was like a force in the corridor, for if the bullets missed, the disorienting effect of all that blast took the fight out of a lot of the men.

But Elmer clicked empty on each cylinder, and knowing that he was now unarmed and would be so until thirty seconds' worth of reloading work, he faded back, rotated around, and headed for cover behind a tree. That is when he was shot in the head.

It hurt mightily. He went down, disoriented, feeling the blood pour from the wound. Next thing a bullet hit next to him, pulling an angry gout of earth, and then another close by. He was being shot at from on top of the building. They had him cooked but good, and it didn't matter because he'd been shot in the brain.

But if he were shot in the brain, how could he think so clearly? He slid his hand under his hat and felt a bloody furrow atop his skull, pulsing with blood. It was a grazing wound.

Another shot tore into the earth, filling the air with dust. Them fellows were not the best shots.

Suddenly someone was next to him, pulling him upward, while nearby, someone very calmly fired, fired again, fired some more.

The girl pulled him upward.

"Mr. Kaye, you are too heavy to carry, sir."

"Sally, watch yourself."

"Now you come on and we'll get you looked at."

She dragged him back to the trees under cover of the very fast fire that Bill Jennings laid over the top of them.

Then Bill faded, slipped around to the other side.

"I take it I am not hit bad," said Elmer.

"Your head is as hard as a potbellied stove," she said. He felt three or four fast pricks.

"Ouch! Girl, what are you—?"

"Hold still. Knitting you up. You'll like to bleed out otherwise. Now this is really going to hurt bad."

With that, she applied some kind of astringent. It stung like holy hell.

"Ow!"

"Ow yourself. Now get back in the fight, sir. No time for lollygagging."

Elmer skootched over with his rifle. The girl slipped away. Wasn't she a heller! That one had some damn grit!

The flames of the burning Store illuminated the scene. Shots came from his left; that had to be Bill. Farther away, it was now the Whipping House that blazed in the night. The whole scene was lit by the lusty flames; the odor of fire and meat filled the air.

Elmer took up his rifle, a Winchester '92 in .38–40. Now and then a figure would appear in an upstairs window with its own rifle, and Elmer was so quick and accurate, he knocked three down in as many minutes. He cranked the lever behind each shot. Then a man emerged, and Elmer drew to him.

But he could not fire.

The man had a woman in front of him, a Negro gal constricted both by his strong arms and by her own terror. She was too far gone to scream much. In the firelight, her eyes shone brightly, all white.

"Y'all come to set the niggers free? Well, we goin' kill 'em all if you don't back away, goddamn your race traitor hides. We goin' to—"

Elmer couldn't get a shot. He slithered sideways, glad that no blood would be filling his eyes, though perturbed at the ruination of a good hat. That hat upset him. It had cost seven dollars in Medicine Bend, Montana, a specially big Stetson that climbed a full six inches above the top of his head. It would be hard to replace, but then it occurred to him that blood-spattered and with a nice hole in it, it would make an excellent souvenir. He'd hang it off the bison head in the dining room.

He had found the angle. Now quickly, he drew the rifle to him, finding the tiny blade of the sight, and pressing it sideways until he lost it against his antagonist's head behind the Negro woman, pressed trigger with ball of finger, and fired. He hit the yelling man under the left eye. What a big soft chunk of .38–40 lead does to a human head at that range is not a pretty thing to see, and skull emptied and tattered, this fellow slipped softly to the earth and went limp, and the colored woman ran away.

"Nice shooting," Bill called.

"Believe I hit him right square."

"Believe he won't be no problem."

The next event was the approach of a horse, driven hard by a rider who knew his business well. Reinforcements? Elmer quickly loaded a passel of .38–40s into the rifle, cranked the lever and watched, hoping he wasn't about to be trapped by shooters on two sides. But of course it wasn't reinforcements: it was Charlie Hatchison, cackling madly, his face lit red by the fire. Charlie seemed to have come straight from hell; he was jabbering as he dismounted his animal and gave it a smack to drive it away. He raced to Elmer.

"Yee haw, ain't this a goddamned picnic. You get any?"

"I got some."

"How many?"

"Charlie, I done what I had to do. Didn't stop to count. We got a batch of 'em in there. Bill's off on the side."

"You been hit?"

"Yes, I have. But where it don't matter. The head."

"Me too. In the ribs."

"Get that girl to look at it. She's good with wounds."

"Hmmm, think I could sneak a kiss?"

"You try, and I'll shoot you, only I'll put it between the eyes and that's an ache that won't go away."

"You are an ornery bastard, Elmer. It was a joke. Say, got any more them firebombs? I say we light 'em off, then gun the boys as they flee. But sometimes them bombs don't work so well and—"

"That's too much like murder to me," said Elmer.

"Hell, son, murder's what we come to do. Cover me as I get closer and toss a few. Though sometimes they don't work too good. That Earl isn't quite the genius he thinks he is." He turned and yelled, "Bill, don't you shoot me. I am going to light up these boys mighty fine."

"You hold on there, you old bastard," said Bill. "I got a play to make."

Bill now did an amazing thing. Ramrod straight, with all his guns holstered, he stood out clear and bold in the firelight and approached the smoky building. No shots rang out, though he was now easy pickings.

"It's that goddamn face of his," Charlie said. "Nobody got the sand to shoot at a fellow looks so scary."

Lanky, Western, his long arms hanging free, his hat set square on his head, Bill walked like a movie gunfighter to the barracks and stood outside. No shots rang out.

"We got you outgunned and overmatched and outmaneuvered. We can shoot the tits off a cow at a hundred yards a hundred times out of a hundred. We have firebombs that can fry you up crispy like catfish. You are already dead. Now you have two choices. You can play it out and be dead in just a little while. Or you can come out buck naked and lie face down in the mud. Don't make no never mind to us."

He stood there.

There was some scurrying inside and then, one by one, they began to file out. Three or four Negro women came out, too, and raced off in the darkness.

"Y'all git nekkid," Bill commanded, "and if you don't move fast enough, I got a crazy redneck over there kill you just as soon as spit on you."

There were eight of them, and they commenced now to pull clothes off, then go prone.

"You, all the way nekkid. You could have a gun in them underdrawers."

The last pants came off, and the guards lay flat in the mud.

"Anybody left inside with fight in 'em?"

"No, sir," came the call.

"Hope not, 'cause we now going to burn her out. Charlie, light the bonfire."

"You do it, Elmer," said Charlie.

So it was Elmer who unscrewed a canteen cap, pulled the cord, and tossed the fizzing thing through a window. It worked perfectly, as did the one that followed and landed on the roof. So Charlie tried one, and when it didn't fizz like it should, he just threw it through Elmer's window so those flames would light it off.

"I musta got all the duds," he said.

The barrack began to fire up, and in moments it was ablaze.

"We should kill 'em."

"Don't you dare, Mr. Hatchison," said the young woman, stepping out of the shadows. "They've surrendered, you can't kill them."

"Girl, what world are you from?"

"The one you'd never understand. Anyhow, let me have a look at that hole in your side."

"It's okay. Say, you're all right, out here in all this, a girl. You're a little bit of just fine."

"Don't think a compliment will git you a kiss, Mister. If I can't see your wound, then you have to get back in the fight."

"We're going to cook, lying here nekkid," one of the fallen men yelled.

"Crawl on your hands and knees then. We got other places to go, other men to kill. Count yourself lucky, boys, you fought so poorly, wasn't interesting enough to kill you all. You crawl to the trees and hide there. In two days a boat comes, there's your way out of here. In a bit, all them Negro men are going to be free, and if they run into you, by God, what we'd have done to you will seem like a picnic. Now crawl, damn you, crawl."

By the time Earl got to the barrack, the flames had eaten it almost to the foundation. He heard shots ahead, in the fields, and knew it to be Audie and Jack finishing their play. He assumed that the others had moved on to join them.

He crouched by the trees. Fires raged everywhere. A few bodies lay flat in the dirt, where the others had potted targets. He checked and by his own vision could sense that none was Bigboy.

Damn!

He edged around the tree line, meaning now to head straight to the prison compound a half mile ahead. But his eye snagged on something white. He focused, unable to recognize it, but saw that it was a human shape. Then he got it: it was a guard, naked, crawling ahead toward the trees. He must have surrendered.

Earl ran to him.

"Hey!"

"Don't shoot! Goddamn, don't shoot, I done give up. My leg's hurt bad, Mister. That fella done shot me 'bove the knee. I may die."

But Earl didn't care. He just saw a bare-ass man in the dirt, crawling ever so slowly ahead.

He knelt by him.

The guard turned ever so slightly, looking up.

"You!"

"Me."

"You's a haunt. You's a ghost. I seen you go down in that black water. I seen the river take you and—"

Earl put his Colt Trooper barrel against the nape of the man's neck and let him feel the slight grind of the cylinder wheeling around as he drew back and cocked the hammer with an oily click that must have filled the vault of the man's skull with its reverberations.

"I am the man who'll blow a goddamned hole in your head if you don't tell me what I want to know."

"Sir, I—"

"You shut up now and listen hard and answer good. Where's that goddamned Bigboy?"

"That's why you're here! You come back from the dead for Bigboy."

"Where the hell is Bigboy? Was he off tonight? Was he in N'Awleens or Jackson, helling it up? Where is that man?"

"Bogart, sir, I don't know nothing. He's here, like every night. He ain't a goer. He's here all the time."

"He worked over that boy Fish?"

"He worked 'em all over. He done been hunting something for three weeks now. Working over colored boys every goddamn night."

Earl blasphemed something dark and evil.

Then he said, "When's last time you saw him?"

"He'd have been in the Whipping House. That's burning now, I can tell. He may be in that fire, sir. That's where he'd be. If he ain't there, sir, no telling."

"Goddamn," said Earl.

"Sir, please don't kill me. I's only doing what they's telling me. We didn't have no choice in the matter neither." But he saw that he was talking to nothing, took a deep breath, and continued his slow crawl.

EARL moved on toward the prison compound, but a noise came from an unexpected direction. He peered into the blackness of the piney woods and saw a small shed. Behind it dogs yowled savagely with fear. Something in their brilliant but tiny dog brains had picked it up, the vibration of disaster. They knew. Somehow they knew.

He drew the Trooper and eased back. The shed was empty, though clearly men had been stationed there. Whether they took off at the first sound of shots, went in and were killed, or surrendered and crawled away stripped naked he didn't know. But the place stank of cigarettes, so it hadn't been abandoned too long ago.

He looked out back. This is where the farm's man-hunting hounds were kept, invisible in the aerial photo because of the tree cover. He remembered them nipping at his ass, driving him forward as he fought Bigboy on the levee road.

They were even madder now. Blood was in the air, and fire and gunsmoke. They seethed and slithered against each other, piling up at the gate for a freedom that would never come.

"You boys are going to die," he said. "It's the way these things happen."

He turned, but then turned back. Dogs scared him,

ever since he'd seen them chewing up half-dead Japs in Tarawa's bunkers. But some odd feeling of remorse came. The dogs only did what the humans trained them to do. They didn't have a choice in the matter.

He walked to the fence, lifted the hasp and opened the gate. If the beasts smelled blood on him or if their aggression would turn them loose on him, he would know in a second. But the dogs were hell-bent on survival that night. They sped out, gray blurs in the dark night, and disappeared.

65

THE two Irishmen had gotten in close. They crouched together under the legs of one of the machine-gun towers. Twenty feet above them, two unknowing guards shifted, spat, drank coffee from thermoses, groused quietly about the endless boredom of the duty, and one even pissed off the platform with a groan.

Then the shots rang out from the Store and the Whipping House. They just started up, a staccato of gunfire, rolling over the fields that separated the two. Audie and Jack heard some scuttling about up top, and one voice said to the other, "What the goddamn hell is that?"

Audie lifted his black German attack rifle, as it was called. He had no hesitations whatsoever, for all hesitations had been ground mercilessly out off him that day in Italy when his friend Lattie Tipton had been gunned down. He fired the whole long, curved clip, and above them, the slugs poured through the floorboards, ripping and splintering as they went, the noise shattering the sleepy silence of the night.

For an old man, Jack moved swiftly. He got into the tower and didn't pause to look at the two freshly killed men. He'd killed a lot of animals in his time, and death held few fascinations for him. Now it was time to shoot.

He swiftly unslung his Model 70 and brought it to his shoulder, his finger flicking the safety off even as his hand guided the stock into the pocket of the shoulder, his knees and feet found a solid kneeling rested position with the forearm of the rifle resting pool-cue-like in the relaxed splay of his left hand on the ledge of the guard tower. His right index finger ran to the curve of the trigger, knowing it so well, so familiarly, and rested firm against it, feeling the slack just go out of it.

It was dim through the Lyman 4X Alaskan scope, but Jack had no problem finding the guard tower one hundred yards across the way from them, over the roof of the Ape House. He made out the silhouette of a moving man and a searchlight came on in that same moment. He squeezed carefully, and had the hunter's deepest pleasure of knowing that his shot had scored. He quickly threw the bolt, ejecting the used shell, lifting another .270 into the chamber, found the second target and put him down.

"Got 'em both, old man," screamed Audie.

Jack shifted fast; the third tower was also one hundred yards away, and quickly enough he found a target there, fired and was rewarded with a cry. He hunted for a second, found none, rotated to the last tower but was too late.

Next to him, Audie fired a long burst with his attack rifle. From the distance, Jack watched the slugs eat the place up. They danced over it, sparking oddly here and there, raising a spew of dust and wood chips. The hot shells rained on Jack, but he was salty enough to ignore the discomfort—pain, even, when one got down his shirt collar and burned the flesh of his shoulder—as he hunted. He saw nothing.

He went back to the tower where he'd only hit one man, and sure enough the second was halfway down the ladder. Jack nailed him good, though he wobbled a few feet on shaky legs before he sat down and collapsed.

"You are a hell of a shot, Mr. O'Brian," said Audie.

"I have shot an animal or two in my time," said Jack.

"Now as I understand it, you're to stay here till them other fellows arrive and cover for them when they move through to free them coloreds."

"That's it. I will hunt for targets as they come available."

"I believe I am to head over into them lean-tos and shanties outside the wire. That's where them women and old men live. I'll be getting them out of here."

"You take that big fast-firing gun."

"Well, sir, I am plumb out of ammunition for it and I can't get no other. I had sixty and I done shot 'em all. Now it's time for Colt work."

"Don't take your cowboy gunfighting style too seriously, Audie. This isn't the movies."

"Well, sir, it isn't, but it sure seems like one."

With a pixie smile on his small and pretty face, America's most decorated hero slipped out of the tower. He had a town to tame.

AUDIE strolled the dark street. He was an apparition in gun-hawk black, from his black hat to his tight black neckerchief to his black shirt to his black pants to his black double gun belt. Only the two Colts, each tied with a thong to the leg, were not black; they were nickel-finished, polished up nice, not a night-fighter's guns at all. But they had their advantages. The great Hollywood gun coach Arvo Ojala had honed and stoned their actions, so they were slick as hog guts. He'd rewelded the hammers on each, so they pronged upward another inch and were smooth there, the point being to draw the palm of the off hand along the top of the rising revolver while holding the trigger back so that no lockage was possible, and the hammer just reached apogee and fell of its own accord. Fanning, it was called, and it was much favored by movie gunfighters. You couldn't get work if you couldn't fan, and fanning took a year to master, for you had to build that callused toughness into the edge of the palm, and you had to build the muscles of the wrist and forearm. Most movie cowboys practiced with blanks, so accuracy wasn't an issue. Audie, Texas-born and war-hard, saw no point in blanks; conceptually the blank made no sense to him. So he shot to hit with live .45s, and by this time was among the two or three fastest gunmen in the world. He had made himself into a different kind of killer than the boy who had thrown grenades and shot men down with carbine, Thompson and Garand; he was the Kid now, not much older than the famous Kid of 1884, Johnson County, New Mexico.

In 'ho-town, four men had gathered. They had enjoyed pleasures accessible to them by right of skin color and the guns they carried. This was no mission of rape; it was simply the way it was at Thebes, and one reason why only the best guards of the Mississippi penal system came to Thebes; its 'ho-town, and the relaxations available, were legendary.

These four were neither braver nor more cowardly than their brethren, most of whom were already dead, the rest of whom had crawled nekkid into the trees; they simply happened to be the ones who were there, and they had gathered at one end of the street in the lee of a shanty as the gunfire and flames had risen all around them. They essentially had no idea what to do: Should they go back or should they flee?

Having no ideas, they did what men in such circumstances will always do: nothing.

They sat and waited to see what would develop.

What developed was a cowboy in black strolling down the street.

"Will ya look at that?" said one. "He stepped out of the picture show."

"He's a little 'un."

"Them guns he's carrying ain't so little."

"If I had a rifle I'd shoot him and we'd ride on."

"You don't have no rifle. You got yourself a revolver like him, and unless you can shoot it well a hundred yards in the dark, you are going to have to get through him to get your cracker ass out of this place."

"I say we run out shootin', and sure enough one of our bullets will clip that feller."

"Yes, sir, but suppose he don't panic, suppose he shoots as good as he looks, and suppose you're so nervous you can't hit nothing. Then what?"

"Let him pass, shoot him from behind."

"That be a good idea."

"It be, but can you absolutely still your breathing and the noise as he passes by? Suppose he hears you? He turns and comes. Then what?"

"What're you saying, Vonnie?"

"I am saying the onliest sure way is to get close up

and face this bastard. He can't take all of us. He just can't. No, sir. We four, he one, that is what it be. We have our guns out. But we have to be so close it ain't about aiming, it's about speed. You got a better plan?"

Nobody did.

And so it came to happen that Audie saw them slough into the street. They had guns in their hands, sleeves rolled up, hats pulled low. A director would have handled it differently, and better. For one thing, he'd have lit the scene more vividly, as the odd flicker of a lamp from the close-by shanties didn't bring enough texture out; and for another, he wouldn't have let them carry their guns, because that violated the code of the movie West. They wouldn't be clean-shaven, and their hats would have more character. He'd also have insisted on better dialogue, for even Audie sensed the banality of the exchange.

"You go on, git out of here, Mister. This ain't your place. You got no business here."

Audie, a fighter not a writer, could do no better.

"This is my business. This is my *best* business."

"You one. We four. You put them guns down, boy, or you will be dog dead in the dust in two seconds."

"So will you."

"You ain't got no cards to play."

At that point, one of the men fell dead. He dropped like a stone, a small geyser of blood pulsing from the side of his head, which had been crushed by one of Jack O'Brian's .270s fired from almost a third of a mile away.

"Odds are a little better now," said Audie, whose best thing as both actor and real-life gunfighter was that in moments of high stress a little smile played across his tight lips and his not terribly expressive eyes came abloom in twinkle. So this was the best line, and the best delivery, of his career.

From the three guards, the three guns came up, on the practical impulse that standing in the middle of the 'ho-town street was no longer a risk-free opportunity, and the faster this was handled the better it would be for all of them.

They moved first, and it is practically true that in such encounters aggression pays dividends; nobody can catch up with a fired gun.

Audie, therefore, could not catch up; however, the shots that came at him missed, not by much, but by enough—a tenth of an inch being "enough"—because the shooters were not practiced at the art of instinctive close-range shooting and didn't realize that unless you've disciplined your trigger finger to come straight back, as if on a pivot, its yank will invariably misdirect the first shot; it comes then to correcting quickly.

That's the quickly they lacked.

Audie drew and fanned so fast his shots sounded like a burst from the German attack rifle. He scored three hits in less than a second, and two were fatals; two men went down, a .45 Colt not being something a man can argue with. The third was gut shot and the big slug hit no bones. He was dead but would not die for another ten or so minutes, and he got his gun on Audie and would have finished the trick but for Jack's finest shot of the night, which hit him in the neck, a split second before Audie recovered and fanned two more, heart and lung, into him, and knocked him askew for all time.

Then it was over.

Gun smoke hung in the air, and dust, too, from the fall of the four.

Again the movies: slowly doors opened and women and kids and old men came out. They'd all seen it, but they knew nothing about Jack. It was just that the stranger in black had gunned four of the hated guards down in the street in but a second, after a dramatic exchange of words.

"Who you be, sir?" an elder finally asked.

"We come in from the river, folks," said Audie. "We come in to serve this place some justice. You see the flames lighting the sky? We're burning it out. So y'all have to clear out and find other lives. In the morning all this is gonna be under water."

"I see by your outfit that you are a cowboy."

"I am, sir. Texas born and raised. Proud of it. Y'all take your belongings now. Have courage. Be bold. This part of your life is over."

"Sir, they won't nevuh let us leave. We owes 'em all money, so we have to stay. The Man work that way."

"Ain't no more Man. Them debts, that's them burning. All your debts are burned to ash. You get what few get, and that is a new start in life. I'd grab it hard, for there ain't nothing here for you or nobody tomorrow."

And with that, the cowboy faded into the dark, a dream, a wish, a myth, but above all a man with a gun.

66

THE world exploded on Jack O'Brian. It just lit up. Suddenly he seemed in a wooden coffin while men shot the bejesus out of the thing, and as the bullets whipped into and through it, they yanked out shards of jagged wood, old chunks of nail and shingle, broken wire, bits of lead and jacketing and a sleet lashed at him.

Jack slid down into the corner as the storm continued. He was aware that somewhere in the region of his lower left-hand chest, a numbness was spreading, though he had no memory of being hit. His hand flew to the spot, encountered something wet and dark and pulled back.

Aw, hell, he thought.

The firing stopped. Jack lay still. Smoke and dust filled the air. He was expecting to die, but death took its time. Oddly, he was not outraged at the world, for as he looked back upon his life, he saw that it had been a good one. Over six hundred game animals taken, the shots all good and true, on six of the seven continents. On top of that his wife loved him and he loved her, and following the advice of various wealthy sponsors, he'd invested wisely; no worries there.

And he'd killed men, now, finally, after all these years, including a great shot on a fellow through a window in the Whipping House. That was a shot to remember. Then the shots on Audie's antagonists.

"He is fixed good," he heard someone mutter below him.

"We got that goddamn jackal but sure. You go on up and git that .30-cal., Ferris."

"You go, Nathan. He may not be dead."

"He is dead," said Nathan. "Plum-jack dead, I tell you."

Jack's numb fingers stole to the huge New Service he carried. He pulled it from its holster, amazed at how big it was. It was a big old thing. He knew if he cocked it, the click would set these boys to shooting him up some more, so he just lay quiet, feeling the slight tremble as somebody placed his weight on the ladder and began the climb up to the tower.

A head appeared in the floor hatchway, pivoted as it sought information, revealing a face and a set of eyes that blinked when they encountered the muzzle of Jack's revolver not three inches away.

The muzzle flash blinded Jack as he sent a bullet the size of a robin's egg into the face: the flash was vast and fired up the night. He did not see the effect, but heard, through the ringing in his ears, a loose thump of body striking ground in complete repose. Someone else scurried away.

"He is still alive, boys. Give it to hi—"

But the shots that followed came not from the sound of that voice but from elsewhere, and Jack recognized the boom of Elmer's .44s and Charlie's .38 and Bill's .357.

"Jack, you all right?"

"Hit pretty bad, goddammit."

"You stay put," came the call from Sally. "I will be right up to you."

"Sally, there may be more of them boys."

"These old farts down here will take care of them."

The shooting rang afresh, but no rounds came through the wood. Sally was up to him in seconds.

"I'm a goner," he said.

"Only if you believe that, sir," said Sally.

She pulled his shirt open and saw him plugged cleanly; a through shot had taken out some lung tissue and opened a lot of veins.

"I believe your poor old wife ain't shuck of you yet," Sally said. "You will be along for many a year to cuss and complain of her."

"My wife is a fine lady," he said.

"Well, whatever, she deserves something more than an old gizzard like you."

"That is certainly true," he said.

"How is he?" Elmer called up.

"He's lost blood and will be abed for a month, but if we can get him out of here and to the raft on some way other than his own two legs, he'll be around for years to come."

"I was afraid of that," said Elmer.

"Damn you, Elmer Kaye," called Jack.

"And the same to you, sir."

Sally put two gauze pads on Jack's entry and exit wounds, then wrapped him tight with yards of linen bandage, running the material up and around his shoulder, tightening one arm to his side. Then Elmer climbed up, and so did Charlie, and between the two of them they got Jack down the ladder and set him against a tree.

"You done some good up there, Jack," said Elmer.

"I think I did hit a few," said Jack.

"Where's Audie?"

"Fool kid was off in 'ho-town playing the marshal. He's got guts, but he's big shy on brains."

"Hey, I heard that." It was Audie, rejoining from his gunfighter's foray.

"Jack's been hit," said Sally. "But he is too ornery to die."

"Son, you are plumb crazy walking down the middle of the street like that."

"I wanted to see if it could work. It works fine as long as Uncle Jack is up top running backup with a bolt gun and a scope. Jack, you don't look so good."

"I am fine, son. Though I am now wrapped so tight my ears might explode."

Then Earl arrived, and he was not happy.

"What the hell are y'all doing? Sitting here yapping as if in the bar over some beer. Jesus Christ, don't you old bastards have a lick of sense among you?"

"Earl, Jack's hit."

"Oh, shit. Jack, how are you?"

He coughed up a little spray of blood, then wiped it off his mouth dismissively with the back of his hand.

"I am fine. No big thing. A lot of blood is all. I've seen plenty of blood before."

"He can't walk."

"Okay, let's clear these buildings and rig a stretcher and get him back to the town."

"That'll work."

"Jack, you stay here."

"Earl, thought I'd go to my dancing lesson, it's all the same to you," Jack said.

"You are a tough old goat, I will say. Now listen up, y'all. This ain't over yet, and it still ain't no goddamn tea

party. We got a sweep to do, and there's still a very dangerous man about who might still get his people together."

"Ain't no people to be got together, Earl. Them we
ain't dropped done fled."

"Hell, I'll go ahead and kill what's left, you say the
word, Earl," said Charlie. "I'm having a grand old picnic and don't want it to end."

Earl saw that this banter could go on forever if he
didn't stop it hard.

"Okay, now. This here's the last damn thing. We open
the gate, sweep the compound, knock open the prison
barracks, and step aside as them black fellows run free.
Then we burn what's left."

"Suppose you got old men who don't want to leave.
Old men can be peculiar stubborn like that."

"Then you make the younger boys take charge.
That's the only way. Come on now, we have to get
humping. We can't be powwowing like this, no matter
what fun it is. Next thing you know, Charlie'll be passing the jug out."

"Didn't bring a jug, Earl. Got me a nice flask, though.
Care for a tot of bourbon and lemonade?"

"Afterward, flying home."

"Be all gone by that time," said Charlie.

"Earl," cried Jack, "you watch that fool kid, Audie.
He wants to get himself killed."

"Aww, I do not."

"You stay under discipline, junior. That's an order.
Rest of you old coots, you listen here. This ain't no
movie. You move slow, in the shadows, in a line abreast.
You keep in visual contact. You shoot what moves, and
ask about it later. You stay down as low as possible,
move from cover to cover. Y'all ought to know that.
Sally, you stay here with Jack."

"The hell I will. Jack don't need me. Maybe some of them old black men do."

"You won't do one thing I say, will you?"

"Not a single one, no, sir."

"Well, can you fire a flare pistol?"

"I suppose."

"Then let's get some illumination and finish this thing and get the hell out of here."

Sally took the flare pistol from Jack's pouch, and, being practically minded, solved its intricacies quick enough.

"See, honey, you—" Charlie began to explain, but she raised the pistol and fired, the soft pop detonating a few hundred feet up, and ever so slowly, dangling from its parachute, a white flare floated down, drifting and swinging pendulum-style, so that the shadows it created danced eerily across the terrain.

"Come on, people," said Earl.

THE gunmen moved easily through the buildings. They could sense eyes from the locked buildings hard-pressing against them, but they were looking for men with guns, not men with eyes.

Charlie, whose senses were still keenest, saw something move and blasted a Blue Whistler at it. So salty were these boys that exactly what a young Marine platoon would have done, these fellows did not, which is open up with a panicked fusillade.

"I think you just kilt a rain barrel, Charlie."

"Was a moving target, goddammit."

"Charlie'd shoot anything that moved."

"Don't kill me, Charlie, for I am moving."

"Keep it down," said Earl.

Where was Bigboy?

Had he missed him? Had he lit out? Had he fled at the

first sign of gunfire? And what about Section Boss, with his Thompson submachine gun he loved so well? On the other hand, maybe it wasn't Section Boss's cup of tea to stand and fight, even with a powerful weapon. With that gun and some luck, he could have done some damage and rallied his own men, but those that weren't dead appeared to be scattered off in the trees by this time, or crawling naked in that direction.

Sally fired another flare, and it began its gentle drift to earth.

But no guards emerged to fight or surrender.

"I think it's clear. Them boys didn't want to fight a bit," said Elmer.

"Okay, let's get these damned things opened and get these boys out of here. Then we got to blow the levee, and we're finished."

EARL kicked in the door of the Ape House.

Lanterns had been lit. He stepped into a cone of yellow light just inside the door, and it all came flooding back: the stench of men living close in terrible quarters, with buckets for latrines, the bunks and cots everywhere, old-sweat-soaked clothes hung out to dry, mildew, woe somehow baked into the ancient wood of the place, the iron gratings on the windows, the smell of old leather from old work boots much cured with blood and perspiration, the sense of density, hopelessness, despair. It was the last place on earth any man would go in a right mind.

But this time he wasn't wearing chains, and he wasn't planned as meat for the strong. He was himself again: Marine-proud and armed, a strong man who was in command.

His presence was greeted with silence.

Then a bell-clear voice called, "You is a ghost. You be dead."

"Well, then somebody forgot to tell me, because here I am."

"What is this? What you doing?"

"This is deliverance. Y'all, I come back to burn this goddamn place, and in the bargain you git your freedom. It's eighteen sixty-five, boys, only I ain't got no forty acres and a mule for you. Only a dark road into town, and off you go to whatever happens next, good or bad. Meanwhile, we'll blow the levee, and come two hours, this place is under twenty foot of dark water. Now you go on, git!"

"Is you from Our Lord Jesus?"

"I doubt an angel would have the notches on his gun I lay claim to. I am a gunman. I am a gunfighter. Now go on, git, before old Bogart changes his goddamn mind because he is sick and tired of yapping."

They seemed not to be happy, not really. It wasn't like a liberation, for perhaps the word "free" had no meaning, and perhaps as well the shock of a Bogart back in the flesh stretched their minds and made no sense.

But someone had to ask.

"You ride in on the pale horse?"

"Son, I *am* that pale horse. And I am done come back as I swore to old man Fish I would. Now, goddammit, get out of here, get your asses going!"

They filed by, carrying nothing, for there was nothing to carry. One by one they filed past, and Earl recognized most, Tangle Eye and Jefferson and Corner Man and James and Willis and Samuel and George P. and George M. and Vonzell and Jacob and on and on; and last of all, somehow, that contingent of sick and injured, whatever would become of them. Earl almost had pity, for what lay ahead would be hardest on them. They jabbered to themselves, or they moved slowly with fused spines, or they seemed dazed. Some would not make it, but that was the way things happened; he had to paint his violence with a broad brush, knowing that in the particulars it would be occasionally cruel.

"Go on," he said, "into town. There'll be rafts of some sort there, I have been told. Whether the State of Mississippi comes looking for you or not, I can't say. I will say all the records with your names on them have been burned to nothing. That, and I can give you a couple days head start and hope you don't kill no folks nor rob none neither. Go on, git. You Grandpa, you go on, this is for you, too."

That was the eldest, and Sally came to him, spoke soft words, and got him mobile. She commandeered two fellows to march with him on the way down that dark road.

Earl watched as the men of the Ape House joined up with the human torrent that had been released from the other barracks and headed off toward the town of Thebes, leaving the penal farm behind forever, not that much of it remained unburned. For as they left, one by one, the barracks went aflame, bursting with cowboy firebombs that lit them from within. The orange glow roared flickery and hot up the sky, burying the stars in illumination, and lighting the parade as the boys went out.

But Earl knew his building was not empty.

With a lantern he walked on back, until at last he found him.

Moon, once so magnificent a warrior, the king of Thebes, had been whipped so hard his lacerations had scarred up. He was a ragged man, with no part of him untouched by the cat's tail. His face a mask of tatters, like a doll ripped up by feral dogs or cats, it now showed not manhood and aggression but fear. He was weeping.

"You come to kill Moon, Bogart? G'wan, kill me. Shoot Moon dead. He ain't good for nothing no more. The whip man done took his soul."

"Moon, you git out of here. You git your soul back in the world. It sure ain't in here. Whip man will win, you stay here. Killing you don't matter a damn to me. Go on, so I can burn this place once and for all."

"You ain't come back to kill me?"

"No, sir. I come to set you free, and only regret them boys I was too slow to help, like old Fish. You go on now. Git out of here. I'm going to pop this here thing, and when she goes, this whole building goes down."

He held the firebomb.

Moon eyed him balefully, as if it made no sense. And by his lights it didn't, but in time he saw where his future lay, and he drew his immense self up and walked out the door.

Without giving it a look, Earl pulled the cord, felt the fuse light properly, and tossed the thing into the back corner of the Ape House. It was fiercely alight by the time he left, where his fellows had gathered.

"Audie, you know what's doing. You blow that levee. You other boys, you gather up Jack—maybe some of them black fellows can help you with the stretcher, and head to town. Gather up Mr. Ed. You got to be upriver by ten hundred hours tomorrow, ten in the morning for civilian types, 'cause that's when our Navy friends come looking for us and they won't have enough time to hang around. Sally, you make sure these old goats don't wander off or lose interest."

"I will run them hard, Earl."

"You go on, now."

"Earl, where you going?"

"I have a piece of business yet to take care of. You go. It don't concern you."

"What, Earl?"

"It's the last place. It's why there's a Thebes on earth. It's what it's all about. The Screaming House."

67

A ROCKING CHAIR was found, and the old man sat in the middle of the street, enjoying the fireworks. Beyond the town, beyond the trees, the whole sky was lit in a glare so powerful it extinguished the stars. That acrid tang of burned wood hung crisp in the air, driving out even the moisture. It was Fourth of July and All Hallow's Night and New Year's Eve combined, the light crackling off the vault of the sky. The old man sat and rocked.

"Sir?"

"Yes?"

"Ain't just got white lightning. Got some fine old Kentucky drinking whiskey, too. Had it many a year, so many a year I don't remember when I first owned it. Be a pleasure, sir, to serve you a drink of it."

"Sir, my drinking days have been many a year past. But tonight I will make an exception. That is on one condition. The condition is that you and your colleague there join me, and that we raise a sip in salute to the burning of Thebes."

"I will take that charge, sir."

"So will I," said the other, and in a few minutes, the three old men enjoyed a fine sip of Kentucky bourbon, fiery in its own way as the blazing sky.

Meanwhile, the citizens of Thebes came from their hovels and dogtrot cabins to see the wonders of the night. They stared and murmured, particularly as by this time the fires had grown so intense that they cast a glow on the river itself at the base of the street, and it now rippled with the orange textures of oxidation. It was quite beautiful, if not so terrifying.

A woman came to Mr. Ed.

"Sir, what is happening?"

"Why, madam, we have burned the prison farm. To the ground, even now. There have been battles, and I am certain that most of the guards have perished and the rest have vanished. The sheriff and his fellows, they, too, have gone on. There ain't nobody here no more but you folk."

"Sir, what do we do?"

"You may stay or you may go. It is your choice. Though there won't be no employment, for those of you who drew a living off that place. That place, it just ain't no more."

"Sir, we can't leave. We owes money. All us."

"No, ma'am. Not no more. Whatever debts was owed was paid up in full tonight. Look up, folks, and see the ash in the wind. That's your debts. The place you called the Store. All gone. Nothing left."

"What we goin' do? How can we leave? We can't leave no way. It take a boat to leave and we—"

The woman stopped.

"Noah built his own, I recall," said Mr. Ed. "I am no carpenter, but I see a barge just offshore, and if my old

eyes still work at all in this light, I see the inscription
TRUGOOD WATERPROOF CASKET COMPANY. And I see a
powerful pile of boxes meant for the dead. Now, seems
to me—"

"You can use them boxes, yes sir! You can run board
between them with only a little hammering, and in no
time, goddamn, you gots a raft. You gots a lot of raft."

"Why," said the old man, "it's almost as if it were
planned that way!"

The people got themselves into action, and if they
were slow and clumsy at first, it was minutes before convicts began arriving in torrents down the dark road.
They too saw the genius of it all, and with their muscle
and skill, with nails reclaimed from dogtrot cabins and
mallets and boots and whatever used as hammers, with
boardage from cabins quickly disassembled, it was not
at all long before a fleet of rafts, each supported squarely
by a squadron of pontoons that had been coffins, came
into being.

"Sir, we going. They be enough for all of us. You
come with us, sir. Ain't nothing left."

But the old man was dozing in the excitement, and
even when three more white cowboys, a wounded man
on a stretcher, and his granddaughter arrived to look on
the scene with encouragement, no one could muster the
nerve to wake the old fellow up, for certainly, all agreed,
he had earned his rest this night.

68

BIGBOY saw him a fair ways off. The flames leaping at the horizon helped, for they threw a wash of light that otherwise would have kept the man invisible. But no, there he was, two hundred yards out, moving swiftly, bent in purpose. Bigboy's heart leapt a little, but he calmed it to quiet by the imposition of his will, and concentrated on the practicalities of the problem ahead.

He was in the gully just behind the toolshed where the axes and shovels were locked each night. He knew it was Bogart by the walk, the manful stride. He could see the cow man's hat low over the eyes and a rifle in his hands, and he guessed there'd be handguns under that big canvas coat. Bigboy knew Earl was dead set on going to Thebes's one last secret place.

With a pop and a hiss, Bigboy let the whip uncoil and snake through the dirt. It had to be loose and ready for an instant's use. He looked left and right to make certain no branches hung low to capture the tail and tie it up, and of course there weren't any. He was free and clear.

His whip hand was strong and his whip had free rein to snap and bite where he directed it.

He tried to dull himself out, reach a kind of no-place feeling, so that he could move swiftly when the time came, use the whip to take the man down, get on him, and disarm him, then shoot him with his own gun or beat him to death. No, not beat him. Bogart was too swift and tough to be beaten, and no one punch would do the trick; it would have to take two or three in a row, and good as he was, Bigboy remembered that the smaller man was equally good and would have a chance at the lucky punch as he had managed before. But shooting him had no pleasure in it anywhere, for it didn't reflect Bigboy's own purity of will and natural propensity for triumph. Bigboy had to kill him with his own hands, that he knew; but he also knew those hands would have a whip in them.

EARL hustled along. He was on the levee road, that ridge of land that bisected the fields and led to the trees that marked the river. Along here somewhere would be the turnoff that led through those trees to the Screaming House, with its polite doctor and his assistants, where the convicts went to die in pain.

He knew also that Bigboy could be out here. It was too easy to believe that the guard sergeant had perished in the fires at the Whipping House or the barracks. The man was too swift, too smart. Had he then fled? That didn't seem like Bigboy either, for if there was a thing he wasn't, it was a coward, and even if he escaped the general slaughter, it wouldn't be his inclination to flee, but to hang around.

But Earl also knew that he hadn't time to smoke the man out, not without dogs and other trackers. Bigboy knew the land; he didn't. Bigboy could make time, he couldn't. You caught Bigboy flat in the surprise or you didn't. He hadn't. Bigboy would survive and come dog him in his real life, he had no doubt. Bigboy wasn't the type to let a thing like this slip; Bigboy would work just as hard to find out who Bogart was as Earl had worked to get back here with gunmen. That was Bigboy's nature.

So when the whip flicked out and smashed against his ear, ripping it in a flash of heat pain so intense it almost took Earl's memory, it was not quite a surprise. The surprise was that as Earl wheeled to bring the rifle up Bigboy got there so fast, for he had never seen the albino run and had no idea what animal speed the man possessed.

Bigboy hit him with the crown of his head under the left eye, and even brighter fires than the ones he'd seen that night lit instantly in Earl's brain, and Bigboy's force carried him onward, crushing him in the rush, until he had the smaller man down.

He cracked him crown to face, crown to face, crown to face three more times, each splitting skin, each knocking Earl's sentience toward chaos and sloth.

Then Earl felt Bigboy's hands on him, ripping at the guns. Earl wasn't fast enough to catch the first one, but he got a grip on the big man's wrist at the second, and so Bigboy crown-butted him again. His grip slipped. In an instant, both handguns had been ripped from the holsters.

But Bigboy did not shoot him as well he could have. Instead, he threw the last one away, following the other, pulled off the pouch that contained the firebombs, tossed it too, then stepped back, leaned to retrieve a thing from the ground, stepped back three more paces.

Earl got himself up slowly.

He heard the flick and whisper of the whip.

"Ever see a man die by whip, Bogart?" Bigboy asked.

"Seen one," said Earl. "An old man chained. Don't take much guts-wise to kill a chained-up old man."

"You'd be surprised. Lots don't have the entrails for the work. But I see he was talking about you at the end. You came back, riding a pale horse, just like he said you would. You've done good, Bogart. The sky is bright with what you've done. You are a hero. But remember once I told you about the hero's flaw. It's his vanity. Do you know what that means? Self-love. Self-adoration. And that's your flaw. You came out here alone. Where are those other fellows with all their guns? I *knew* you'd come alone, even if you didn't, for what good's being a hero in a fairy tale if you don't face the beast? That's what's ticking away inside you."

"This ain't no fairy tale."

"No, it ain't. This is the whip man with nine feet of cat rawhide for you, delivered in licks so perfect you won't believe it. I took one ear. I'll take the other. I'll take the nose and the fingers and the eyes and the knees. Then I'll put such a roar of lashes against you, you'll pray to die. I'll take each of your nerves. Then I won't kill you. Then I'll leave you blind and tongueless and paralyzed and hideous ugly as a human stump. That'll be Bigboy's bequest to the world."

The whip snaked and this time it cracked at Earl's good ear with a sound so loud it all but busted the eardrum.

"Who are you?" Bigboy said. "Tell me that and I'll hit you so hard upside the head you'll go unconscious, and I'll get one of those guns and shoot you neat in the heart. Who are you?"

"Bogash. I'm a truck driver. I hope to run a hunting lodge down here for rich sportsmen from Little Rock."

"You are a stubborn bastard."

Earl rushed. He wasn't fast enough. Bigboy pin-wheeled the whip and flicked three cuts into Earl so explosively he knocked Earl down in the dust. Where the cuts were it hurt so bad he thought he'd die. Who knew a thing could hurt like that?

"Bad, huh? Yeah, it gets worse. You can't do it. No man can face up to the whip man, no matter how tough and quick he is. It can't be done."

Earl came again and learned the same lesson, only worse. This time the whip man lashed him perfectly on the top of one hand, opening a deep cut. That hand went numb and useless at once, as if it had been stung by a hundred bees. It swelled into something fat and puffy and yellow.

"You still ain't close enough. You think you can get inside the whip? That's what they all think. But no one can take the pain, no one. And no one's got that kind of speed to him."

"One of my boys'll be along soon. He'll shoot you dead and laugh about it. He's killed plenty in his time."

"That little kid?" said Bigboy. "He looks like he'd wet his pants you yell at him. Only that one's long passed. I take it he's going to blow the levee and flood the place. A good plan. It'll let me slip away, too, and start again, and wouldn't you know I've got a pretty penny cached in New Orleans banks. You're really doing me a favor and—"

Earl's fingers scooped and tossed a cloud of dust toward Bigboy's eyes, but it didn't produce blindness, only laughter.

"That's a good one. Oh, ain't I seen that in two hundred pictures or so. And I'm so stupid I'm going to fall for that one! You must not even yet know who I am."

Think! Earl demanded of himself.

Read him! What's he going to do next? Anticipate.

Earl stood and backed off a few feet.

"Oh, you think you can get away. I'll take you down across the ankles and whip your back so raw you can't move a bit. You want that? It could be so easy. You tell me who you are and the lights go out. No pain."

"Except after I tell you, you tell me you're going to kill my wife and boy after you kill me. Then you whip me slow, laughing."

"You got an imagination," said Bigboy. "That I give you, an imagination."

An insight passed into Earl's mind. He is a fighter. He is a fighter with a long right-hand punch. You rotate away from it.

He began to rotate to his own right.

"Where you going, son? You think this is a boxing match? You think you can out-think me?"

With that Bigboy pivoted to his own left, and snapped the whip into the dust to Earl's immediate right, to stand him still. But Earl saw it coming, for that was Earl's gift, and though he knew he'd never be fast enough to catch the whip with foot or hand and pin it, he might bring that trick off with his whole body, and even before Bigboy had pivoted for his strike, Earl had started his dart to the ground, and in the same second the whip lashed the dust, he landed on it, stilled it, and rolled three spins toward Bigboy and came up until they faced each other across three feet of dead whip now wrapped tight to Earl's body.

A flash of panic hit the big man's eyes, but Earl stepped in and hit him hard in the nose, breaking it, and the big man recoiled, roared in pain, and grappled bearwise against Earl, his big strong arms crushing the smaller man.

Earl bit his fucking nose. Didn't know where that trick came from, it was just what he did.

Bigboy loosened his grip and the two spun, groping for advantage, until it arrived at Bigboy, who lifted Earl off his feet and threw him seven feet through the air, where he crashed into the shed of tools, splintering it.

Bigboy waited for the man to pull himself up so that he could finish the job, and had even begun to move in for the kill, when he came to an abrupt halt. Earl staggered from the wreckage, but rotated slightly, blinking to clear his mind, and as he turned he revealed that in his hand he held an ax.

"You want your whip back, sir?" Earl inquired. "Come on over here and get it."

Bigboy's eyes dropped and he feinted a retreat, but Earl had seen this move, too, and as the big man came at him full bore, too close for Earl to swing the blade in an over-the-shoulder arc, Earl dipped under the rush and heaved through his arc horizontally. It lit with a thunk and was then torn from his grip.

Bigboy stepped back and looked with curiosity at the ax blade sunk into his hip, and the black blood that welled from it, and the two feet of wooden haft that hung off it. He went to one knee, groggy, shaking his head as if to make the spiders and firecrackers leave his mind.

Earl had another ax by this time, and when the big man regained his sense of purpose and came at him, Earl was fast enough to sidestep, and go top to bottom with his arc, and bury this one in the shoulder.

The two axes stuck deep in the big man, each slightly aquiver. Bigboy turned, spied Earl with ax Number 3.

"You goddamned bastard," he said.

He lurched, with enough power still but no speed,

and Earl planted this one in his stomach, hanging it up among the loops of entrails which split open, and it wasn't just blood that came out, it was also shit and turnips.

"You bastard," he said again, and Earl was amazed that the man was so tough. He had never seen toughness like this, not even from the Jap naval infantry. But that didn't stop him from seizing another ax from the pile. Bigboy staggered left, and reached for his own ax, and Earl chopped off his right hand. Bigboy looked at the stump, as if to waggle phantom fingers, but became fascinated with the arterial spray spurting from the wound. Then, once more he launched himself, and Earl teed off with the fourth ax, a ballplayer with a fat pitch too slow to miss. He felt like DiMaggio. It went with a noise that was new to his ears, unheard even in all the close combat of the Pacific, on the diagonal across Bigboy's face, tearing out eye and nose and cheekbone, and he stepped groggily away as if he couldn't yet believe this thing had happened to him and looked at Earl, face halved like a melon by the last of the axes, which all still lay set in him.

"Earl Swagger," Earl said. "United States Marine Corps."

Bigboy fell at last, as dead as they get.

69

SOMEHOW the town itself became engulfed in flame. No bombs had been thrown. But evidently in the melee, as the convicts ripped lumber from the dogtrot cabins and hammered them into frameworks on the pontoons of the waterproof coffins, a lamp was spilled over. That flame caught, and a wind or whatever propelled its jump to another cabin and another.

The conflagration didn't matter, though. By this time, far into the night, the original townspeople had long since departed, taking with them what they could, cached money and food, old photos, a treasured Bible. Sally had been everywhere among them, cajoling, speaking gently, helping the elderly, giving guidance or medical help or benediction as the circumstances warranted.

"That girl is some kind of angel," said Elmer.

"She is pure goodness," said Jack, from his stretcher. "Her grandad would be proud for her," said Bill. "Should we wake him?"

"Let him sleep some more," said Elmer.

And the convicts labored hard and well in their own

benefit, some of them proving master carpenters as well, and indeed their rafts were even more soundly engineered and constructed than the first generation.

The plan was simple; it was hardly even a plan. No, they would not drift into Pascagoula, all two hundred of them, and hope that nobody would notice. Instead there were three or four Negro towns in the great swamp, and segments of them would make landfall at each of these, and there gather wits and disperse overland. They'd have at least a couple of days' head start, and if they didn't bunch up and stayed cool and kept moving, they'd have disappeared so totally Mississippi would not have the energy to look hard for them if it ever quite caught on that they were not dead and not drowned by a flood.

So they had it at last: freedom. It was worth working the long night for, and so they did, and not soon but soon enough, they were gone and on their way, without a farewell, leaving the three awake white men, the girl and her sleeping grandpap.

Sally and the old men watched them go.

"Well, that's the last goddamn act. We done what we come to do."

"We done it good," crazy Charlie said. "I ain't had a ball like this one in years, if ever."

"I hope it turns out for the best, 'cause there's no going back."

"I'd bet we done the right thing."

"I hope you're right," said Elmer, "but my theory of the human heart may be darker than yours."

"Mr. Elmer, you should believe in the good," said Sally. "If you believe in it, maybe it will happen."

"But Sally, most people ain't like you. You're special. Most are like us, crabby old men who don't care much about nothing except what's in it for us."

"Wasn't nothing in it for you as I can see," said Sally. "You did it because it was right, and I did it because it was right, and who can ask for more?"

"I did it because it felt so damn good," said Charlie.

"Charlie, underneath it all I don't believe that's the true you."

"No, honey," said Elmer, "underneath it all that *is* the true Charlie."

Of course all the time they were talking, the modest, humble, silent Bill was working. He had carpentry skills, too, and he threw together a raft as fine as any of them in an hour's worth of labor, a platform on a frame nailed neatly to four strategically placed coffins. He worked hard and steadily.

"Y'all can sit there yapping, but if you do, you ain't riding on *my* raft," he finally said, and the two other gunfighters wearily arose to join him.

"Problem is," he said, "we got to go upstream. Them other fellows, they all headed downstream."

"Bill," said Charlie, "whyn't you build us a Johnson outboard? That'd get the trick done right fine."

"No oil," said Bill. "If I built it, we couldn't run it, 'cause we got no oil to cut the kerosene with."

"Good point," said Charlie.

"Can we pole?"

"*Have* to pole," said Bill. "No other choice."

"What's 'pole'?" asked Charlie.

"Don't you know a goddamn thing?" Bill said.

"We stay close to shore and sort of push ourselves upstream."

"I got it."

"It ain't all that hard to get."

"I'll go into the woods and look for saplings we can cut into them poles."

"Charlie, that's the first smart thing you've said all week," said Jack from his stretcher.

Charlie went off, Jack rested, Bill worked on the raft, Elmer helped, Sally helped—she couldn't be ordered to rest—the town burned to ash and chars, the sky began to lighten and the old man dozed contentedly.

In time, Charlie returned, and with his knife set to hewing the instruments of their deliverance. He did a good job and was finished just as the dawn was breaking.

"Want to go?"

"It's not seven yet. I figure two hours to get upstream. We—"

A boom cracked the air, far off. That meant that Audie had blown the levee.

"Best wake your grandpap, sweetie."

"Yes, it's time."

She walked up the incline to the old man dozing comfortably in the rocking chair in the middle of the empty street in the town of burned-out buildings and returned in a bit.

"What'd he say? Want to snooze some more?"

"Grandpap didn't say a thing," she said. "He's dead."

"Oh, Lord," said Elmer.

"At least he died happy," said Charlie. "Hope I die that happy, though it'll happen in bed likely, after a crotchety decline and lots of hell thrown at and received back from damn women nurses and wives."

"Are you all right, Sally?" Bill Jennings asked.

"Yes, I'm fine. Give me a moment please, is all."

She walked off and faced the river, the dawn, the far shore, the rest of her life.

"Well, whatever, she don't have to spend the rest of her life caring for an old man. She can find a young one now."

"Doubt there's one good enough for her," said Jack. "These kids these days, if you catch my drift."

"I do."

"All right," she said, returning, "I am all fine now."

"Let's wrap Mr. Ed carefully."

"He sure deserves that."

"He surely does."

And they set about to prepare a funeral shroud and then place the old man in one of the Trugood waterproof coffins.

70

EARL pulled the coiled whip off him as if it were an infected snake whose very skin contained poison. He hated the gnarly feel of the thing, and threw it as far as he could off into the fields, with a shudder of revulsion. Then, quickly, he went to look for his revolvers and found one, the Heavy Duty Smith. The Colt Trooper was evidently gone forever, for he did not have a night to hunt for it. It would rust away to nothingness in the coming years. He picked up the pouch with the last few firebombs.

Then at last he touched his face. There wasn't much blood, except at his ear. His sorest spot remained the top of his left hand, where the whip tail had cracked deep. That one was almost useless, and the ear, with a deep and bad tear, was equally a mess, though for some odd reason it didn't hurt as much. The openings on his face had coagulated and ceased to bleed. Stitches would close them up, but stitches were still a day or so away.

Settled, he turned and headed down the road. Not once did he look at the ax-burred body of the big man, as if it didn't exist, and as if therefore his barbarity, and the hunger and glee with which he'd planted that last blade deep in the face of the man, didn't exist either. He pressed along, wondering how much time he had before Audie blew the levee, and how much after. How quickly would the lowlands go under? Would the water have the force of a moving wall, a pure destructiveness, or would it seep slowly forth, rising in increments until it soaked the world? He didn't know. He really didn't care all that much either. If he made it out, wouldn't that be a treat and a half? And if he didn't, that was the way the cards sometimes came to lay on the table.

He found the turnoff, took the new road, which led back into piney woods that gradually yielded to more jungly growth. The fires still burned on the horizon in one sector of the sky, but not nearly so brightly. He didn't care. He didn't look at his watch either, because he didn't care what time it was. He didn't pay attention to the possibility of ambush by yet still-unaccounted-for guards, because he didn't care much about that either.

At last he came to still another smaller road behind a gate and realized that the Screaming House lay behind it; but this road, followed another few hundred yards, led to the Drowning House, where the prison launch was moored and the concrete blocks and chains were stored. He saw now what he'd have to do if he had the time.

The gate was locked. He shot it off, not caring about noise. He walked boldly up the road, and any man hiding in the bushes or the building with a rifle could have shot him. He didn't care. He came then to the building. It was the newest structure on the property, giving ample evidence of sound U.S. Army Engineer Corps design and construction. He heard the generator going out back, which explained the electric lights blazing in a region yet to be electrified.

He kicked in the door.

No one greeted him, but the place was neat, almost antiseptic, any government building foyer, from the Marine Corps to the Civil Conservation Corps. The swirls of a wax buffer on the green linoleum testified to the spic-and-span efficiency of whatever labor detail attended. From far off came a loony tune of music, though of the higher form, that orchestra stuff, that spoke to Earl only of balls and fancy snoots in fancy suits. He had no idea what it was and no curiosity.

He opened the door and walked down the hall, as the music rose, until at last he reached the room where he had been examined all those weeks ago. He kicked it in.

It was empty. Whoever had staffed this place, they had fled, leaving almost nothing. A few papers and towels lay on the floor, evidence of a hasty retreat. Who knew where they went?

Then Earl heard soft music. It came from one more door.

Earl kicked it in.

AUDIE dug.

He was excavating an ever expanding hole halfway up the inside lip of the levee, where the ground was softest. Audie was young and strong, and his system was choked with the power that all his adrenaline and testosterone—considerable in both cases—had generated over the past few hours. He was also weirdly, fabulously happy. He could have whistled while he worked.

He had no idea how deep he should go, but after a furious forty minutes of work, he was a good five feet into the levee, and he figured that was enough.

He already had retrieved the bundled sticks of dynamite from the raft. The stuff was waxy and had an unpleasant odor. It amounted to five bundles of ten sticks apiece and awkwardly, he planted them in the bottom of the hole. Then he took the detonating cap, opened the waxy paper at a central stick in the central bunch, and plunged it in, twisting it against the cakelike consistency of the explosive itself. He twisted till the cap nearly disappeared, leaving a residue of ground powder on his fingers.

Next came the fuse. That was neatly wedged into the well at the top of the cap and screwed tight itself, so that the connection was solid.

The long green waxy twine of fuse curled up out of the hole. Audie climbed out carefully, so as not to kick anything with a foot or bring down a rush of earth from the hole and disconnect things. He wanted to do this right the first time, and not have to come back. Filling was easier; ten minutes of easy shovel work at the hole filled it in again.

He pulled out his Zippo, flicked it once. It whooshed healthy flame, which he quickly cupped to the frazzled end of the fuse. That waxy twine glowed red once, and then at last sparked to life and began to sputter away toward detonation.

Audie raced up the levee and stood for just a second. The broad black flat river stood on one side, placid in the moonless night. On the other side, beyond the levee, stood the reclaimed fields with their drained swamps and okra crops.

He thought: the world is going to look a lot different in ten minutes.

He climbed into the raft and paddled to the center of the dark river.

THE music was sweet and sickly, full of tinkly piano passages.

The doctor sat at his table under a single-bulb lamp which bent on a curve to illuminate his work. He was writing with a fountain pen in a notebook, and Earl could see a piece of meat in a dish in front of him, uncooked. Then he realized it was human meat: it was a liver, with a kind of pale crust spotted with green at one end. The doctor was describing it in his ink scribbling.

Beyond him, on a morgue table, far in the darkness but clearly not quite indistinct, lay a black man. Earl didn't recognize him. His chest had been bisected surgically then splayed backward, so that all his innards lay before the world. Some of them had been removed.

The doctor said, "Schubert."

"What?"

"Schubert. On the Victrola. Schubert's 'Fantasie.' Do you like it?"

Earl put a bullet through the Victrola, smashing Herr Schubert's beautiful notes into a million pieces.

The doctor winced, for he was not used to such noise so close, so loud.

Then he said, "I don't know what you think you're doing. But even a man like you will understand this."

He pushed a document across the table.

"Go on, read it. You can read. You are or were military. You know the meaning of orders and the higher good. Read it. Go on."

Earl seized it and noted the heavy embossment of the United States Department of Defense.

TO ALL LOCAL, STATE AND FEDERAL LAW ENFORCEMENT AUTHORITIES, it began.

The bearer of this document is a participant in an operation that is classified HIGHEST TOP SECRET and has been officially deemed In the National Interest. As such it—and the bearer of this document—fall under the full protection of the United States Government. It and the bearer of this document have been granted a priori immunity from all state, local and federal laws.

Any violation of this policy on the local level will be prosecuted to the full extent of the law by the United States Attorney's Office in your jurisdiction. You are hereby ordered to cease and desist all law enforcement or other activities involving the program at Thebes State Penal Farm (Colored) in Thebes County, Mississippi. You are ordered to release the bearer of this document and leave the area immediately.

For further clarification of this policy, call the duty officer at the Defense Intelligence Agency at WE-5-2433, Arlington, Virginia, using the code name BLUE TUESDAY for authentification purposes.

THIS IS AN OFFICIAL POLICY OF THE UNITED STATES GOVERNMENT AND THOSE IN VIOLATION OF IT WILL BE CONSIDERED TRESPASSERS AND FACE ALL LEGAL SANCTIONS.

"You know what that means, don't you," said the doctor. "You are up the river in more ways than one. See, you have no idea how *valuable* this is, how *important?*"

Earl just stared at him. The moment seemed to go on and on.

"Suddenly you see your duty and you're brought up short. The best thing you can do is escape again, with whatever men you've brought, and leave us in peace. This is too important for a little man like you to destroy. Too much is at stake, as that document—and you don't doubt it, do you?—makes clear. You've killed all the rednecks who beat you, so you should be satisfied with your meaningless vengeance. Now, either you leave or I will make a phone call and in twenty minutes I can have the Marine Corps here."

Earl held the document up to his gun muzzle, and fired. The flash ignited the paper; he let it fall from his hands to the floor, where it was devoured crisply in a quick spurt of flame.

"You are trespassing on a *Top Secret* government—"

"What you're doing is wrong," said Earl.

"No, what we're doing is right," said the doctor. "You have no idea what this is all about."

"I know exactly what this is all about, Dr. Stone," said Earl. "Or is it Dr. Goodwin, whatever the hell you're calling yourself these days? You been injecting these colored men with syphilis. I believe it's called *Treponema pallidum*, or some such. But it ain't just any syphilis. It's some kind of supersyphilis. You're trying to turn the clap into a germ warfare weapon. That's why the Los Alamos Plutonium lab and the people at Fort Dietrich in Maryland are involved. Dietrich is the Army's germ warfare installation. That's why the infected convicts are painted with big numbers, so your boys can watch them die or sicken through binoculars from a long way out and take notes. That's why the contaminated bodies have to go underwater. You're making atom-powered syph to fight the commies, and you're testing how it kills on American Negroes."

Now it was the doctor who could think of nothing to say.

After gibbering ineffectively for a second or two, he recovered enough to say, "How did you know that? That is *Top Secret*. You are not supposed to know that. You cannot know that! How dare you know that? Who do you think you are to know that? This is the most secure—"

"I saw the red radiation marking on a package shipped to you some months back. Didn't mean a thing then. But then someone you don't know nothing about ferreted you out, and saw you's receiving correspondence and shipments from Los Alamos and Fort Dietrich. It wasn't hard to put two and two together. But tonight it comes out zero. I'm ending it."

"Look, you idiot, stop and consider. Yes, what has happened here is monstrous, and I am the monster in charge. But the bigger picture, the only picture that counts, is the war we will fight sooner or later against people who would destroy us. We must stop them. We must. We will fight it in Asia or Africa or South America. And what if we have become so comfortable we lack the will? And what if we can't use atomic bombs? A biological weapon, untraceable, undetectable until too late, could decimate an enemy force. It could save the lives of hundreds or thousands of American soldiers. That is my humble contribution to our survival. I am building a weapon that will destroy our enemies. I am almost there. And you come along and destroy it in a single night."

He stood.

"You started out to cure the disease," said Earl, "after

what it did to your wife and child. Now you're turning it into a weapon. You're killing American men, same as you and me, to test it, and you say it's for commies. But I know soldiers and I know whores and I know it can't be controlled. It'll just go on and on and on."

Far off came the sound of detonation.

Everything in the lab rattled a little and leaped ever so slightly from its place, including the liver on the plate. The vibration rolled through the room.

"That's the water," said Earl. He reached into his case.

"What is that?"

"That's the fire," he said.

"You cannot—"

Earl unscrewed the cap, pulled the cord; this one worked just fine. It sputtered, spraying sparks this way and that, and he tossed it deep into the room.

"Stand clear," he said. "It's burning time."

The doctor did an insane thing. Earl had heard of such a thing in the war, and knew that men were capable of such commitment, or bravery. And it was bravery. Nevertheless, it stunned Earl; it was the last thing he figured on.

The doctor threw himself on the canister, to muffle its destructiveness. He was atop it when it detonated, and the radiance of the flame blowtorched him alive and swallowed him in incredible destruction. He burned, screamlessly and passively, his body just absorbed in the totality of the fire. He melted like a witch in an old movie.

And in his insane courageousness, he succeeded. The fire simply expended its entire force on him until nothing remained but a smoking carcass.

Earl turned away. He'd seen Japs fried crispy with

the flamethrowers and hadn't liked it. This was all that, only concentrated on one figure. He fought a surge of vomit in his throat but then regained control. He had one more bomb left. He removed it, pulled the cord—it worked just fine again, and tossed it. The device ignited, and the room filled with its illumination. Earl now saw in the light that the place was a kind of museum on the theme of atomic-powered *Treponema pallidum:* along the walls on shelves stood jar after jar, each full with liquid, each with its biological treasure, a harvest of items from inside the body, dense, meaty, placid. Or outside it: several large diseased penises were included.

The fire's heat was explosive. It burned furiously, spewing gobbets of itself about, lighting the room in just seconds.

Earl beat it to the door, and by the time he was outside, the building was gone in fire.

71

SECTION Boss had no taste for battle. When he heard the shots, he knew immediately that one loomed. It so happened that he had drawn duty that night in the dog kennel, a job he hated and felt should be beneath him, given all his responsibility. His job was to beat the dogs with rawhide soaked in Negro sweat, not care for them. But as the firing mounted and mounted and the glow of flames began to light the horizon, he understood how lucky he had been in being way out here, away from the prison's central structures.

The dogs yowled. He didn't care. He just wanted to get the hell out of there.

He took Mabel Louise, of course, his treasure: the Thompson submachine gun. He took a bagful of thirty-round magazines brimful with ammo and all the food he could carry. His damned horse was back at the corral, so he couldn't ride. It was simply a question of following the river upstream, staying calm, and living to live another day.

He stayed close to the riverbank, and came soon to the big levee the engineers had built in '43. It was grassy and broad, and walking it was no difficulty. At the center he halted. There he could see it and . . . My God!

The whole sky was lit up with flames. Knowing the place as intimately as he did, he could place each blaze to a building and figured in a second that his intuition had been correct: the whole place was going. It was over, razed to the ground, forgotten and flattened to ashes.

Glad I ain't there, he thought.

Turning, he continued his way along the levee, the gun in his hand, the going easy.

But soon levee gave way to riverbank, and the going got tougher. Sawtooth cut at his legs and boughs whipped his face. The ground here was infirm, a soupy insubstantial margin between earth and water. But onward he went, at a considerably reduced pace.

Sometime toward dawn he heard an explosion. It shook the trees and rattled the leaves. Dust seemed to be torn from the earth by its vibrations, and he realized what had happened: they'd blown the levee and whatever remained of Thebes State Penal Farm (Colored) would shortly be gone completely. One thing about them boys: they did the job up right.

But he continued on, now altering his plan. He'd just get far enough out and go to ground for a bit. No sense in trying to fight his way out of this place, and getting torn to shreds.

Then, maybe in a day or so, he'd work his way back. He'd shoot off a couple of clips, dirty his face, and by the time he returned and the state authorities had found out and taken over the site of the disaster, he could represent himself as a weary veteran of the fight who'd stayed at his post 'til it was overwhelmed, then heroically fought his way out of there and laid up.

Hell, he guessed there'd be no other damned witnesses. This thing could play out right swell for him.

So it was that he found a dry spot off the riverbank and set himself down for a nice nap in the cool pines, far removed from the violence.

He dreamed of glory and escape and a better life and at some point people were cheering him madly. But then he realized the cheering was in the real world, not the dream one, and he blinked awake to the sound of voices.

He fought his panic as he looked around. He checked his watch. It was nearly 10:00.

The voices seemed to be coming from the river. He snaked his way forward, and then he saw them.

Cowboys.

There were six of them, sixty feet out in the water. They were in the prison launch, which they had commandeered. They were laughing and joshing loudly among themselves, having a fine old time.

Then he recognized that goddamn Bogart.

That one!

Still alive!

Suddenly it made all kinds of sense. Bogart had somehow survived his murder, and as everybody said he was a trickier man than he let on. Back in the world, he recruited these bandits, and they came back in the dead of night for the dark pleasures of retribution. Now on the stolen prison launch they were escaping, heading upriver.

Section Boss had a machine gun.

He could kill them all. Even if he didn't get them all, he could shoot the shit out of the boat and sink it dead in the water. Then if there were any left alive, he could finish them, or simply vanish before they could get organized and come after him.

He *would* be a hero. An actual, real-life hero.

He hunkered down behind the gun, began to check off the firing requirements. Steadily, he drew the bolt back, till it clicked. He looked at the two levers above the grip on the left-hand side, the safety (off) and full-auto (on).

He checked the sight, that fancy Lyman job, and diddled a bit with it to make certain the gun would shoot to point of aim at less than fifty yards.

He had them.

He brought the gun to bear, and at that moment beheld an amazement. A thin cowboy stepped out of the cabin of the craft, and took his hat off, and cascades of blonde hair fell out, and Section Boss saw that it was a girl!

A goddamned girl!

For some reason this infuriated him even more profoundly. A girl! A girl had been among the raiders, and had brought all this hell upon the place.

A girl!

He squiggled and wiggled gently, oriented the big gun this way and that, until he'd put the big sight blade square on her and had it centered in the peephole of the Lyman sight.

Gun braced tight, he began to squeeze the trigger.

He was a hero!

72

THE birds sensed it coming somehow, and the dark night was full of them, seething and cawing, wheeling and darting. Amazing how many birds a piney woods could contain, and how mysteriously they could read the future and know it to be tragic. They launched, like carrier planes, before the water arrived.

Earl wondered how it would come as he labored at the prison launch, trying to find fuel to add to the tank, mixing some oil in, studying the primitive controls so that he could understand it well enough to run it, and finally cracking off the control panel at the keyhole (he had no time to look for a key) and trying to hot-wire the tangles to spark, and get out of there.

He tried to concentrate, but he could not. The world was about to end, this world at any rate, and by his hand. He somehow had to see it, know it, watch it finish and drown.

Birds in the air. Animals scurrying through the brush. A sense of disturbance in the universe, as the animals understood flood as well as fire, and made to flee.

When it came, it came stealthily. He thought of Japanese naval infantry moving through the fog, knowing how to use the land, geniuses of concealment and silent movement. The black water was not there and then in the next second it was, though at first only the oddest sense of shimmer or vibration where there should be none gave away its presence, and then it was everywhere, unstoppable, remorseless, powerful in its quiet, insistent way. It didn't rush or gurgle or throw up sprays of white; it boasted no waves or tides; it just rose in the trees and spread with devilish speed until in seconds there was no ground visible but the trees stood sunk halfway in black water. Its current was strong, for boughs and chunks and pieces hurled along its surface, and here and there the corpse of a dead animal.

Earl knew it was time.

Come on, goddamn you, he said, jerking two splayed wires together. At last a spark, just a tiny twitch of light in the dark chaos of what had been a control panel, and the old craft heaved, shuddered, coughed up a throatful of blue, dense smoke, and then began to roar.

Earl steered straight into the channel, hoping there were no secret impediments or secret passageways concealed by the still calm water that he didn't know (he hadn't been paying much attention the last time he'd gone for a ride in this particular boat) or that he wouldn't encounter some kind of supercurrent set off by the broken levee that would suck him in and down.

The old scow lurched into the dark water under a spray of stars, and Earl held her steady, aiming for an opposite shore, where there should be as much safety as possible.

He looked back and saw that the Drowning House had now been taken, its foundations eaten away by the flood; it fought its destiny but then gave up, tumbling into collapse as the water claimed it.

The sun was coming up. Its brightness oozed out of the east, and soon enough the water began to sparkle. The disk itself was shortly visible, and the sky began its run from black to gray to pewter to blue.

In the increasing light, Earl watched the clouds of birds circling the opposite shore, although shore wasn't quite the right word. Remnants of the levee stood all along it, though here and there, by natural forces difficult to comprehend, it had been breached, and yet more water poured into the lowlands of Thebes State Penal Farm (Colored).

Earl navigated a course south, toward the town or what would remain of it. This took him along the whole course of the prison installation at which he looked for signs of destruction. They were ample. Of the four machine-gun towers only one still stood, the others having given way to the water; and that one looked ready to go at any second, twisted crookedly as its supports washed away. The air was full of the sense of water unleashed, and yet still whiffs of the night's fires remained. Above it all the birds rotated in the sky, trying to figure out a new destination.

When Earl passed what should have been the Big House, the Store and the Whipping House, he could see nothing. But of course he hadn't looked for them from the river before, and so he didn't know if this signified their ruin or not. But he heard the rush of water, and that was enough to suggest they were inundated.

The last mile was calm, and he could tell from the columns of smoke of fires still burning that the town was gone, too, somehow. But at last he saw what he had come to see: a raft, poling its way up the river on this far bank, holding three cantankerous white fellows, cursing at each other loudly, a man on a stretcher, and a girl, who stood apart from them.

She took off her cowboy hat and waved, and her survival, honestly more important than any of the others, filled him with sudden joy.

"Say there," he hailed.

"Damn, Earl, where'd you get that damn boat?"

"Picked it up somewhere in the night. Here, let me get y'all aboard."

"Be careful now. There's a fifth."

Earl wondered what Elmer meant, but then he saw a coffin on the raft that wasn't being used as a pontoon.

"Oh, hell," he said.

He maneuvered close enough, and throttled the engine back, afraid to turn it off. Elmer and Bill seized his gunwale and mated the two craft in the center of the current. Then Charlie and Sally helped Jack across, and though the man had difficulty with his pinned arm, in other respects he seemed spry enough. He was a tough old bastard. Then Elmer and Bill got the coffin up and slid it over the gunwale, with Charlie and Sally pitching in on their side, until it rested on the deck of his own boat. Then the two men threw rifles across, and came themselves.

They released the raft, and Earl steered hard a-starboard to reorient upstream, and the current was much stronger running against than running with, but the old scow plunged ahead in the increasing light and heat, back in the direction he had come.

"Glad to see you, Earl," said Elmer. "We's getting tired of that poling and goddamned Charlie wasn't pulling his own weight on his pole. And Jack wasn't worth a damn."

"Hell I wasn't, old man. These two old coots let me do all the work."

"What happened to Mr. Ed. He catch one?"

"No, sir, not by a damn sight. He faced his fellas and done that job up right good. He told all them colored men how to put a raft together, and they all been gone for hours now. They downriver a far piece. Then old Ed just passed, with a smile on his face, in a rocking chair. He went gentle into the good night, I'll say."

"I'm sorry, Sally. I never meant—"

"You never mind, Earl. Now what on God's earth happened to you? Looks like you put your face in a meat grinder."

"Had a ruckus with a fellow."

"Someone else can drive this boat. Earl, you come here and I will stitch that ear on or it will fall clean off and you will look like a circus freak."

"I—"

"Earl, you do what I say."

Earl did. Charlie took over the steering, and Earl sat still as Sally ran a needle and thread through his ear and scalp, and it hurt like hell, but not nearly as bad as when she doused the stuff in some kind of disinfectant that made it burn like pure hell.

"Goddamn," he said.

"You can get through it, cowboy, big man like yourself."

"Oh, Christ, that hurts."

The others laughed.

"Some damn hero. Earl, maybe you ought to give that medal back."

They plowed up the Yaxahatchee, once again passing the flooded prison farm, which was now to the left. The fourth tower had fallen, and more of the levee was gone.

It was all reverting to savage swamp. Everything would be buried under the water, and in months the silt would build up and all traces of a fight would be gone, unless Navy divers decided to make a million-dollar salvage project out of it, which seemed unlikely.

"Don't hardly seem like nothing was there now," said Elmer.

"Nope. It's all gone to hell. We wiped 'em off the face of the earth." This was Charlie.

"Hey, I see the kid," shouted Bill.

And, yes, there he was, Audie paddling furiously in a yellow Navy raft. When the sound of the engines reached him, he turned and saw Bill waving wildly from the prow of the craft, and waved back. He steered out to the stream, and Earl guided the launch toward him.

"Hey, you fellows."

"Look at him, out for a Sunday boat ride."

Again, Earl came close and went to idle, and Audie transferred. He left combat knife slashes in the raft before he made his move, ensuring that it would deflate and sink in time.

"Where's the old fellow?" Audie asked.

"Didn't make it through the night," Elmer said.

"Oh, Christ," said Audie. "Sally, I'm sorry."

"Thank you, Audie. I will be fine."

Upstream they went, for another half an hour, until they were lost in trackless piney woods and silence, as if no other humans existed on earth. Earl retook the wheel and navigated to the pickup site, and checked his watch. He saw they had some time.

"We'll just lay up here," he said. "I think we're home free."

"Home free," said Charlie. "Goddamn, how I like them words."

73

IT all danced before Section Boss: how he and he alone had tracked the Northern communist night riders who came South with fire and brimstone. How he slew them in the river. How justice was served. How he became a hero in the white South, the king of N'Awleens and all them pretty gals, how he was elected to the state legislature and then the governor's mansion and then who knew what.

How he killed a damn girl who humiliated the great white South!

And all he had to do was squeeze a trigger and hold it down for a few seconds, as he had done so many a time.

He felt the trigger yield to his steady pressure and . . .

And then he heard a crash as something or some fleet of things blasted from the piney woods upon him.

The dogs. The dogs came out of the brush like rifle shots, all snarl and teeth and blood hunger. Somewhere in the swamp, they had picked up the scent of the man who beat them all those months, and hunted him hard.

They hit him with a frenzy, and he screamed as the fangs drove into him, though in his pain he could not hear it and neither could anyone else, over the arrival of another sound, the roaring of engines, loud and low and close.

74

THE call came at half past noon. Sam picked it up quickly.

"Hello?"

"Mr. Sam?"

"Earl! Jesus Christ, man, what happened?"

"It's done. It's finished. We hit 'em hard and got out pretty clean. Ain't no more Thebes prison farm. It's destroyed twice, by fire and flood. Destroyed three times, really, the first by gunmen."

"You're all right?"

"Have some stitches in me."

"The others?"

"One man died of a heart attack. Three others were hit but should recover. We're all beat to hell. And I'm sorry to report that Mr. Davis Trugood didn't make it. I found him dead in the upstairs bedroom of the old house when I went looking for the warden. He found the warden first, but what happened between them or why, I have no idea."

"Earl, I have found out much about him you should know."

"Later. I'm too tired to remember. You can move your family back to Blue Eye. It's all over. It's finished."

"Earl, you . . . I don't know what to say."

"Don't say a thing. We all agreed. After today, the words Thebes penal are never going to be said. I'm going to rest a spell, then go back on duty. No more gunfighting. That's all over, unless the gunfight comes to me, and I don't think it will. At least I hope it never does."

"Earl—"

"Mr. Sam, you keep this under your hat. I'll see you in a few days. I have to set my adventuring right by Junie, and I'd prefer to do that face-to-face than on a phone."

"Of course."

Sam hung up and looked about himself, to a little messy Little Rock office-bedroom. He meant to call his wife first.

But he couldn't.

Some things never change.

He called Connie.

BILL Jennings and Jack O'Brian didn't leave the helicopter at the farm; instead, they were flown on to Pensacola, under the advice of Sally, who urged that Jack needed to get plasma into him as quickly as possible. The word came that night from Bill that Jack would be all right, the doctors in Pensacola said, and would be three weeks in the hospital. Jack's wife, Sarah, was headed down. Earl knew how much was left in the fund from Davis Trugood and knew that there'd be enough. He told Bill to tell Jack and wondered if Jack had a last message. Bill said that Jack sent his best to all the boys and hoped to see them again, maybe sometime in the 1970s or '80s. The boys got a laugh out of that, especially since they knew they'd see him at next year's NRA convention and could josh him merrily.

Meanwhile, Charlie and Elmer, with their lesser wounds, saw no need to rush. Charlie had a rat's amazing ability to recover. He would be bruised for a month, but his cracked ribs would heal, and the two flesh wounds sealed themselves up and didn't infect. Elmer had a whopper headache, so bad that for the first time in years he let his correspondence languish. He just sat on the porch, drinking whiskey and swallowing aspirins. But he wasn't grumpy a bit. He actually seemed to enjoy it all.

At night, much drinking was done, though not by Earl, and much retelling around the campfire. It seemed Charlie had killed hundreds and he would have re-created each of them if he weren't hooted down by the others. But the cowboys were happy, to a man. Audie said he hadn't been so happy since V-E day, and he'd spent that in the hospital with a chunk of his hip shot away. This time, he got to celebrate it up right! They almost seemed in the end as if they couldn't quite let go of it. But already they missed Bill and Jack, though they knew the two weren't coming back. There was a sense, somehow, that this was it: a last roundup, and they'd never be together again, at least not like this, in the lassitude of survival, thankfulness and drunkenness.

The next day Sally made the arrangements for her grandfather, and a hearse from a mortuary in Pensacola came by to pick up the body. The mortician had the death certificate, and nobody seemed particularly bothered by the legality of it. Old men died, it happened all the time, and this fellow was in his eighties without a mark on his body. The mortician—he seemed somehow to be a deputy sheriff, too—assured Sally there'd be no problems at all, especially when Earl paid out a nice lump of change for him.

The next day, it was Earl who drove Sally to Pensacola for the long trip to Montana by train, and for burial for Mr. Ed.

Earl parked in front of the station, which was all jammed up with Navy personnel in their whites and their girls and folks and kids. A lot of hubbub floated in the air, and Earl could see the big steam train hissing and puffing at the head of its cars.

"You are a special one," he told her.

"So are you, Earl."

"Where will you go? Have you a place?"

"My aunt. Grandpap's other daughter. She's been after me for years. It'll be fine. I'll be all right, Earl, don't you worry. Don't I seem like the type who makes out just fine?"

"You do. But let me tell you this: Young men are going to come courting hard now. You pick the best. You deserve the best. If you wind up with some no-good, old Uncle Earl will visit you and kick his butt and give you what-for, do you understand?"

"Well, Earl, as I have not done a single thing you ever told me, why should I do that?"

"I'm hoping you'll change your wild ways. Lord, I wish I was twenty years a younger man. I'd give them young bucks a run for their damn money."

"Well, guess what happens now? You have to kiss me. It's how the story ends. Don't you see? Prince Charming kisses Snow White and releases her from her spell and so she doesn't have to live in the woods with the Seven Dwarfs anymore."

"I ain't no prince and I certainly ain't charming. Though I would admit them other fellows was mostly dwarfs. And you're not a princess. You're a queen, you just don't know it yet. So I shouldn't be kissing so far above myself."

"Well, as I sewed your ear back on and did a nice damn job on it, I will determine what happens, and for now you will kiss me. And that will be that. The queen has spoken."

"You were the toughest and the bravest. Do you know that?"

"I just tried to live up to grandpap's standards, and then to old Uncle Earl's."

"You done that, and how."

He kissed her, hard, just to see what it would feel like, and of course it felt exactly as he knew it would, and an electricity of regret flashed through him and then it was over and no more. She smiled and laughed, and got out of the car.

"Do you need help?"

"Earl, if I don't get away, I'll never leave. You go on, I can handle this little suitcase."

She grabbed it and took off, without looking back.

He watched her go, and damn, as had happened so rarely in his life but happened this time, some kind of grit came sailing through the window and clouded up his eyes, and the thin young woman walked away and back to whatever her life would be, disappearing in a squall of sailors.

When Earl got back, Audie and Charlie had left. Audie had made a phone call, and he yelled out a big whoop-de-do when he hung up. He had gotten that big part in that Civil War picture. He'd play a hero. He had to leave right away, as he had to get back for what Elmer reported was called "wardrobe" by the end of the week, and since he was going west, he'd drive Charlie back to Texas.

Anyhow, those two boys would have some fun together. And maybe it was better that all the parting took place in this strange way, without much of a final ceremony, just in little dribs and drabs. These were not men who spoke clearly of things they felt, and more often ran from them. So it was best for everybody that they just separated without much palaver.

Only little Elmer was left, and he helped Earl clear the house. All the leftover provisions were buried, the beds stripped, everything returned to normal. The lease still had some time to run, and Earl allowed it best to let it run out, so no authority could ever link the abandonment of the farm in Florida with the strange events in Thebes two states over, though the only news so far was something Elmer heard on the radio about a flood in southeastern Mississippi, and the destruction it had wrought. It didn't seem like anybody was making a big to-do about it.

And then they were done and each was set to head off in a different direction.

"So Earl, tell me now: Was it worth it?"

"I think so," Earl said. "But it all fades from memory fast, don't it?"

"Yes, it does. But I want your conviction, Earl. We did the right thing, didn't we?"

"I would say we did."

"A lot of men died that night. I never killed a man before. It's different than a game animal, who's lived a magnificent life and whose meat will honor my table as his head will honor my medicine lodge. But you don't put no human heads on no walls, and maybe those boys thought they was serving a moral purpose."

"Maybe they did."

"So I don't know, Earl. Maybe we'd have been best off to leave it all alone."

"I think we done right, Mr. Kaye. Something bad ugly wrong was going on down there—you could sense it yourself."

"That I could. It was the last stop at the end of the world, where there are no rules."

"Well, we were the ones that stopped it. Maybe there were other ways to stop it, but I don't know them. And maybe what follows won't be much better, but by God, one thing I know is it'll be different. Maybe different is better enough."

"We shall see."

"We shall, indeed."

"I will say this, Earl. It was a hell of a fight. I will always take pleasure in the fight I fought and in the men I fought it with. It was a hell of a fight."

"Yes, sir," said Earl, "it was the best damned fight I ever saw, that I deeply believe. And I've seen some fights in my time."

And with that, they parted, sworn between themselves by deepest bond to never speak of such things again.

75

THE boy was watching. He sat alone in the late afternoon, intent upon his task on the porch of the white house on the hill. He never spoke much, but he'd been speaking even less since his father had disappeared. But he was a noticer, a collector of information. He saw things, he tracked things, he filed them away for later recall and examination.

He could see a flock of black crows in the trees off to the left. He knew they'd flown in from the west and would settle the night and fly out to the east in the morning at dawn. He could see the yellow thatch where the dried-out grass had lost its color, but knew also that it contained teeming wet microscopic life under the apparent dryness. He could see the occasional southward flight of Vs of high geese and duck, their trumpeting far off and incomplete. It was getting cooler. He sat, he watched, he waited. He thought.

He knew other things. He knew his mother was desperately unhappy. He felt her tension, and it frightened him. She wasn't speaking much these days either. The two of them lived in silence, ate in silence, slept in silence. His mother had become a different kind of watcher; she was the sort who watched, but never saw. She would stare for hours out the window and see nothing at all. Her fear had made her haggard. Though to the boy she was beautiful and would always be beautiful, he saw enough through his idealizations to realize that she was losing weight, her bones were showing, the knobs in her face were sharpening, and there was an emptiness coming into her eyes.

The father was simply gone. It had been weeks now, and it cast a dark spell across the farm. It seemed even the plants felt it, and they withered in the sun, and now that it had begun to cool with the coming of autumn, everything seemed in a rush to go to brown.

The boy would wake up in the night, sure he'd heard his father's voice, rumbly hoarse and powerful, yet always with a kindness under it.

"Daddy! Daddy!"

"Bobby Lee, it isn't your daddy," his mama would call from her bedroom down the hall, where again she was lying but not sleeping.

"I heard my daddy."

"No, Bobby Lee. You were dreaming, honey. It wasn't him, I'm sorry."

So he would ask the next morning.

"When is Daddy coming home?"

His mother would stare off into the distance.

"Honey, I do not know. He will come home when he is ready."

"Is he all right, Mama?"

"Sweetie, it would take a tank to kill that man."

But the boy knew this was no answer. Yes, it would take a tank or something big and powerful and mean, but he had figured out that there were tanks in the world, as there were big, powerful, mean things, and that they killed people. There was a war in some place called Ko-ria and the older people and most of the boys talked about it every day, about how we had to stop them yellow commies and drive them back or they'd come over here and take over.

Now he sat on a day like all the others, rotten in its sameness, and he watched as a car turned up the driveway and began to crawl toward the house.

It wasn't Mr. Sam's car, that he knew. It had an aching familiarity about it, and in his heart, a thought exploded so fiercely he thought he'd die, but at the same time he fought it, for he knew he couldn't face another disappointment.

He prayed: *Dear God, please let it be my daddy.*

This one time God listened, or so it seemed. The car pulled up, and Bob Lee now confirmed it was his daddy's, and in that second, lumbering, strangely stiff, his father climbed out.

"Daddy!" he screamed, loud enough to wake the dead, or even his mother from her solemnity, "Daddy!"

"Well, howdy there, young man, say, ain't you a big

'un. You know a boy named Bob Lee? Used to live here. Little squirt, whatever happened to that boy?"

"Oh, Daddy!"

The boy threw himself at the father, who swept him up, gave him a hug that was urgent in its intensity, then held him up to the sky at arm's length in his two big hands.

"Lord, you look good to this old man."

"Daddy, what happened? Was you in a fight?"

His daddy's ear was bandaged as was his left hand. His face was oddly swollen about the eyes, one of which was badly bloodshot. There was a darkness visible in the flesh of his face.

"It's nothing, Bob Lee. It's all over. Don't mean a damned thing. Oh, it's good to see you, son! Say, what good would I be if I didn't bring you something. Here, you see if you like this."

Earl took the boy to the trunk of the car, opened it, and there was a two-wheeled Schwinn bicycle, gleamy new, the twenty-four-inch model, purchased with the last few dollars in the late Davis Trugood's operating fund.

"Oh, Daddy!"

"Yep. Figured it was time you learned to ride a two-wheeler." The father pulled the bike from the car and dusted it off. "I will teach you—"

This may have been the happiest moment in Bob Lee's life. He already knew how to ride a two-wheeler. Jimmy Frederick, a school buddy, had one, and had showed him how, and for some reason Bob Lee just took to it so fast and natural it amazed Jimmy Frederick. Now Bob Lee climbed aboard, set the pedal, pumped hard that long first move, and shoved off, riding with no uncertainty about the farm yard.

"Damn! Where'd you learn that trick?"

Bob Lee's face lit up in a blaze of intense pleasure.

"He's a champion," his mother said from the porch, her own voice lit with pleasure.

"Howdy, ma'am," said Daddy. "I brought you something, too."

"A new Crosley refrigerator, I hope."

"Naw, just some old flowers!"

He pulled out a bouquet from the backseat of the car, a batch of roses red and dark as blood, and walked over to hand them to his wife. Then he kissed her hard, in a way that Bob Lee had never seen him before. His mother perked up something wonderful; it was like a parched plant getting a shot of water, and the leaves changing immediately.

"Now you come here, Bob Lee."

Bob Lee obeyed.

"I just want you both to hear this from my own lips. I had to go away, but now I am back. I will not be going nowhere again. I will be here with you forever and ever. Do you hear me? My adventures are over."

"Oh, Earl," she said, as if she believed it.

That night Bob Lee heard his father and mother talking earnestly. He knew something was different somehow. He could feel it in their voices. His father had changed in some small way, and that in turn led to a change in his mother. Whatever it was, Bob Lee couldn't say, but he felt it. It scared him a little.

Please God, he prayed, *please don't never take my father away.*

ACKNOWLEDGMENTS

So many people came up with so many good ideas on this project I began to question, toward the end, whether I had anything to do with it at all.

The great Weyman Swagger, one of the world's finest natural editors, brought considerable intelligence to bear from start to finish. Behind that grizzled countenance lurks penetrating insight; he really gets it.

Then my friend Lenne Miller, in the throes of a divorce, took time out from his anguish to pitch in a key idea and to remind me that I couldn't write a book where the hero hates dogs.

Usual suspects Mike Hill and Jeff Weber were there as needed.

In my journalism life, I went to my editor, John Pancake, and said, "John, I have a question that the Arts Editor of *The Washington Post* certainly ought to be able to answer. How do you drain a swamp?"

Here's the scary part: he knew.

He also was, as always, somewhat forgiving in his definition of acceptable time-in-office, which provided me the freedom to have the two careers going simultane-ously and puts off that Big Choice another year or two, if not forever. Gene Robinson, Deb Heard and Peter Kauf-man were equally forgiving on the present/absent issue.

Cellmates Henry Allen and Paul Richard were enthu-siastic, which is a great help, believe me. Bill Smart, an-other great old *Post* guy, loaned me certain shooters' biographies helpful in concocting my old men; and when office politics in the Style Section grow wearying, I can always turn to him for an illuminating discussion on much more important subjects such as: 9-mm vs. .40 S&W for personal defense, or 7-mm Remington Mag—enough for elk?

Randy Mays, retired from a certain agency he can't talk about, supplied me with a Department of Energy book on Los Alamos science that I kept too long, as I usually do. Sorry, Randy, but thanks so much.

Also in Washington, Mike Jeck of the American Film Institute came up with that wonderful use for old cow-boy movies.

I should also mention the late Jim Schefter. Jim, au-thor of *The Race,* and several other volumes, died before he could read this book, I'm sorry to say. But he caught a huge geographical mistake in *Hot Springs* that would have made me the recipient of dozens of snippy letters. I'm sure he's up there in Writer's Valhalla, taking his red Corvette through 180 fishtails on gravel roads whenever possible.

In cyberspace, my thanks go to Bob Beers, who voluntarily runs a Stephen Hunter website at Wbanet.com/hunter/. Why I don't know, but he seems to enjoy it. My appreciation.

I should mention also that the prison work songs are taken from the Alan Lomax collections—"Prison Songs

I and II," recorded by the great Mr. Lomax at Parchman in 1948—and are available from Rounder Records.

In the gun world, I was able to spend a morning on the range with Jerry Miculek, the world's greatest revolver shooter and the heir to Ed McGivern. Jerry, and his wife Kay Clark-Miculek, are fabulous people, and I had to pinch myself several times to remember that I was hanging out with someone at the level of Joe DiMaggio, who was nevertheless decent, approachable, helpful and whose insights on the care, feeding and fast manipulation of a revolver were of great help.

Jerry came into my life through the good offices of Ken Jorgenson of Smith & Wesson, and Michael Banes of the National Shooting Sports Foundation, who convened a writers' play-day at the Fairfax County Rod and Gun club. And to Ken, thanks so much for other considerations.

My good friend John Bainbridge spent a wet, cold, muddy week with me in Mississippi, most of it perched in tree stands on Steve McKenna's ranch, waiting for the legendary Mississippi white tails to appear. If you spend time in a deer camp, you're a lucky man if you have a buddy as congenial, decent and amusing as John Bainbridge.

Professionally, those two legends, Michael Korda and David Rosenthal, editor in chief and publisher, respectively, of Simon & Schuster, were steady hands, true believers and highly accomplished facilitators; they made this book as good as it could be. And of course my agent Esther Newberg was always around to say gently, "Stop whining and get back to work."

I was particularly emboldened when I explained to my daughter Amy what I wanted to do in this book and she said, "Dad, works for me."

And of course the great Jean Marbella, one of the funniest, smartest, most beautiful women who ever lived, was supportive from the first and until the last.

And I should say finally that while some readers may recognize the real life antecedents of my six old gunmen, there is no evidence at all, and this book was not meant to suggest, that they ever took part in such an enterprise as I've invented, technically illegal no matter how morally upstanding.

And also to them—my heroes in the '50s—I have to say, "Gents, I'd ride the river with you anytime."

ABOUT THE AUTHOR

STEPHEN HUNTER won the 1998 American Society of Newspaper Editors Award for Distinguished Writing in Criticism for his work as the film critic at *The Washington Post*. He is the author of several bestselling novels, including *Time to Hunt, Black Light, Point of Impact,* and the *New York Times* bestseller *Hot Springs*. He lives in Baltimore.